THESEUS
AND THE SKY
LABYRINTH

I0582756

GWENHYVER

SKYDOG
BOOKS

THESEUS AND THE SKY LABYRINTH

First edition July 2025

Published by Sky Dog Books

Copyright © 2025 Gwenhyver

ISBN (eBook): 978-1-916644-08-3

ISBN (Print): 978-1-916644-09-0

This is a work of fiction. Names, characters, places, and incidents either are the product of the author's imagination or are used fictitiously. Any resemblance to actual persons, living or dead, events, or locales is entirely coincidental.

Story inspired by the myth of Theseus and the Minotaur.

Cover illustration © Alyssa Winans.

Developmental, copy and line editing by Kat Stainforth of Foxglove & Folio Editorial Services.

Visit the author's website at www.gwenhyver.com

For Jen,
Who makes navigating the labyrinth of life
the greatest adventure!

CONTENT NOTES

A few spoiler free things for you to be aware of before you embark on your adventure to the Sky Labyrinth.

This book contains swearing. It also contains a swaggering lesbian monster hunter,* a princess who can rescue her damn self, and a whole lot of sapphic yearning. There's snark and general horniness, as well as intimacy/sex. And there's a real risk of swooning, so please be warned!

If you'd like more in-depth/specific content notes, including **trigger warnings**, you can find those on the final page of the book, or by visiting *www.gwenhyver.com/theseus-notes*.

*a monster hunter who is a swaggering lesbian, not a hunter of swaggering lesbian monsters. A subtle, but very important difference!

PART I

SKY LABYRINTH

1

SPACE

If there's one thing Theseus knows, it's how to kill a monster. If there's another thing, it's how to not get sentimental about it.

But it's difficult not to feel *some* pesky emotions when faced with the strange, ever-shifting beauty of space. She's travelled the stars before; of course she has. She's not a hermit. She can boast first-hand knowledge of several star systems under the Seven Suns. (Or she would, if she were the boasting type.) It never gets old, though, this feeling. Drifting in zero gravity, suspended in everything and nothing, surrounded by infinite skyscape.

Daunting. Isolating. *Exciting.*

Still, it could be argued that the beyond-the-upper-stratosphere entry platform to the inescapable Sky Labyrinth, home to an un-killable beast, is not the most sensible place to be. But sensible isn't in Theseus's cache of skills and weapons. Instead, she wields a short-sword, a dented circular shield, a rucksack of (mostly) essentials, a desire to make the universe a better place, and—as per usual—a death-wish. She's as surprised as anyone that the latter hasn't got her killed.

Which is why, unlike the thirteen other doomed individuals just deposited at the entry platform, staring up at a gargantuan gateway to certain death, she's pretty calm. Well, not *calm*—that would be unhinged—but not freaking the fuck out like the others. Beside her, the sobs of the man with face tattoos might be silent—thanks to all comms being rendered mute—but puffy eyes, streaming tears and a vibrating torso aren't subtle. And he's not the only one suffering in forced silence. Because their punishment is underway in an overtly Minosian fashion.

According to one prison guard with a passable hold on Athenian, the invalidation of being silenced is akin to the loss of identity, being less than nothing: a curse worse than death on a world that prizes being seen and heard.

Which is why their astro-helmet comms are now muted. Their auditory input too.

It's not clear whether the guard was intentionally being an asshole, or just prone to nervous chatter. He probably hadn't known whether to treat her like a criminal on a one-way journey, a potential hero who might upend the heavens, or just an idiot.

Heavens above and below. She wishes the others would get a grip. The thing about a bad situation is, once you're in it the only productive option is to make the best of it. So as their sky-shuttle makes a swift retreat, and the drawbridge reels them in like bugs on the tongue of a cosmic giant, they may as well enjoy the view.

Below, the coal-like boulder of the planet Minos glows with webs of orange light, clustered like starbursts where there are cities and civilisation—though in Theseus's view, the two can be mutually exclusive. It could be her senses heightened by the circumstances, but the lights of Minos seem to pulse brighter.

Theseus returns her focus to the path ahead.

Given its form and positioning, some refer to their current location as 'Minos's mechanical moon'. Some refer to it as 'the unforgiving one-mile spherical island in the sky'. All refer to it as the Sky Labyrinth; an architectural wonder, a work of art. Myths of Minos—mazes, battles, heroes and victory—are etched into the monument's surface, framed by maze-like formations of luminescent stripes battling the darkness. It's a mighty feat of engineering—and also... honestly, *a bit much*. There are far better uses of a world's resources, surely. A gateway has no business being this big, unless it wants you impressed or quaking in your boots.

Which—now that she thinks of it—is probably the point.

Theseus tugs at the metal torque about her neck. According to the skyport control official who'd welcomed her to Minos in one breath and noosed her in the contraption the next, all citizens and tourists are required to wear them. She'd read in her tourist guide-Shard, the torques are meant to stop the Minotaur stealing citizens' Minosian Flame—their individual life force, their spark of life (she'd learned after cross-referencing the glossary). Apparently, the Minotaur uses their Flame to power its Sky Labyrinth. That hadn't exactly made a whole lot of sense, but—at the time—Theseus had been wedged between empty fuel barrels and too busy battling a bout of motion sickness en route to Minos to think further on it.

The torque might be for protection, but—right now—it feels more like a choker.

As the drawbridge platform reels them towards the opening doors, Theseus spares a look up at the prominent sculpture looming at the apex of the gateway. The famous creature with a bull's head and a human body: all muscles, sinew, and strength. The eyes exude an otherworldly glare. Judging her. Judging them all.

Theseus's deep breath whispers against her helmet's invisi-visor. She might manage a practiced calm in the face of impossible odds, but she's not quite arrogant enough to think she's invincible. According to legend, only the worthy—heroes and the innocent—emerge from this place with their lives intact. And so far, no-one has. If tavern whispers and legend are true, this place will be the death of all of them.

But no-one, not even criminals deserve to live in the shadow of this beast.

As the gatehouse seals them inside, stealing the vista of space, the idiocy of this mission settles into her bones. To risk her life for the greater good is one thing, but to do so to impress a princess... well, that's downright reckless, isn't it?

2

THE GATEHOUSE

As Theseus's friend and mentor Herakles always says, *First rule of monster hunting: Take in your surroundings.*

Well...

If a sky-ship were to procreate with a cavernous ancient vault, this chamber would be the result. Dull metal walls of varying hues meet a dark stone floor threaded throughout with linear channels of pulsing lava, save for a six-foot circular indentation at the chamber's centre. There must be some kind of invisible barrier between the channels and her boots, because the floor is merely warm underfoot.

Is the lava-free circle functional or decorative? Either way, Theseus doesn't trust it. Better keep an eye on the others in case anyone's foolish enough to wander across it.

She trails a whisper-mesh clad finger over her forearm, just above her armoured cuff, where the multicoloured shafts of light—emanating through stripes and blocks in the Labyrinth's outer-shell—toy with the hue of her bronze skin. Her forefinger rucks the whisper-mesh covering her arm, but it reforms tight to her skin as soon as she leaves it alone.

Anyway. Best not get distracted, because already they're faced with their first fork in the road: two grand doors set into opposing interior walls. The group flit from one to the other, their torques sparking like frantic fireflies at the hollows of their throats.

Before long, the bravest—or most foolish—unseal their face obscuring astro-helmets to engage in—judging from the wild gestures—fraught conversation.

Still encased in the silence of her own astro-helmet—of open-faced, Athenian design—Theseus inspects the one direction none of the others are observing. The closing of the entrance gateway has blocked out the skies, yet the interior surfaces are all decorated with glowing constellations. The Architect either wanted to highlight what may never be seen again, or to remind them of the threat that lies beyond.

Of course, there's always the chance they were just trying to make things pretty. And in that, they have succeeded.

In the centre of the outer-shell gateway, at about chest height, the chamber's colourful luminosity picks out a strange, irregularly shaped hollow, its opening about the size of a coin. Theseus might have landed herself in a cosmic death maze, but she's not so daft as to prod mysterious gaps in its gateway. She does rather like possessing all her limbs and digits, thank you.

Still, it's curious... unique enough to suggest it has a purpose, and deep enough that her rucksack's shoulder torches throw its shadows into sharp relief.

Theseus smirks. Bizarrely enough, she might have just the right tool for this task.

From her rucksack, she unspools a hand's width of luminous thread: as thin as medi-thread, with a glow about it that makes it appear as thick as twine. The Minosian Princess had given her the strange material to 'guide her path'. Theseus had already pushed her luck a little far to ask how the fuck it was going to do that. She'd decided it'd just have to be one of those quest things she has to figure out.

Well, here goes.

Cutting a length with her short-sword, she drops the thread into the opening, where it pools inside it.

And...

That's it.

The thread sheds light within the smooth, dead-end hollow, but no light at all on its function. It just sits there, coiled in on itself.

Theseus shrugs. *Worth a try, wasn't it?*

She leaves the cut length of thread where it is. For all she knows, the Labyrinth might contain dozens of identical chambers. At least now she'll be able to tell if she happens across this one again.

She returns the spindle to a hidden compartment in her rucksack; because there's nothing worse on a monster hunt than being unintentionally lit up like a target.

Though, skyport control hadn't considered any such practicalities when they'd clamped the damn torque about her neck. It's tight enough that she can't remove it—she's tried—but loose enough to grab. It's lighter than it looks, but it's still an unfamiliar, unwanted distraction. The most pressing issue, though, is its intermittent frazzle of electricity. It doesn't hurt, but it hampers Theseus's usual ability to camouflage.

She retrieves a black neckerchief from her rucksack and wraps it about her neck, covering the torque's electricity. Once it's clear the sparks aren't going to set the fabric alight, she fastens the knot. If she had more than the one, she'd be handing them out to the rest of this sorry bunch.

The chamber's light and shadows are disturbed as the

group's gestures grow more unsettled. Some of the group prod at the walls and doors; others stand back, deferring to a man in astro-armour so golden and gleaming it's more of a challenge on the eyes than the stripes of colourful labyrinth light.

Minos's Chosen Hero.

Of the fourteen sent to prove themselves against the beast of Minos, he is the only one here officially by choice. For the rest of them—all less opulent in their astro-attire and armour, with dull metal devoid of sparkle, and astro-helmets instead of his more theatrical astro-mask—this is their punishment, as decreed by the questionable Minosian judicial system. But him? He's here because he nominated himself as worthy of trying his wits against the monster in the sky, and the people of Minos agreed.

For a world obsessed with appearances, that prizes confidence and victory, he is the result.

At the celebrations of the Righteous Path, he'd been enjoying the spotlight on the main stage in the capital's plaza. His proclamations of how he planned to 'return with the bloody heart of the Minotaur', 'free Minos from tyranny' and 'be the hero the Princess needs' were relayed to the crowds by a theatrical troupe of interpreters.

Bleugh. Overconfident, patronising jerk. He's not Theseus's Chosen Hero, that's for sure.

While she'd been put off by his parading, his elaborate but redundant swordplay, the audience had... well... not. The frenzy with which citizens and tourists alike had cheered his posturing had made her wonder whether she was on a different planet. And wish she was *on* whatever they were.

Because, seriously... This guy?

He makes strutting look like a life skill.

Okay, so there's nothing wrong with wanting to make the

worlds of the Seven Suns better. There's nothing wrong with taking charge and leading the way. And, yes, stopping the beast, freeing Minos and its princess from its tyranny, that's what Theseus is here for, too. But you don't hear her going on about it on a stage in front of thousands of people.

Doesn't he know that arrogance is simply irony's setup to making a joke of you?

Perhaps he has reason for such confidence. He is the Chosen Hero, after all. Or perhaps he's not too bright, because he hadn't seemed bothered then—nor does he now—that this is the nineteenth Minosian sun-orbit this barbaric event has taken place: that before them, two hundred and fifty-two people have been lost to the Labyrinth.

At least she can't hear him. Although...

Ordinarily, silence isn't a problem—though silence chosen is better than silence forced, of course. But with the group so agitated, she'd rather have some warning if they're about to do the Labyrinth's deadly job for it. If her own idiocy ends her life, that's fine. She'd just rather be at the helm of her demise than a mere spectator.

The helmet stats scrolling across her invisi-visor confirm the air is safe to breathe. Theseus risks unhinging her jaw guards, losing her protective whisper-mesh, and committing to the air of the Sky Labyrinth in one deep breath.

It's stale, with an odd metallic tang that puts her in mind of sky-ships. Injuries. Mortality.

A tirade of Minosian echoes through the chamber. Sure, it's always clever and sensible to speak the language of a world you're visiting, but Theseus has never claimed to be either of those things. Though, if there's one thing she's discovered in her short time on Minos—a beautiful planet by external and engineering standards, full of epic cities and complex architecture—

it's that its various dialects can be misleading. Only days ago, she'd been approached by a Minosian woman who'd appeared to be choking. Theseus had been midway through wrapping her arms around her to thrust her lungs into expelling the cause— wondering whether she might require the kiss-of-life—when she'd realised the woman was in fact propositioning her. She'd thought Theseus's response a little odd, but put it down to her being from a different galaxy. And after some more successful communication, and a change of location, there had been much thrusting *and* kissing... but now's not the time to be thinking about that.

The point is... perhaps the group are dealing with this situation better than she thinks they are?

Or... not...? The jerky gestures of the group can only be distress. The Chosen Hero's monologue cuts through their clamour. His puffed-out chest and over-polished armour are presumably meant to be impressive, but only remind Theseus of ridiculous statues that supposedly represent *victory*.

Theseus's chest tightens. *Don't laugh... don't laugh...*

But the way his palms rest against the hilt of his broadsword and the shaft of his spear, almost caressing the things...

Don't. Laugh.

Theseus stifles her outburst a moment too late. The sudden snigger echoes about the cavernous chamber, returning to her own ears as the group and the Hero's attention swerve to her.

Oops. Where's a noise-cancelling astro-helmet when you need one?

Hero's eyes scour over her until every inch of her suffers the abrasion. She doesn't typically make enemies this fast. But she's all for beating her personal best.

Strutting toward her, his bejewelled armour glinting, he growls something as cutting as his glare. Honestly, felines hock up hairballs with less guttural sounds. Even his astro-mask, clipped to the front of his chest-plate—a creepy face that should have been nixed at the design stage—is snarling at her.

She might not know enough to translate, but the way he's gesturing at her torso-armour and general attire suggests he's criticising the unpolished state of her.

Rude.

Dark and dented. That's how she likes the metal and leather of her armour. Polishing armour is up there with spending hours braiding hair. It might look pretty, but since when does that help in a confrontation?

Well, there'd been that one time she and her buddy Herakles had had to dress up in garishly opulent garments and elaborately plaited hair in order to infiltrate a Marathonian sky-ship... but that's a story for another time!

Shiny armour is for being seen. Long hair is for being pulled. It's why Theseus keeps her armour tarnished, her steel-toed boots scuffed and her hair—naturally as dark as a cosmic abyss—buzzed at the sides and short on top. Armoured cuffs protect her forearms. Her dark trousers stretch with her movements. Sure, they may also shape to her muscles and show off what she's working with, but that's *not the point*—as a skyfarer, it's astro-compatible. And, crucially, can't be grabbed.

All the better for survival.

She might be cavalier with her life through her monster hunting missions, but she won't be made a fool by the functionality of her outfits. She'd much rather be battle-ready than strutting around in shined boots with lavish buckles.

Unlike some...

The Hero's torque is fraught with electricity as she holds his glare with a practised coolness that's landed her in more than a few tavern fights over her twenty-nine sun-orbits.

A quick glance to the group lets her know their eyes are

pinging between them as though they're watching contenders in some arena battle.

Theseus can do politics and de-escalation when she can be bothered. Right now, she probably *should* be bothered. Shared words might be useful. But while Theseus is skilled with her tongue, it has never translated to an ability or inclination to learn more than a few choice words of any local language. Besides, Minos is so well geared to tourists that few learn the language. The Athenian Expanse is only one sun over, but its languages aren't widespread here, even amongst those in the tourist trade.

In a professional capacity, it's crucial to be armed with at least a few sentences when venturing to unfamiliar worlds. Phrases like: "I'm just here to kill a monster," "*How many* heads?" and "No, please, don't erect a monument in my honour," are helpful, while, "Do you have a spouse or partners you've promised yourself to?" can help avoid unintended turmoil when it's time to relax. There'd also been that one time she'd wished she'd asked: "If we have sex in the arena's sky box, will I be chased across the galaxies by your mother's fleet of wrecker ships?" But hopefully that one never rears its head, or several—like some mythical beast—again.

Other words, like "Yes," "No," "May I?" "More," "Harder," "Right there," are immensely useful in a variety of circumstances. And her vocabulary of anatomy... well... that's important should anything be injured on a mission, of course.

But uttering any of her stock phrases right now will only anger the beast. Though it's tempting, just to see what he'll do.

Instead, in her best impression of someone with a phlegm issue, she tells him in the most basic Minosian: "I—no speak—Minosian. Speak—you—Athenian?"

The Hero stares at her, as if trying to catch her in a lie. Interesting. He might not be as surface deep as she'd thought. But wherever this delightful exchange is headed, the spectacle is interrupted by simultaneous *clunks* from the two internal doors.

All eyes swerve to the colossal structures as a *tick-tick-tick* from beyond them... or within them... punctuates the passing moments. Mechanisms *click-clunk* into place. A lock engaging or disengaging? Something waltzing into alignment?

With a mighty groan, both doors swing open.

3

DANGER

While everyone else—the Hero included—recoils from whatever perils lie beyond the doors, Theseus steps forward.

Both passages appear almost the same: as in the gatehouse, luminous, multicoloured blocks line the walls, lighting the way. And though pulsing veins of orange lava thread both the walls and floor, giving the corridor a furnace-like hue, it remains only comfortably warm.

Both directions are populated with neatly painted signage in a host of languages. The majority feature the flowing pictography of Minosian, but there are at least half a dozen others, including Theseus's own. The left-hand corridor warns:

DANGER

TURN BACK

SERIOUSLY!

DON'T BE AN IDIOT

Theseus smirks. She's never felt *seen* by a sign before.

Oof. A solid blow to her shoulder jolts her forward. The Hero and his heavy rucksack are forging a path straight through her, apparently. What is his problem? And what in the heavens has he got in his bag? She catches the Minosian word for 'tourist' in his disdainful mumble, his sneer directed both at her and the Minotaur plushie hanging from the strap of her rucksack.

Jerk.

She knows it's all kinds of wrong to punch someone in the face for being subpar in the personality department, but it is tempting. Still, there are more important things to be getting on with.

The righthand corridor is more inviting, with signs that say things like THIS WAY and SAFE TRAVELS.

It should take no more than five seconds to sprint from here to the end of either corridor. Unless there are... surprises.

The massive doors are ticking again. Mechanisms shifting into place? A countdown? Nothing speeds things up like a deadline.

Not trusting the signs, Theseus untucks her cord necklace from beneath her armour and unclips the coin-like pendant. When the way forward isn't clear, may as well flip a coin.

Heads—that is, a creature with one head lion and one head goat—for right.

Tails—that is, rear end of a creepy goat with a serpentine tail —for left.

She flips it.

Smoothed over time and pressure from her thumb and thoughts, the coin is dull but has enough of a gleam at its edges to accentuate the strange glint in the Hero's eyes. Watching her.

As if the coin threatens his authority, the Hero takes a decisive step towards the left corridor, summoning his followers to... well, follow.

The coin lands in Theseus's palm. She flips it onto the back of her opposite hand to read the result.

Creepy serpent goat-butt. Left. The same direction the Hero has chosen. It irks her, even though it shouldn't.

She steps up to the threshold, level with the Hero, while the twelve shuffle behind them. Well... more behind him, really.

Is that fear hovering beyond his veneer of charm, or calculation? With a winning smile, he gestures in a manner that can only mean 'after you'.

How fucking kind.

Well, whatever. She was going this way anyway and it's both a hobby and a profession to be swaggering head-first into danger. Tucking her pendant beneath her armour, she steps into the corridor.

No footsteps follow. Which is... fair enough. Her hand hovering above the hilt of her sword, she treads past the dark stone walls with their luminous, colourful stripes—seeking any visual, auditory or atmospheric clue as to what in Hades and the Heavens is going on here.

Behind her, the ticking stops.

When she glances back, the door is closing, and the group shuffles like a herd of herbivores at the threshold, uncertain which way escapes the slaughterhouse. The Hero steps into the corridor and the rest of the company follows. With the grinding of internal mechanisms, the gateway shuts.

Reaching the end of the first corridor, Theseus rounds the blind corner to find more signage insisting she TURN BACK and...

A tree?

Its canopy of dull gold and silver leans out across the middle of the corridor like an archway. Its charcoal roots are sprawled, clinging within the wall's lava-channels, interrupting the path of the liquid fire. Nature versus architecture—it's not clear which is in charge here.

The Hero struts past her, broadsword drawn, but he pauses only a few strides ahead, nodding for Theseus to go first.

Seriously? What a hero.

Theseus passes cautiously beneath the branches, half expecting the tree to *do* something. She has no fucking idea what, but with its roots dipped in lava it might be made of sturdier stuff than this 'tourist.'

Though, it's possible this labyrinth is merely a bunch of illuminated corridors whose only threat is their ability to unravel the mind with the false promise of danger. But her instincts say otherwise.

There's a fine line between panic and actual warning. But right now, there's something... different. Her arm and neck hairs prickle. Her stomach tightens as a growling roar rumbles along the corridor, rebounding from the walls.

Is that the roar of the beast, or the Labyrinth?

Her hand gravitates to the hilt of her sword as she holds her breath and swivels, checking all directions as the roar continues to reverberate.

Disquiet sinks bone deep. Some would call it fear. Whatever. It'll keep her alive. There's a warmth at her neck; her stupid torque. Great. A distraction is just what she needs right now. And, she's not the only one tugging at the uninvited jewellery. Behind her, the group's torques are all frazzling electric-blue, jagged and agitated like their movements and mutterings.

The Hero cuts across them with something that sounds sharp and unsympathetic. Yeah... Theseus really should have learned more Minosian.

She turns the next corner, and stops. Because a fast-approaching wall of mist rolling toward you is never *good*, is it?

She retraces her steps at a sprint to alert the group but—she skids to a halt, because *oh shit*—a second bank of white cloud folds in from behind them.

It's too late. They're already surrounded, the mist obscuring everything.

The tainted, shimmering air hits Theseus's lungs. Bitter with a sour tang, it clings to her pores like sweat in a tropical storm.

She reinstates her jaw guards, triggering her invisi-visor and the whisper-mesh spanning out from her armour and helmet, hugging invisibly to her. She curses herself for her rookie error, but there's no point in dwelling. At least there are no immediate or obvious effects. There's a vague buzzing beneath her skin, but that could just be adrenaline.

And, damn, she'd forgotten about her muted helmet. Her stampeding heartbeat and uneven breaths crowd her.

Theseus winces as a flash of gold sizzles through the churning mist. *Stars above,* does he have to be so *shiny*? Perhaps it's tactical. Perhaps the Minotaur will be blinded by his opulence. Or perhaps she's getting a damn migraine—

Blades slice the mist—

Tiny bursts of torque-lightning skitter within the storm as Theseus dodges three wayward sword swipes. *This* is why civilians shouldn't be allowed the pointy weapons—and why she usually goes on missions alone. Devolving into chaos didn't take long, did it? She's seen ice dams in a wildfire melt more slowly than this lot.

These so-called criminals are probably farmers, miners or in the tourism trade; swords to them are a decoration, not a tool with which to prove self-worth.

It's a good thing the only weapons allowed on this ceremonial journey towards redemption or death are blades—they'd all have been mown down by bullets by now, otherwise.

Clunk—

The hit is so ineffectual, Theseus can only raise an eyebrow at the blade resting against her torso-armour, cutting the whisper-mesh briefly before it self-heals. The man with the face tattoos looks at her with terror in his eyes. When Theseus shrugs to let him know 'don't worry about it', his brow quirks with a mix of apology and utter relief.

As Theseus navigates through the mist, he remains within her orbit, as if his panic is lessened by Theseus's calm in the face of the group's fast unspooling sanity.

Theseus has no problem with that—so long as he keeps his blade to himself.

A sudden shift in the shimmering mist—

Is that the creature? Sprinting? Darting through the mist? Churning it? All the while hidden by it?

Theseus steps towards the movement and stumbles as the toe of her boot meets something in the swamp of mist. Recovering, she crouches to inspect it.

Vacant eyes stare up at her as the fallen's torque's electric wisps extinguish to nothing. Their face is rigid with panic and death and striped with blood. There's nothing she can do.

Fuck.

No-one deserves this.

At the injustice, her jaw clenches. Her fists do, too. She stands, silently promising the deceased that she'll end the beast. End this place.

She unsheathes her short-sword and flips it. The blade slices the mist and the hilt lands in her palm as she tests the weight of her tool of choice, recalibrating to the Labyrinth's gravity. As expected, it's damn near perfectly aligned to Minosian standard.

The tangled mist unknots a little but horror and guilt twist inside her as she swivels to take in the aftermath.

Blood. Everywhere.

Tattoo, Hero, and four others are still standing, but as Theseus wades through the lingering mist, her steady motion parting it, she discovers the four... five... six more fallen, all striped with blade marks, their armour punctured and buckled.

Did the Minotaur's horns do this?

Bile taunts the back of her throat. She came here to save these people, and look how that's going. One encounter with the hidden beast, and already half their company has fallen. She should be scared, but instead her pounding heart is fuelling her inner rage, shifting it into something lethal.

She tugs at her heated torque, as pinching and unwanted as a noose, just as a disruption in the mist—about twenty paces away, maybe—summons her attention.

A figure takes shape.

A crown of thick horns, curled forward like weapons, pierce the thickened air. Fast, hard breaths churn it. Glowing eyes as cold as ice, as hot as blue flame—whichever is worse—cut through the haze. Its skin, tar-like. Solidly built, muscular, and tall, the creature's epic stature haunts the mist.

As still as a predator, the creature is staring right at her. Something about its posture, the tilt of its head... it's *assessing* her.

And, for a moment, Theseus can only stare right back.

Sure, all the legends say its horns are sharp as razors and that it eats human flesh, but— *Pfft*. She's not worried.

Aaaaand it's running right at her—

Well, shit.

4

MINOTAUR

First rule of monster hunting: Survive first. Have feelings later.

Theseus grips her sword and shield, knuckles set, her every muscle ready, and launches herself at the charging beast.

It weaves and veers and ducks as they barrel towards each other, tying the mist and Theseus's focus in knots. She tries to keep her eyes locked on it, but—

Hades and the Heavens. Her head spins as its glinting horns slice the mist to ribbons.

The thing is fast. It's nimbler than it looks, too.

But she refuses to be outwitted by a creature with hooves for hands.

Her blood thumps like a war drum in her ears as she accelerates. Only ten more paces away—

But pain flares through her shin as something hits her. Legs knocked from under her, she slams into the floor, rolling with the momentum.

The beast must have thrown something.

Stars above. A weapon-throwing hoofed creature? That's the last thing she needs.

Whatever it threw, there's no blood... she's still intact.

The air above her glints like a blade—

Another thrown weapon?

Theseus springs to her feet, but before she can fully rise, a flash of glowering blue eyes accompanies a *thud* and her own *oof*, as the world-upending momentum of the creature's shoulder knocks her off her feet and lands her firmly on her back.

It's not a position she usually lets herself get into.

A solid arm clamps about her chest, pinning her sword-wielding arm uselessly beneath her shield as the creature drags her across the stones, back the way she came.

Shit.

Don't get skewered on your own fucking sword. That's not even a rule of monster hunting. That's just common sense.

She angles it away from herself.

The creature is so fast, so purposeful, Theseus wouldn't be surprised if a secret passage opened up, swallowing her into its den.

The scuffing of her boots as her legs paddle against the floor vibrates through her. The creature's breaths steam against her neck. Its jaws are too fucking close.

"*Don't wait for death. Make your move.*" Herakles's guiding voice again: wise, calm and frustratingly obvious.

Thanks for the wisdom, *buddy.*

"*Well, if you only got on with it, I wouldn't have to—*"

Yeah, yeah.

Theseus thrashes her legs out, jolting her body up. The creature stumbles and falls, and the arm across Theseus's chest disappears as the creature flails. They both land heavily, skidding across the floor in opposite directions.

But the creature is back on its feet with the kind of solid agility athletes dream about. And it's not just being winded that has Theseus lagging behind... It's just that... the creature's legs are... human-shaped, encased in trousers and capped boots not dissimilar to Theseus's own. *Stars.* Yes, the Minotaur is reported to have the head of a bull and the body of a person, but Theseus hadn't expected they'd have similar, sensible footwear.

"*Focus, Theseus. It's trying to kill you,*" Herakles' imaginary voice reminds her. "*Get up.*"

Theseus leaps to her feet, adjusting the sword in her grasp. If she'd been looking to impress anyone, keeping hold of her weapon in such a circumstance might do the trick.

"*This is no time for gloating.*"

The creature lunges.

Theseus sword-swipes, but sizeable bull-horns deflect the strike. She lashes out with her shield instead, an uppercut to the creature's bull-nose. If the creature cries out, Theseus can't hear it.

It recovers too fast, knocking her sword and shield aside, its hoofed arms clamping around her, lifting her and slamming her against the opposite wall—

Theseus's stomach flips. *Please don't vomit—*

Gravity tugs her insides and balance in a new direction. The wall the creature just shoved her against is now the floor. So multidirectional gravity is a thing here? Good to know.

Directly above her face, the creature's shoulders are heaving as Theseus's sword and shield drop down beside them.

Bracketed by the creature's limbs, Theseus grabs her sword and slashes up at its solid neck—

A forearm—distractingly human-like in its musculature—strikes the sword from Theseus's hand, but not before her blade makes contact. The creature jolts back, but any sounds are silenced by Theseus's helmet.

The corridor lurches, sudden enough and angled enough that blood drips from the red slick line across the Minotaur's right upper arm—likely only a surface wound, but a wound all the same—to splatter across Theseus's torso-armour.

Gross.

The creature recoils and Theseus scans the ground for her sword.

Shit. *First rule of monster hunting: Don't lose your fucking weapon.* Easier said than done when there's a Minotaur standing with surefooted ease on your new horizontal, between you and said weapon.

"*Use gravity to your advantage,*" suggests the imagined voice of Herakles, and Theseus lunges from her floored position, boot-swiping the creature's legs from under it, felling it so suddenly that her own back twinges in sympathy.

Theseus scoops up her sword, but—quick as lightning—the beast knocks her off her feet, its solid weight landing atop her, its hooves anchoring her arms.

Fuck's sake. Good thing she's not on a mission to impress a Minotaur!

The corridor trembles.

Her captor's arms ripple with muscle. Its tar-like skin pulses with orange veins. It's like she's not fighting some creature, but some impossible creation of science or sorcery that lurks only in nightmares.

Theseus strains her every muscle, uselessly, against the impossible beast, but she can't move her arms an inch, and her hips are so heavily pinned her legs can't do a damn thing.

A torturous heat sinks through her. Rage at the creature's crimes. Shame at not being able to bring Justice. Embarrassment at being so easily and thoroughly bested. And the heat at her throat is choking; her torque sparking enough that even she can see the electricity spiking.

Fuck.

She's met her match.

And all the creature is doing is watching her. Is it savouring its kill? Its victory?

What's it waiting for?

Her breath stutters. It could be her last—

But the creature leaps away, retreating into the lingering mist.

...the fuck?

In the moments it takes Theseus to recalibrate and steady her breaths, the shimmering mist unravels, and the corridor un-tilts itself.

Where did the creature go?

And for that matter, where is everyone else?

5

THESEUS, MONSTER HUNTER

It's not like Theseus *wanted* to be rescued, anyway.

She's suddenly bone tired. Who knew that wrestling the Sky Labyrinth's very own, very murderous house pet would be such great exercise?

It's unsettling, though. It wasn't skill or strength that won her the scuffle, but... luck? The creature getting spooked? Its boredom? Or its desire to prolong the chase?

Whichever it was, it's sure dented her pride.

But enough of that. *First rule of monster hunting: Keep your wits about you.* (There are a lot of 'first rules' of monster hunting, most of them relevant to self-preservation. All of which Herakles is equally emphatic about. It's like she thinks Theseus has a death wish or something.)

With the strange mist gone, Theseus unclips her astro-helmet to listen, but discovers only gentle creaks and groans from the labyrinth. She takes a few sips from the hydration tube attached to her ruckack's sternum strap, then scoffs a nutrition bar. That'll keep her sharp for a while, despite the lingering buzz that's been needling beneath her skin since the mist hit.

The floor's dark, irregular, stone-like material gives the place a fortress feel. The uneven walls and their occasional stripes of colourful light add to the shadows. There's a gnarled tree protruding from between the bricks, clinging in place with solid roots. Surely that's over nineteen sun-orbits of growth?

But the most unsettling detail, the one she can't get her head around, is the damn signage. 'THIS WAY'; 'SAFE PASSAGE'. Are they part of the Architect's design? Are they a cruelty or a kindness? Do they reward trust or punish it? *Is this all some mind game?* Theseus has never been a fan of those. She's more of a throw-a-sword-at-a-problem type than a navigate-mind-games type.

Perhaps some of the Labyrinth's past victims took the time to share their knowledge of the safer paths? But it's a rare person who prioritises others during their own peril, let alone creates extensive signage in the circumstances.

The others must have followed the signs, too, because it's not long before familiar Minosian voices—sharp and agitated—reach her from the corridor ahead.

It takes longer than it should for the Hero and the six remaining others to notice Theseus emerging from the shadows. When they do, several of them startle as though *she's* the Minotaur. One even throws—with thankfully appalling aim—a dagger, which lands with a *clang* a full sword's length to Theseus's right.

Theseus raises an eyebrow at the blue-haired, blue-eyed knife-thrower, who looks more alarmed than sorry. Theseus shrugs at her, pointing a thumb back over her shoulder. "Minotaurs. Am I right?"

The Minosians' general response to her still being alive seems to be confusion and, possibly, awe?

According to her tourist guide-Shard, no one has faced the Minotaur and survived. Though, since the only ones to witness the events of this place are those who never return, it's not clear how that would be known. Those who have faced the creature might have done so and survived... they just didn't survive *in the end*. Anyway, the point is she's not sure she merits praise right now.

Which is why it's a little jarring that the blue-haired knife-thrower's alarm morphs to an attentive intrigue, like she wishes she'd thrown herself at Theseus instead of the knife. Which she basically does: pawing at Theseus, as if her biceps are in need of thorough inspection. She doesn't need to speak Minosian to understand Blue's thinly veiled intent. And, if they were literally anywhere else under the Seven Suns, Theseus would probably be open to something... energetic.

It so happens that her approach to bedding women is not dissimilar to her approach to monster killing. Both involve a notable amount of screaming, though the former involves zero weapons and fewer restraints. But even Theseus isn't stupid enough to get frisky in a death labyrinth. And, besides, she's got a princess to save.

Still, it's an ego boost.

The Hero, meanwhile, is glowering at her like she's grown another head. Theseus squints, because either the mist is still affecting her, or he's just way too shiny. Seriously. His armour is a literal eyesore right now. He schools his expression into socially expected relief at her presence, but she catches the split-second detour via something to be concerned about.

She's seen eyes like his before. She knows not to trust them. The sharpness beneath is a hidden spear.

Perhaps she's underestimated him. She'd pissed him off before, sure—he hasn't hidden his dislike for her—but to be actively disappointed by her survival? Yeah... that lumps him into a whole new category of asshole.

Maybe it's best if she curbs her enthusiasm for winding him up. *Maybe.*

He asks something that might be, "Is the Minotaur dead?" Someone else blinks at her hopefully, calling out something with the word 'kill'. Maybe, "Did you kill it?"

Theseus shakes her head and stretches her aching shoulders. "I didn't die. And that currently feels like an achievement." Though not an earned one, but nobody needs to know that.

Blue beams at her, saying something about 'love' and 'accent'. Minosian dialects are surprisingly ugly for such a beauty-obsessed world, but to outsiders, apparently, Athenian sounds like poetry; philosophy in motion, with a musical lilt. Which is ill-fitting: Athenians might be philosophical, but they're also known for their military might. And if there's one thing Theseus isn't, it's fucking poetic.

Though tell that to Blue who's practically eating her with her eyes.

The tattoo-faced man rumbles something. There's a tremor in his voice and worry in his eyes. She thinks he's asking, "Are you okay?" If the group had been debating whether to go back for her, she'd guess Tattoo would have argued for her rescue.

His eyes lower and his concern seems to be aimed at her armour. Theseus wipes at her chest-plate. "It's not my blood."

The group's sudden utterances almost have her reaching for her sword, until she recalls some of the words. In amongst the noise, there are curses that roughly translate as '*Confound and flummox*'. Minosian swear words tend not to land in translation.

She follows the group's widened eyes, glued to the patch of armour she's just cleaned. Well, *cleaned* is a loose term...

Oh. Now she sees it.

The next words she doesn't understand entirely, and it's not clear whether they're talking to her or about her, but the overall tone seems more excited than panicked?

Either way, she knows the Minosian for 'Athenian Expanse' because it's basically those same words. *Shit.* Serves her right for parading around in armour with stupid royal insignias on. She'd chosen to wear it only because it's *good* armour, and because the insignia had been hidden by its tarnish.

She doesn't particularly want the attention of the six circling her—or the Hero's unsettling gaze.

"Theseus," says one of the six, with a twinkle of reverence in his eyes, followed by the next choking cough, which... yeah... would be Minosian for 'Monster Hunter'.

Well... it looks like tales of her adventures have reached Minos. Theseus squirms. For some reason, people love a bloody tale, and monster hunting happens to generate the kind of stories that amplify with distance and repetition. When she—on occasion—is regaled with tales of the mighty Theseus, they're always exaggerated, often crediting her with the impossible. She hasn't yet defied gravity, but it's embarrassing—for them *and* her —what people will believe. That's why she'd rather she and her armour blend with the shadows, thank you very much.

From the Hero's forced smile, he'd rather that, too.

Anyway. Enough dithering. They can't keep shuffling about hoping to avoid the Minotaur forever.

She reclaims her sword from its scabbard and chooses a direction, determined to discover what else this place has up its whisper-mesh sleeve.

The six follow as if magnetised to her, as Hero trails with obvious reluctance. Having followers isn't ideal for stealth, nor for using herself as bait, but each time she tells them to stop, with obvious gestures too, shooing them away, they wait until she carries on and damn well follow her again.

She had a similar *follower* problem once before, back when she'd been less purposeful. She'd passed out, drunk, and awoken to find a gaggle of goslings had imprinted on her. It wasn't ideal, but she'd made sure they found safety. If only she could reason as easily with this lot.

She's made it hardly any distance at all—a mere two corridors—before Hero steps in and demonstrates he can't stand being anything other than in charge. He barks out what can only be orders. Blue clings to Theseus's arm, just a little too tight.

Obviously not one to risk his authority being undermined, Hero lets their pairing be, while he selects Tattoo as his companion. Once Hero doles out which corridors each of them are to investigate, the group disperses.

As soon as Theseus and Blue are alone, Theseus resolutely ignores Blue's intense gaze and leads the way. If it can be called that, when Blue is essentially attached to her.

Theseus clears her throat, about to beg the woman to stop stroking her arm so she can concentrate—but Blue, misconstruing her intent, lunges forward and plants a hungry kiss against her lips.

It's not a *bad* kiss, just... unexpected and overenthusiastic; enough to tackle them both to the floor like Theseus is back wrestling with the Minotaur. Blue grins, a wild glint in her eyes.

Stars above. Now is really not the time...

First rule of monster hunting: Don't get caught with your trousers down when—

An echoing roar summons their attention, snapping Blue out of her stupor and Theseus into action.

6

LURE

Theseus understands the Minosian for 'Quick' and 'Help', which is what the Hero is bellowing from the distant end of the curved corridor.

Tattoo's cries reach for her as she skids to his side. He's on his back, blood soaking his front and pooling beneath him; his armour split by two deep puncture wounds. Shit. The creature must have had some momentum to run him right through.

Next time she sees that thing—

She shakes herself.

Survive first. Feelings later.

She swivels her rucksack onto her front and retrieves her medi-kit. The beast might be hiding mere paces away, watching. This could be a trap. But she can't leave Tattoo like this.

Her focus skitters up and down the curved corridor. About fifty paces away, there's a ceiling hatch, but nothing else. No sign of the beast. Perhaps the Hero scared it away. Fair enough. It wouldn't surprise her if he'd pushed Tattoo into the path of danger to save his own damn skin.

She crouches beside Tattoo, angling herself to keep the Hero and the hatch in her line of sight. "Keep watch," she tells him, with words and gestures, and he plainly understands because he scoffs.

Blue catches up, distress contorting her face, but keeps her distance as Theseus tends to Tattoo's wounds as best she can. There's only so much she can do when the wounds are organ-deep. She's saved—and lost—enough lives to know on which face Tattoo's coin will land.

He reaches for her, tears and panic in his eyes. Is he telling her to stop? Or begging her not to? Theseus squeezes his bloody hands, wishing she could make it all okay.

"You'll be out of here soon enough," she tells him in Athenian. Doubtless he has no idea what she just said, but he stills, like all that remains is the inevitable.

And there's nothing Theseus can do as the light in his eyes dims.

Theseus springs to her feet, destined to throw or punch something—*fuck*—but tamping down the urge. Her resolve solidifies to something sharp and unforgiving. She'll show that creature what death feels like if it's the last thing she does.

The remaining four rush towards them. The relief in their postures must be from returning to the flock, their panic-widened eyes from the gruesome tableau before them.

That Tattoo's death could be a trap settles in her veins like ice. They shouldn't be here. They need somewhere to hide.

Shoving her medi-kit back into her rucksack, Theseus surveys their surroundings.

The hatch at the curve of the corridor, fifty paces away... Beneath it, embedded in the wall, there's a ladder-like series of protruding bricks. While the Hero regales the group with what appears to be—judging from his gestures—a grandiose retelling of events, Theseus climbs the ladder.

Of course, a switch in gravitational direction when she needs it would be too easy, wouldn't it?

The hatch is too narrow for a creature with a crown of horns to climb through. She peers up through the opening. Her shoulder torches aren't angled right, so she uses her spool of luminous thread like a fire-torch. She'd rather be venturing sword-first, but she needs to see and she needs to hold on, so...

But there's no need for her defensive approach. Because up here, there is nothing but space.

Literally.

The alcove is some kind of observation platform. A floor-to-ceiling porthole occupies the outer wall, framing the planet Minos like an oversized lump of coal webbed with bursts of light. But it's the stars that capture Theseus's attention. *Sky glitter*, her mother used to call them, before Theseus had learned not to be taken in by pretty things.

She checks the area for any surprises, then returns to the group and points up, trying to express that this is a hiding place where the Minotaur can't get to them because of its wide-set horns. She never was any good at charades. Still, the group, rattled by—well, everything—seem relieved at the chance to be tucked away for a while. Even Blue joins the others.

Hero, meanwhile, follows her, watching as she unspools her medi-thread from beyond the hatch, down the corridor and along to Tattoo. As she'd suspected, the thread isn't long enough, so she adds to it with the luminous thread to cover the rest of the distance.

Is Hero staring at her or the thread? He seems the sort to be taken with the shiny things in life. Armour. Accolades. Luminous thread. The look of hero-worship in gullible eyes.

A warning chill reminds her to keep him in sight.

She ties the glowing thread about Tattoo's ankle, hiding it beneath his boot and tucking it out of sight, beneath him. At least this way there's no lit-up trail leading to their hiding place.

The trap is set.

Moments later, alongside the rest of the group, Theseus tries to get comfortable up in the alcove beyond the hatch. All they have to do now is stay quiet and wait.

Because monsters don't give up, not without a fight. It's about the only thing about them Theseus understands.

And the Hero needs to back the fuck off. Slumped against the sizeable porthole, his silhouette hides all but the essence of his face. His eyes glimmer, but it's not magical like sky glitter. It's dangerous, like the space between stars.

He watches her as she loops the end of the dull thread about her wrist, his attention as unwelcome as the torque around her neck.

What in the Seven Heavens is his problem?

The glare of his armour pulses in line with the prickling buzz under her skin. Is this the mist's effects or a migraine?

Theseus schools her features into calm disinterest. She won't give him the satisfaction of showing her discomfort. They could be here a while, and there are far more attractive topics she could be thinking about.

Keeping him in her peripheral vision, she hides the luminous spool in her rucksack's secret compartment and plumps her bag like a pillow. Settling against it, she gazes out at the burning coal of planet Minos, floating in its sea of stars, its skyports teaming with activity as the sun sets on the planetary horizon.

7

PRINCESS

The night before entering the Sky Labyrinth...

"Are you enjoying your stay on my world?" asks Princess Ariadne, Minosian and Athenian tussling under the translation tincture, the toying lilt in her tone loud and clear.

It's the sort of translation tincture that's hard to come by in much of the Seven Heavens. Certainly not cheap. That she would use it on a criminal... that's... interesting...

"I am now." Theseus's playful smirk is counterbalanced by a solid thump to the back of her shoulders. Her ankle-cuffs hold her in place while her upper body cants forward. *Hades and the Heavens*, she hates having to bow to arbitrary power. Especially when someone shoves her from behind to do it.

Theseus casts a scolding glance over her shoulder at the official oaf with the personality of a brick and a grip like iron who'd fetched her from the subterranean prison where she's been kept since committing her crime.

She's occupied more than her fair share of cells and has to admit the Minosian prison is more aesthetically pleasing than most of the places she's lived in her life, even if the ubiquitous geometric patterns are challenging on the eye. Though it's nothing compared to the lavish living chambers she's standing in—vaulted ceilings, marble pillars, precious metals gleaming—waiting to discover why the Minosian Princess has summoned her.

Lounging in an oversized gilded throne, Princess Ariadne appears more focused on something outside her window than Theseus or her servants. Is she admiring her sizeable balcony and the golden sky-motor that's a crime against taste? Or is her gaze on the star-studded night sky and Minos's mechanical moon?

She looks a little younger than Theseus's twenty-nine standard sun-orbits, but she likely has a youth-preserving trick or two up her satin sleeve. She's still decorated in the same flowing charcoal and sea-green tuxedo-gown she'd worn for the day's celebrations, but now her golden wreath-crown sits askew, and her posture is no longer as straight as her gleaming honey-coloured hair. She's been on display all day, and now she looks royally fed up.

Great. The last thing Theseus needs is to be subject to the whims of a cranky princess, even one who occupies her throne with an admirable dose of *fuck you* attitude. It's rare to find someone in possession of *swagger* when sitting still.

With the kind of sweeping gesture only royals can get away with, the Princess summons her closer. Theseus's gravity-cuffs remain heavy about her wrists and ankles, but their strength dials down enough, apparently, for her to obey.

Obey with her own dose of swagger, obviously.

The warden follows like a shadow.

The servants keep their eyes lowered as Theseus passes them. Either they have no wish to acknowledge a criminal, or they're in no position to interact. She might be the one in literal chains right now—well, gravity-cuffs—but the servants lack their freedoms too.

At the foot of the steps to the throne, the gravity-cuffs reassert themselves, pinching her in place so abruptly it threatens her balance. For the sudden tension to have somewhere to go, her arms strain and her teeth grit.

The corner of the Princess's mouth curls, electricity rippling from the elaborate torque at the hollow of her throat. If Theseus isn't mistaken, Princess Ariadne is assessing her. She's taking her time about it, too. Is she questioning Theseus's capability to undermine her laws, or does she like what she sees?

The Princess leans forward, her loosened gown falling open to reveal a silk waistcoat embroidered with intricate designs. She's too far away for Theseus to decipher the detail of the patterns, but the fabric has a lustre to it that would have her reaching out, if she weren't in these cuffs.

And with royal permission, of course.

The Princess's growing smirk suggests she knows exactly where Theseus's mind is wandering. "Tell me. Why are you here?"

A good question.

Theseus's travel agent had done all they could to steer her towards any other place: "Hesperides is wonderful at this point in its sun-orbit," "The mountains of Erymanthos are simply breathtaking. Do pack a fully oxygen-stocked astro-suit." If Theseus had listened, she could be hunting an escaped giant rodent at the Thessalian amusement moon, or decapitating a multiheaded serpent in the sweetly fragranced swamps of Lerna. But perhaps she's the one who's lost her head, because voyaging to the galactic region of the Fourth Sun and committing a crime to infiltrate the deadly Sky Labyrinth to try her skills against the infamous Minotaur, probably wasn't the wisest of moves. Even if it's earned her an audience with a formidable and attractive princess.

"The celebrations of the Righteous Path are a wonder to behold," she says. "So I was told."

Princess Ariadne raises one perfect eyebrow. "Did you not enjoy our celebrations? Too busy testing boundaries, perhaps?"

If Theseus had to guess what a festival of the Righteous Path would look like—an event that is essentially a celebration of mass murder masquerading as Justice—well, she'd have thought it to be a more sombre affair. That there'd be less singing, dancing and all-round pageantry, much less vibrancy and artistic flare in the costumes and interpretive re-enactments.

Children and adults alike had seemed to take pride in strutting about the architecturally overcomplicated streets, playing out the battle of mortal-versus-Minotaur with toy weapons, as if that's what it means to be *a hero*. But there's no denying that the 'Minotaurs'—conveyed through all manner of masks from the morbid to the monstrous—had been having an enjoyably unhinged time.

Perhaps everyone on Minos just needs to let off a little steam.

Theseus knows what it's like to have a monster constantly occupying your thoughts as you go about your day: taunting you, daring you to let your guard down. It's exhausting—no wonder Minosians all look so tired—but it can be such a relief to let your frustrations loose, too.

"You know..." begins the Princess, standing slowly, one hand in her tuxedo-gown pocket, the other placing atop the hilt of the sword at her hip, as if purposefully drawing Theseus's attention to it. *Heavens, please let that sword be only for show.* "...most in your position throw themselves on their knees and beg my forgiveness."

Theseus buries her smirk. She wants to find the Princess annoying—princesses *are* annoying (she should know)—but the glint in Princess Ariadne's eyes is either mischief or the spark that precedes a wildfire.

"*This is dangerous*," warns Herakles' voice, in her thoughts. "*Perhaps more dangerous than the Sky Labyrinth.*"

Shut up, Herakles. Theseus has already destined herself to a probable grisly death; she may as well have a little fun first.

Theseus leans forward, just a little. "I can think of far more interesting things to do on my knees than beg forgiveness, Princess."

Oof! With a solid thump to her back, Theseus jerks forward, her knees slamming against the first step of the stairway. Thankfully, the oaf in charge of her gravity-cuffs must have been awake enough to have temporarily released them, otherwise she'd have dislocated a few limbs. The cuffs tighten again to anchor her squarely in place: on her knees before the Princess, fists weighted at her sides.

The Princess's torque emits distracting blue sparks, but when Theseus meets her eyes, there's no sign of the anger Theseus had expected. Instead, there's... amusement?

Huh. Perhaps she's the one controlling the cuffs?

"You like to play with fire?" asks the Princess, sauntering down a couple of steps, accompanied by green flames in the gullies that flank the stairs.

Theseus squints, uncertain whether the question is rhetorical.

"Let me put this another way. What is the daughter of the Athenian Expanse doing running around my world, breaking my laws?"

Shit. Theseus schools her features, a little too late judging from the Princess's satisfied smile.

"I might live within these gilded walls, but even I have heard of the great Theseus. Monster Hunter. Athenian Princess.

Making quite a name for yourself, searching the skies for wrongs to right and monsters to vanquish."

Theseus swallows the lump in her throat, the one that always appears when someone brings up her heritage. The heritage that had landed in her life one day, and she's not known what to do with since.

"And now—lucky me—you're here, clogging up my prison cells." The Princess studies her so intently, it's almost enough to make Theseus squirm. Almost. "If I were utterly mad, or you were downright stupid, I'd think you had engineered circumstances to deliver you to my very own monster."

The Minosian Princess certainly isn't stupid. "Anyone that idiotic deserves the inevitable outcome, Princess. And it's not for me to say whether you're utterly mad—"

She doesn't flinch as the warden raises his hand to strike, but the Princess shoos him away with a *back the fuck off* gesture. A regal one, obviously. "Oh, calm down, warden. Anyone would think you're enjoying this."

The warden steps back, mumbling an apology. Theseus chews her cheek to bury her smirk. She doesn't want to overplay her hand.

The Princess descends a couple more steps before perching, lounging almost, putting her gaze level with Theseus's.

"Well," she says, "since you're on your knees..."

Theseus loses a breath. If the Princess expects to escalate their game of flirtation, Theseus sure won't be doing it in restraints, or in a room full of onlookers. She's only into that if onlookers and restraints are consenting and consensual, respectively. And she'd much rather not be the one in the cuffs.

"Aren't you going to list all your strengths for me?" The Princess's tone is less teasing, suddenly, and more... awaiting disappointment? "Why I should expect you to succeed where all others have failed?"

"Why would I? I've never faced a Minotaur before. I can be arrogant, Princess, and I can be stupid. But I try to never combine the two."

Princess Ariadne opens her mouth, but no sound emerges. Theseus might label her reaction as shock if she understood what had caused it.

"Well." The Princess clears her throat, standing again. "Thanks to your crimes, tomorrow you get to discover first-hand why the people of Minos stay within the Righteous Path. The Labyrinth is the ultimate judgement."

Theseus scoffs. The warden steps forward again, fist raised, but the Princess interrupts. "Everyone out. You too, warden."

Without protest, every servant files out in a swift and orderly manner. Only once the doors shut and silence rings out does the Princess gesture for Theseus to stand.

The Princess's hand emerges from her pocket with what must be the control for Theseus's gravity-cuffs, because the weight lessens once more. Theseus rises slowly, in case the Princess tries to catch her off-guard. She could do without pulled muscles or torn tendons the night before she heads to her punishment in the skies.

The cuffs anchor her again as the Princess descends another couple of steps. How in the heavens does she not trip in that gown? The thing is as ridiculously impractical as manoeuvring in it is impressive.

"Do you always question the ways of worlds you are a guest upon?"

A guest? Is that what they're calling it? The lodgings are exceptional. The gravity-cuffs, not so much. But in truth, Theseus generally likes to be respectful of customs. "It's usually my mouth that gets me into trouble, Princess." Theseus adds a cheeky smile for good—perhaps unwise—measure.

"I have no doubt." The Princess's eyes flash with amusement

before turning more serious. "You have a problem with our system of redemption?"

"From what I understand, no-one has yet been redeemed. And I would question whether a creature in a labyrinth is the best judge of guilt or innocence."

The Princess narrows her eyes. "You are quite the puzzle. If you'd wanted to risk your life exploring my labyrinth, Theseus —Monster Killer, wayward daughter of the Athenian Expanse— you need only have asked. You could have ventured under the banner of Chosen Hero, rather than criminal."

"I've seen this sun-orbit's nomination. I'm not sure I fit the mould."

And how in the heavens the citizens of Minos believe that being sent to the Sky Labyrinth is both the worst punishment imaginable, and an honour worthy of the Chosen Hero, is a mind-fuck wonder of the universe.

"You're of royal blood, you have your own domain." The Princess completes her journey down the steps, her gaze now level with Theseus's again. "And yet you're here for mine?"

Heavens above and below, please don't let this escalate. Being of royal descent is the worst. Can't her actions just be her own and not be interpreted as political manoeuvrings?

Theseus shrugs. "My bio-father's the royal. I've never even met the man. Look, I'm just here to kill a monster. I have no interest in the prize of titles."

"The prize isn't merely a title. You must know that?"

Theseus's heartrate rallies as the Princess steps within arm's reach... or sword's reach... The torque about Theseus's neck grows warmer. The Princess's eyes flick to it, an unsettling smile on her lips.

Theseus clears her throat. How to tell a princess—an Architect, no less—that your only interest is in doing the right thing, which includes not *winning* her as a prize?

"There must be a better way to choose your bedmates, Princess." The Princess's grip tightens on the hilt of her sword, and Theseus's lungs constrict. She speaks fast. "My interest is only in seeing Minos freed from the Minotaur. I'm not here to marry a—" She swallows the word *spoiled*; even she isn't foolish enough to test the waters of this dynamic any further. "—uh... princess."

Princess Ariadne scowls. Is she pissed off or mystified?

"Others have all been more focused on claiming my world and occupying my bed. Anyone would think it's not really the creature they're looking to conquer. But you?" The Princess observes her coolly. "If I were prone to self-doubt, I might be offended."

"No offence is intended, your highness."

"Thank goodness." The Princess gives a smirk. "Otherwise we might have a diplomatic incident on our hands."

Playful. Yes. Theseus can do playful. She arches an eyebrow. "Like a daughter of the Athenian Expanse being put in gravity-cuffs?"

Princess Ariadne *hmmms* her amusement. "It would be a crime to miss seeing you strain against them." She makes no apology of trailing her gaze over Theseus's arms.

Stars above. Mirth sparkles in the Princess's eyes, rippling in the blue-green depths like lagoon waters stirred by a creature lurking. Her skin looks as flawless and smooth as the gemstones for sale in the tourist districts.

Now that Theseus is closer, it's clear the intricate patterning on her gown is some sort of puzzle—in fact, it's a labyrinth. *Of course it's a fucking labyrinth.* Theseus is a little worried at her own mental dexterity, though she can hardly be blamed for being distracted.

The Princess shrugs free of her tuxedo-gown, letting it pool on the floor without a backward glance, like maybe she'd expected a servant to step in to collect it mid-fall. *You did send your servants away, Princess.*

The shimmering gold thread woven through the fine material of her waistcoat follows the same labyrinthine design as her discarded layers. The ruffles adorning her stark white shirt are almost ridiculous. But Theseus can't keep her eyes off her. Her demeanour, her swagger; her slender folded arms and the assessing gaze that reminds Theseus she's being judged right now.

Green flames ignite in the floor furrows, following the Princess as she circles Theseus, inspecting her from every angle.

Theseus clears her throat. She's not here to play games, or to be toyed with. "The Labyrinth is your creation? You're the Architect?"

"The Labyrinth is mine. But I am an Architect-in-waiting. I will only ascend to the full title when someone solves my Labyrinth."

"It's very impressive, Princess. You creating such a structure and trapping the beast within."

There it is: a flicker of suspicion. The Princess's torque flickers too, along with the flames surrounding her. A natural flourish in the fuel supply, perhaps?

"You have some burning questions, Monster Hunter?"

"As I understand it, you discovered the Minotaur in the deepest of Minosian mines." Why do mythical beings always emerge from mines? And deep ones, too? "They say it's uncatchable, unkillable. That no-one knows whether it's a creation of science or magic, or simply a deadly design of the universe."

"Do you enjoy lecturing your hosts on the facts of their own worlds? What a bore you must be at dinner parties."

There's that fine line between pissed off and playful, and Theseus can't help but bite, holding their delicious, dangerous eye-contact. "I admit *dinner parties* aren't my forte, Princess."

A flash of intrigue lights Princess Ariadne's eyes, like she might be imagining exactly what Theseus's *forte* is. *Stars above and heavens below.* What is with this flirting? And is Theseus's thumping heart telling her to jump on the Princess, or run from her?

"I don't suppose you're heading towards a point?" The Princess sounds... intrigued?

"How? How do you catch and imprison an uncatchable beast?"

As if Princess Ariadne herself has the power of the Sky Labyrinth and its pet, to weigh and judge, she observes Theseus, cooly. "Perhaps you are lacking in imagination, Monster Hunter?"

Their gazes lock, and Theseus isn't sure whether she's captive or captivated. Her skin feels as hot as the flame-furrows at the Princess's feet. Fuck. She'd welcome showing the princess exactly how much of an imagination she has...

"Perhaps you are lacking in answers, Princess."

Well, she hasn't got this far without being *bold*, has she?

8

CHASE

Back in the Labyrinth...

The thread about Theseus's wrist twitches.

Immediately, she cuts the dull thread, letting it drop through the hatch. To remain undetected by the creature, and to not startle the already frazzled group, she calmly collects her gear, checking to ensure that the tools of her trade aren't going to give her away at an inopportune moment.

Her sword is secure in its scabbard, her shield over her rucksack like a tortoise shell. She tucks her dangling Minotaur plushie beneath the rucksack strap her astro-helmet is affixed to, like the toy is hitching a ride, and peers carefully down through the hatch.

She's half-expecting to get a face full of Minotaur. Instead, she finds the corridor dimmed; its lighting must have adjusted with Minosian night. And fifty paces away, where they'd left him, is the shadow shape of Tattoo's corpse, down-lit by the burning blue eyes of the looming beast.

Even from here, the creature's breaths are loud, like it's been running hard. When the creature lowers its head further, inspecting its prize, Theseus takes her opportunity to drop down to the corridor in practiced silence.

With its back to her, the Minotaur lifts Tattoo's boot, anchoring Tattoo's leg beneath its armpit and slowly, purposefully, drags him away.

It's not the frenzy Theseus would have guessed. And it's not just the Minotaur's lack of urgency, its slow procession, that's tugging at the threads of the uncanny.

It doesn't move like an animal.

Yes, Theseus has seen depictions of the Minotaur in various places under the Seven Suns, and in them the Minotaur is ordinarily upright, with a human body, hooves for hands, and the head and horns of a bull. All this checks out. But what's clear, now that Theseus isn't too busy being pummelled to notice, is just how *human* its gait is.

There's jostling above. The group must be growing impatient. She gestures for them to *quiet the fuck down*—that gesture is universal, at least—while, up ahead, the Minotaur pauses.

Theseus loses her breath somewhere in her chest. Maybe it didn't hear anything over the scuffing of Tattoo's armour against the ground?

The creature continues and Theseus lets herself breathe—quietly—as, one discreet footstep after another, she follows.

That is, until the Minotaur stops.

What's it doing?

It sure seems interested in Tattoo's boot and the glowing thread Theseus tied there. In fact... it's examining it on its hoof, tracing the line that's now no longer beneath Tattoo, but trailing alongside him.

Theseus has observed Nemean lions toying with yarn like a bunch of overzealous kittens, but she's never watched a predator so dexterous in its assessment of a situation.

Dexterous. With hooves!

The Minotaur looks up and burning eyes lance right through her.

She expects the creature to lower its horns and charge, like it had before. But, instead, it turns and bolts.

The fuck—?

Theseus races after it.

At each turn, the beast is already at the next. Theseus ups her pace, ignoring muscle burn and need for breath, but when she reaches a crossroads, the Minotaur has vanished.

Theseus skids to a halt, listening—

Hoof steps? Boot steps?

Running. Fast.

From...

Above?

Theseus looks up.

Heavens above. The creature is racing *up* the wall.

Guess that's multidirectional gravity for you.

Theseus throws herself at the wall and groans as gravity plants her face down on her new horizontal. Yeah, she'll need to work on that.

Theseus scrambles into a sprint just as the Minotaur disappears around the next corner in a blur. She hurtles after it, stumbling on something but recapturing her balance as she goes.

She glances back—

Is that a book protruding from the ground, set in the stone?

Weird...

Eyes forward. Theseus rounds the corner, and—

Shit.

She skids. She stops. Because... *huh?*

All she can see up ahead is a dead end.

She looks up and down and all around... But all she's chasing, apparently, is her own breath. She clenches her fists, tamping down that familiar urge to throw her sword at something... or nothing.

The walls—all stonework, dimly lit colourful stripes, and lava-channels—give no clue where in the labyrinth she might be. An outer corridor or several layers in? It all looks the same.

Something scuffles behind her. She whirls to it, sword raised, but—a blazing golden interruption—it's only the Hero stumbling to catch up.

She gestures for him to *keep fucking quiet.* He obliges, but the scowl he hurls her way demands, *'What's your problem?'* and the arched brow that follows questions: *'How'd you lose the Minotaur?'*

A fair fucking question.

She's missing something... What does the beast know that she doesn't?

Treading carefully, Theseus surveys the stonework for a clue, and the Hero sticks to her shadow like she's a canary-goat down a Minosian mine.

Something about the air in this corridor has the hairs on her arms and neck bristling. Who in the Seven Heavens knows what air should and shouldn't be in this place, but Theseus is pretty sure it's not meant to be hazing.

And is it just her, or is it hot as fuck in here?

There are lava-channels in the walls and floor, but all are beneath a protective layer. The stifling heat is emanating from the dead end.

In a kerfuffle of stumbling boots and clattering weapons, the rest of the company catch up. They look about as green around the gills as Theseus does when she's on bumpy voyage between worlds.

Hero struts like he's centre stage and addresses them in a booming voice. *Fuck's sake. Has he heard of stealth?*

With a sigh, Theseus forges towards the heat-hazed wall.

There. Boot prints in a dark sand-like residue. She treads closer. She looks up again, in case she's missed something. Nothing.

But another step closer and—there it is. The gap between appearance and reality.

This isn't a dead end, but three irregular pillar-like stacks, staggered to create the illusion of one solid wall.

It's hotter here, that's for fucking sure.

While the group all have their eyes on the Hero, Theseus presses on beyond the pillars.

Heat bites within her nostrils. And the smell? Well... there'd been that time Theseus had had a talented bladesmith reform her sword, only to find herself distracted by knowledgeable hands turning both her and the metal molten. That's what this smells like: heated metal and mistakes.

Her eyes must have widened, because even her eyeballs are feeling the heat. Of all the perils she's imagined the Labyrinth might hold, a full-on lava river was not one of them. You'd think someone would have mentioned: *oh, by the way, there's a fucking murder river running through it.*

Please, gravity, don't get creative in here.

The river flows like a red flag, burnt black and ripped with orange stripes. It's wide enough it'd need a ferry to cross it. But there's no sign of one of those! The dark volcanic stone bank on which she's standing is more like a ledge: there's no route the creature could have taken either side. Or up—Theseus checks. There's no sign of it on the curved, cave-like ceiling.

It looks like there's nothing but stone wall on the opposite bank, too. But there is a ledge. Perhaps that leads to a way through, also disguised by a trick of perspective?

If so, how did the Minotaur get across? It's too far to jump, even with an athletic disposition and lack of sense. Is the creature so monstrous that its hide of tar can swim through lava?

No. Theseus scolds herself. That's ridiculous.

Isn't it?

She scours her surroundings for clues, finding boot prints in the thin layer of volcanic sand. She tracks them to where they end at the 'river' edge.

When she aligns her own boot with one of them, the solution rises from the lava; rocks, flat-topped and wide enough to stand on. The rocks must repel the heat, somehow, because the thick, molten rock sludges away from them.

Theseus used to love hopping between stepping stones as a kid. Probably still would, if she were facing a normal river instead of a fiery pit of doom.

At least the stones are equidistant. All she has to do is keep an even stride and a cool head.

Ha. That might be a reach, since it feels like even her brain is sweating.

"Deep breath. One step at a time." Theseus can practically imagine Herakles behind her, leaning on the entryway. Nonchalance personified, Herakles smooths her hand through her shock of sculpted neon-blue curls as she advises: *"Just don't fall in."*

Theseus snickers. *Helpful, Herakles. Helpful.* But Theseus nods at her friend's words—imagined words, but still—as she takes the first step.

One— Just don't think about slipping...

Two— Don't think about being immersed in molten rock...

Three— Don't think about your insides flash-boiling to steam...

Four— Or what flame does to skin...

Five— Fuck. When a bladesmith with her fingers buried in you answers your morbid question about what happens if you get distracted around molten metal, it hits different to when you're the one who's about to meet an agonising end.

Theseus might not like the over-inflated stories of her exploits, but she sure as Hades and the Heavens doesn't want to end up a cautionary tale either.

Six— Her boots are sticking to the stone... *Shit.* Better speed this up.

Seven— Eight— Her breaths scorch in her throat—

Nine— Dizziness shrouds her vision. She stumbles, teetering—

Ten— Eleven— Twelve— Her sword counterbalances her, just... Her vision spins. Her torque is practically searing her skin.

She leaps.

Her arms paddle the air, willing her forward. Her nerves bristle. Her jaw clenches. The landing judders through her. Solid ground. *Oh, thank fucking fuck.* Her knees scuff against sand and rock.

Heavens above and below. She can breathe again.

But she's got to get away from this heat.

Sweating like some ill-acclimatised ice-dweller in the tropics, Theseus stumbles further onto the ledge and against the stone wall.

Up close, they're staggered pillars—as she'd suspected—that mask the way forward; the dark tunnel beyond. And there's a breeze, thank the stars.

The beast must have gone this way, but—as ever, it could be a trap. This dark, cramped pinch point would be the perfect place for a monster to lure its prey.

Lava one way, rock the other... Isn't there a famous saying about that?

She ignites her shoulder torches, but their light only reaches a few metres into the winding tunnel. They'll only light her up as a target, so—sword angled, eyes trained on the untrustworthy shadows—Theseus retrieves the spool of glowing blue thread from her rucksack.

Clutching the loose end of the thread, she casts the spindle into the dark, letting it roll and drape light across the uneven contours of the rock in the tunnel's depths.

No beast.

No triggered traps.

She breathes slow and steady. The only footsteps are those behind her, echoing from the far bank of the lava river. Presumably the group are trying to figure out where she's gone.

She retraces her steps and, sure enough, Hero, Blue and the others cluster together on the distant ledge. With big gestures, Theseus communicates for them to 'wait there.' To make her point extra clear, she claims her Minotaur plushie from her rucksack strap and points to the hidden tunnel, then reiterates for them to 'stay the fuck where you are.' Collectively they blink at her.

They're not going to follow her, right?

At least there's a lava-river blocking their path. So long as they don't find the stepping stones... So long as they're not clever or foolish enough to follow her actual footsteps.

Clipping the mini-Minotaur back in place, Theseus returns to the winding tunnel. She follows her trail of thread before kicking the fallen spool further, flooding the tunnel with blue light one stretch at a time.

The cool breeze is soothing to her heated skin. The air is fresh and rejuvenating. She'd expected the labyrinth to be full of stale air. She hadn't thought she'd be breathing deep on air reminiscent of summertime hilltops in foliage-rich worlds, of expanses of nature protected from industry and pollutants. Such worlds are rare, and a far cry from the over-mined husk of Minos, no matter how decorated its veneer.

When she reaches a slight bend in the tunnel, up ahead something glistens, rippling like a large puddle under a night sky. Theseus blinks to decipher it. It takes a moment for her eyes to adjust.

It's not a puddle, it's an opening.

She picks up her glowing spindle, winding the thread and storing it in her rucksack. Now she knows the tunnel is clear, she can use the shadows to her advantage as she navigates the final stretch.

When she peers out of the opening, invisible forces urge her back in, tugging her equilibrium in different directions. She steadies herself against the tunnel wall, letting the cool air calm her nausea.

She's used to different worlds having different predilections for gravity, but *multidirectional* gravity is unfamiliar territory. Turns out it's a bit of a mind-bend.

Right. She squares up to the tunnel opening. *Let's try this again.*

9

AMONGST THE STARS

Theseus's biceps protest at the weight of body plus armour plus rucksack of mostly-essentials. It's all of that versus the insistent push of gravity, as she hoists herself out of the tunnel onto the new horizontal, like she's surfacing from an in-ground drain.

Not the smoothest manoeuvre, but she'll settle for not losing her head and being side-swiped by a freight train of vertigo.

She unsheathes her sword and stands, warily. The surface is sturdy, like metal or stone, though the shadows are so thick it's impossible to tell which.

As far as she can see, the shadowed ground is scattered with pin-prick twinkling lights. Those furthest away seem to be angled, suggesting that the ground curves. And amidst all this, three chimney-like, circular light wells punctuate the darkness with beams of milky light.

A gentle lap of liquid reminds her to look up.

Theseus flinches. She doesn't mean to. But in her defence, when you look up and find an arena-sized expanse of water where the sky should be, it's hard to trust that it's not going to collapse onto your head.

The lake ripples, reflecting the lights in the surface she's standing on like stars and moons.

Well, that's... something.

If she didn't know better, she might think she's landed amongst the stars.

Surrounding the lake, long grass—wheat, perhaps?—sways as though subject to a normal planetary weather system. Where the meadow ends, there's a cliff face that meets the sky in one direction, and dense woodland draped in shadow in the other. And she's never before had reason to wonder what an upward-flowing waterfall would look like. It's ethereal, like a lone stalagmite in mist, but there's something about it that makes her gut churn. It's too similar to plumes of smoke, billowing but contained like a house fire.

Stars above—or, more accurately, *stars below*. As much as her brain is protesting that the ground is upside-down, if she's stood amongst the 'stars', she must be the one who's the wrong way up.

If multidirectional gravity boggles her mind, an entire outdoor ecosystem within a death maze is... a challenge.

Though... There's no rustle and chirp of creatures, only the rush of water. But still, this place has a certain beauty about it. A tranquillity.

No doubt designed to trick those who make it this far.

Don't be taken in by the pretty things. Perhaps that's the point of this inner layer: to lure her into a false sense of security, wrapping her in wonder and awe until the Labyrinth tightens its grip.

Up, on a silver-grass knoll near the lake, sits a cluster of trees. The most prominent tree shimmers with a confusion of colours, more like a massive lantern than a tree; its light throws the meadow's shadows into sharp relief.

Something near it moves in the grass: a glint of metal.

Theseus squints up as the distant Minotaur slices at the

wheat with... is that a scythe? Some movements are lost to distance and shadows, but the creature's sedate pace is clear. As is its ability to bundle the harvested crop onto its back.

That's... mighty nimble.

The creature must think it's outrun her, to be so calm. But how did it get down there so fast? It'd take Theseus a while to sprint the hemisphere surface of the 'sky' and the horizontal of the fields to reach where the creature is.

Disguised by the shadows in the night sky, Theseus isn't worried about being seen. So long as she's quiet, she can go undetected. And, for now, she simply keeps still and watches as the Minotaur kneels at the moonlit lake edge. She expects it to bend to drink like an animal—but instead, with two practised hooves, it retrieves a canister from a bag on its shoulder and dunks it under the water.

As the creature observes the faux sky, Theseus swallows against the lump of uncertainty in her throat. She's battled enough monsters to recognise those driven by maiming and destruction. The Minotaur had seemed more set on escaping than hurting her.

But Tattoo hadn't deserved his violent death. And Theseus refuses to be tricked by the creature's human qualities, its capacity to gaze up at a sky in wonder—

A cacophony of footsteps echoes from the tunnel, announcing the ungraceful arrival of the group. Fuck's sake. They're as subtle as a herd of bulls. If only Theseus could have existed in the peaceful silence below the midnight meadow just a little longer.

Hero climbs out first, grunting as he strains against new gravity. He ignores Blue as she tearfully reaches out for assistance, but those behind her must help because she flops out into the shadows, as if bundled through.

With a glance at the sky—or, well, the *ground above*—

Theseus hopes the creature won't hear them as she strides over to help the new arrivals to their feet.

But... only a further two flounder onto their new horizontal.

Maybe the others actually had the sense to just stay put? No... it's unlikely Blue's tears are only the result of being put through the wringer by gravity. And the other two are breathing unsteadily, like they're dealing with challenged fitness *and* utter shock meets grief.

Hero merely shrugs like it's all part of the process.

Theseus's jaw clenches. She should have tried harder to convince them all to stay put.

But she can feel bad about that later. Right now, the dwindled group's cries tug at her, but they're also loud enough to travel.

Up at the lake, though, the creature isn't looking at them. It's still. So still. Is it watching them in the reflection? Or is it merely admiring its own image? Are its eyes glinting like therma-stones, or is that Theseus's imagination? It looks up at the sky, and for one heart-hammering moment Theseus is certain their eyes are locked.

Then, like a spooked deer, it bolts.

Shit.

There must be a way to get down there fast—

The Hero hurls his spear up at the creature. Either he's an optimist or that ego of his knows no bounds.

But—

Theseus is glad she kept her thoughts to herself, because instead of dropping back down, the spear keeps hurtling upward, picking up momentum until at last it pierces the ground metres from the fleeing Minotaur.

Well, that's actually helpful: now Theseus knows how to get up—or down—there. Even if the journey is going to suck.

She sheathes her sword, tightens her rucksack straps,

gestures for the group to stay back, and returns to the tunnel, bracing for the—*urghhh*—stomach flip of the gravity change.

She remains upright this time. *Progress.*

Multidirectional gravity is an unwieldy beast. You think you've got the logic nailed down, and then those nails go flying in a whole new direction. The great thing about it, though—or so she's heard—is that at speed, it's possible to punch through it.

So she gives herself a good run-up, heaves in a fortifying breath, and sprints for the tunnel's edge.

At the opening, she leaps.

And...

For a heart-thumping moment, she's sure she's about to get tugged back and have her life ended by a tunnel that ends in lava, or have her ego dented with a face full of stars.

But she keeps going. Up, up, up, until the maelstrom of gravity grabs her, whirling her inner axis until *up* turns to *falling* up, and then something in her head realigns to down, down, *down* towards the lake—

It's not her first time plummeting from the sky—or even from a false sky—but it's never a sensible or strong position to be in. You never fully know how it's going to end.

Almost there—

Theseus stretches her arms, elongating her body—

And slices through the lake's surface.

The water rushes and roars in her ears. She'd expected a shock of cold, but the temperature is pleasant enough. What isn't pleasant is the weight of her drenched clothing. And in the water's depths, a frantic rippling stirs: something, or some *things*, disturbed by her presence.

The feeling is mutual.

She heaves herself upward, exhaling deliberately to clear her nose as she breaks the surface. At least now she feels the right way up.

As she pulls towards the shore with confident strokes, she zeroes in on the twitch of tall grass where the Minotaur is racing for the shadowy woodland.

But something needles at her thigh.

What the fuck—?

Kicking to stay afloat, she looks down, expecting some sort of aquatic weeds.

Bulbous, translucent eyes stare back.

Oh, fuck no— Theseus shoves at the water to put space between her and the palm-sized skeletal fish, its lower jaws flanked by sabre fangs.

No... No thank you.

She cuts through the water towards the shore.

Another sting at her thigh. Keeping her strokes even and her breath held, she opens her eyes under water. It opens its jaws to bite anew, and Theseus slaps the creature away—only for it to latch onto her wrist-armour.

With a violent flick of her wrist, the creature tumbles towards the depths... where more bulbous eyes glint up at her.

Kick harder.

She does, until she's in the shallows and her boots finally touch the bottom. The creatures circle and disperse on repeat as Theseus sloshes her way through them.

As she emerges onto the shore, she closes in on a warning sign with a silhouette of a fish with sizeable fangs.

Yeah, no shit.

As soon as she's on dry land, she strikes her shoulder torches into illumination with one hand, unsheathes her sword with the other, and sprints toward the twitching grass.

This isn't her first rodeo.

The golden grass swipes at her already drying clothes. There's seldom a mission where she doesn't benefit from her speed-drying gear and watertight rucksack.

A splash from behind—

Theseus glances back as more splashes punctuate the others dropping like fledglings from the sky. She hopes they can swim fast, but beyond that she hopes they don't catch up.

Up ahead, a glinting scythe and the flash of blue-fire eyes confirm her target just as it disappears into the dark woodland.

Within a hundred hurried strides, Theseus crosses the thicket threshold of overlapping coniferous trees. Her boots churn the undergrowth, tripping on roots and sending her ricocheting off trunks into low branches, and snagging on the shawls of moss.

She has little choice but to slow, using her forearm cuffs to guard against branches and foliage intent on knocking sense into her.

The solid trees stretch higher than her illumination. Some trunks are arches, more like overgrown roots—is that a gravity-direction thing?

It's not the time for curiosity.

Theseus's boots spring against the moss-carpet. Branches sweep the air ahead and the undergrowth rustles as the creature weaves between the trunks.

Damn, this thing is quick.

Several splashes behind her suggest Hero and the Three are following.

All this stalking and chasing has Theseus a little queasy. Monsters, true monsters, tend not to run or hide, unless it's some trick. So why is the beast running and not charging right at her? Is this all part of its game?

She slams to a halt to avoid a face full of branches. Her chest and shoulders heave as the shadows knot beyond her light.

Where did it go?

There are no snapping twigs up ahead, no rustling. Everything is silent. Theseus reins in her ragged breaths and switches off her shoulder torches. Everything shrouds in stillness and shadow.

Until...

Near and far, half-moon shapes staircased around tree trunks bloom into ethereal illumination. Shields and domes—all manner of fungi—cluster on every branch and exposed root like a thousand miniature lamps, sickly green to neon blue, violet and a smattering of pinks and purples.

Damn. Theseus is no poet, but this is fucking beautiful.

Moisture drifts in the air. The scent of soil and the tang of something more pungent. But before she can take in more of her surroundings, a jolt to her back sends her splashing into a cluster of sloppy, shimmering fungus.

Yeah, the source of *pungent and putrid*...

Theseus just full-body landed in it.

Urgh.

Muscles coil, ready to take on the monster, as the luminosity of the fungi highlights the culprit.

Hero laughs as Theseus slip-slides back to her feet. Her gear might be water-repellent, but there's little she can do about mud and gunk. The staccato glow of Hero's torque painting shadows across his face only highlights his grin. Even his laugh is a parade of self-indulgence.

What is his fucking problem?

She's about to demand precisely that, but the undergrowth quivers. Right fucking next to them.

And in a flurry of activity, the Minotaur dashes away—

Shit.

Theseus races after it, as much as is possible in a tangled woodland, and when caked in unknown slime.

But the creature must have triggered something, because the

trees of epic proportion are suddenly draped in a towering and expanding oblong of blue-white light. The walls are opening to a bright chamber, into which the distinctive silhouette of the Minotaur takes a confident lead.

It's a stark reminder that they're not in some magical forest, and everything is not as it seems.

10

TRAP

Oof! Theseus skids on the ice-slick floor as her breaths plume around her.

The walls and ceiling are too far away to decipher. The only discernible details of this new avenue are the icy floor and the distant ice-monoliths pointing at them like a wall of sideways stalactites through freezing fog.

While the creature up ahead strides into the fog—more gracefully than anyone has a right to on ice—Theseus and the Hero sprawl like snow-fawns on ice.

Shit, shit, shit.

Theseus grits her teeth and levers herself up an inch at a time. The slime caking her boots and astro-suit isn't helping matters, but she makes it to her feet first, keeping her smirk to herself as Hero flails. She could help, but... he did just shove her into fungus slime, so...

In the bright light of this winter chamber, the marks on his neck and face are red and raw. Damn. Those fang-fish have sure got some bite.

At least all that's biting them now is the frigid air.

The remaining three of the group skitter into the chamber. When one of the company slips at Hero's feet, he sneers. Theseus hoists them up, just as an otherworldly groan shudders everything.

Even Theseus's hands tremble.

The bellowing is the sort she's only encountered from beasts with size and mythology on their side. But it isn't coming from the monster up ahead. It's *everywhere*.

And it coincides with the chamber's gargantuan door sliding closed behind them.

Okay. That can't be good...

What is the Labyrinth up to? Have they triggered something? Is the Minotaur doing this?

Theseus's inner axis tilts—

Her heart rate ratchets into survival mode. She widens her stance, holding out her sword to counterbalance her skidding feet and—crucially—not fall on it.

The others are sliding forward in a squall of Minosian curses, prayers, and outright screams.

Shit, shit, *shit*. Theseus can see where this is going. The epic cries are mechanical; the Labyrinth is turning. And there's nothing to hold on to. It won't be long before the sideways stalactites become life-ending spears from below.

There's only one way to beat this.

"This way. Quick!" Theseus strides down the slope as fast as she can, beckoning the others to follow her.

But they're too slow. The chamber is tilting too fast, too steeply.

Theseus wraps both hands about the hilt of her sword and plunges it into the ice behind her.

Out of the corner of her eye, she spies Hero copying her, digging the tip of his spear into the ice. The other three attempt the same with their weapons, with varying degrees of success.

Theseus hooks her left boot into the palm-grip on the back of her shield, then drives the shield's edge into the ice beside her sword. Thank the heavens for those sand-surfing lessons on the volcanic dunes in the Tartarian Constellation.

But the gradient is growing ever steeper.

Fumbling her own shield, Blue free-falls past her—

Theseus yanks her sword free, angles her shield, and plummets past Blue, grabbing her by her belt as she overtakes her. She digs her shield back into the ice to slow them both.

As Theseus pulls her closer, Blue drops her own shield, which disappears into the fog with a distant, reverberating *clang*-clang-clang... clang.

Blue kicks out, almost knocking Theseus's shield from under them both. Theseus crouches to compensate, but the shield isn't made for two...

Or for this purpose.

Blue's wild eyes connect with hers and for a moment Blue must glimpse through her terror to find comfort. She wraps her arms around Theseus, clinging like a limpet—throwing Theseus off balance—

The shield spins, sending them plunging toward the ice-spears—

Theseus drives the shield hard into the sheer wall, hauling their combined weight back towards the slope—

Blue's grip tightens, her cheek pressing against Theseus's.

It's difficult to see—

Theseus adjusts—

A spear of ice dead ahead.

She ducks, pulling Blue down with her, unbalancing them both. Blue's body vibrates against her, her panicked breaths hot against Theseus's face.

Theseus shifts her weight again, scoring a trail down the wall with her sword. She risks a glance down over her shield edge, keeping her weight above her heels. How far is there to go?

The stalactite-fangs widen towards their bases, now more like triangular trees of ice and stone. Fog obscures the ground. Their landing could be five metres away, or five hundred.

Either way, they need to slow if they're to survive and remain intact.

Screams echo through the ice forest, ending abruptly in two crunching thuds. All Theseus glimpses as she and Blue swoop past are flashes of red dripping down upward-pointing ice branches.

Blue lashes out in panic. Theseus tries to hold her still, but Blue shoves her away, her elbow cracking solidly against Theseus's cheek.

People do the strangest things when drowning in adrenaline.

Theseus dips down to right their course, but Blue is still flailing. Panic flares in Blue's eyes as she realises she's off-balanced. Theseus grabs for her outstretched hand—but it's too late.

With a nerve-scraping scream that will haunt Theseus forever, Blue plunges into the fog below. Theseus listens for a thud, but none comes. Only silence as the screaming suddenly stops.

Fuck.

The angle of her descent is still too steep—

With the shroud of ice fog only a metre below, Theseus jumps for the shallower angled ice-trunk opposite.

She digs her shield edge into its sheer surface, slowing her enough—

With a bone-shuddering thud, the shield beneath her feet hits the ground, casting her into the fog.

Uncomfortable and ungraceful. But not deadly.

That'll do.

Her skin turns to goosebumps with the chill. Her eyes on

every direction, Theseus stands and reclaims her shield from the briefly disturbed knee-high swamp of fog.

This fog is nothing like the sour, smothering mist that had enveloped them in the corridors, that still buzzes uncomfortably in her pores. This... well... it's like a winter's morning mixed with icing sugar.

At a movement in her peripheral vision, Theseus spins—

But it's just her own movements reflecting at her. Down here, the sheer surfaces of the ice-trees, stalactites, whatever they are, are like frosted mirrors.

Amongst the forest of her own reflections is a flash of blue hair. Theseus starts towards Blue, but a sinking nausea in her gut stops her. Her breath flails from her lungs as her mind processes what her body has already pieced together.

An empty-eyed stare. A mouth mid-scream. Blood congealing against ice.

Never mind the screaming. The sight of Blue's lifeless body impaled on a jagged ice-branch—*that* will haunt Theseus forever.

Fuck. This. Place.

"You tried your best," says Herakles's gentle voice in her thoughts. Theseus can almost imagine her friend behind her, with her neon-green curls and her comforting hand on Theseus's shoulder.

Trying isn't good enough, though, is it? Theseus wants to say as she shrugs Herakles's imagined hand away. There isn't time for this... Those who dwell in the realm of monsters always end up dead.

"Survive first. Have feelings later?"

That's more like it.

Footsteps echo in the frozen hall of mirrors. A voice calls out in Minosian. Is that Hero?

Theseus turns, but only her own face stares back, grimacing at her from a dozen directions.

Beyond one of the reflections, though, deep within a trunk of ice, something is frozen. Theseus steps closer, squinting. Is that a book? A paper-made case-bound book?

Why is it inside a tree of ice?

This place is weird.

That self-important Minosian voice meanders between the ice-pillars again—somehow both near and far—as Theseus's neck itches, the fine hairs bristling: she's being watched.

But by who, or what?

It could simply be her own reflections...

Theseus pauses her breaths and yet she can still hear it. Breathing. Slow and heavy, with a growling edge that's something other than standard Minosian.

Theseus's fingers flex against her sword's hilt as she stills ...

Footsteps. Behind her.

She ducks and turns—

A blade parts the air above her head—

The Minotaur's scythe?

How in the heavens does it wield a blade?

Theseus can't get a good look through the fog. She dodges again and collides with a frozen tree, nearly head-butting her own reflection. She stumbles back, and—

Heavens-a-fucking-bove!

Pain lashes up from her lower leg, ripping through her body like a vengeful lightning bolt. The heavy snap of mechanisms registers only distantly against the searing agony.

First rule of monster hunting: Don't let the monster know you're caught.

But the bellow that erupts from deep within her scours her throat like a thousand ice shards, rebounding off surfaces and ricocheting back to her as a taunt.

She dares look down.
Red. Blood. *Her blood.*
Teeth. Metal.
Fuck.

11

LOST

This monster hunt could be going better right now.

But even if she'd been wearing her astro-helmet and been protected by her whisper-mesh, it wouldn't have helped against metal jaws. She grits her teeth to stifle her whimpers.

Footsteps. Behind her. Again.

Sneaky beast.

Theseus tries to twist, but the trap's teeth gnaw deeper. Her muscles spasm, branching agony to every frazzled nerve ending. A blinding sharp, deafening tinnitus whines in her ears. She can't even mop the sweat dripping from her brow.

"Do something," Herakles pleads, and even her imagined friend blurs with the pain.

She needs something to lever the trap, but her sword and shield are lost to the fog. Should she risk reaching for them?

Faces dance around her. Hero? The beast? Merely her own twisted reflection? Where does one face start and another end?

She tugs at the torque gripping her throat, uncomfortably hot against her chilled skin. It's meant to keep the Minotaur from stealing her life force. It's hardly going to help now, is it?

Footsteps snow-crunch closer...

Usually, creatures with mythological stature fail to live up to the stories, but there's something distractingly otherworldly about this beast. With one upper arm striped with the blood Theseus drew from it, its tar-crackled biceps ripple with muscle as its fists (well, hooves) hang at its sides. Its solid stance is more like a gladiator in an arena than a creature in the wild.

The imposing bull-headed silhouette glowers down at her, blue fire in its eyes.

Bull-headed. Ha! Theseus sniggers at her own pun and the creature tilts its head. Is it wondering what's so funny? Does it have a sense of humour? Theseus's laughter dies. Because soon she will, too.

Unless—

A rush of movement from a dozen directions. Something soaring. Hero's gloating grin and gleaming armour flash amongst the dizzying reflections as a spear embeds itself in the sheer surface of a nearby ice-trunk, turning its reflections to a blood-spiked web.

With a bellow that could almost inspire sympathy, the Minotaur dips to one knee, wrist pressed to its left shoulder, where blood now drips. Hero calls out, celebration in his Minosian growl.

Did he just punch the air, like he's already won the battle? Urgh. Theseus would roll her eyes at him, if they weren't already busy blurring her surroundings as pain threatens to pull her under.

The beast snarls, whipping its attention towards Hero. It stands taller. Defiant. Scythe at the ready in a stance that says: *It's not going to be that easy.*

If only Theseus had her sword right now. But instead, turned to a seething, quivering, wheezing mess, all she can do is answer gravity's insistence—and lie the fuck down.

It's moments like this she wishes she wasn't driven by her misguided need to conquer monsters.

She's never known a pain so deep, so sharp, burning and ripping through her like wildfire while whispering the promise of death. She's never been so choked by agony that—for a torturous second—she'd invite that promise to hurry the fuck up.

Footsteps. One set running away. One set crunching towards her. Theseus must have closed her eyes for a few seconds or longer, because when she opens them, scuffed boots stand just beyond her reach. One boot has a sliced line through the tongue, just above the laces. An odd detail to notice, but whatever.

Theseus flinches, sending fresh pain biting up her already gnawed nerves.

A guttural growl—

Is that her or the Minotaur?

Shit—

She can't die like this—

Fuck the pain—

She claws at the ground in search of her sword, but her co-ordination is as lost as her weapon. Her own strangled cries tumble from her as she paddles at nothing and the metal jaws ravage her leg. Judging by the sound, she might be the beast in need of taming.

Through pain blurred eyes, she stares up as the beast looms over her. *Don't pass out. Because that'll be it...*

But the thundering heart that had set her to survival is losing its battle to something stronger. Time becomes elastic. Everything darkens.

No, no, no...

Theseus hadn't expected this to be easy. She's travelled the galaxies in search of wrongs to right, monsters to vanquish; it's no shame that the one to end her is the infamous Minotaur.

But—*still*—she'd really rather not die like this. And not today. There are too many monsters out there in need of her specific combination of bravery-meets-stupidity.

Pain flashes through her, fierce and unforgiving.

She must have lost consciousness for a while, because now there's momentum. The ground scratches along her back, grit or ice scuffing her armour.

There's a pressure about both her ankles, both legs angled upward. The agony from her right leg ignites over and over, like some echo location reminding her where all her pain receptors are.

Dragged... She's being dragged...

Her eyes crack open. Her rucksack trails along beside her, her astro-helmet's whisper-mesh sparking like an extension of her overloaded pain receptors. The soggy, goo-covered Minotaur plushie stares at her with its button eyes. It's definitely seen better days.

You and me both.

When she'd first seen the palm-sized, scowling toy at the tourist market, she'd been amused. But as the real Minotaur pulls her towards heavens knows where, and the pressure in her head pushes her towards unconsciousness, she's sure not laughing now.

PART II

THESEUS AND THE MINOTAUR

12

THE THREAD

The night before entering the Labyrinth...

Theseus probably shouldn't be questioning Princess Ariadne, the Architect-in-waiting, about how she managed to catch and imprison an uncatchable beast, much less telling her she lacks in answers. Especially not when she's bound by gravity-cuffs in the Princess's palatial chambers. But Theseus does many things she shouldn't do.

And damn, if the Princess biting her lower lip like she's wrestling a beast in her own thoughts isn't giving Theseus *ideas*.

Princess Ariadne must decide *something*, because she strides to a wall and opens a drawer—the seams of which hadn't even been visible in amongst the chamber's geometric patterns. She retrieves something dark and palm-sized before returning to within an arm's reach of Theseus.

"This will assist you in your quest," says the Princess, her tone hushed as she empties the pouch into her palm.

Theseus raises an eyebrow at the spindle of neon-blue thread. "I wasn't planning on sewing a decorative border to my pockets, Princess."

Instead of chastising her, or expressing anything resembling amusement, the Princess glances over Theseus's shoulder, toward her chamber's grand, closed entrance. Is she worried they'll be overheard? Theseus had assumed the Princess to have all the royal power of an Architect-in-waiting, but perhaps she's not as powerful as her guide-Shard has led her to believe.

When the Princess's eyes lock onto hers, Theseus can't tell if her expression is beseeching or mischievous. Perhaps a little of both.

"Use the thread to navigate your path," the Princess whispers.

O-kay...? How in the heavens will it do that? Theseus bites her tongue. Perhaps it's something symbolic rather than actually useful?

"Why are you helping me?" Theseus asks, instead.

"Am I?" The ripple of the Princess's torque is as distracting as her scorching smile. "Perhaps I am merely prolonging your suffering."

The Princess keeps holding out the spindle but doesn't bring it closer.

"My hands are bound, Princess."

Without breaking eye contact, Princess Ariadne traces the shape of Theseus's upper thigh with her knuckles. Theseus's heartbeat stumbles against her armour as the Princess slips the spindle into her trouser pocket.

"Please," Princess Ariadne whispers, her breath caressing Theseus's cheek. "Only the heart of the Minotaur will set you free. Kill the beast. Bring me its heart. *Set me free.*"

13

DELIRIUM

In the Labyrinth…

Theseus blinks back to consciousness with a bone-deep dread. There's pressure about her left ankle and her wrists, anchoring her in place. It's not the *worst* feeling, unless—

Fuck-fuck-fuck. She's in restraints. She tenses, and—Heavens above and below and every fucking place in between—pain rips up from her right leg, which is still weighted by the metal bite of the trap.

Gritting her teeth, she stifles her gasps. What kind of monster doesn't free their prey from its trap when dragging it to…

To where? Where is she?

She'd assumed a Minotaur den would be as cold as the creature's heart, but an intricately carved stone fireplace licks its heat towards her, wrapping her in warmth. In any other circumstance, she'd love to get cosy by that fire.

Fuck you, universe.

Her thoughts snag on the question of how a hoofed creature can create a fire—not important—before landing on the matter of the palatial bed she's in, or on. Beasts don't sleep in beds, do they?

Depends on the beast. Some monsters can act so human no-one would guess their true nature. Perhaps it's not so strange that a creature with a partially human body might sleep in a bed.

Which leads to the uncomfortable question: What is she doing in this one? Does the Minotaur make a habit of offering guest quarters to its captives?

Unlikely...

Theseus squints at the flickering yellow light. Fire-torches? Electric ones? Whatever it is, it's not strong enough to cut through the shadows, but...

The Minotaur. It's there.

At some kind of... workbench? Desk? Whatever it is, the gentle rustle of movement suggests the beast is busy with something. Deciding how best to eviscerate her, probably.

What does it want with her? Why hasn't it killed her yet? Is that what it's about to do? No doubt it won't be long before she gets answers she doesn't really want.

Best to stay still and not disturb it. If only the agony weren't roaring and clawing within her, demanding all her energy and more not to yell out. Her jaw clenches so hard she might break teeth. How can she make life-saving decisions when she can't even see or think straight?

The creature turns, shadows shrouding its face, and heads across the chamber towards Theseus with a fluid grace. Theseus's hands clench in the sheets—soft, silken sheets...

No. Focus. Because what she's about to do is going to hurt.

One kick; that's all she'll get. It's better to lose a leg than a life.

Just a little closer...

The firelight illuminates the Minotaur's hands, manipulating a pestle and mortar more dextrously than a beast has any right—

Wait...

Hands?

It must be her pain-blurred vision...

The hearth's light falls on the Minotaur's face.

Theseus gasps.

Lagoon-blue eyes: familiar, yet strange. Human features, wary and lacking amusement or swagger. Her practical, short blonde hair is wavy instead of pin-straight, and without the sheen of endless preening. A thin line of scar tissue interrupts her top lip; Theseus hadn't noticed it when they'd met before. Her freckles, too, must have been covered. And in her simple vest and trousers, both the colour of ash, she's not as regal or polished.

This has to be Theseus's imagination, right?

"Princess?" she croaks. "I didn't recognise you without all the ruffles."

Why is Princess Ariadne here? Has she grown tired of sending others to brave the Labyrinth, and chosen to take on the Minotaur herself? Has she conquered the beast and rescued Theseus?

Theseus is all for being rescued on the odd occasion— particularly by dashing princesses when it's a life-or-death situation—but *this doesn't make sense.*

"What are you doing here? How did you...?" Theseus splutters. If Princess Ariadne has saved her from the beast... well... she can only be grateful and impressed. But she can also question her judgement. "Princess. Risking your life in this place..."

The Princess tilts her head, as if she, too, is confused. Perhaps she can't understand her. They need that extortionately priced translation tincture. Her blue eyes flicker, though with what it's difficult to tell.

Theseus grits her teeth, sweating. *Gaaaah*, her nerve endings are being taunted like there's two dozen carving knives intent on completing their journey through flesh and bone. Not far from the truth.

The Princess sets aside the pestle and mortar and pulls up a chair to the side of the bed, her gaze skittering past Theseus as she perches. What happened to all that royal arrogance?

Perhaps encountering a deadly sky labyrinth and its beast will do that? Though that doesn't explain why the Princess's arms are taut with muscle in a way they definitely hadn't been when Theseus had seen her last.

"When did you get so buff, Princess?" Theseus hears herself say, in a clumsy mix of flirtation and currently-lacking-a-filter. *Stars above.*

But. Really. Such a physical transformation would take months, at least. Has Theseus been here that long?

Impossible. Her wound is still fresh.

In reply, the Princess reaches for Theseus's trapped leg, and for the length of carved wood Theseus had failed to notice at the foot of the bed. She can guess it's intended as a lever.

Oh, *shit.*

Theseus isn't confident she's going to get through this without passing out. Again.

But best get it over with. Theseus presses back into the bed, trying to dull her sounds and keep as still as possible. The more she kicks, the more it's going to hurt. She grits her teeth half a second before the Princess levers open the metal jaws.

Within five long, excruciating seconds, the trap's teeth slide from Theseus's flesh, slicing as they go. The shock floods her system, rendering her mute for an eternal moment until the agony unleashes in a guttural scream that scrapes the roof of her mouth raw.

Muttering in Minosian, the Princess casts the metal contraption aside. Theseus wheezes. She has no idea whether the Princess's words are meant to be critical or calming.

The Princess retrieves the pestle and mortar, mixing what is hopefully some tincture to ward off infection, or at least dull the pain. From their previous encounter, Theseus would have expected some banter, telling her she's making a racket, or even just a withering eyebrow raise, questioning her bravery credentials. But there's only an uneasy glimmer in the Princess's eyes. It's enough to hoist Theseus out of any potential relief, enough for her twisting vision to narrow in on the dimly lit workbench...

A beastly mouth hangs open, inanimate. Its eyes inert, empty sockets filled with shadow...

What... the... fuck? The decapitated head of the Minotaur?

"You *killed* it?" The words leave Theseus on an exhale.

Confusion flickers across her rescuer's features as she turns slightly to follow Theseus's line of sight, shedding firelight on her arms, shoulders and neck—all smeared with the remains of a dark camouflage. But it's the seeping wound across the Princess's upper arm that underscores an unwelcome realisation.

No...

The Princess hasn't killed the beast.

She *is* the beast?

What—?

The Princess reaches out with whatever the mortar concoction is. Theseus swipes at it, at her, only to miss both targets and jar her shoulder instead. She thrashes, unwilling to be touched or tricked, but the restraints anchor her. She tries to scramble backwards, only to slam her weight onto her shredded leg instead.

Fresh agony shoots through her as she collapses onto the bed with a strangled cry, tugging desperately at her restraints.

Either they weren't too tight, or Theseus is impressive as fuck, because she slips free.

The Princess doesn't try to stop her. Her brow is buckled with something gruff and unsettled, but with nothing to suggest she considers Theseus a viable threat.

Rude.

But of course she's not worried. She knows this place and Theseus is acting wilder than a cornered Minotaur with the precision of an over-served drunk.

She claws back, tumbling from the bed onto the flagstones, slamming the air from her lungs as her leg screams its protest.

The chamber's previously dim fire-torches blaze bright. When the Princess approaches, her shadow looms large.

"Stay away from me," Theseus splutters. She struggles to stand on her injured leg, only to be greeted by pain so blinding, the undertow of her waning consciousness pulls her back down.

As shadows bleed into her vision, the silhouette of the Minotaur-Princess offers no answers, only an infuriating head tilt.

Well, fuck...

This sure as Hades and the Heavens wasn't in the guidebook.

14

FEVER

Snarling fangs. Saliva dripping. Veins burn like lava. Sapphire eyes blaze, smudging to nothing on a blink—

A sickly swirl of colour.

Arms flailing. Legs stomping. Frenetic dancing.

Banners. Streamers.

The capital's streetlights surge brighter with the mania of celebration as the many masks of the Minotaur take shape in the blur of the crowds.

Morbid. Monstrous. Magnificent.

It's enough to fuel a fever dream—

✦

HER LUNGS LIKE LEAD, Theseus heaves in an unsatisfying breath.

She doubts the people of Minos would have such colourful festivities for their so-called Righteous Path if they knew the reality of their Labyrinth. Or maybe they would. They already understand it to be a place of death. But do they know it's their precious Princess Ariadne, their Architect-in-waiting, masquerading as the beast?

Sweat crowds Theseus's brow. Passing out is never a *good* idea. She clenches her jaw in annoyance; at her body, and at herself for getting into such a vulnerable state in the first place.

But beating herself up won't help her now.

She tries to listen for her captor, but all she can hear are her own laboured breaths, her own heart storming her ribcage as if it too is trying to escape this predicament. Her head lolls the other way. Flames rage in the fireplace, hurting her eyes more than Hero's over-shined armour.

She needs to get out of here. Obviously. Wherever *here* is. The Labyrinth? She must still be in the Labyrinth. She just has this *feeling*: the same itchy pressure under her skin she experiences when her monster hunting excursions take her deep underground; that odd, bone-deep knowledge that she's subterranean and that escape won't be simple.

Add that to the pain spilling up from her leg, and the strange buzzing that's been needling beneath her skin ever since being immersed in the shimmering mist.

And where is the Princess?

Theseus should have listened to that inkling of disquiet in her gut when she'd first met Princess Ariadne. But no, she'd wanted to toy with the fire, to wade into the deadly stillness of those lagoon eyes. She'd wanted to play the hero. And look where it's landed her: in a world of pain, confused as fuck, and tripping on too many metaphors.

She presses a hand to her heart-hammering chest. Her wrists are no longer tethered. That's the only positive of this moment. That and the fact that the Minotaur—the *Minotaur-Princess,* apparently—is currently elsewhere. And that the trap is gone.

Thick puncture marks, crusted red and black, remain, with a strange sparkle around them, but the injury no longer spews sparks like a severed electric cable with a direct line to her nervous system. Her leg may be clean, but the rest of her is still caked in foul-smelling fungus goo.

Yeah, it's fair to say she's had better days.

The shadows writhe. Theseus's attention snaps to them—but there's nothing there. Only a sickening, familiar laughter, snagging at her insides like poison-tipped brambles, delighting, as always, in digging into her self-esteem.

"Idiot. Useless. What even is the point of you?" She's never known shadows to be so *mean*. Nor for them to twist and sway.

But the voice isn't really there either. It's not possible.

Stars above, her senses are swimming. She's had fevers before, but this is something else. Something unique, personal and scathing, from the buried recesses of her mind.

Such things are temporary. *Temporary, temporary, temporary,* she chants to herself, hoping it'll see her through. She tries to breathe through it, but it eases nothing. Whatever the cause—internal or external—it looks like she'll have to ride this out.

Some animals derive comfort from being contained; others would chew their own arm off for freedom. Unfortunately for Theseus, she'd rather escape into a verified death trap than sit in a cage.

Squinting past the tapestry of dancing firelight, Theseus spies her sword and astro-helmet across the room, piled neatly along with the rest of her belongings. The Minotaur-Princess must have a sense of humour, because the weapons are being 'guarded' by her Minotaur plushie. In different circumstances, Theseus might find that amusing.

This is going to epically suck. But death—or being kept as the house pet of some spoiled, macabre princess—will suck more, so Theseus hazards to her feet. Well, foot.

So much for her injury having calmed. Every movement towards the tools of her trade lances through her like lightning.

Mind over matter. Mind over matter. Grinding her teeth, she reclaims her rucksack, astro-helmet, and sword, leaving her armour, shield, and the Minotaur plushie—which looks far cleaner than she does right now. Useful though armour may be, trying to layer up will only alert the Princess. And she doesn't have to try putting on her boots to know that they're too heavy for her injured leg. And she can't hold a shield if she's supporting herself against a wall, can she? Which... yeah... doesn't bode well...

She hops for the door, every step like daggers—dimly aware that any captor worth their currency wouldn't accidentally leave weaponry within reach. Either the Princess's increased muscle mass has choked the blood supply from her brain... or this is all part of her game.

There's always the slim chance that she's not expecting Theseus to be capable of fighting. Theseus clings to that idea as tightly as her sword.

The windows are barred and boarded; presumably the door is locked as well. Theseus steels herself to scour the chamber for some point of weakness—but she doesn't have to, because when she stumbles against the door and grabs the handle to steady herself, the door just... opens.

Well, that's underwhelming.

She keeps her relief in check, however: this could simply be a tick in *the Princess likes to play games* column. Or she could just be making her great escape into a storage cupboard.

Wouldn't be the first time.

She peeks through the door into a corridor, simultaneously answering her question and almost impaling herself on her own sword. She catches herself on the doorframe. It's a good job she's no longer bothered about impressing a princess, because her current achievements are definitely sub-par.

Dome-encased electric fire-torches lean from the corridor walls. Like the rest of the labyrinth, the floor and walls here are patterned with narrow, glowing lava-channels. The combined light isn't enough to douse the shadows completely, but enough to see the shape of a path. There's a vague breeze, too. A way out? Or a route into a trap?

Theseus begins her stilted journey, the floor slightly cool beneath her foot. The irregular brickwork is useful if you're an injured monster hunter in need of something to grab onto, but progress is painfully slow. She's seen sleep-walking tortoises—*don't ask*—travel faster than this.

As she rounds a bend in the corridor and exhaustion crashes over her, she leans against the wall, clutching the stonework as she tries to steady herself and her ragged breath. How long is this corridor? Its curve makes her feel like she's going in circles. And does she have to breathe so damn loud? She's going to give herself away.

Under the racket of her breathing there's something fluttering, flapping… a scratch-scratch-scratch against stone.

Something is moving in the shadows, back around the bend in the corridor. Is it her imagination? Or is she being followed?

A flare of blue and orange flames throw the creature's shadow across the uneven walls. Its shape indecipherable as Theseus winces; the glare too much for her sore eyes. *Please let this be a hallucination.* None of the myths said anything about the Minotaur breathing fire, but they never mentioned the fact that it's a princess playing dress-up either.

More scratching… More fluttering… The creature in the shadows draws closer.

Burning orange eyes pierce the dark as a demonic creature bursts forth—

Theseus instinctively throws her forearm over her face, pain skittering through her as her forearm sears with flame.

What the fuck? She swipes at the creature, but it's already roaring a retreat into the shadows.

This is a place of nightmares. Theseus limps away, faster this time. Whatever it is, the creature doesn't pursue.

It takes a million sun-orbits, or thereabouts, before the corridor opens into an entrance hall. Her vision skews like she's on some storm-tossed sea-faring vessel. Through the blur, she can make out a grand, intricately sculpted doorway of wood and metal on the outer curve of the corridor: twice her height, but still without the opulence of the Minosian palace.

It's only ten more paces away.

But there's the unmistakeable sound of boots on stone, closing in. Back along the curved corridor, the fire-torches flare. In a matter of moments, the Minotaur-Princess will find her.

This is going to hurt...

Theseus gulps two quick, steadying breaths, then hops for her target. She hopes no-one ever finds out that the 'Great Monster Hunter Theseus' hopped her way to an escape. This is all embarrassing enough.

One—*Stars above, the pain.*

Two—*Mind over matter.*

Three—*Mind over fucking matter.*

Four—*Fuck mind over matter.*

Five—*Fuck-fuck-fuck-fuck—*

She lumbers into the door, gripping the intricate metalwork for support. The door would be more useful if it had a doorhandle. Through her swaying senses, the patterns are too complex to follow, though the four deep indentations are clear enough: two at waist height, a shoulder width apart, and two lower down and closer together.

She pushes the door and it doesn't move a Minosian inch. Fuck-fuck-fuck. She pushes again with the same results.

There's no way out.

It could be the fear flooding her system, or the heavy thrum of pain clouding her thoughts, but Theseus doesn't think through what she's doing—as she does something she told herself she'd never do. She fishes the coin pendant from beneath her shirt and twists the two semi-circles about their axis.

All the coin does is darken. And before she can regret her choices or question what it all means, a shadow falls over her.

The Minotaur-Princess is *there*, and far closer than Theseus had expected.

Not within sword-swiping distance, Theseus discovers, as she commits too heavily to her swing. She plants weight on her injured leg and pain spears up through her, folding her to the warmed, lava-furrowed flagstones.

So much for mind over matter. Sometimes the matter *matters*. She bites down on her cries, refusing to give the royal beast the satisfaction of her distress. But she can do nothing about the dark waves of agony pulling her under once again.

This is the last fucking time Theseus tries to impress a princess.

15

FLIP A COIN

Theseus has had about enough of passing out. It's not a winning strategy in the realm of monsters, that's for sure.

It must be her overly optimistic imagination, but as she clambers up and down the slippery slope to uninvited slumber, she could swear there's something cooling against her forehead, dulling the bite of her fever. Or attempting to, at least.

Perhaps the Minotaur-Princess and all that previous chaos was just some nightmare. Perhaps she's been rescued by Hero—*barf*—and is recuperating back on Minos. Or maybe for once she took her travel agent's advice and she was never trapped in a death labyrinth at all, except in some hangover-fuelled bad dream after too much indulgence.

Hangover sounds about right, because she's got the *monster* of all headaches, boring into her brain like a ravenous Iolcian vole-rat, and her throat and lips are as dry as a sun-scorched plain.

But that throb in her leg... the blazing heat in her forearm... When you meet some weird fire-creature in your nightmares, they don't actually burn you, do they?

Far from ready to contend with reality, Theseus squints

against the light. She's back in the bedchamber, in the oversized bed. Alone, thankfully. Something like daylight hazes between the bars of a window that's not in her current skill set to reach. If there's daylight, she can't still be in the Labyrinth, can she? Although if a moonlit meadow and woodland exist in the Labyrinth... perhaps sunlight isn't impossible?

Heavens above. Critical thinking has her head thumping. How long has she been out? Long enough for dark to turn to light, for the buzzing beneath her skin have subsided, and for her leg to only be aching, now.

Headache aside, she feels clearer.

When she adjusts the soft blanket, discomfort slithers through her; she's only wearing her undershorts and vest. Her skin is still sticky from whatever she landed in back in the woodland, but her leg and forearm are wrapped in clean bandages.

What in the Seven bloody Heavens is the Minotaur—the Princess—playing at?

Theseus runs her dry tongue against her lips. She's never licked sandpaper before, but now she can imagine what it might be like. A glass of water taunts her from the bedside table, its exterior beaded with cool moisture.

It could be a trap.

How could it not be?

But dying of thirst while venturing to challenge the renowned Minotaur reeks of absurdity. The thought of her own demise has her fingers gravitating to the coin pendant tucked beneath her vest. Its dullness body checks her into panic—

+
.•

Several sun-orbits ago...

Herakles demonstrates 'using momentum and gravity to your advantage' by throwing Theseus over her shoulder as easily she might slap a high five, before landing her in the training sand with an *oof*.

"See?" Herakles grins down at her, her dimples popping and her shock of bright purple curls bouncing with the residual momentum. "Easy."

Monster hunter training is never *easy*. Their lives depend on being prepared, but having no idea what to be prepared *for*. And apparently it involves Theseus getting a face full of sand. Repeatedly.

Their sky-cruiser might be out for the count until their engine-savvy co-captain shows it who's boss, but that doesn't mean Herakles and Theseus have to wait around like spare parts. There's always an opportunity for self-improvement, and a quiet skyport with landing bay training-sand facilities is a better practice ground than most.

"It's alright for you," Theseus grumbles from the ground, "you're made of muscles, skill and confidence."

"Why, I thought you'd never notice." Herakles accompanies her flirting with an infuriating bicep flex.

"Shut up." Theseus can't decide whether to stare in appreciation or roll her eyes, so ends up with an awkward face twitch instead as she stands and brushes off.

"You have muscles." Herakles claps her on the back, trying to help with brushing off the sand, but almost proving the superiority of her strength and gravity in the process.

And yes, she is *technically* right. Theseus works hard; stood beside anyone else, she might even be physically impressive. But next to Herakles, she's an Athenian string-bean competing with an Olympian marrow. Though that could just be her dented self-esteem talking.

"I guess one out of three isn't bad," Theseus mutters.

"The whole point of this exercise," continues her friend and mentor with an eye-roll, "is to work on your skill and, therefore, confidence. You don't have to have the biggest muscles. You just have to be... you know... not the most idiotic." She shoots Theseus a smirk. "If you can manage it."

If anyone else said that to Theseus, she'd show them a closeup of her fists. But such words from Herakles are only ever meant in jest.

"Gravity can be your enemy, but it can also be your friend." Herakles underscores her lecture with a smile so winning Theseus could almost believe her. "And in any fight, it's good to have a friend on your side."

"Failing that" —Theseus grins back— "I could follow your example and lecture them into submission." She feigns dropping dead from boredom.

Herakles's eyes narrow, but then brighten again at a snort-laugh from beneath their sky-cruiser. Herakles's co-captain, otherwise known as her spouse (she has a name; she just prefers 'co-captain') knows how to overhaul an engine *and* listen in on their conversation. Skills.

"Smart ass," Herakles mumbles, swigging water and nodding for Theseus to join her at the sidelines, where her midnight-blue waistcoat lies on a bench. She digs something from the waistcoat's pocket and presents it to Theseus. "For you."

Theseus turns the item over in her palm. It's a pendant of some sort: a coin, clipped onto a simple black cord. Jewellery's not really Theseus's thing. Carrying around precious metal is reserved for weaponry; armour at a push. Herakles *knows* that—

though if she had to choose something, it would be simple, understated, like this.

She raises an eyebrow. "Do we give each other jewellery now?"

Herakles cuffs her gently across the back of her neck. "Don't be cute. Doesn't suit you."

"I think it does." Theseus grins. She doesn't want to be an asshole about the necklace if it is actually a gift, but it's also too fun an opportunity not to mess with her friend. "So, you're giving me this because it brings out the steely determination in my blue-*blue* eyes? Or to confess your undying love for me?"

Another laugh carries from beneath the sky-cruiser, fuelling Theseus's smirk. Herakles rolls her eyes with faux exasperation. "Against my better judgement, this is to keep you safe."

Theseus whistles. "It's magic, then?"

Herakles blinks at her. "Sometimes I don't know whether you're thick or just pretending." Yeah, sometimes Theseus doesn't know either. "It's a Locator."

"A what now?"

"How have you got this far through your skyfaring life and not heard of a Locator? The clue is in the name. It's Arcadia-tech. If ever you need help, all you have to do is activate it."

Herakles reclaims the pendant and twists the coin, splitting it into two semi-circles along its centre. Theseus expects it to light up or bleep or something that would make it seem like it's a beacon. But instead, it darkens, like flame-tarnished metal. Makes sense. If she were in danger, she wouldn't want to visually broadcast her precise whereabouts to whatever she were hiding from. Hiding in a tough manner, of course.

"See?" says Herakles as she digs her own darkened pendant from under her vest.

"So this will let me communicate with you, no matter where I am?"

"Think of it more like a cosmic flare that pinpoints your location and calls for help." At a press of Herakles's thumb, a simple sky-map appears on the coin's flip side, showing their locations as adjacent dots, while glowing co-ordinates appear on the coin's edge. "Once you activate it, it can only be reset by me reaching your location." To demonstrate, she taps her own Locator to Theseus's, returning both coins to their shiny states. "Set this off and I'll know where to go to get you out of trouble."

Theseus scoffs. "I can get myself out of trouble, thank you very much. You worry too much."

"I worry the right amount." Herakles rubs the back of her neck in that way she does when she's nervous or bashful. "You're an unstoppable force, Theseus. This is for the day you meet an immovable object." She drops the Locator back into Theseus's palm, clearing her throat. Her next words have a forced lightness to them. "And you're not very well going to make the universe a better place if you're dead, are you?"

Theseus can hardly disagree with that.

Herakles wanders toward the landing bay, as if sensing Theseus needs a bit of space to reflect. Her friend will be there for her, no matter what, and something about the sentiment brings a lump to her throat.

Don't cry.

The last thing she wants is for Herakles to worry about her. And if wearing this Locator thing helps, she can do that. She fastens the cord about her neck. Swallowing her emotion, she presses her palm to her chest, pretend-swooning. "Happy? Now we're matching!"

The muscles in Herakles's neck and shoulder relax as she returns with an appreciative grin. "You're right..." says Herakles, stepping a little closer than Theseus expects as she reaches out and examines Theseus's new pendant. And—damn—is

Herakles gazing at her? She sure knows how to escalate their game of flirtation. "Steely determination. Blue-*blue* eyes."

Theseus's heart quicksteps even before Herakles leans a little closer and whispers in her ear. "It even monitors your heartbeat."

Herakles pulls back, comparing their pendants and—Theseus can only assume—observing Theseus's mutinous heart rate.

She throws Theseus an infuriating wink. "You know, so I know you're not dead before I rescue you."

Theseus scoffs. "Don't think I don't know you're trying to spy on me and all my *activities.*" Theseus leads the way back to the training sands. "And you're basically affixing a tracking device to me, which is... you know... creepy?"

Another snort-giggle emanates from the sky-cruiser.

"Let's see if you're still quipping when your face is in the sand, shall we?" Herakles swings a lazy punch in Theseus's direction. "Come on, Thee. Time to get that heart racing."

✦
•

OH, *fuck.*

Theseus tenses, prompting vehement protest from her leg and head. She activated her Locator last night, didn't she?

She presses her thumb to the dulled coin, then flips it. On the opposite face, her location dot blinks into existence. At the far edge is the dot that represents Herakles, while around the coin's circumference, co-ordinates for their relative positions glow.

According to those, and their last real-life conversation, Herakles is currently somewhere under the Sixth Sun. It's not an impossible journey from there to the Fourth, where Theseus is... but what then?

Herakles could handle the Labyrinth. The great Sky Captain, Killer of Monsters, wouldn't be known far and wide, up and down, over and under, if this weren't the sort of situation she could swagger her way through.

But *could* is not certain enough. And by the time Herakles reaches her, Theseus will either be a dehydrated husk of Minotaur captive, or dead.

If there's one thing Theseus has learned from her friend—aside from how to flirt, how to use gravity to her advantage, and all the numerous first rules of monster hunting—it's to never forget that life and luck can run out. Reputations are built on past actions; that doesn't mean you can't still make a wrong turn. And there's a strong chance that Theseus has summoned Herakles not to a heroic rescue, but a brutal death.

Theseus always endeavours to get out of the chaos she lands herself in, but this time—for Herakles's sake—it's more crucial than ever that she succeeds.

16

TACTICAL

Theseus wraps the torn scrap of blanket tightly around the wide end of a broken shard of glass and clutches it like a dagger. Hopefully, when her captor returns to find her still in bed and her weapons across the bedchamber with her rucksack, she'll assume Theseus is unarmed.

The heavy thrum of her heart rate accentuates the persistent throb of her headache. She tugs at the stupid torque around her neck. If she gets out of here, she'll be having words with whoever designed the damn things.

The chamber door opens and Theseus tucks her hands beneath the covers, watching as the Princess concentrates on carrying a metal tray. The tray holds a water jug—even from here, Theseus can see the beads of condensation clinging to it—and a bowl with steam rising from it.

Savoury notes tease her nostrils, putting her stomach on growling high alert. Is that... soup?

It doesn't matter. Theseus won't be lured into trust.

Her grip tightens about her hidden weapon. Her limbs feel... unwieldy. She's not convinced she's up to any kind of confrontation, let alone with the person who managed to slam her off her feet even when she was fully functional.

The Princess is a little shorter than she recalls—but then, she's not wearing the bull mask right now. She's not as heavy-set or bursting with muscle, either. Theseus's adrenaline-riddled mind must have embellished somewhat—though she suspects that strange buzzing sensation wasn't *just* adrenaline. What was in that mist?

That's not to say, however, that the Princess's physique isn't well-defined. Her broad shoulders stretch her long-sleeve shirt, showing off the contours of her arms. Which Theseus is only taking a lingering note of for tactical reasons. Obviously.

Because. Actually. It doesn't add up. When they'd met at the Minosian palace—okay, when Theseus had been *hauled into the royal chambers in gravity-cuffs*—Princess Ariadne's musculature had been that of someone who'd only ever had to exert herself picking up a quill. Not that there's anything wrong with that. It just doesn't fit with what she's seeing now.

In the new light, Theseus could almost be convinced that the Princess before her isn't a monster. But she'd seen that damning injury on her arm... and the Minotaur head that's nothing more than a mask... *she* is *the Minotaur*.

Tattoo's bloody, nightmarish demise headbutts into her psyche. Beast or human, anything capable of *that* doesn't deserve mercy.

But something is out of alignment. Something Theseus doesn't currently have the mental dexterity to put her finger on. The Princess's face doesn't hold triumph or bloodlust, or anything else Theseus had expected. Instead, there's... apprehension?

Theseus's head throbs. She wishes this made sense.

The Princess reaches the bedside, but she doesn't place the

tray on the bedside table. Instead she pauses, observing the furniture in question. Shit. Has she noticed the missing glass?

Theseus tries to look innocent when the Princess's head snaps up, but—

Oh, fuck it—

Theseus upends her tray with a left-handed punch, sending soup splattering across the room. Theseus grasps the Princess's open shirt and vest and drags her closer while slashing at her with the glass shard clutched in her right hand—

But her weapon meets only metal. The Princess still has a grasp on the tray and is using it as a shield.

Damn, she's quick.

Theseus hisses as the shard slips from its protective wrapping, cutting into her palm, but she hardly has time to wince before the weight of the Princess is on her.

She swipes again. Or tries—but there's a firm grip about her wrist, pinning it and the weapon to the pillows.

Theseus's other hand is wrapped in shirt material and pressed between their bodies. And with the Princess's solid thighs straddling her hips, her legs can't do a damn thing. Again.

Fuck.

The Princess squeezes her right wrist, forcing her to drop the glass shard. It slips from the pillow and clatters to the floor, along with Theseus's self-respect.

The Princess's lagoon-blue eyes are wide with shock. She's so fucking *close*. And Theseus's misinformed pulse beats *everywhere*.

It's a distraction from her headache, at least.

She tries to wriggle her left hand from between their bodies, but no sooner has she freed it than the Princess has it, too, pinned to the pillows, bringing them closer still.

Theseus lets a knowing smile slip. Her fight response is simmering down. Maybe because the Princess's grip is assertive, but not cruel. Maybe because her scowl is of curiosity rather than rage. Or because Theseus is normally the one in the Princess's position—albeit in more recreational endeavours—and she hadn't expected her body's *reactions*.

Maybe she doesn't *always* have to be on top...

In their scuffle, the Princess's shirt has pulled askew, putting shoulders and her collarbone on display... Muscular shoulders, scattered with freckles like star systems that could inspire a voyage... And oh, heavens, she smells like summer. Like clean linen drying in sunshine.

Fuck. What is *wrong* with her? Being so thoroughly pressed to the sheets is obviously cutting off blood-flow to her brain.

Do. Not. Sniff. Her.

Light dances beneath the Princess's chin; her torque is glowing. What's *that* about? But yeah, electricity... that's about what's travelling through Theseus right now. So much so, she must short-circuit—because instead of trying to put distance between herself and the Princess, she flexes her hips and presses up against her.

The wildfire blush up the Princess's neck isn't her imagination. And the gasp on her lips, echoing Theseus's own, is tinted with a moan that makes Theseus's pulse go rogue.

You might be on top, Princess, but—

But before Theseus can consider her next move, sensible or otherwise, the Princess releases her. Theseus flexes her fingers, appreciating the returned circulation. She should do something useful, like clock her attacker across the temple.

Only... the Princess isn't attacking her.

And Theseus might start a fight, but she won't keeping fighting someone who isn't fighting back.

The Princess's nose scrunches, which Theseus should absolutely not be finding cute. Though it's not her fault if the Princess has an inconveniently *cute nose*. Fact of the universe is all. Doesn't mean Theseus won't put her in her place. When she's ready.

The Princess mutters... something. In Theseus's revision of phrases that could be useful in a narrow set of circumstances, she'd learned the Minosian for 'you smell so good', but this doesn't quite match. *You smell so...* sounds right, but the last word isn't *good*.

The Princess has really committed to that nose scrunch. So ... *not* good?

What's also *not good* is the abrupt upending of her perspective. In quick and unceremonious succession, she's scooped—*scooped!* Nobody *scoops* Theseus!—lifted, and thrown over the Princess's shoulder.

Theseus grasps for something, anything, to retaliate, but only achieves bunching the Princess's shirt up her back. Her well-defined, mighty impressive back.

Oh.

Fuck.

Face burning hotter than the Seven Suns, all Theseus can do is flail—how fucking *embarrassing*—as the Princess carries her into an adjoining chamber, its walls decorated with a maze of pipework, and deposits her on the tiled floor like a sack of awkward potatoes.

What—the—fuck? Is this some sort of cell?

While Theseus shuffles herself into a sitting position against the warm wall, the Princess retreats a couple of paces. There's no arrogance in her posture, only the air of a seasoned fighter unwilling to be goaded by a lesser opponent.

A stench meets Theseus's nostrils like a slap. Urgh. What *is* that?

Oh, no. It's *her*. How had she not noticed sooner? She smells worse than an Arcadian bog monster in heat.

At least she now knows the Minosian for 'terrible' or 'disgusting' or maybe even 'worse than decay'. But never mind that; right now she needs to figure out how much on the back foot she is, before—

The Princess presses a triangular wall tile. Shit. What's going to—?

The air overhead churns, thickening like captured storm clouds. Theseus tries to stand, but topples like she's never experienced gravity before.

The Princess tilts her head, watching with arms crossed as if wondering: *What the fuck are you doing?* Okay. If earlier had been embarrassing, this is mortifying.

As the first droplets hit her, Theseus tenses, ready to throw herself to safety, but as the water cascades over her... as she spies the washbasin and latrine... she dies a little more inside. Because this isn't some death cell. It's a shower.

Well, at least she's cooling off. If only she had some—

A bar of soap glides across the floor to her through the thin layer of surface water. When Theseus looks up, the Princess is already heading back to the bedchamber, saying something in Minosian about... clothes?

The floor tiles are rough enough for Theseus to lever herself upright onto her good leg and lean in one corner against the slippery wall. The shower is both the best and worst thing in the universe. The water's temperature and pressure are both perfect. Even her headache is letting up.

She hisses with pain as the water channels through a cut in her eyebrow she hadn't known was there. Her lacerated palm stings a little. And, yes, when the water's steady stream hits her injured leg and forearm, she wants to claw out of her own skin for five searing seconds. But the enveloping steam is like a warm, cleansing hug—and, right now, she could really do with one of those—and once she's figured out how to angle away from the jet, and the water frees her from the worst of the grime, this could even be the best solo shower she's ever had.

Theseus has always found water soothing—unless she's sharing it with something fanged. Back before life got complicated, rivers, waterfalls, and the ocean were all her playground, her sanctuary. Showers, too, have always brought her a sense of calm.

She pulls off her sodden vest and eases down her shorts, clenching her teeth against the pain as the sodden fabric drags past her bandaged shin.

First rule of monster hunting: Survive first, then check your wounds when there are no weapons being thrown at you. Or something like that. Now would probably be a good time, but the bandages look to be those moisture-repelling ones that keep wounds dry even when immersed in water. Messing with them could cause more problems than leaving them be.

She runs the soap through her short hair and scrubs her face. It smells like the Princess: like sunshine and summer. And at that, Theseus's pulse goes wandering without her permission.

She really needs to focus.

As the soap dissolves the layers of filth, the water's heat penetrates her muscles, waking up their tenderness and reviving her from her stupor. Perhaps because she spends her days wading through swamps and burrowing into slime dens for the greater good, cleanliness is high on her list of priorities. It's such a *relief*—though her mouth tastes less appetising than a shit-beetle's hind legs. Yes, there was that one time she had that pleasure. And no, she doesn't want to talk about it.

She could stay here under the cascade forever. But shit—What if the steam is laced with something? What if she's relaxing into a trap?

That thought gargles her ill-advised relaxation down the

plug holes. In her sudden need to flee, she almost slips, but catches herself on the wall.

As she's debating how best to escape on one leg without jolting herself—again—into unconsciousness, she notices that just beyond the cascade her rucksack is hanging on a wall hook. The Princess must have put it there.

Which is... helpful?

Helpful is confusing...

The Princess must have placed it there when Theseus's eyes were closed under the water. Which is not a ringing endorsement of Theseus's current situational awareness.

What's even more confusing is that, next to her rucksack, leaning against the wall, is a crutch: three thick sticks, stripped of bark, smoothed and bound together.

Did the Princess make this for her? Or does she host enough victims of the Labyrinth to have such items readily available?

When the water stops, a uniform arrangement of coin-sized holes appears in the floor and wall. Before Theseus can panic—or do anything else—a whirlwind of air blasts around her.

It's honestly the most thorough post-shower air-blast she's ever experienced. Her injured limbs bristle beneath their bandages, but at least she's dry.

Now what?

Her pile of sopping, stinking astro-attire might be swift-drying, but her clothes won't be wearable without considerable scrubbing first. Her stock of mostly-essentials doesn't include a change of clothes, but Theseus unclips the hydration tube from her rucksack and sucks down several gulps before sifting past her guide-Shard to find a nutrition bar, tearing it open and shoving it into her mouth. It might not taste of much, but captive monster hunters in specifically this predicament can't be choosers.

What a fucking mess. She'd wanted to kill a monster and

free the Minosian Princess from the invisible chains of royal expectation, only to end up captured by that very royal monster. And, yes, maybe she'd wanted to impress the Princess, which was idiotic. Obviously. Because so far, all she's managed to do is embarrass herself.

On the plus side, as she rummages in her rucksack, locating the items she needs: she can *finally* brush her teeth.

17

STITCHES

Theseus finds the bedchamber empty, but the Princess has clearly been busy in her absence. There's no longer soup splattered across the floor, the bedsheets are crisp and clean, and there are fresh clothes set out—for Theseus, presumably. She limps closer, her scratched palm smarting as she grips the crutch.

On inspection, the outfit is not too distant from the sort she'd choose for herself: three-quarter length trousers in a dark stretch material, a vest, and a light, collarless long-sleeve shirt. Even the undershorts are the kind she likes, not the tiny triangles of fabric that many seem to prefer.

First rule of monster hunting: Try not to be naked when you shouldn't be. Herakles had declared that one specifically for Theseus.

Theseus pulls on the undershorts, which is a challenge. She's only got them halfway up her good leg when the door opens and the Princess's shadow looms over her—though the looming could be more to do with the flickering corridor lights and Theseus's discomfort at being caught literally with her trousers down.

The Princess, however, seems more preoccupied with balancing the tray she's carrying than Theseus trying and failing to dress herself. She doesn't even glance at Theseus until she's halfway across the room. When she does, she stops and outright stares, her jaw dropping enough for it to clearly be a compliment.

Undershorts finally in place, Theseus almost wraps her arms around herself—but why should she? She isn't bothered about her body. She's rather a fan of it, in fact. It's not arrogance; well, not entirely. She just rather appreciates that without it, she wouldn't exist. It seems right to be thankful for that. Besides, she's got more pressing things to be embarrassed about. Like having got herself into this mess in the first place. Like having dragged Herakles into danger. Like how she, a supposedly great monster hunter, has let a mere princess floor her several times now.

So, whatever. The Princess can stare if she likes. The blush on her cheeks is doing wonders for Theseus's ego.

But...

Um...

Maybe that's *enough* staring?

Theseus clears her throat and the Princess's eyes snap up to hers. Theseus can't help raising an eyebrow. "Like what you see, Princess?"

The Princess's torque sparks. She mumbles something Theseus doesn't catch, hurrying to set the tray down on the bedside table, keeping the bed a barrier between them. Theseus pulls on the vest and perches on the bed, trying to wriggle into the trousers without touching her wounds.

Which is easier said...

The Princess strides around the bed towards her, saying *something* in her sandpapery voice. Theseus flinches away. The

Princess's hands raise in placation, gentle eyes seeking her permission to...

What? Help?

What's more confusing still is that Theseus lets her. She lets the Princess kneel before her, lets her guide the trouser leg up her calf with one warm hand while the other holds the fabric away from her wound. Gently, the Princess growls something which Theseus guesses means 'stand up'. She does so, balancing on her good leg. She reaches to brace herself on the Princess's shoulder—

But the Princess flinches under her touch.

Instinctively, Theseus grabs for her neck—

But—again—the Princess is quicker, pushing Theseus down and pinning her to the bed. Pain shoots from her calf, making even her toes ache, and Theseus yelps, letting rip a torrent of curses that would make even a monster hunter blush.

The fireplace roars about as much as Theseus's leg injury as the Princess growls something back at her. Several somethings. Gone is the gentleness, replaced with wide-eyed exasperation.

Okay. Maybe that's enough belligerence for now. At least until the odds aren't quite so stacked against her.

When the Princess releases her, Theseus attempts to sit, only to discover that she's cuffed to the headboard. *Again.*

"How the fuck—?" Theseus's heart rate scrambles but the Princess isn't escalating this further. She's just... pacing.

Theseus's heart-thumping panic at being bound calms at the Princess's huff of irritation. On closer inspection, what she'd assumed to be purpose-made restraints are in fact just belts. Well, they do the job, don't they? Here she is again, this time with her trousers undone.

Not exactly progress, is it?

The fireplace calms, flickering but not flaring. As the

Princess finally settles, she grumbles a question that seems to be, "Shall we try this again?"

Theseus gives a single nod. Both eyeing each other warily, the Princess approaches her and unwinds the bandage around her leg, revealing a wound that's red, raw, and... neatly stitched? It's calmer than before, with the same shimmer at the edges of the stitching. It matches the tincture the Princess is showing her now in a small dish from the bedside tray.

Is she asking permission, or just checking Theseus isn't about to lamp her? Theseus nods, and the Princess begins to rub the balm around the perforations in her shin. Theseus tenses at the initial shock, letting out a growl of pain. But after a second, the balm is cooling, the Princess's touch to her ragged flesh soothing enough that she lets out a sigh.

But she can't let herself relax with a stranger poking her raw wounds; never mind a stranger who casually murders people while dressed as a half-bull. She can't relax when she still doesn't know exactly how fucked she is.

She doesn't want to, but it's necessary. She flexes her leg right down to her toes, clenching all other muscle at the radiating ache that follows. It hurts worse than a chimera kick, even numbed by the balm—but she can move her toes, lift her heel. She's not broken beyond repair. *Thank fuck.* She'll still be able to show the monsters who's boss, if she can escape the one who, for some unknown reason, is tending to her wounds.

After binding Theseus's lower leg with a fresh bandage, the Princess moves on to examine her forearm burn.

"You know," Theseus rasps, "if you want me in restraints, you should really buy me dinner first." She smirks at her own stupid joke, recalling the time when a very charming woman from—

The Princess looks pointedly between her and where the soup had decorated the floor. Oh, yeah. There had been dinner, technically.

For some reason, the Princess is blushing profusely. Seriously? The Minotaur infamous for murdering all who enter her domain gets bashful at one mention of power play?

But wait...

That means—

"You understand Athenian?"

The Princess shrugs. Fucking *shrugs*. What does that mean? Yes? No? A little?

Having re-dressed Theseus's arm, the Princess turns to her restrained palm, dabbing the shimmering balm onto a clean cloth and wiping the cut gently with it. It stings for a only a moment before the pain dulls. Without fuss, the Princess covers the wound with an adhesive bandage, then turns to the cut in Theseus's eyebrow, squinting at it for a few moments before reaching out to hover a tincture-covered fingertip above her brow.

Permission. She's seeking permission.

What the actual fuck?

Theseus should pull away. Eyes are the windows to truth, and Theseus doesn't share hers so readily.

But she's so confused, she just nods.

She winces at the first touch. Then she winces at her own wince. She *is* tough. Honest.

The sting is already gone. All she can do is watch, half suspicious, half bewildered, half awestruck, and fully ignoring mathematical reality, as the Minotaur-Princess tends to her wounds with a touch so gentle, Theseus could cry.

She absolutely is not going to, though. Obviously.

What is going on? Is the Princess trying to lure her into a false sense of security?

Is it working?

Theseus only ever gets this close to people she's about to kiss or kill. And in either situation, she rarely takes note of the shifting hues in their eyes, like tropical ocean waves in sunshine.

"Why are you doing this?" Even to her own ears, Theseus's words are a confusing mix of soft and exasperated. *Why are you keeping me captive? Why are you pretending to care about me? Why do you prance around dressed as the damn Minotaur?* Is Ariadne nursing her back to health simply to have a more challenging target to hurt through the endless corridors?

"You—hurt," says the Princess in stumbling Athenian, frowning as if Theseus had asked something ridiculous. Energy shimmers along her torque, dancing at the hollow of her throat. Close up, its lack of opulence is plain to see.

The Princess frees her from the restraints. There's no warning, just simple freedom as she steps beyond Theseus's reach.

Theseus's eyes flick up to meet an expressive blue-green gaze. Only now is her head clear enough to hear what her gut has been shouting at her.

Back in the Minosian palace, Princess Ariadne's royal swagger had been buttressed by arrogance as she toyed with Theseus. Even when she'd been flirting, she'd needled at Theseus like a Nemean lion assessing its prey. This princess wears her every emotion scrawled on her face—including, so far, annoyance, confusion, surprise and disgust, all aimed at Theseus. She holds herself with a rigidity that could be arrogance, but... it's different.

Honestly. Sometimes Theseus can be denser than a solar core.

"You're not Princess Ariadne."

18

THE PRINCESS PUZZLE

But if this isn't Princess Ariadne... who in the heavens is she?

The stranger's eyes light up. A stream of Minosian erupts from her: "*Something-something* Ariadne? Ariadne *something-something*? Please, *something-something* Ariadne—okay?"

"Uh..." Theseus's response is universal for 'I haven't got the first fucking clue what you're saying.' Nor does she understand the desperation in those blue-green eyes.

Stars above; she looks so much like Princess Ariadne—and yet, now that Theseus has seen the obvious, she can't unsee it—nothing like her at all. Their features match, but though their eyes have the same colouring, what lies behind them is worlds apart. Where Princess Ariadne had been all confidence and fire-crackling flirtation, the eyes before Theseus now hold only uncertainty and battle-weariness.

"You're..." Theseus gestures to her generally, then more specifically to her face. "...Ariadne's twin?"

The stranger's scoff puts her in her place. "I—her—twin—she—*my*—twin."

"Okay. You're each other's twin. Got it."

Another stream of Minosian follows, from which Theseus can only decipher the repeated word 'Ariadne'.

Does Princess Ariadne know her sibling is here? *Kill the beast. Bring me its heart. Set me free.* That's what she'd challenged Theseus to do. Does Princess Ariadne think the Minotaur is real? Or does she want her sibling dead?

Theseus huffs. It's a lot of questions when there's a language and trust barrier larger than any sky labyrinth.

When it becomes clear Theseus doesn't have any answers, mostly because she doesn't understand the questions, the enthusiasm in the twin's eyes dims and her shoulders slacken. For a moment, Theseus sort of feels *sorry* for her.

But fuck that. She will not get sucked in to caring about a murderer's feelings. Besides, if anyone deserves answers, it's Theseus herself.

"Who the fuck are you?" she demands.

The twin's brow creases. "The... fuck...?" she repeats, scratching her head. It's possible that not everyone who learns a new language decides to start with the swear words.

Whatever.

Theseus makes a point of pulling up her trousers properly. It involves some uncouth wriggling, but she's not having a frustrating, existential conversation or another altercation, or whatever all this escalates to, with her trousers undone. It is a rule of monster hunting, after all.

Hades and the Heavens, the fabric is soft. And the material stops just above her calves, leaving her injury free. Was that a purposeful, thoughtful choice?

Seriously, who *is* this person with the princess's face and the bull's head? And what is her game?

The stranger's mouth snaps shut, her cheeks tinting in a way that suggests she's recalled *one* meaning of the word she's been murmuring.

"Will you stop that?" Theseus shouts. The stranger recoils, her features pinching with unease. Her apparent compliance only makes Theseus bristle more. Why in the heavens is the person who dragged her here to do *who knows what* to her the one who looks startled? "Stop! Stop pretending to be... whatever this is. Stop pretending to care. Just tell me—*why did you bring me here?*"

"Why...?" She's trying out words again. For fuck's sake.

"Why did *you*" —Theseus points to whoever she is— "bring *me*" —she points to herself— "*here?*" She gestures around them.

The stranger's gaze flicks back and forth, as if trying to decode the questions. Finally, she gestures to the window. Which, it's now clear, isn't barred with metal at all, but decorated with carved wooden shutters over a light-well.

"Monster." The twin's statement is so matter-of-fact, and all the more maddening for it.

Theseus can't help her mirthless laugh. *But* you're *the fucking monster.*

The stranger's narrowed eyes search her face. Theseus tries again: "Why bring me here? Why stitch my wounds? Wounds *you* inflicted. *Why did you kill everyone?*" It's too many words, and all too quick. Theseus knows it. But the twin *has* to know she won't take this lying down.

Even though, *technically*, she is still lying down... Right now she's not even amused by the irony.

The stranger repeats some of the words under her breath, as her brow ripples with frustration. "Perhaps, I... not understand?"

Theseus sighs, heavier than shadow-gravity. She'd expected torture in the den of the Minotaur, but *this*? "If you're not Ariadne, who the fuck are you?"

"Who...?" The twin tries out the word as though examining it, and for the longest time, Theseus is sure she's not getting an answer. But finally, the twin takes a deep breath.

"My name is Asterion."

PART III

THESEUS AND ASTERION

19

WHO?

Mumbling in Minosian, Asterion shows herself out. Theseus isn't sure why *she* looks like the one who's just discovered her survival depends on solving puzzles she's not cut out for, but maybe she's just projecting.

Although Theseus is known for charging into chaos, she does—on occasion—do her research. She'd absorbed as much as she could from her guide-Shard on her connecting astro-flights to Minos, but she's not cut out for rattling off specifics. And to be fair, her brain's been dealing with a lot in the last few days.

Time for some revision.

Getting to grips with her crutch, she's halfway to her ruck-sack when a percolating growl, too fucking close, stops her in her tracks. After a momentary diversion of her heart to her throat it's confirmed that Theseus is more of an idiot than a monster hunter. Though there is often overlap between the two.

The growl isn't some beast, but her own stomach. Apparently a single nutrition bar wasn't enough.

The fresh bowl of soup and another cup of water—metal this time—wait on the bedside table. Theseus hesitates, her stomach aching with temptation and her mouth salivating its support while her brain insists it's all a trick.

It looks like soup... It smells like soup... The water is clear and doesn't smell like anything it shouldn't. But the part of Theseus that wants to believe in the goodness of people is tainted by suspicion, myths and first impressions.

Why anyone would toy with thoughts and trust, she cannot fathom, but there are those who thrive on such things.

However... even if this 'Asterion' has dark plans for her, she probably wouldn't have taken the time to sort her wounds if she were about to poison her. Right?

Carefully, Theseus tastes the soup. It's almost thick enough to slice, just how she likes it. It's perfectly seasoned, too. This place is better catered than most establishments she frequents.

Weapons within reach, door within sight, soup bowl in her lap, Theseus settles back onto the bed with her guide-Shard. She navigates past the section on why the bull is the symbol of a world known for mining and monuments (it's an echo from Minos's farmland past, before its raw materials had been discovered) to the BE AWARE section, the addendum that tells tourists all the things they should avoid if they don't want to embarrass themselves or their hosts, get marched back to the skyport, or—in Theseus's particular case—get sent to the death maze in the sky. A useful resource, for sure. It always helps to know what counts as a crime on a world when you're seeking to commit one.

Anyway. In the SOCIAL FAUX PAS section, under the DO NOT MENTION subheading, she skim reads about:

THE LOST PRINCESS
Progeny of the late Architect-monarch...
(blah, blah, blah)
...the Princess's mysterious death at a young age... victim of

the Minotaur... deep in the Minosian mines... Labyrinth
constructed to contain the unkillable beast...

So... apart from wondering what a child was doing in a deep
mine... If Asterion was 'killed' by the Minotaur... how and why
is she here? And why in the heavens does she roam the place
dressed as the beast that's meant to have killed her?

Theseus is going to have a word with her travel agent about
these guides. It doesn't even explain *why* not to mention the Lost
Princess, or to whom.

Asterion. She hadn't introduced herself as 'Princess Asterion'.
Just 'Asterion'.

And Theseus is still no closer to answering the most pressing
question of all, which is: what does Asterion want with *her*?

The chamber has darkened. Orange flames continue to
flicker in the fireplace, while cool blue light stripes through the
shutters in a convincing impersonation of moonlight. But there's
no chance Theseus will be sleeping. Her thoughts are too unsettled, her heart thumping too hard.

Rain patters against the window, which doesn't make a
whole lot of sense. But then, neither does so much of what she's
witnessed here. There are creaks and groans, too, similar to
those she'd heard in the outer corridors. At the time she'd
thought them the roars of the Minotaur, but now it seems more
likely they're just the labyrinth in motion.

And beyond the rain, beyond the distant rattling of the walls,
there's something else. Something that has her bolting upright,
straining to listen.

Sobs. Inconsolable human cries from somewhere beyond
her chamber. The sound lights a fire in her with no heed to her
current capabilities. Grabbing her crutch, she hobbles to the
door, reclaiming her sword on the way.

Once again, it's unlocked. The curving corridor beyond, lit

by stuttering fire-torches and warmed by the lava-channels in the floor and walls, appears to be clear. At least now her senses aren't drowning her in shadows and her inner equilibrium can keep her upright.

The cries echo louder as Theseus crutch-limps as swiftly as she's able, careful not to tap-tap-tap it against the stone floor and give away her location. The more she listens, the more certain she is. This isn't the sound of terror, but of grief.

When she reaches an open door, the sobs are louder. She peers through into a lamplit chamber. It's similar in size to her bedchamber, with a fireplace to match. In place of a bed fit for a monarch (or several, if that's your thing), it's packed with *things*: everything from clothing, toothbrushes and cleaning implements, to notebooks and writing paraphernalia, all neatly ordered and arranged like with like. It's mostly Minosian in origin, but not exclusively.

The only thing not neatly catalogued is the heap of weaponry in the centre of the chamber. It's taller than she is and obscures where the crying is stemming from. Theseus's leg throbs its disgust, because the trap that had bitten into her flesh is glinting at her from the top of the pile. It looks cleaner now than when it had been cutting through her muscle and scraping at bone.

And that's not all that's churning her stomach: some of the armour and astro-helmets, all lined up, all cleaned, are familiar. Some are dented, punctured where something sharp has pierced through.

The sobbing stops.

In silence, her stealth abilities returning—finally—Theseus rounds the weaponry pile, one crutch-aided step at a time. There, sitting at a workbench with her back to Theseus, is Asterion, surrounded by her claimed treasures, her inventory of the fallen.

Theseus's attention snags on the scythe glinting from its storage hook on the wall above the workbench. Acid sours Theseus's stomach. Is that what she used to killed Tattoo? Or was it the mask's horns?

Alongside the scythe hangs a selection of other weapons: levers, screwdrivers, wrenches, hammers... Okay, maybe they're more tools than weapons. All include an attachment at the handle that looks the right size to affix to a hoofed arm.

Theseus edges forward. Bile burns her throat. The loss of all these people... the grief of their loved ones... How dare Asterion take not just their lives but their belongings too?

Theseus's fingers tighten around the hilt of her sword. She's close enough. One swipe, and Minos will be free.

Free of the monster—

The monster who... dressed your wounds?

The monster who's not actually doing anything monstrous right now. The monster who—with a snort and a snuffle—is blowing her nose?

Theseus steps even closer, trying to peer past Asterion to see... There's *no victim* lying on her workbench. There's only a selection of—

Asterion turns.

Toe to toe and eye to eye...

And Theseus the fucking Monster Hunter should be putting the business end of her blade to use...

But Asterion's eyes are red-rimmed, tears tracking down her cheeks. Sad eyes flash at Theseus's half-raised sword. Asterion's forearm lashes out, striking Theseus's wrist so hard that her sword clatters from her grasp, towards the weaponry pile.

Her crutch slips, her world upturning in a swirl as she lands hard on the stone floor, pain juddering through her leg and arm —mostly her leg—before she discovers that, yet again, Asterion has her pinned. This time to the flagstones.

Deja-fucking-vu. Does she *always* have to be on top? Theseus huffs. It's embarrassing how off her game she is. She's never been so much on the back foot—or so much on her back full stop—on a mission. If she could just stop ending up *beneath Asterion*, that would do wonders for her apparently fragile monster hunter ego.

Asterion's breath brushes her cheek and Theseus's heartbeat squirms like it's in restraints and it's *fine* with that. It's really not the time for such reactions.

Because—

All these people...

Theseus wrenches her right hand free and grasps blindly toward the weaponry pile, somehow not losing all her digits in the process. Her fingers wrap around a piece of blunt metal. She plucks her new dagger-sized weapon free and angles it against Asterion's stomach, just beneath her ribs—

The lamplight trembles. And Theseus can only stare as, instead of retaliating—or even trying to defend herself—Asterion's shoulders shake with a fresh flood of sobs. The same sounds that had drawn Theseus here.

Oh, fuck.

Monsters don't cry like that.

Between Asterion's body-shaking sobs, all the more unsettling in the frazzled and faulty electricity, Asterion chokes out words... only some of them familiar: 'What'; 'more'; 'you want'; 'me'.

What more do you want from me?

The hurt in those words is like a sword through Theseus's chest.

Which is why, when Asterion rests her tear-stained cheek on Theseus's shoulder, she lets her. She's almost tempted to give her a hug with her free arm; Asterion obviously needs one.

No. She must have hit her head, because that's ridiculous.

Isn't it?

It takes several seconds for Asterion's sobs to lessen and for them both to look down to the weapon pressing beneath Asterion's sternum. It would have been a deadly strike with a blade. But with Theseus's weapon of choice... not so much.

They both blink at it.

Theseus's cheeks blaze.

She's tempted to point out that the weaponry filing system needs an overhaul if *that's* what she came away with in her lucky dip amongst the blades, but instead she just feels—as is increasingly the case around Asterion—completely an idiot.

Because. Yes. Apparently, her chosen weapon is *a spoon*.

Asterion sob-gasps, as if she's not sure whether to laugh or cry. She manages a strangled version of both before climbing off Theseus and escaping the chamber at a fast clip. Fair enough. If someone tried to kill Theseus with a spoon, she'd need a moment to regroup, too.

Theseus needs more than a moment just to feel like less of a fool. It's not that these things *don't* happen to famous monster hunters—they do, more often than you'd think—it's just that they're the stories you try to make sure people don't hear.

With Asterion's departure, the lamps have simmered down until only a whisper of light remains. The chamber is cooler, too. Theseus reclaims her crutch and hauls herself over to the workbench for a closer look.

The items Asterion had been crying over? Portrait-shards, lockets, family action shots captured in the ether of thumbcoins. Keepsakes.

Only now does it occur to her that, compared to the organised shelves stocked with bandages and medical supplies, the weaponry pile is a mess. The blades are all sparkling, yes—it's always wise to free a weapon from blood and grime—but they're not filed away for reuse like everything else. Clearly, they're not Asterion's priority.

She'd been so blinkered in her pursuit of the monster, before, she'd failed to notice the signage in the corner of the chamber, with paints and brushes nearby. Theseus recognises enough of the wording to know the consensus is to guide people towards safety. If Asterion created these signs...

That confusion from her first encounter with the Minotaur resurfaces. Asterion hadn't been *attacking* her, had she? She'd been trying to divert Theseus from the path of danger.

Asterion has cleansed her wounds, stitched them, fed her, even. And all Theseus has done in return is push her, threaten her, and generally act like the kind of nightmare she spends her life trying to defeat.

Well... fuck.

It's entirely possible Asterion isn't the monster, but Theseus is.

20

BREAKFAST

Feeling less like a captive and more like a conclusion-jumping murderous asshole, Theseus takes Asterion's hint and leaves her alone. Her injured leg isn't up to pursuing anyway, so she returns to the bedchamber, climbs under the covers without even bothering to undress, and tries to bury the inner voice hissing *idiot, idiot, idiot.* Hopefully tomorrow will be a better day.

She must find sleep, because she wakes to find the rain and darkness replaced by early morning sunlight. Despite rolling around on the floor last night with Asterion, her clothes are still clean.

Oh, *shit...*

She owes Asterion an apology. Or several.

There are so many questions, and she's not going to get answers if she luxuriates in the soft sheets forever. Everything takes longer with her leg injury, but the crutch allows her to roam the fortress's singular curved corridor that—as far as she can tell—links all the rooms. Her bandage-covered palm smarts only a little with each step. Asterion didn't have to give her the crutch or the bandages. *Stars*, she could have left her in the trap to bleed or freeze to death. Instead, Asterion had dragged her here... which can't have been easy, despite her powerful physique.

Theseus usually swears by gut feelings. They've got her where she is today. Which, okay, might be hopping along in a den of confusion—but she's alive, isn't she? Still, ingrained patterns of thinking are difficult to escape, and hers often have her assuming the worst in people. Which, in a place like this, just makes sense, doesn't it?

But now she's warring with this new notion that Asterion isn't the beast she'd thought. And it's not like the truth can be determined by the toss of a coin.

The corridor opens into a vast banquet chamber. Though the long table down the centre of the hall is simple in itself, the size is... a bit much. Theseus hadn't expected this sort of grandeur—but then she hadn't expected the Minotaur to be the spitting image of Princess Ariadne either.

The chamber is so long, it takes her a moment to notice Asterion sitting at the far end of the table.

Okay. Let's get this over with.

But then she notices that the seat nearest to her has a place set for breakfast: a tall glass of multicoloured juice, plus... is that porridge? The smell alone has her stomach growling like some labyrinth creature.

Theseus shudders as something dead-eyed stares up at her from a plate beside the porridge bowl: a fang-fish from the lake. There's one in front of Asterion, too, so it must be food.

The invitation is clear. Theseus takes her seat. She's fairly sure the porridge isn't poisoned, though less convinced that the fang-fish isn't either a challenge or a punishment.

It'd help if she had something to eat with, though.

Asterion must have something to say, because she's standing... walking—evenly, calmly—towards Theseus. Her dark trousers are tucked into black capped boots, her belt with its simple buckle practical rather than fancy. Her powerful shoulders stretch her grey long-sleeve, enticing Theseus's pulse to voyage to ill-advised places.

First rule of monster hunting: Know your parameters.

Asterion might not be a monster, but apparently Theseus still can't help observing her 'parameters'.

Asterion stops just a pace away. Her eyes are a little red; she looks tired, like she's had a fitful night. Something a lot like guilt slithers in Theseus's gut. But Asterion is also... suppressing a smile?

She says something in Minosian— "...you smell..." One of the words is 'better'. 'You smell better today.'?

Bloody cheek. True as it may be.

Theseus squirms in her seat as Asterion, with a sarcastic flourish, produces a piece of cutlery and places it on the table beside her bowl.

Oh, heavens. A spoon.

Renewed embarrassment burrows through her. What kind of monster hunter tries to stab someone with a *spoon*?

Though thank the heavens the blades had evaded her. Killing monsters is noble. But to get it wrong... well... that's just murder, isn't it?

An apology hovers on Theseus's tongue, but she doesn't voice it because Asterion is making a show of stepping back, raising a playful eyebrow as she pretends to cower from the stupid spoon, before returning to her end of the table.

Damn. That's some snark. If Theseus were more surefooted right now, she might have let her amusement show. Instead, all she can do is gawp.

Asterion utters a single word in Minosian, then starts on her breakfast with royal finesse. Theseus recognises the word for *eat*, though those of a prudish persuasion would blush to know why.

But that's not something to be thinking of right now.

She looks down at her porridge. All the healing must be taking it out of her, because she's famished. She endeavours to match Asterion's dignified pace of food consumption. Though Theseus herself is technically of royal heritage, she never received that kind of upbringing. Still, she can feign poise if she has to. Usually.

It's only when she pauses for breath that she notices Asterion staring at her like *she's* the beast. She must have been furiously paddling the porridge with her spoon. Oops.

"You have—name?" Asterion's question is gruff, as if making conversation is the worst kind of torture.

"Theseus." She watches for a reaction, but her host only nods: acknowledgement rather than recognition. *Huh. Guess she hasn't heard of me.* Probably a good thing.

Maybe it's best not to announce that she's a monster killer.

Apparently that's all the conversation Theseus is getting. Asterion returns to her porridge, eyeing Theseus warily. Which is understandable given everything. Theseus follows suit, enjoying the porridge's creamy texture and the sweetness of shredded apple. For a while, they eat in silence. The skeletal fish might haunt her nightmares, but it tastes delicious. Though she can only eat it if she points its eyes and fangs away from her.

But she's not here to enjoy a hearty home-cooked meal. She's here to kill a beast that... doesn't exist?

Of all her missions, it's the ones where the monster doesn't exist that are the most challenging. How do you prove something that *isn't*? How do you convince a village, a city, a world, that their fear is of something imagined? Wild imagination and misplaced fear fuelled by those in power can be stronger and more damaging than any beast.

"Why do you wear the mask?"

At Theseus's question, Asterion looks up from her elegant

eating. She's too far away for Theseus to decipher the emotion behind her scowl. Perhaps she's puzzled by her Athenian or the question. Each to their own, of course, but masks are quite a niche enthusiasm, so the associated Minosian vocabulary hadn't made the cut during Theseus's minimal brushing up.

Theseus repeats her question, supplementing the words by pointing to Asterion and using both hands to create a vague imitation of bull horns.

Asterion nods her understanding. At least, Theseus thinks that's what that is. By the time her brain and mouth have conferred, her host has strutted past her with a certain "follow me" air about her.

Theseus reaches for her crutch and does so.

21

MASK

Theseus's crutch co-ordination is far from second nature, but Asterion doesn't seem vexed, waiting until she's within sight before continuing along the dark stone corridor to the entrance hall.

A spine-chilling awareness of being watched steals over Theseus. She turns, and—there. Someone is standing beside the gateway.

No. Not someone; it's a life-size portrait. She hadn't noticed it when she'd been here last. Either it was draped in shadows, or her fever-vision had her blinkered.

Theseus shivers. With those cool green eyes and lavish attire, the figure in the painting is undoubtedly Princess Ariadne; her features more youthful by a handful of sun-orbits. But the painting is not what she's here to look at.

Asterion is waiting beside the double-her-height wood and metal door. The one that has complex patterns, no doorhandle and four mysterious holes in it. On the nearby wall, hanging from hooks, are the rucksack Asterion had carried in the labyrinth, and the Minotaur mask.

Theseus almost drops her crutch.

"Is this a joke?"

Asterion's nose scrunches. "Joke?" Her intonation suggests she doesn't understand the word rather than the context.

Steeling herself, Theseus squares up to the mask. The Minotaur doesn't look like this. Well, the features are the same: the bovine snout, the scowling forehead, the dagger-like horns that could gut a person... Did they gut a person?

She isn't sure of anything anymore. But in the light of day, without the adrenaline and whatever else had been fuelling her in the labyrinth corridors, the mask is just that: a mask.

Its skin likely is leather, so in that sense it may well be made of actual bull. Its lifeless gaps for eyes are creepy enough to make her shudder, but not to unbalance her into the depths of terror. It's the horns that give it height. They're a dull silver, indented with ridges that appear pattern-like, purposeful.

As Theseus thumbs a neatly stitched line across the nose, Asterion—perhaps subconsciously—scratches at the scar intersecting her own lip.

"But the Minotaur looked more ferocious than" —Theseus gestures— "*this*." It's just a bunch of material. A costume. How had she mistaken it for a mythical beast?

On the floor beneath the rucksack sits a bucket of tar-like slop partially covered with hessian. It looks similar to the woodland mud, but darker and lacking the stench. It's more earthy and sweet.

Asterion dips her fingers into the clay and smears it over her own forearm, as if to demonstrate its purpose.

Out in the labyrinth, Theseus might have imagined fiery veins wired through tar-like skin... but the reality of Asterion's forearm muscles flexing beneath the camouflage is just as captivating.

Theseus clears her throat.

Asterion appears to be too busy stretching—not distracting

at all— to notice how flustered she is. She lifts the mask atop her head and clips a brace from her back across her chest. It tightens around her like a noose, and Theseus's own chest tightens at the way Asterion stiffens. With a series of clicks and clunks, the mask goes from hanging limply to adhering rigidly to her frame.

Empty eye sockets flare to blue flame. The electric bright-ness of the beast's eyes must be the light from Asterion's torque. A beastly growl erupts from the mask and Theseus nearly fumbles her crutch. Stars above, is that what she'd heard in the labyrinth? It's not as monstrous now, but it's still fucking creepy.

The mask must have some sort of sound alteration mecha-nism, turning Asterion's words to growls and roars. Even her breaths are animalistic.

But the puzzle is still missing too many pieces. *Why* would Asterion wear this?

"Why...?" she asks, uncertain whether Asterion will under-stand the word, or if she can even see Theseus's confusion from within her mask.

Asterion squares up to the gateway. For a few moments, she angles her head like she's... listening? When Theseus holds her breath, she hears clicking... or ticking...

Asterion bows, as though asking the gate's royal permission. *O-kay*... But the reason for the bow becomes apparent as Aste-rion leans closer, slotting the mask's horns into the holes in the door. They're... keyholes?

Mechanisms *clunk-clunk* within the door, but it doesn't open. Asterion places her hands deep into the two other cavities in the door. Theseus has witnessed similar stances from unlucky citi-zens on backwards worlds who'd found themselves punished with the stocks. When her host's forearms are fully buried in the door, mechanisms churn, the metalwork realigning. Asterion's arms jolt as if something within the door has a grip on her.

Fuck. Theseus's own wrists ache at that. Either this is some torture device, or—more likely given that Asterion has willingly put her limbs at risk—these events have something to do with those hoof-like cuffs Asterion had been wearing out in the labyrinth.

Whoosh—

In a sudden flurry, Asterion and her mask are gone. And Theseus can see it now: the carved stone turntable on which the door stands.

Okay... so this is how to open the fortress gateway? This is how to get back into the labyrinth?

It's only seconds since Asterion disappeared, but it sure feels longer. Long enough for the facts to take hold in Theseus's chest: the only way to access the world beyond the fortress is by wearing a mask that's a cruel mix of punishment and theatre. The only way is by being the Minotaur.

Is it possible the person she'd recently thought to be her captor is, in fact, captive?

A series of clunks precede the sudden turn of the gateway and its stone platform. Theseus stifles a gasp. Asterion is there, her head locked in the mask, the mask locked in the turnstile. Theseus shouldn't be this pleased to see someone who's been gone only a few seconds; who she'd suspected only last night of being some trickster or worse.

Enough of this.

"I have to go," says Theseus, pointing between herself and the gateway.

The brace disconnects in the door mechanisms, freeing Asterion from the mask but leaving the mask anchored in the keyholes. Asterion liberates her arms from where the cuffs—the *hooves*—must remain, and emerges with a face full of... what? Confusion? Worry? Irritation? It's entirely possible she's just always perturbed when looking at Theseus.

"I have to go." Theseus points more emphatically between

herself and the closed exit. She reaches for the mask, only for Asterion to block her path. Their statures aren't dissimilar. Without recent evidence to the contrary, she'd have assumed she could take her. "I—go," Theseus insists, attempting to crutch-step past her. Honestly, she's usually better at diplomacy, but all this Labyrinth chaos is exhausting.

She must be overzealous, too, because Asterion and gravity work in tandem to unbalance her. She must still be sluggish, because by the time she's taken her next breath, her functional leg and crutch have been knocked from under her, and her right wrist is above her, tethered to the wall by Asterion's rucksack.

And there's not a thing she can do but grind her teeth and fail to wrangle her rampaging heart rate.

"Arrgh. Stop tying me to things!" Theseus kicks out a border-line tantrum.

"*You*—stop." Asterion's words are more a plea than an order.

Theseus catches her breath. If someone tried to take her stuff like that, she'd have introduced their face to the wall. Asterion paces before her, her torque frazzling with electricity, disgruntled confusion morphed to outright distress like she's just realised she's told pirates where she buried her treasure. "You—no—open." Asterion points emphatically between the mask and door. "You open—I here? Trapped."

Okay. Theseus can understand not wanting to be trapped. But there's enough space on that turntable for two. If Asterion won't take her out with her... well... that answers the question: *Am I captive?*

To communicate this, Theseus points between herself, Asterion, the mask and the door. In response, Asterion points to Theseus's injured leg.

"Exit far. Obstacles. Many. Danger. Stupid."

It sounds like she's saying that the exit is far and there are many dangerous obstacles, which it would be stupid to tackle with such an injury. Or maybe she's saying that Theseus herself is stupid.

Either way, she might have a point.

"When good... You—go."

Theseus isn't sure what it is about her host who's barking worried words at her while she's expertly tied to a wall by a rucksack strap, but—for some reason—she believes her.

Perhaps it's because, once again, Asterion's expertly tied makeshift restraint is only loose. Perhaps it's because—of the two of them—Theseus is the one who's proven herself time and again to be the feral one. Perhaps it's because she's right. If Theseus ventures out into an assault course of the unknown in her current state, she's unlikely to make it out alive. At the very least, this doesn't feel like one of those *I found you therefore I keep you* icky scenarios. So...

Asterion growls something in Minosian. Theseus doesn't understand the words, but the exasperation lands well enough.

"Okay." Theseus clambers to her feet.

Asterion must see the sincerity in her eyes, because she lets out a sigh and her shoulders relax. A little. And Theseus has no idea what should happen next. They're just kind of... standing there.

It's kind of cute how Asterion is wringing her hands, like she's trying to figure out *what next?* too. She certainly isn't giving off monstrous captor vibes, that's for sure. Monsters tend not to doubt themselves.

Asterion's eyes light up. "You want... tour?"

22

TOUR

Asterion shows Theseus another gateway, this one less grand and requiring no mask to open it. When they step through, it takes more than a few moments for Theseus to decipher what she's seeing.

She squints against the light beaming down from the channel at the centre of the domed roof, so much like daylight. A network of grassed and paved pathways threads through a geometric patchwork of cultivated beds, all bursting with an entire rainbow of different fruits and vegetables.

A garden?

But it's more than that; an orchard lines the furthest reaches of the green expanse. Its size is difficult to tell from here, but... *wow*. Because not only is everything bathed in light, the domed roof—embellished to look like sky—suggests that *this* is the centre of the Labyrinth.

Asterion leads the way between the vegetable beds, waiting every few steps for Theseus to catch up, showing her vegetables and fruit. Theseus mostly has no clue what she's saying, but her chatter is oddly calming.

Sheaves of wheat rest beside a machine composed of an

input hopper, cylindrical rollers and a turning lever similar to a sky-ship's helm. A wheat mill, Theseus assumes.

Asterion points to a selection of mirrors dotted about the gardens, on the ground, up the walls and even in trees, and Theseus wishes she understood what she's saying, because *why are there mirrors everywhere?* Asterion moves on to the stone well at the centre of the garden. Its stonework is different to the fortress walls: more decorative, with a distinctive emerald hue, and Asterion must be explaining something about it, but Theseus, frankly, is distracted. Partly by the sight of her original clothes drying on a clothing line—which means Asterion must have done her laundry—but mostly by the chickens with blue and orange feathers parading about the place.

She's so distracted, in fact, that she—*oof!*—limps right into Asterion's back. As she stumbles, Asterion whirls around, panic flashing in her eyes. She lashes out—but instead of thumping Theseus unconscious or shoving her down a well, she catches Theseus's upper arm, keeping her from falling.

"Sorry." Her whisper caresses Theseus's cheek. Her shoulders are heaving. "I—um—not do—not done this—before."

Theseus's breath is lost somewhere in her chest. *Done* what *before?*

But before she can ask—no doubt in an embarrassingly breathy manner, because *damn* they're close—an explosion of blue and orange wings and disgruntled chicken noises interrupts.

Asterion strides over to the anarchy, where four, maybe five, chickens appear to be ganging up on the smallest one. It also appears that this is a situation Asterion has dealt with a hundred times before.

With what sounds like the mildest of Minosian swear words, she emerges with the bullied chicken, feathers sticking out like a bad haircut, tucked under her arm. The aggressors go about their business with clucks that could also be Minosian swear words, while the rescued chicken looks rather startled by the experience. Or maybe that's just its face.

Asterion murmurs soothingly to the creature. It seems to work; the chicken relaxes, and Theseus does, too.

How had she ever thought Asterion to be a threat?

Asterion kneels in the soil, ignoring the mud on her practical trousers. It's possible Theseus has had one too many knocks to the head lately, because she's never before thought anyone both handsome and dashing while talking to a chicken. As Asterion sets the chicken down, her shirt tightens across her upper arms—which Theseus is absolutely not dwelling on. Nope. She rolls her eyes at herself. Asterion's choice of attire is probably limited to whatever arrives on the backs of doomed travellers. Still, evidently she's good with a needle and thread; she could make other clothes for herself if she wanted. But somehow Theseus can't imagine her parading around in ornate gowns.

It's difficult to know what goes on in the mind of a chicken. Especially when it sets its burning orange eyes on you, its weird beak opening to squeak-squawk like you've offended it.

The chicken launches forward, wings flapping and—*what the fuck?*—flaming at Theseus.

The fire. Those eyes. Was *this* what she'd battled in the corridors while wading through her own delirium?

The chicken shakes its feathers, and the fire that burns in its lungs flickers within it. Wow. Theseus has heard of Roasting Chickens before; of farmers trying to turn them into food only to become a meaty carcass themselves. She'd just assumed such a creature wouldn't be so... small.

Theseus is learning all sorts about assumptions in this place.

The chicken closes in, wriggling as if building up to something.

Uh oh...

But Asterion grabs a pail from the well, dousing the chicken just as a fireball barrels from its open beak and reducing the potential inferno to a smoky plume.

"I... Tour..." Asterion continues as Theseus gawps, as if she hadn't just saved Theseus from a renegade arsonist chicken. "I— not—tour. Give tour. First time."

With a disapproving '*bok-bok!*' and a swish of soggy feathers, the chicken about-turns and stomps off. Theseus can't help but burst with laughter because, of all the things she'd thought she might witness in this place, a disgruntled chicken with a fiery personality was not one of them.

She laughs even harder, then, because she's faced down monsters in masks and multiheaded beasts, but she is undeniably afraid of this one chicken.

Asterion observes Theseus as if she is the strange occurrence, before her frown softens to a tentative smile. When she laughs too, the tension that's been coiled around them ever since they first crossed paths starts to unwind.

23

ROAMING

Theseus lies on top of the bedsheets, flipping her Locator coin over the backs of her fingers, mulling over what to do. Pressing her thumb to the coin-face, the co-ordinates at the circumference detail that Herakles has started her journey across the heavens. It's difficult to tell how long it'll take her, because touring between galaxies rarely involves a direct route.

Guilt knots in Theseus's stomach at the idea... no, *the reality*, of putting Herakles to any trouble, or indeed landing her in it. And how in the heavens is she going to explain how she, a monster hunter, got caught in a monster trap, without sounding like an epic waste of space?

Herakles will only be glad that she's okay... but, still...

At least the galactic distance between the two of them gives Theseus time; to heal, to get out of this place before Herakles tries to get in it.

Asterion is right. She needs to recuperate. Best she accepts it. She could probably do with a break, anyway. This could be just what she needs.

Right.

It's the adventurous thing to do...

She's so used to being on the move, navigating from one danger to the next. Throw her into the path of a monster—fine. Force her to stay still for any amount of time—now there's the real challenge. So if the definition of adventure is to experience something out of the ordinary, then Theseus is still very much the adventurer.

That's what she's telling herself, anyway.

She should brush up on her Minosian so she can talk to Asterion and try to suss out the truth of the situation: Why in the heavens the Lost Princess is the 'beast' in a mask? How long has she been here? Has she ever tried to leave?

Theseus groans. *Stars above and heavens below.* Her leg thrums like a nest of fire-ants have taken up residence beneath her shin. If her leg would just stop hurting, if her thoughts would stop *wurring* like a poorly maintained sky-motor, if she could just rest a little while...

+
∴

EARLY MORNING LIGHT spills through the window. She hadn't meant to sleep so long. Stupid body needing stupid recovery. She shifts the blanket from on top of her. She doesn't recall getting under it, or arranging it so it wouldn't touch her injuries. Did Asterion do that?

There's a tray of food on the bedside table, too: scrambled eggs, fluffy bread and chilled multicoloured juice. Theseus's stomach leaps in appreciation.

She devours the food in a fraction of the time it would have taken Asterion to harvest the eggs, make the bread and press the mystery fruit. Maybe that's something Theseus can help with, to be of some use while she's here.

She crutch-limps to the washroom and freshens up before venturing out into the corridor. She might not be a captive, but if she has to stay in this chamber any longer she's going to feel like one anyway.

Following the flow of warming lava-channels, she finds Asterion in the workshop where they'd had the—*mortifying*—spoon incident, hunched over the workbench as though concentrating hard on something. At least she can't see Theseus's tinted cheeks. Theseus rarely embarrasses so easily, but then she rarely does so many embarrassing things.

She intends to thank Asterion for the breakfast, and—well, she can't think of a not-strange way to say *thank you for tucking me in*—but instead she's just standing here like a weirdo-creep who can't think of words. A shiny piece of golden armour near the weaponry pile distracts her. It reminds her of Hero, though the embossed markings and inset jewels are different.

She'd forgotten about him. Oops. She should be worried for his safety, should feel grief, sadness, righteous indignation, or *something* about his likely demise.

But he hadn't bothered himself with anyone else's. And there'd been something about him...

Does that make her a monster?

Perhaps she should reflect on it further, but—what is Asterion doing? She's pulling threads from fabric, soaking them in a bowl of liquid one meticulous strand at a time. This must be where the thread for Theseus's stitches came from. Judging by Asterion currently wearing a vest and no over-shirt, and the bandage at Asterion's upper right arm, dappled with red, she must be preparing for her own wound repair.

Suddenly, the sheer quantity of armour and personal belongings filling the chamber dawns on her. Everything here, all Asterion's supplies, must have been stripped from someone's body. Raided from the dead.

"You killed all these people?" It's less a question than a verbal vomit of horror and confusion.

Asterion flinches, looking up wide-eyed. Then she scowls, shaking her head. "No. They kill—Labyrinth kill. I—only—" She wrings her hands like she's frustrated. "I—no hurt. But... I choose—my life."

Oof. That's a gut punch if ever there was one. Because if that's true... that's fair enough, isn't it? Choosing her life over those of people who've travelled here to kill her is more than justifiable. And harrowing for her, too, no doubt. The quest of the Labyrinth must have forced her hand too many times.

The tortured uncertainty in Asterion's eyes confirms it. Though Asterion has knocked Theseus off her feet and pinned her to the floor on multiple occasions—she hasn't once tried to hurt her.

Theseus had been so sure it had been the Minotaur who'd murdered Tattoo and the others in the mist-filled corridor... but now, with Asterion before her... Theseus can't imagine her hurting anyone.

She gestures around the chamber. "What is all this?"

Asterion stops wringing her hands. "Is—no use—to dead."

Slowly, Theseus nods. What good is it to abandon items that may still have a use? Especially since, presumably, resources here are limited.

But what happened to the bodies? She doesn't want to ask, especially with their limited language overlap, but she needs to know. What happened to those she couldn't protect?

"The people... Where...? What happens to the dead?"

Asterion bows her head a little, wringing her hands again. "Fire—chamber...?"

Fire chamber? Does she mean the lava river?

Well... given the circumstances, it's possibly the most respectful send-off in a place like this. Stars above. One body to lay to rest is too many for anyone in a lifetime, and Asterion must have dealt with hundreds.

There's nothing Theseus can say to make that okay, is there?

"Thank you," she says, her voice choked, and Asterion's eyes flash to her like it might be a trap. Theseus clears her throat. "Thank you for rescuing me. For stitching my wounds. And, uh..." *Tucking me in?* "...everything. Uh." *Okay, calm down.* This is too many words and Asterion is squinting like only half of them make sense. So she concludes, in Minosian: "Thank you."

And Asterion's uncertain smile feels like the beginning of a sunshine-filled day.

24

OFF-KILTER

W hether the day was in fact filled with sunshine, Theseus hasn't a clue, because all she's done since barging into Asterion's workshop is sleep. She'd fully intended to do *something*—though what one does when contained within a fortress at the core of a sky labyrinth, she has no idea.

Well, she'd planned to try to make herself useful and then learn more Minosian, for starters. Find out *stuff*.

Her stomach growls, letting her know she has to at least do something about that. After some careful stretching, her muscles protesting their forced inactivity, she goes in search of food and Asterion.

Following the curved corridor that—she finally discovers—literally loops back on itself, so she can't get lost even if she tries, she locates the kitchen, where Asterion already has things underway, standing at a counter chopping carrots with her back to the door. Like her workshop, everything in here has its place. Stacks of carrots await chopping; woven baskets of apple-like fruit in a spectrum of solid colours sit beside the sink. A tall window looks out over the garden, which is as colourful as the neat array of jams, pickles and dried fruits stocked in glass jars on the shelves.

Just as Theseus is about to make her presence known, a growl more monstrous than anything her stomach can create shudders the room, clinking the glass jars against one another. An invisible force lifts Theseus from the floor, her feet paddling empty air as her stomach somersaults in protest.

She only manages swallowing her instinctive curses purely because she doesn't want to startle her host who has a knife, and because Asterion is hovering mid-air, too, and is too fucking calm about it.

Then gravity resets, planting her back onto her crutch and foot. She remains upright, which is—frankly—a surprise. And Asterion lands with grace, casually resuming her chopping as if nothing had happened.

"The fuck was that?" Theseus gasps, completely forgetting her intention not to startle anyone.

Asterion whips around, knife clutched tight. When she sees Theseus, her wide eyes dial down from startled to vaguely suspicious. She seems more concerned by Theseus's presence than anything. Theseus checks that the ceiling isn't about to fall in—you never know in this place—and looks to Asterion, waiting for an explanation.

Well, it's not a Minotaur, is it? In truth, when she'd still been roaming the labyrinth and not been privy to the Minotaur's true face, she would've thought that's precisely what the sound is.

The kitchen lurches a few crucial degrees. While Asterion easily catches her carrots as they roll from the counter, Theseus clings to the doorframe like she and the Labyrinth might both fall off their axis.

Finally, the rumbles cease and the kitchen *thunks* back into place.

"The Labyrinth—it moves," explains Asterion, still peeling carrots as if all of that was fucking normal. "Sometimes—it—bit stuck."

Okay... Theseus lets her heart rate settle. She'd read something about the Labyrinth being in a geostationary orbit with Minos. Perhaps the gravity fluctuation is related to that?

She inches further into the room. It somehow feels safer to be closer to her host. "Can I... um... help?"

Manners cost nothing, after all. The least Theseus can do is pull her weight.

Asterion side-eyes her as she takes up residence at the wooden counter. Theseus presses on—though she keeps her distance, because there's no mistaking Asterion's *fuck off* vibes.

But after what appears to be a thorough assessment, Asterion pushes a trio of peeled carrots in her direction. The relief of being allowed to help is soon quashed by her inability to be— well, helpful.

"Erm... I might need something to chop with?" Theseus mimes 'chopping' with her palm. She clears her throat, racking her brain for any relevant Minosian words. It's completely understandable if Asterion doesn't trust her with sharp things, but if she's to help...

Asterion opens a drawer, selects an implement and pushes it across the counter to her. Theseus is about to get chopping, but—

It's a spoon.

Theseus stares at it. Vague embarrassment and sincere guilt at their tussle in the workshop are won over—thanks to Asterion's poorly stifled smile—by utter amusement. And amusement paves the way to her heart doing some weird leap-constriction thing. *Because Asterion has a sense of humour.*

Theseus chuckles as Asterion passes her an actual knife. If

their roles were reversed, Theseus isn't sure she'd be so trusting. Then again, it's possible Theseus has been so consistently
inept that Asterion doesn't see her as a threat. Either way, right
now, she's glad to get to work.

+
. •

AT DINNER, Theseus devours the carrot soup, albeit in a more
socially acceptable manner than she'd tackled her breakfast.
Their shared laughter from earlier has tapered off into a silence
that's only amplified by the vastness of the banquet chamber.

It occurs to Theseus that if Asterion were dining alone,
presumably she'd choose the seat she's given Theseus, the one
nearest the door, rather than trudging all the way down to the
far end. Is this another act of kindness and consideration, or is
the idea of watching Theseus's painfully slow journey to the far
end simply too tedious to contemplate? Perhaps she just doesn't
trust Theseus to cross her path without event?

No matter the reason, Theseus, her leg and her stomach, all
appreciate the gesture. But it's difficult to gauge Asterion's mood
from the far end of this much-too-long table.

Before the silence can stretch beyond this galaxy and the
next, Theseus picks up her plate and cup and—leaning on the
table as a crutch—hobbles to a seat closer to the middle of the
table. She doesn't want to encroach too much.

Asterion's widened eyes seem to ask: *What are you doing?*

"Do you mind?" asks Theseus.

Asterion doesn't answer. She just returns to her food,
keeping an eye on Theseus. Perhaps she's tired. Perhaps it'll take
more than a couple of shared laughs to build a bridge between
them after the way Theseus has been first-rate feral to her.

But silence is notorious for filling with unwanted thoughts.
That's presumably why Theseus starts chatting about her past

adventures, about worlds she's visited. Anything to distract herself from the fact that the moonlight pouring through the floor-to-ceiling window is bathing the banquet hall in a soft, romantic glow.

Nope. She's not thinking about that. Her ordeal, combined with being cared for by her dashing host, has all just... made her strange.

It's daft that's she's even considering the moonlight romantic. It's just coming from a fucking orb in the sky. Not even that: it's from an engineered light-well or something. Anyway. Whatever.

"You know, when I was surfing in the volcanic dunes of Tartarus..." She's waffling. She knows it. "I was knocked from my board by sand-dwelling, fire-breathing spiders as large as my head—"

Asterion's spoon pauses before her open mouth, her brow contorting to something a lot like disgust. Soup droplets landing in her bowl punctuate the silence.

Great social skills, Theseus. She clears her throat. "I was just going to say... maybe they could've been friends with your chicken?"

Theseus focuses on her soup. Maybe silence is the way forward.

"Bok-bok—eat—spiders," says Asterion.

Okay, gross. Well, at least now they're conversationally matched. "Maybe not, then."

"It would—not—be—long friendship," Asterion agrees, and her words are so earnest, so concerned, Theseus wants to hug her.

She doesn't, obviously. She just eats her soup.

"What—you... uh... what were you—do—in Tartarus?" asks Asterion. "What is—like there? What happen—with spiders?"

Okay, so Asterion can understand and speak more Athenian than Theseus had thought. Theseus tamps down her grin, because apparently Asterion doesn't mind her weird ramblings.

It's odd; normally when she does bother to share stories of her adventures, she focuses on the heroic exploits, or the foolish ones that somehow turned out to look impressive, because that's what people want to hear. But Asterion's more interested in whether Theseus and the spiders ended up getting along (they did not), and in Tartarus itself, its topography and weather, and what the journey was like to get there.

The conversation is stilted, but whenever Asterion doesn't understand something, Theseus rewords or acts it out. At a certain point, she becomes convinced that Asterion does in fact understand quite a lot of what she's saying, but is enjoying Theseus's questionable skills at conveying the weather and beasts of Tartarus. Her quiet smile suggests she rather enjoys Theseus making a tit of herself.

But once they've finished their meal, the open enjoyment on Asterion's face shutters.

Has Theseus said something wrong?

Asterion scoops up Theseus's plate as she passes, disappearing towards the kitchen so fast Theseus doesn't get a chance to ask her, or to insist that she should be the one to clear up.

By the time she's managed to hobble to the kitchen, it sounds like Asterion is in her own world. Unfamiliar Minosian words drift along the corridor: a rich, layered melody, smooth like velvet. Asterion is singing to herself.

She doesn't sound unhappy, so hopefully Theseus hasn't annoyed her? And that voice... Theseus could stay here all night, leaning against the door jamb, listening.

But what is she doing? She's never been this much of a lurker. And *no more gazing.* Even if Asterion is impressive and beautiful and totally fucking cute.

Theseus chokes on her own thoughts. Literally, it turns out, because at the sound that escapes her malfunctioning throat, Asterion flinches and the crockery she's holding slips and smashes on the stone floor.

Shit. Theseus flinches too as Asterion grumbles. Probably swearing, too. She lumbers into the kitchen to try to help as Asterion gathers the shards, but the awkwardness of her crutch and a flare of leg pain halts her. But it's Asterion's sudden withdrawal, her full body flinch, and the alarm in her eyes—like Theseus had just drawn a blade—that has Theseus retreating.

She hadn't meant to scare her.

The seconds pass. Asterion returns to picking up the broken crockery, growling something that must be, "Go away. You've done enough."

It's not like Theseus can blame her for being wary. She just thought they'd moved past that. Clearly, it's going to take more time.

With a sigh, she begins the journey back to her bedchamber.

What a confusing day.

As she makes her slow, arduous way along the curved corridor, Asterion's footsteps echo behind her. When Theseus peers back along the corridor, to where visibility is almost lost to the bend, Asterion seems to be in her own world. She's humming to herself, albeit with a serious expression, her eyes angled to the corridor's inner curve.

Not wanting to startle her—again—Theseus isn't sure whether to announce her presence or stay very still. She could just carry on... but she's intrigued by Asterion tracing a pattern on the wall.

Inner-wall mechanisms *clunk-clunk* and a hidden doorway opens—spilling warm light across Asterion as she steps through —and closes seamlessly behind her.

Okay... she should probably expect hidden doors in a

labyrinth... right? But what in the heavens does a Lost Princess keep in a hidden chamber?

For the first time, Theseus's instinctive assumptions aren't anything horrific... And not knowing has her curious.

It'd be too precocious to hammer on that door to find out what's in there. It's clear Asterion won't welcome company right now, so Theseus lets her curiosity go unanswered.

For tonight, at least.

25

OH NO

B eing still is not Theseus's forte.

Despite having slept with ease before, sleep has become a difficult beast to wrangle: her brain won't switch off, homing in on every click and groan of the labyrinth. Which is why, as soon as light hazes through the shutters, she gets up and starts exploring the fortress.

Though she's curious about the hidden chamber, she doesn't want to overstep and upset her host, so she leaves it be. But, finding the doorway to the garden already open, she investigates.

The central garden is bathed in a peaceful morning glow. It's mind-boggling to think of the precision that must have been involved in engineering this place. Not only is it a technical wonder, it's beautiful.

Breathtaking.

As is the rather more energetic sight of Asterion racing circuits around the sizeable boundary between the garden and orchard. As Theseus watches, Asterion switches to lengthways sprints across the garden, weaving between vegetable beds, her feet always finding the path. When she reaches the well at the garden's centre, does she go around it? No. She leaps over it and races on. *Damn.*

Breathing hard, Asterion skids to a stop in front of a stone slab as tall as she is, barely pausing before bending to lift one end. It must be a chunk of labyrinth wall, repurposed as exercise equipment, because she overturns it again and again, first one way, then the other, the muscles in her arms, neck and shoulders —the sort of muscles it takes time, energy and dedication to build—flexing with every move.

It's a Herakles kind of workout. Powerful. Demanding. And, in this instance, captivating.

There's a shimmer to Asterion's skin. And Theseus is absolutely not going to think about Asterion's sweat licking a pathway down her throat, or the raw power in her limbs, or the way her rolled-up trousers display her well-defined calf muscles. Nor is she going to *ogle* the strip of fabric wrapped around Asterion's chest.

This is all just because... Theseus is suffering from her leg injury. It's making her restless. And... inappropriate.

But Asterion is almost vibrating with energy, and Theseus cannot look away. It's both exhausting and invigorating to watch. But *she's not going to ogle—*

"Bok-bokkkkkk!"

Theseus jolts. She'd been so busy *not staring* that she hadn't noticed a judgemental chicken taking up sentry duty at her feet.

"Bok-bokkkkkk!"

Theseus winces and cringes all at once. She doesn't need to speak chicken to translate: *"Look! Here! Look! I caught her! I caught this weirdo staring at you!"*

Bok-bok's squawks are so loud and obnoxious, of course Asterion has stopped her activities and is squinting at Theseus from afar. Theseus should do something... like move... or ask the ground to swallow her. Though she should be careful what she wishes for in this place.

Shit. Where's a hidden doorway when you need one?

Stars above. Asterion is strolling towards her. Okay. Don't panic. Even if it is doing funny things to Theseus to have Asterion staring at her so intensely while her sweat-sheened upper body is heaving in breaths.

Calm down. Asterion is just catching her breath. Doesn't mean you have to go and lose yours.

To save herself the embarrassment, as well as escape the risk of death by flaming chicken, Theseus retreats to the kitchen. She can't pace—*stupid leg injury*—but that doesn't stop her berating herself. Because this will not do. She will not be having a crush on the person she believed until recently was a murderer. The person she's stuck here with until her leg is healed. The person who rescued her from the labyrinth.

Monster Hunter Theseus does not swoon over her rescuer, thank you.

Absolutely not.

People have crushes on *her*. Not the other way around. Mostly.

Whatever. Right now, she needs a nerve-soothing snack.

She rummages through the kitchen's harvest containers to find a carrot and chomps on it like a neurotic rabbit. Maybe if she keeps out of Asterion's way, there won't be any need to acknowledge that she'd stared at her slack-jawed like some utter perv.

Is it perverse to gawk at a sculpted work of art?

Urgh. Yes, it's perverse to think of someone as *art*, to objectify, to reduce a person to their physical attributes. Even if they are *objectively* stunning.

Theseus crunches her carrot a little more rabidly. Or rabbit-ly, perhaps. She chuckles at herself. She needs to get a grip.

Appreciation. That's a better word. She was *appreciating* Asterion's impressive form from afar—

Asterion strides into the kitchen. Startled, Theseus squeaks —for fuck's sake, what is *wrong* with her?—and Asterion falters like she's just found an Iolcian vole-rat in her kitchen. *Rude.*

Asterion's bemused expression turns to an equally mysterious smile. Is it knowing? Is it merely polite?

Theseus's heart is tripping over its damn self, and all Asterion is doing is reaching past her for a cup and filling it at the tap. Of course she's thirsty after that workout. And here Theseus is, getting in her way.

But damn; those arm muscles hadn't been a trick of the sunlight and Theseus's daydreams. Droplets of sweat highlight their sinuous contours as Asterion gulps her water, and Theseus's mouth is so dry, and her skin is as hot as a lava river. Is this what bashfulness feels like?

Fucking snap out of it!

She steps aside, to give them both some space, but stumbles and catches herself on the doorframe. "Sorry," she says. Fuck. *Stop being weird.*

Asterion says nothing, merely scowls at her like she's got two heads and has lost at least one of them. Though it's not like Theseus is adding anything to this non-conversation either. It's not the language barrier that's the problem; it's that her own tongue isn't connected to her brain. And her brain has wandered off. If this is what a crush feels like, Theseus wants none of it.

And most probably neither does Asterion.

Just leave her alone. Theseus mumbles another apology, before fleeing to the bedchamber as quickly as her crutch will allow.

26

BRIDGING THE GAP

Not sure what to do with herself, Theseus is halfway through burying herself under blankets on the bed when the door opens and Asterion strides in, stripping off her sweat-sodden wrap vest.

Oh... fuck...

Theseus almost falls off the bed she's barely climbed onto. It takes several heart-racing moments to process that Asterion isn't about to jump her bones, but that she simply hadn't realised Theseus would be there. And that the stripping—unfortunately—isn't for Theseus's benefit, but—judging from Asterion's trajectory into the wash chamber and the smooth sound of cascading water—for the rather more practical activity of a shower.

Is there only one wash chamber in this place or something?

The way her cheeks are blazing and her heart is scrambling over itself, trying to figure out where in Theseus's chest it should be, anyone would think Theseus had never seen a naked woman before. Though, of course, she has. Several. More. She doesn't like to brag... or count. But for some reason, her brain is crumbling like a faulting Minosian mine right now.

The least she should do is give Asterion some space.

She tries hobbling to her feet, but at the shift in blood flow, her leg throbs with a vengeance and she falls back on the bed. By the time she's psyched herself up, Asterion has finished the galaxy's swiftest shower and is striding back into the room. Naked.

Asterion is totally, entirely, sublimely naked.

Because she's just had a shower, not because she's interested in... other adventures. Right?

It's not like she's looking at Theseus, or even acknowledging that she's there...

Only when Asterion opens a decorative wall panel—which is in fact a wardrobe; how had Theseus missed that?—and sources a selection of practical clothes from it, does it dawn on Theseus that this isn't some guest room she's been recuperating in.

This is Asterion's room.

Which means Theseus is more than encroaching.

With difficulty, Theseus averts her eyes as Asterion struts around the chamber getting dressed without paying Theseus even a *lick* of attention. A poor word choice, perhaps. *Fuck. Just... get a grip, Theseus.* Asterion isn't parading her nakedness for her, so Theseus needs to chill the fuck out and not possess a face as heated as a screeching fire-chicken. She should be able to handle a couple of days of recuperation without her body yearning to fling itself at her rescuer.

She gulps. Would it be weirder to leave the room now or to stay?

She wishes she'd purchased a paper-book from one of the overpriced Minosian gift shops, just so she could bury her nose in it and hide her burning cheeks. She'd have to risk the pages catching fire, but...

She fumbles for her guide-Shard on the bedside table and

starts swiping. Better than nothing. And at least Asterion is in undershorts now, tight to her legs and—

Stop looking!

But Asterion is very distracting as she angles her head left and right, stretching her neck and grimacing. Muscles tight from her workout? An injury from the labyrinth?

When she steps into the window's light, the bloom of bruises across her back and shoulder blades cut into Theseus's awareness. Because those are the injuries she can take responsibility for, aren't they?

Not that she can really be blamed, of course. When a Minotaur charges full pelt at you, it's a given that one or both of you will end up getting hurt. Even so, seeing the result of their encounter aches like a bruise beneath Theseus's own skin.

Of all of Asterion's injuries, one shouts louder than the rest: the angry slash across her left shoulder from the Hero's spear. Asterion is straining to see it in the mirror, but it's difficult for her to reach. It looks fresher than it should, like it's just reopened after never fully closing in the first place. *Ouch.* There's not a chance under this sun or the next that the wound will heal well without intervention. And it'll be impossible to stitch herself.

As Asterion twists to inspect her wound, her eyes meet Theseus's in the mirror, holding her gaze like she's trying to puzzle her out.

Theseus squirms and looks away. *Oh, get a grip.* She forces herself to look back, refusing to be *that* pathetic. She might be utterly useless right now, but perhaps this is one way she can help. Not by staring, obviously, but by—

But before she can finish her thought, or work out how to communicate it, Asterion's brow pinches as she marches over and sits on the bed. The mattress shifts under her weight, tilting Theseus a little closer as Asterion leans towards her. Nakedly.

Which is... fine. Totally fine.

Theseus grips the sheets, maintaining eye contact like some absolute warrior.

"You—are hot?" Asterion asks, or states, or... something?

Well...

Theseus's focus lands on the pendant Asterion is wearing: a lump of stone hanging low on her sternum. Then, realising where she's staring, she hastily raises her eyes.

Sorry, what? Something about being hot?

Asterion points to Theseus's cheeks, then to her own, then to Theseus's injured leg. Her brow is rucked with worry. "Is—okay?"

Oh, she's saying Theseus looks flushed? Asterion thinks she's got some fever from her leg injury. *Stars above.*

"Is fine," says Theseus, abandoning her sentence structure. Then, to change the subject, she points to Asterion's shoulder and blurts: "Um. I—I can stitch that for you...?"

You don't survive all manner of monsters without occasionally having to get creative with a needle and thread in your own flesh. Stitching someone else's wounds? Easy.

To demonstrate, Theseus grabs her rucksack from the floor beside the bed and hoists it between them. Asterion watches with interest, her eyes flashing warily as Theseus digs out a pocket blade she'd forgotten was in there—*oops*—but she doesn't recoil. Theseus casts the blade aside pointedly, hoping Asterion will understand the message that her murder attempts are all in the past. Promise.

Finally, from her rucksack's hidden compartment, she retrieves her medi-kit, needle and the empty spool of her medi-thread.

Asterion tenses, but doesn't flee.

"You trusted me with a vegetable knife," says Theseus, and Asterion scowls as if reassessing her past choices. "You may as well let me repair your wounds." Now, how to say all that in Minosian? "Besides, I always have my wit. That's damn sharp, too."

"Yes." Asterion's scowl doesn't shift. "Is painful."

Does she mean her injury, or Theseus's wit. Asterion's quiet smile lets Theseus know which. *Utter snark. Sublime.* Theseus buries her grin and mumbles, "I, uh, need to wash my hands and disinfect this," as she holds up the needle. "Also, I've run out of thread." She indicates the empty spool.

"No." Asterion points to the luminous spool of thread that's now peeking out from her rucksack's hidden compartment. "You —use—this?" Asterion's eyes light up, in part because they're reflecting the glowing thread, but also with... awe?

Theseus frowns. "It's a bit flashy, but—"

"You know—what is?"

Theseus looks between Asterion and the thread. Why is Asterion being so... enthusiastic? And is it a trick question? "Uh... Thread?"

"It—" Asterion beams. "It—heal."

The stitches will help her heal? Well, yes, that is the point...

Asterion remains adamant that the needle and thread don't need disinfecting, but Theseus insists. Asterion rolls her eyes but disappears to the kitchen with the equipment while Theseus washes her hands, and returns with the supplies they need, including the tincture Asterion had used on her.

Right. They're doing this.

Asterion sits on the edge of the bed and Theseus considers how to position herself to best reach Asterion's injury. The best way is to sit right next to her, with Asterion's muscular back angled toward her.

Well, the *best* way would be for Theseus to sit behind her, with Theseus's legs either side of her... but that's not going to happen, for so many reasons. Not least that the last thing Asterion needs is Theseus drooling over her when she should be tending to her wounds.

Her poorly timed fantasy is expelled faster than a trespasser on a sky-ship when she begins to examine Asterion's skin close up and realises just how many injuries, historical and recent, are imprinted in her flesh. Puncture marks, blade scars, burns... The whispers of past pain.

Theseus hates this place more than ever. She'd tear it from the sky, if she could.

She clears her throat and applies the tincture to the area around the angry wound. Asterion's sigh suggests the balm is working its magic—or science, or whatever. Still, every pierce of the needle through Asterion's skin turns her stomach. Theseus might hunt monsters, but that doesn't mean she's not squeamish.

She forces herself to focus on each stitch of luminous thread, doing her best to be considerate and quick about it.

"Why doesn't the tincture make my fingers numb?" she asks, mostly to distract herself.

"It—affect—injury only."

"Oh." Impressive stuff.

But—*Oh!* Theseus's jaw drops—not as impressive as—

She can hardly believe what she's seeing...

A sparkle sizzles as the thread pulls the edges of the wound together; reforming fibres glowing as they seek connection, bridging the gap in Asterion's flesh.

Heavens above. The wound is already healing.

27

BLOSSOM

Asterion turns to her—still topless, because... yeah... she hasn't seemed to notice or doesn't care that she's not wearing much—and says... something? Something about her wound glowing blue and already being healed? And Theseus should respond, but—

Breasts.

No. Stop it. Asterion is speaking.

But all Theseus can hear is her pulse thudding in her ears.

Stop looking. They're just breasts. Even if the gentle swells against Asterion's athletic frame are worth admiration. And her skin looks so soft...

How about making eye contact, dumbass?

Theseus tunes back in. Asterion is saying something about... using the thread on Theseus's wounds...?

"Um..." *Great response. Strong.* Theseus clears her throat. She could do without her inner critic right now, even if it is trying to stop her from being a creep.

Asterion's looking perplexed as she muses that she's not sure how it would work with Theseus's leg wound already stitched, but that it's worth trying...?

Theseus is too preoccupied, her honourable aspirations keeping her gaze where it should be, to formulate a reply. She scrambles to her feet—fuck, her foot—and grits her teeth as pain flares.

Asterion's face pinches in what looks like sympathy-meets-confusion. But Theseus can't linger. She grabs her crutch and stammers, "N-no, thank you," as she puts some necessary distance between them.

┼
˙•

IT'S THE WRONG DECISION, she realises as she wakes in the middle of the night, her healing body having dictated that she sleep through much of the previous day.

Theseus groans as she stretches. It's a wonder of the galaxies that she managed to reach adulthood with mush for a brain.

At least it hadn't been the strange clicks and groans of the Labyrinth that had interrupted her sleep. What a difference a day makes. Now she's awake, she can hear the background hum, the distant mechanical *tick-tick* and *click-click*—but somehow, it's not freaking her the fuck out.

Her thoughts are ticking over too, however.

It's incredible how rapidly the thread had healed Asterion, how her body had absorbed it. Theseus's own stitches will need to come out soon, but it looks like Asterion's are a permanent feature.

If she'd known how precious the luminous thread was, she wouldn't have casually dropped a length of it into that mysterious hole in the door of the outer-shell gatehouse, and been more thoughtful in its usage since. But it's too late now.

Does Princess Ariadne know what it does? Had she intended for Theseus to use it to heal injuries and save lives? If she had, she would have been clearer than a fucking riddle about it, wouldn't she?

Use the thread to navigate your path; that's what she'd told Theseus. And sure, it's been a useful enough torch, but either Princess Ariadne knows nothing of its function, or she revels in toying with the people she sends to the sky.

The spool sits on her bedside table, an extra length wrapped haphazardly around it. Is that the piece she'd used to tether herself to Tattoo? The thread Asterion had so easily discovered? Did she venture into the labyrinth to retrieve it? Does that mean she's dealt with Tattoo's... remains?

What a task.

Is Asterion okay? It's dark. She's presumably sleeping... somewhere...

Stars above. This place.

Never mind healing; there's so much Theseus needs to understand before she can leave. She can hardly come up with a plan for rescuing Asterion—and herself—until she knows the parameters. Has Asterion ever tried to escape? Surely she must want to leave. Who would want to live in a world surrounded by a death maze? Even if the living quarters are an aesthetically pleasing fortress and gardens.

Theseus can't stay here. And she can't leave Asterion behind either.

Asterion must have tried to escape. The more Theseus can find out about her attempts, the better. But that's a lot for two people who are only just learning how to communicate.

Theseus reaches for her guide-Shard and swipes to the LINGUISTICS section and the YOU-KNOW-LINGO add-on her travel agent had insisted upon. She can absorb the information, if she applies herself; she learns lots of things all the time. All she has to do is pretend she's learning the stealthiest route to a monster's lair, or the best techniques with weaponry, or creative ways to make a woman—

"*NU-UH!*" the device shouts at her. Apparently Theseus has selected an incorrect subject-verb conjugation. She tries again. "*NU-UH.*" Fuck. She repeats the lesson, but the harder she concentrates on how Athenian words relate to Minoglyphs, the less information goes in.

She's all about perseverance, but—damn—does the device have to sound so disappointed in her? After a dozen rounds of trying and failing, she finally gets one right—"TA-DA!"—and an animated star twinkles in the ether-screen.

"About fucking time." Theseus casts the stupid guide-Shard aside, refusing to be beholden to a piece of travel-tech.

Fuck, that's wound her up.

There's no hint of light through the window shutters, but Theseus's tight muscles demand movement, as does her dented ego. So she grabs her crutch and roams.

The corridors are lit with blue fire-torches and the orange glow of the lava-furrows. She assumes Asterion is still asleep, so she's intrigued when she explores the garden and spies the luminous line of Asterion's stitches at the distant orchard's edge, near the chicken coop, spotlit by moonlight or something like it.

The only other illumination comes from a tree with glowing leaves which ripple in a confusion of colours. In amongst the greens and yellows, there are flourishes of pinks and purples. It's strikingly similar to the tree she'd seen— upside down—beside the lake when she'd been chasing the Minotaur.

She's too far away to hear Asterion's words—not that she'd understand much anyway—but it sounds like Asterion is talking to someone.

A small hatch opens in the chicken coop, glowing like a blue and orange furnace, and a fiery chicken hops out: the bullied one with the questionable personality. It lands on Asterion's shoulder like a sentient lantern.

Asterion strokes the chicken's ember-like feathers in a way that suggests she's used to being a perch. She must be letting the chickens out for the day.

And that's when it happens.

Light drizzles down from the dome's central channel until it spotlights the emerald well and—reflecting from its stonework—darts across the garden like shooting stars in search of new directions, rebounding again and again from mirrors throughout the garden, until the entire expanse is drenched in light.

So that's how sunrise works here. The Labyrinth's geostationary orbit with Minos accounts for the day-night cycle, though how sunlight reaches the *centre* of the structure is still mystifying. Celestial mechanics isn't really Theseus's strong suit. But apparently, staring at Asterion is.

Theseus diverts her focus to the obstacles in her path and heads for Asterion, ensuring not to be too quiet about it. *No startling Asterion today!* By the time Theseus winds her way across the garden with her crutch, Asterion is on her knees in a vegetable patch, tending the greenery, with Bok-bok supervising from her shoulder.

"*Bok-bokkkkkk!*" The chicken squawks its belated alarm as it jumps from its human perch.

Asterion looks up. She doesn't seem affronted by Theseus's presence. In fact, there's even the hint of a smile. Though Theseus fears they both might die a fiery death soon. She'd had no idea chickens could hiss, but right now this one is emitting a sizzle-hiss like an overheated frying pan. Should she be terrified or hungry? But Asterion, apparently unconcerned, utters a single word of reprimand, at which the chicken snaps its beak shut.

Theseus keeps a careful eye on the creature. The feeling is very mutual, apparently: that's quite the beady-eyed glare.

Trying to put her studies into practice, Theseus tries for a Minosian accent and greets Asterion, "Good—morning," only for Asterion to tilt her head quizzically.

"I wasn't moaning."

Theseus's cheeks heat. Why is Asterion saying anything about moaning? "Uh... What?"

"You said 'good *moaning*' in Minosian."

Oh, heavens above. "No, um. I meant—" Did it just get warmer out here? "I meant good *morning*."

"Oh. Yes. That—make more sense."

And this is why Theseus doesn't do the languages. Where's an obscuring, cheek cooling ice fog when you need one?

Asterion brushes off her hands as she stands and gestures to the chicken. "Is—Bok-bok," she says, before gesturing to Theseus, too. "Is—Theseus."

She's being introduced to a chicken? Okay. That's better than Theseus's conversation starter, for sure.

"Bok-bok?" Theseus asks.

"*Bok-bok,*" echoes the chicken.

Ah. Okay.

Theseus navigates the paving slabs and plentiful produce to edge closer to Asterion, keeping as far away from Bok-bok as possible. Asterion resumes plucking colourful carrots from the soil, whispering under her breath.

"Are you talking to the vegetables?" Theseus doesn't expect an answer.

"Yes."

Oh.

Asterion sits back on her heels. "I—apologise. And thank," she says, mopping her brow. "I'm—thank—for eat. I apologise— no more grow."

Stars above. What to do with *that* information? Body-checking and disarming aside, Asterion might be the gentlest person Theseus has ever met. Come to think of it, even the body-checking and disarming wasn't aggressive. It was as gentle as anyone can be when they're trying to stop you from murdering them.

"I know—is strange." Bashful, Asterion carries on digging. She's a damn sight better adjusted than Theseus would be if she'd spent a lifetime trapped in a sky labyrinth.

Asterion continues whispering, and it might just be the first time Minosian has ever sounded... sweet.

Theseus flounders for something to say. *Great.* It's going to be one of those days.

But then Asterion leaps to her feet and lunges toward her. For a split second, panic rears its ugly head: *see, you got it all wrong, the Minotaur is going to show you her true colours.* Is Asterion going to whisper apologies while sacrificing *her* for food?

So Theseus should do something other than hold her breath.

But as Asterion continues past her, she says something in Minosian and her bright eyes are more distracting than the most expertly engineered sunlight-well.

After remembering how to breathe, Theseus limps after her to the orchard as the sunlight spreads further across the greenery. Asterion is talking excitedly in Minosian, gesturing at the trees.

Is she talking about the blossom? About the fact that there is blossom?

Theseus must look like her last brain cell just packed up and exited through her open mouth.... because now the 'beast of the Labyrinth' is getting excited about blossom.

"Is sign—season change. New food—soon."

Theseus has questions about how seasons work here, but

mostly her attention is being diverted to the warmth taking up residence in her chest. She's only known Asterion for a matter of days, but she already knows, on a cellular level, that if anyone tried to hurt her, Theseus would body-check them from the skies.

Asterion must notice something is amiss, because the sparkle in her eyes dims. She scratches her head. "Did I—do— talking wrong?"

Theseus shakes her head, mentally kicking herself into gear. "No... No. Perfect. You did talking perfect." Stars above. That last brain cell really has upped and left.

It's just that... she'd come here expecting a monster, not *this*. Kindness and concern, snark when deserved, humour and gruff- ness, all wrapped in muscles, sinew and—

No, no, no. Stop right there.

Asterion squints at her, shielding her eyes from the sunshine, and smiles; the kind of smile that can heal wounds or light up an entire Labyrinth.

Fuck. Do not *fall for her.*

28

DIGGING

K eeping greenery alive is also not Theseus's forte, which is likely why gardening is not one of her skills.

Her only run-ins with flowers are when she's slicing them from their stalks to gift to someone she's set her sights on. But she wants to be of use somehow, and eventually, with the aid of some choice gestures and a chaotic mix of Athenian and Minosian, Asterion had understood this. Which is why Theseus is currently on her knees in the dirt, wondering whether she should be whispering to the seeds or whether she can get away with not making a tit of herself.

At least Asterion isn't overseeing her every move, but has trusted Theseus to get on with the task at hand while she tends to the next vegetable bed over. The same cannot be said of Bokbok, who is staring at her with nostril-flaring demonic intent. Do chickens usually flare their nostrils?

With a groan that sets Theseus's senses on high alert, Asterion stretches from her crouch and strides across the allotments, mopping her brow, sweat glistening in the sunshine.

It turns out Theseus's defiantly averted gaze and determined fixation on her task aren't that useful in helping her keep herself to herself, because suddenly Asterion is at her side, offering her a metal mug of water. When she doesn't take it straight away, Asterion must interpret her hesitation as suspicion, because she points to the well. "Is from—lake. Clean. Filtered for purity."

The well gurgles, as if in agreement. Asterion takes a swig from the mug before re-offering it to Theseus.

Filtered for purity? That's mighty specific for someone who's not fluent in Athenian. Why is Asterion so damn impressive?

To cool that line of thought, Theseus accepts the water and takes a generous gulp, accidentally clearing her throat at the same time as trying to swallow as she concentrates on valiantly *not* thinking about how the mug had just been touching Asterion's lips. She splutters, but recovers soon enough. "Did you learn more Athenian overnight?"

Asterion grins. "I—try... tried. *Am trying.* Lots to learn."

Even her accent is pretty good. There's a classic Minosian rumble in there, but Theseus likes it. It shows Asterion's efforts in learning the old-fashioned way: no tech or sorcery, just hard work and *knowledge.*

If only Theseus's own efforts were going so well.

Asterion must deem that the end of their interaction, because she's already back at work tilling the soil. It's kind of hypnotic, the way she moves. Theseus has seen first-hand the scars on her skin, the evidence of her life's hardships, and can only admire the confidence with which she carries herself. A royal poise, but with none of Princess Ariadne's flamboyance or arrogance.

Theseus really needs to stop staring at her like a creepy demon chicken, albeit one with romantic, rather than murderous, intent.

No, not *romantic...*

Obviously.

Theseus doesn't do romance. She does fun, fleeting experiences with a sensible expiration date. She might travel the heavens to kill monsters, but she's never once met someone she'd move the heavens for. Well, maybe Herakles. And even then, she'd only admit to nudging the heavens a little...

"You are allowed, you know." Imaginary Herakles—and her bright mop of multicoloured curls—is suddenly there, nonchalantly kicking the dirt beside her.

Allowed what? Theseus only has to think the words, because Herakles isn't really there. She knows that, at least. She's not lost touch with reality yet. She just... sometimes hears Herakles's voice in her head. Usually—if she's being self-aware about it—when she's feeling torn.

"To have emotions. To see where things lead."

Theseus scoffs, which only serves to attract Asterion's attention from behind a cluster of oversized lettuce leaves one row over, and to elicit another *"Bok-bokkkkk!"* from Bok-bok, who's been scrutinising her from its perch on a makeshift shovel as though waiting for Theseus to give it an excuse.

Asterion scolds the creature softly, and it shuts its beak. It keeps glowering, though. Theseus had better keep her inner monologues more *inner* in future. She keeps digging, planting the seeds the way Asterion had showed her.

Having emotions and seeing where things lead. That's the kind of advice Herakles gives after a few beers, around the time she starts wielding her encouraging back-slaps with a little less restraint. Theseus has face-planted off enough bar stools in taverns across the galaxies to know when to start sitting just out of arm's reach. It's precisely the advice that had landed her in an unfortunate, life-challenging situation on an entertainment moon under the Sixth Sun, where the attractive woman who'd set her sights on Theseus had turned out to be the daughter of the infamous Ring Leader of the intergalactically known Sky Circus. One night of fun, which was all Theseus had promised, had resulted in the hangover of a demand for *forever*, coupled with the threat of her lover's mobster mother exacting revenge if she didn't marry her immediately. Apparently, having an Athenian Princess as her daughter-in-law, was the kind of currency she wanted in her pocket.

Needless to say, Theseus and Herakles had made a swift getaway, and won't be visiting said moon again any time soon.

That debacle had only cemented Theseus's belief that people cannot be trusted to say what they mean. She's tried giving the benefit of the doubt, only to be disappointed over and over. It's safer to assume that everyone is wearing some sort of mask.

Not *everyone* is like that, though. Herakles deserves some kind of friendship award for sheer bone-headed perseverance. But for the most part, letting people in isn't what Theseus does. Emotions are like a maze; hard to navigate and easy to get lost in. She might gamble on fleeting experiences for the sake of her libido—she wouldn't be much of an adventurer otherwise—but trust isn't within her arsenal anymore. If it ever was.

Asterion might not be a monster, but that doesn't mean she won't challenge Theseus by seeking more than Theseus is willing and able to give. That's what people have done all her life. Why would Asterion be any different?

Besides. Her gut is telling her, in no uncertain terms, that it's not sensible to become entangled with a possibly exiled princess who lives at the centre of an infamous, deadly labyrinth. Even if said princess is distractingly handsome and sparkly-eyed. Even if parts of Theseus's own anatomy have other opinions on the matter.

And why is she even letting this mental and emotional maze tie her in knots? It's not as if Asterion has shown any interest in her, is it? At best, Asterion is tolerating her, letting her be useful. Well, letting her try to be useful while she's lost in thoughts of—

Oh, fuck the heavens.

Asterion is right next to her.

Her face is a crinkled picture of... mystification? Theseus follows her gaze to the ground in front of her. Skies above. She's dug a hole so deep Asterion must think she's trying to escape through it.

Slowly, as if she's still getting used to the concept of closeness, or perhaps still half-thinks Theseus might attack her with her trowel, Asterion kneels beside her.

Asterion is saying something in Minosian, but all Theseus's focus is on is how Princess Ariadne's eyes had been biting, like infested waters, but Asterion's are as clear and warm as an Arcadian lagoon.

Theseus swallows as Asterion gently takes her hands and guides them to the soil, pressing them to the dirt. Has she just filled in Theseus's unnecessary ditch without Theseus even noticing?

She's noticing everything Asterion is doing *now*: her warm hands covering Theseus's, showing her how to spread the soil over the seeds. And wow... Apparently things grow fast here. The seeds they've just sown in the moist ground are already sprouting: the greenery of the carrot tops unfurling into the light.

And how is that not the most wondrous aspect of this place? She should be captivated by the marvel of accelerated growth, not by Asterion's whispered Minosian, as soothing and sensual as a caress.

Theseus's breath exits her lungs. Thank goodness she's already kneeling, because this...

This.

Her hands between mud and careful fingers...

How is *this* the most intimate moment of her life?

No. It can't be. She's been in much more physically adventurous positions with plenty of—

"*Stop overthinking.*" Herakles's voice is soft but insistent.

And Theseus jerks away from Asterion's hands, her proximity. Asterion looks startled, a little uneasy, perhaps, but seems to accept Theseus's retreat, leaving her to carry on unassisted.

And while Theseus gives herself a stern talking to, Herakles sighs, and Bok-bok glares at her in withering judgement.

29

SPARKS

It should be difficult to avoid someone when you're locked inside a fortress together, but somehow, over the next few days, Asterion manages to evade Theseus almost entirely. Mealtimes are quiet and Asterion eats her food faster than her gut must appreciate before exiting as swiftly as possible. She still gives Theseus the much-needed opportunity to be useful; she leaves the used crockery for Theseus to wash up, while in the garden she issues brief instructions before leaving Theseus to get on with it. And, in the evenings, she retreats to her mysterious hidden room.

So that's how things go: Theseus doing her best to be *helpful*, and Asterion keeping her distance. So much so, Theseus can only assume that Asterion is the one who wants her damn space.

She wishes she were up to pacing, but her leg is taking a million sun-orbits to heal.

"You know how to get out of here quicker," says non-existent Herakles, as Theseus tries to bury her frustrations in a book. Yes, an actual tree-made book. Asterion has left her one—heavens

knows where she got it—and Theseus keeps trying to concentrate on it because reading can be fun, and paper is a rare treat.

But perhaps this is Asterion's idea of torture, because the book is written entirely in Minoglyphs. As far as she can glean, the book's topic is Minosian mineral formation, but the shapes on the page make her own brain feel like a square trying to fit inside a circle.

Theseus sighs. *Why not use the sparkly thread, you idiot? That isn't even Herakles. That's all her.*

Yes. Why doesn't she?

"*Bok-bok!*" A burst of sinister flapping from her bedside table jolts her back to reality. Theseus flings her book aside, scrambling to grab her crutch. Not only has she left her door open, the demon chicken has shown itself in.

"*Scared of a chicken?*" She can hear Herakles's imaginary laughter.

Shut up. You'd be afraid too if you'd had your forearm fried like an egg.

With the fiery chicken looming behind her, Theseus has little choice but to flee along the corridor to the kitchen, where a savoury aroma invites her into the safe haven.

Asterion is at the counter, chopping vegetables while overseeing a pan simmering on the heat cradle.

But that's not why Theseus is smiling.

A wind-up music player on the windowsill plays piano mixed with a heavy bass beat. Asterion's head is bopping, and she's bouncing a little in time with the music. It's the kind of dancing that isn't about impressing anyone, it's just about enjoying music and movement. She looks so... absorbed.

And Theseus can't help absorbing everything about her. Her bare feet dancing happily on the stone floor. Her grey trousers, held by a simple black belt, sitting low on her waist. The oversized white shirt flows loose over her black vest, the blue stitching of her shoulder glowing through the fabric as her short, choppy hair shimmers gold in the torchlight.

Even with the cool blue moonlight bathing the garden beyond the kitchen window, and the distant tree flickering multicoloured in the orchard, Asterion's reflection shows how relaxed she is.

Only in this moment does it occur to Theseus that Asterion is happy here. And although she can't imagine being content in a place like this, she's warmed; glad of Asterion's happiness.

Though she's only loitered in the shadows for a second, her inner *don't-be-a-creep* alarm is sounding. So she retreats.

Or she tries to.

She fails because there's a chicken-with-intent charging at her, squawking, "Bok-bok-bok-bok-bokaaaawwwww!" and chasing her most ungracefully into the kitchen. She's not sure who looks more ridiculous: her, or the boggle-eyed chicken.

Asterion stops dancing. Her brow pinches with confusion or surprise. Or both.

"Sorry," says Theseus, trying to retreat but blocked by the chicken flapping at her from the shadows. "I think your chicken hates me."

"Yes." Asterion nods.

Theseus hadn't expected outright agreement. Asterion's face twitches. Was that almost a smile? Is she amused? Well, then…

The music is still playing quietly. It's arguably unwise to blast music when beyond the fortress walls there might be people seeking to hunt you down and make a trophy of your heart. Though, Theseus strongly doubts anyone has survived this long.

Bleugh. How had taking a creature's heart ever seemed like a normal, *noble* challenge? Even if the Minotaur were a beast, how does claiming a literal bodily organ as a prize achieve anything other than *ick*?

Asterion slides a knife along the counter to a colourful pile of vegetables. The invitation is clear. *You want to be useful? Time to get chopping.*

Okay... Good. Just because Theseus has an ill-advised crush, that doesn't mean she can't function like a normal, helpful, polite human in Asterion's presence.

Right?

Bok-bok side-eyes her from the doorway, as if answering that exact question.

As they prepare the food, Asterion stretches out her neck with a grumble, pressing at the muscles in her shoulder. She must be tense. Yeah. Theseus is pretty tense, too.

Asterion's still nodding along to the music, but her movements are a little more guarded than before. It sums up how Theseus's presence must be affecting her. She'd had free rein of this place before Theseus interrupted.

The music has a pleasing rhythm: not too fast, but thumping enough to move to. And there's a vocalist, though not singing a language Theseus recognises. She doesn't know what the words mean, but they repeat, and she gives singing them a good go.

Asterion watches her with cautious, wry amusement. Wanting that smile to bloom, Theseus's vague shuffling in time to the music, evolves to something more goofy and cleansing. When Asterion finally joins in, mirroring her moves, Theseus's heart dances, too.

Which startles her enough that she slips—

As she grabs for the counter, Asterion's firm hands clasp her waist, righting her on her feet.

Okay, that's... fucking suave.

The music is still thumping in time with her heartbeat as they both chase their breaths. Asterion must be made of electricity, because that's what's tingling through Theseus from the point of contact between them.

She swallows. Because that's what gazing looks like, isn't it? Those lagoon eyes, inviting her in. It's not just wishful thinking or projection, is it? They're on the precipice of something.

Theseus could be convinced that they're not in the kitchen of the infamous Sky Labyrinth, but in a dance den, intoxicated, one step away from discovering each other.

Asterion's strong, gentle hands on Theseus's hips aren't pulling away, but they're not drawing her close, either.

It would be so easy to lean in...

Did the Labyrinth just groan, or was that them? Asterion's torque stutters with electricity. Theseus's torque has grown warmer, too.

"I think—we—should—do it..." Asterion's whisper is enough to make Theseus question the direction of gravity.

Thankfully, Asterion has a hold on her. Which doesn't half feel like the world is upside down and inside out. Because when has *she* ever been the swooning mess held steady in someone else's arms?

No. Absolutely not.

But what her traitorous mouth and tongue verbalise is an outright breathy: "You, um, think we should...?"

Theseus tears her gaze away from Asterion's fascinating mouth to curious eyes shimmering like ice in sunshine.

"Only if you—are happy—for it?"

Happy... yes...

"I'm..." Theseus swallows. "...open to—doing it. Yes."

Okay, apparently she's left all her own suavity back on Minos.

Asterion nods, perhaps more seriously than the situation calls for. "But bed—will be—easier."

Theseus's mouth opens and shuts. *How... practical...?*

But before Theseus can muster any evolved thoughts, Asterion strides out of the kitchen, leaving her windswept.

Well, if Asterion thinks they should...

30

FIRE

By the time Theseus reaches the bedchamber, Asterion isn't there. Perhaps she intended for them to get familiar in whatever chamber she's been sleeping in? But then Asterion strides in, past Theseus, the hearth flaring at her arrival.

It's not like Theseus can't relate.

Her back to Theseus, Asterion rummages through the items on the bedside table. "This—make you feel—much better."

Theseus has no doubt. But she stumbles a little over the threshold, her sense of propriety not only catching up, but slamming into her.

Sure, freeing the universe from monsters is a noble profession, but she's not above distractions. There's admittedly a certain fanfare that comes with being perceived as brave, noble, undefeatable. She might not be sentimental with lovers, but people want to be in her orbit, and sometimes she wants that too. But if she's not honest about what she wants, what she can offer... that makes *her* the monster, doesn't it?

She clears her throat. "I'll be going soon."

She wishes she could see Asterion's expression.

"Yes," Asterion agrees, still rummaging. "Is—why we do this."

Oh.

Okay. Sure. That makes... sense...?

It sounds like they're on the same page. Which is... good.

Better than good. It has Theseus's heart thumping.

But there's something else knocking at Theseus's sense of decency. How long has Asterion lived here alone? Theseus doesn't know. But given that the Lost Princess was supposedly 'lost' at a young age, presumably it's been... a while. The injustice of that grips Theseus's insides like some mythical clawed creature trying to break free.

Given the facts, it's likely Asterion has never experienced what Theseus's libido would have them racing towards right now. And the last thing Theseus wants to do is take advantage. She doesn't want to pile on indecency to injustice. Because that, too, would make her a monst—

"I've got—supplies." Asterion's words are so matter-of-fact, Theseus's whole body shivers.

Supplies. Those aren't the words of someone naïve and inexperienced, that's for sure... And though Theseus's more logical brain—currently overwhelmed by the less evolved parts of her —is attempting to question how in the heavens *supplies* of this nature are available in the Sky Labyrinth, anything resembling logic tumbles out the window when—

"On the bed."

Asterion's instruction short-circuits her brain. Being told what to do isn't something Theseus is often into. She's usually the one damn well taking the lead... but judging from the fact that she's already shuffling backward up the bed, with Asterion, apparently, she likes being told.

Who knew?

But... nobility... propriety... decency...

All she can do is swallow as Asterion settles beside her, lifting her injured leg so gently Theseus isn't sure what to do with herself. It's only when she spies the pestle and mortar, along with the needle already threaded with luminous thread, that she realises what's actually happening.

Theseus lets out a strangled exhale that's almost a laugh. She's in a labyrinth that's been trying to kill her, so it totally fits that she's dying inside right now.

As Asterion applies cooling balm to the jagged, angry skin of her lower leg, Theseus bites down a groan, trying not to think about the gentle precision of Asterion's touch. It's a medical procedure. She should *not* be enjoying it.

Well, she's not *enjoying* it. Not exactly. The wound and sensations relating to it are making her nauseous, but Asterion's touch... well, that's soothing her a whole lot. And she's pretty confident that's not solely to do with the balm.

"Is—okay?" Asterion's worried eyes look up at her. "I—hurt you?"

Theseus clears her throat. "No. Is—okay."

Asterion examines the wound more closely. "I think— remove stitches—first?"

Theseus nods, but she has no idea how the glowing thread works. Who's to say what will and won't work?

And that's a knife in Asterion's hand. A sharp one. *Don't think about where that's going...*

Asterion must notice her tensing. "Is just—stitch removal."

Mmhhmm. Theseus nods, but doesn't unclench. She is brave, honest. "I think I preferred being unconscious for this."

"Can—be arranged." Asterion is deadpan, but there's a playful glimmer in her eyes. *Phew.* And at Asterion's humour, Theseus can't help smiling, just a little.

Brow furrowed in concentration, Asterion removes the old stitches. Though the area is numb, the skin tugs a little; an odd sensation. The wound has closed, but it's red and raw still. Far from healed. The thought of her skin rupturing turns Theseus's stomach. There's a high chance she might vomit.

Okay, this is the opposite of alluring.

"You—not have to—" Asterion pauses, clearly thinking. "You do not have to watch," she says, in almost perfect Athenian. It's a sensible suggestion. "You—brave warrior?"

Theseus doesn't appreciate her smirk. "You try getting your leg almost cut off and see how brave you are," she mutters, sounding more like angst personified than a brave *anything*.

But Asterion's words make her think...

"Warrior?" Theseus keeps her eyes on Asterion, whose concentration on her task is unwavering.

"Mmmhmm. Sword. Shield. Armour. Determination in eyes. If not warrior—you are what?"

Now hardly seems the time to tell her she's a monster hunter sent here to take her heart as a trophy... Though Theseus does need to tackle that topic soon. Asterion must have figured out that people come here to defeat the Minotaur, right?

"You are good," says Asterion.

That was quick. Theseus braves a look. Like Asterion's shoulder injury, Theseus's flesh is already absorbing the thread, transforming her wound to a glowing scar. There's a gentle heat there; it's as though she can *feel* herself healing from within.

That's something.

It's only Asterion's words gnawing at her now.

You are good.

She'd likely meant *You're good* as in, *I've finished with your gross wound*, but the other meaning needles at Theseus. Because Asterion won't think she's good when she discovers what the plan had been for the organ in her chest. Asterion shuffles closer, and Theseus's breath barricades itself in her lungs. *What is she—?*

Asterion holds out her hand like she's asking Theseus to dance. And Theseus only stares at it. They're sitting down; how are they meant to...?

But she obliges, placing her hand in Asterion's. And for a long moment they stay like that, frozen: somewhere between a handshake at best, and Theseus looking fucking demure at worst.

Then Asterion turns Theseus's hand palm up, and tenderly removes the adhesive bandage.

Oh.

Of course. That makes more sense. Theseus outright cringes, which only makes Asterion more gentle.

"I—try?" she asks, dangling a short length of thread from her fingertips.

Theseus nods. She'd agree to anything right now.

Asterion trails the thread over Theseus's part-healed palm. The glowing fibres latch on and sink into her skin, erasing the cut and leaving only sprinkles of glowing blue flickering within her flesh.

Asterion smiles, as if Theseus's healing is her own. At Theseus's nod of approval, she unbandages her forearm next and drapes the thread over the burn wound which also sparkles and heals. The remnants of the thread's fibres look like luminous freckles.

Her arm sure feels a lot better now. Though that could be the effect of Asterion caressing her healed skin with her thumb. It's just... curiosity in her eyes. Awe at what the mysterious thread has achieved.

The need to confess the truth of why she's here, what Asterion's sister sent her here to do, bubbles like lava in Theseus's chest. Asterion's Athenian far outstrides her Minosian. But perhaps they can communicate enough to understand each other now?

She places her hand over Asterion's, and Asterion stills, staring at their hands. To say that Theseus's heart is glowing would be ridiculous; far too poetic for anything Theseus has ever experienced. But that's exactly what the pendant that's fallen from beneath Asterion's vest is doing.

Is it just happenstance that the stone hangs, blushing pink, in line with Asterion's heart? That it's irregular like the organ it aligns with? And is it Theseus's imagination, or is it the right shape and size to fit the mysterious gap in the Labyrinth's outer-shell gateway?

Only the heart of the Minotaur will set you free...

Theseus has so many questions, but she's too distracted by the glow of the pendant, flickering like a trapped firefly, to ask any of them.

Without thinking, she reaches out to touch the stone. As she thumbs its smooth surface, warm from Asterion's body heat, her knuckles unintentionally brush Asterion's chest.

Asterion gasps as if Theseus had been bold enough to touch her much lower, blue sparks sizzling across the torque at her throat. But before Theseus can wonder what that means, a seismic rumble trembles the chamber.

Asterion's eyes dart to their surroundings, and her unease sails Theseus's panic skyward.

Is the labyrinth turning? Has something snagged?

Her inner compass whirls as the chamber upends a good thirty degrees, unbalancing even Asterion as she scrambles, wide-eyed, to grab the illumi-thread. Her full weight lands in Theseus's lap as the spool skitters past them, tumbling toward the flaming hearth.

Which is where they'll be headed too, unless—

Theseus lashes out both arms, latching onto Asterion's belt with one, gripping the headboard with the other. Asterion might have her stumbling on her thoughts and words, but—*finally* —reflexes are something she can do.

Asterion lunges off the edge of the angled bed, but her reach isn't quick or far enough. Theseus's insides lurch with guilt as the illuminated spindle, the legendary thread of healing and life, lands unceremoniously in the blazing hearth, turning to ash in a roar of flames.

Gone.

Just like that.

This is why Theseus should not be trusted with magical treasures.

Asterion spews several Minosian swear words as Theseus hauls her back onto the bed, muscles burning with the exertion; the chamber's tilt isn't making it easy. Asterion is still reaching toward the flames as if she might change the outcome.

"Asterion... Please..."

Her words seem to snap Asterion into action as she scrambles back onto the bed, gripping Theseus's shirt and shoulder to steady herself. Theseus wraps an arm around her, holding her in place.

The bed doesn't shift. It must be fixed in place.

Their bodies are pressed together, Asterion's thighs wrapped tight about Theseus's hips. Their startled breaths mingle, and Theseus's heart races. They're so close, she can feel Asterion's doing the same.

Seriously, universe...?

This has to be a dream. Maybe she passed out on watching her leg being stitched. Some warrior. But dream or not, it's the best kind of torture. An oddly specific fantasy she never knew she had.

If this were a dream, she wouldn't think twice about placing her lips against Asterion's. And ignoring the surrounding chaos would be fine, because it's *just a dream...*

But Theseus isn't the one leaning closer. She isn't the one adjusting her hips. She clenches her muscles, trying not to show that Asterion's proximity is driving her just a little wild, in case it's all just wishful thinking.

The blue sparks of their torques dance between them as Asterion's eyes roam Theseus's face from only a breath away. Surprise progresses to something heated and inviting, and Asterion's hand—*fuck*—is stroking up Theseus's neck, sending her senses reeling more than any impromptu chamber tilt.

Asterion's nose brushes hers, then across to her jaw, lingering in the best way before venturing to stroke her cheek. Electricity dances in Theseus's chest. It dances elsewhere, too. It must supercharge and short any link to her brain, because she tilts her face to catch Asterion's lips with her own.

The moment of weightlessness stretches. The labyrinth might be snagging, but with their soft lips gliding, and their bodies pressing against each other, the universe is in perfect alignment.

Theseus wishes she could hold on to this moment.

Her grasp on Asterion's over-shirt tightens, bunching the fabric. When Asterion deepens their kiss, their tongues caressing tentatively, Theseus could fold in on herself like a dying star.

The Labyrinth groans as if in apology—though of course it's not actually apologising; it's a fucking labyrinth. It's course-correcting. The chamber creaks and lurches, tearing them apart, shunting them to opposite sides of the bed.

Axis adjusted.

Asterion's breath is shallow, her eyes alight and wild. Theseus can barely think. No fucking change there.

She needs to find some words. To say what? To ask what in the actual heavens is going on with the Labyrinth? Or what just happened between them? To suggest they do it again, like, right now?

But Asterion is already standing, fingers pressed to her lips. "I—need—um—figure this out," she mutters, as she leaves without a backward glance.

Okay...

She could be talking about the labyrinth malfunction, or the malfunction in Theseus's brain that just let that kiss happen.

31

MONSTER

U ncertain whether she should give Asterion space, Theseus lingers in the bedchamber. Lingering turns to pacing, which is not something she could do even ten minutes ago. That's some powerful thread.

If she weren't so preoccupied with what just happened with Asterion, if her body weren't pulsing with desire and something that's resonating a lot like guilt, she'd be more astounded by the first-hand experience of healing this damn fast. There's still the numbed memory of metal teeth in her flesh, but it's a massive step in the right direction.

If only Theseus knew what direction she should step in.

Asterion is upset. Or she's just on a mission to fix the faulting labyrinth. Either way, if she'd wanted Theseus's company, wouldn't she have invited her? But the possibility of Asterion's disquiet twists Theseus's stomach. She'll make sure Asterion is okay, and then she'll leave her alone—if that's what Asterion wants.

With no need for her crutch, Theseus steps out into the corridor and the clue to Asterion's whereabouts is rather obvious.

Along the corridor, there's a stripe of vertical light in the opposite wall. In her haste, Asterion must have neglected to close the hidden doorway. Or perhaps she doesn't mind Theseus joining her?

Theseus hazards into the mysterious chamber. The doorway that's twice as tall as she is opens with ease and doesn't creak in the manner she expects of a door so grand. Or a door that looks so much like a *wall*.

Fire-torches lick light across the chamber and its walls of books. It's more bound paper than Theseus has seen in her whole life—which is more a comment on the quantity of books, than on Theseus's literacy, *thank you very much*. Most worlds use screens and ether these days. It's rare to find such a collection.

Each of the wooden shelves is engraved with a series of uniform vertical lines, each line no taller than a card deck. The treelike pillars bookending each section are far more decorated, with paint and etchings: stars, galaxies, and one sun for each of the seven. If Theseus squints, she might imagine this place to be some sort of planetarium, as well as a library.

She scans the room, not seeing Asterion, but discovering two wingback chairs arranged to form a bed of sorts; with a footstool bridging the middle, and a blanket and pillow situated on top.

This is where Asterion has been sleeping?

So Asterion *had* given up her bedchamber for Theseus to recuperate. Theseus doesn't want her heart to squeeze at that, but it does. But before she has a chance to either explore or avoid her feelings, there's movement up on the mezzanine.

Okay, so... this library has a mezzanine. And Asterion is up there, her back to the rest of the library. Perhaps she's pulling out books that can help with the labyrinth fault? Whatever she's doing, she's either absorbed or intent on blocking everything out.

A spiral metal stairway accesses the mezzanine, and despite

her leg functioning much better, Theseus takes the steps slowly, one at a time. As she conquers the last metal rung, she finds Asterion drawing an intricate pattern of stars on the wall. Which is... not what she expected...

Her back is to Theseus, and her focus remains on the charcoal decorated wall, but Asterion must know she's here. Her journey up the stairs won't win any awards for stealth. Theseus observes as Asterion smudges ash with her fingers, adding to the depiction of a picturesque night sky.

Where to begin? What to say? *I'm sorry? My intention wasn't to upset you? Have I upset you? Why are you drawing stars?*

Perhaps she should just leave her be...

Theseus's stomach tangles. Because beyond Asterion, eyes are staring from the shadows. Two sets of eyes.

Theseus grasps at her hip for a sword that isn't there.

Despite being unarmed, she steps between Asterion and potential danger. But then her logical brain catches up, pointing out what should have been obvious: the eyes, the people, they're paintings.

They're so lifelike. A man with a caring gaze who looks like all he wants to do is offer hugs and encouragement. Theseus doesn't mind being in his presence. Though she doesn't want a hug.

The other person—the other *painting*—could be a slightly younger Asterion, etched and painted into the pillar. And much like the portrait in the entrance hall, there's something about the eyes, stormy blue and cold as marble, powerful and forbidding...

There's no doubt in Theseus's mind: this is a depiction of Princess Ariadne.

How did one twin end up imprisoned here, while the other rules Minos?

"Your sister..."

Asterion's ash-covered fingers pause as she looks upon the

portrait of Ariadne. The warmth and affection in her gaze is heartbreaking.

She doesn't know...

Asterion returns to the ash on the wall and Theseus swallows hard. She has to tell her. She doesn't want to complicate Asterion's world, but she needs to know the truth.

If only she could meet Asterion halfway and utter some Minosian. But funnily enough, her guide-Shard doesn't have the Minosian for *Your sister either believes you're a monster or has tricked Minos and beyond into believing you to be one. She sent me here to kill you.*

"Asterion. Your sister..." Heavens, Theseus doesn't want to tell her this. "She challenges heroes and criminals to conquer the Labyrinth..."

"No-one—can conquer—Labyrinth—all die trying." Asterion's words are curt as she rubs her forehead, smudging ash adorably across her skin.

No, not adorable. Theseus. Focus.

"Kill the beast. Bring me its heart. *Set me free.* That is what Princess Ariadne challenges those she sends here."

Asterion half-turns to Theseus, unease in her eyes. Fear, too? Of Theseus? Of this conversation? Whoever said honesty is the best policy was never a monster hunter looking into so-called Minotaur eyes as they turn from curious and confused to rueful and defensive.

"I live—in Labyrinth—*you* talk in riddles."

Asterion reaches out to her sister's image. Ash-covered fingertips smear across Princess Ariadne's face. Asterion's frown deepens, and she retreats. With a rag, she attempts to remove the blemish, but only smudges the ash further. Her movements grow erratic.

"She... Sh-she... she know—knows I am strong. She knows —I am safe."

"Are you? Safe?" Theseus asks, softly. "Your scars suggest otherwise."

Asterion's pendant darkens. Her torque ripples with sharp tremors as the chamber stutters and groans like a world suffering fault lines.

"She give—gave—given me—mask. To protect."

How can she think that?

"That mask is the reason people hunt you!" Theseus can't help the exasperation in her voice. "You live in a death maze, Asterion."

Asterion whirls around, every muscle coiled. "*I live in a palatial puzzle!*"

Theseus holds her ground, waiting for Asterion's quivering scowl to double down into rage or fold into sobs of despair. But Asterion holds her ground, too.

Theseus hates all of this, but she has to be clear. She has to be certain Asterion understands.

"Ariadne sent me here to kill the Minotaur." Her voice isn't loud, but Asterion flinches, her eyes flashing with all the hurt and betrayal under the Seven Suns.

Asterion about-turns, strides and descends the spiral stairs so fast, Theseus is still on the top rung when Asterion bursts out of the library.

Minutes later, following the chaotic clatter, Theseus locates Asterion in the entrance hall, already in her torso-armour, her bare arms and shoulders smeared with dark clay. Her eyes are shut, her head angled like she's listening for something

"What're you doing?" Theseus's question is redundant, of course—with the Minotaur mask under Asterion's arm, it's clear what she's doing—and Theseus's presence only serves to propel Asterion further towards the exit.

Shit. Theseus should have been careful to clarify—in

amongst the *I'm here to kill you* speech—that her objective has changed now that she knows Asterion isn't actually a monster.

No wonder she's running away.

Nice one, idiot.

Because now, not only are her words evading her, so too is Asterion. And it's all happening so fast. Asterion pulls on the mask, and Theseus can only wince at Asterion's hiss when the straps and collar tighten automatically about her chest, shoulders, and—from the grinding sounds of it—within the mask itself.

Asterion is so swift at becoming the beast, it's only a matter of moments before the mask's eyes glow with all the energy of her torque, and she's guided the bull's horns into the keyholes. Her forearms clamp into the inner gateway cuffs, and the doorway's mechanisms are in motion.

No.

Theseus can't let her go out there like this...

But she can't stop her, either.

She doesn't overthink it. She joins Asterion on the turntable, a half-second before it clicks into gear—

The turntable spins, casting them both out into the dizzying darkness of the night-time labyrinth.

PART IV

ASTERION'S WORLD

ASTERION

32

DESIGNS

At eleven sun-orbits old...

Little Asterion never means to upset her sister, but is apparently skilled at doing so all the same.

"What have you done?" Ari sounds so affronted, Asterion can only tilt her head in confusion, squinting past the sheen of her sister's structured silk court gown and its overcomplicated ruffles.

Ari's cutting glare seems to be trained on Asterion's designs. "It's a sky palace," explains Asterion. She's been working on the fortress at the centre of the puzzle-world for a while now. The mix of sketches and technical blueprints satisfies her need for both creativity and precision, as well as the possibility of positive change.

There's nothing Asterion wants more than her sister's approval. Well, apart from societal reform, of course. But she's only eleven, and it's not society staring her down right now, it's Ari. And Asterion can't for the life of her work out why she's so angry.

"It's for you and me to live in," she continues, hoping it will make Ari smile. "A whole new world with different biomes and climates, like they have on other worlds. And there's a labyrinth in the outer layers, like a moat, and—"

The sharpness in Ariadne's eyes turns to daggers.

She hasn't always been so severe with Asterion. They used to play together, laugh together. Playing chase was fun; so was 'the floor is lava'. They both used to complain about the ridiculous attire they were forced to wear, both preferring simple, comfortable clothes like the trousers-shirt-blazer combination Asterion still opts for when she's allowed to choose such things. But now Ari chooses the most uncomfortable, impractical outfits, the more elaborate the better. Maybe that's why she's snippy so often.

It's only recently that she's been this way. Just as solid rock can change under heat and pressure, Ari, too, is changed.

Ever since it was announced, officially, that they were old enough to compete for the role of Architect-in-waiting via monumental designs (whoever achieves the most impressive wins), Ari has been *different*. Walking and talking like she's... taller or *better* than Asterion, or something. Which is silly because they're the same height.

"Those are my drawings!" Ari shouts, pointing a shaking, accusatory finger.

Asterion flinches. It takes a moment to look past her confusion to the sketches beneath her own. Ari's designs had been presented to the royal committee and rejected, so it made sense to repurpose the pages.

On a technical level, Ari's designs for an automatic-locking mask are impressive. But theming it as a Minosian bull—a fictitious Minotaur, no less— had been an unimaginative choice, in Asterion's opinion. (Which perhaps she shouldn't have voiced in front of the royal committee. She hadn't intended to be unkind, only honest.)

Minotaurs are a cautionary tale for children. *Don't veer off the Righteous Path, or the Minotaur will get you.* Perhaps 'unimaginative' isn't quite the right description. *Cruel* is more like it.

Neither Asterion nor the committee had been able to stomach the mask's intended purpose. Corporal punishment via the denial of identity—hiding someone's face and garbling their voice, making them not just unseen and unheard, but terrifying —that was too cruel, even for criminals. And their father, the Architect, had agreed.

The committee had been more impressed with Asterion's designs for an apparatus that would repurpose an individual's Minosian Flame as usable energy, without affecting that individual. Resource-torques, she calls them. There's likely a better name, but she'd been more focused on finding a solution to Minos's dwindling resources—for the benefit of all— than making it sound good.

All of this is to say: Asterion had assumed Ari's pages weren't needed anymore. "I thought they were scrap," she says, which does nothing to lessen the wildfire vitriol in Ari's eyes. Clearly, her assumption was wrong.

Ari snatches the pages from her. "What is wrong with you, Asterion?"

33

HEART OF THE MINOTAUR

Later that same sun-orbit...

In the Minosian palace, in the corner of the siblings' bedchamber, little Asterion nestles in her pillow fort and cries.

When there's a light tap-tap-tap at her chamber door, followed by the approach of familiar footsteps, she knows it's Nanny before he peers under her accomplished structure.

"I did it again, didn't I?" Asterion doesn't hide her quivering chin or the tears forging down her cheeks. She hadn't meant to upset Ari. Again. Nor had she meant to follow that up by being such a nuisance that Father sent her away from the royal committee's consultation. *Again.*

It isn't her fault that what the Quantifiers and Constructionists were discussing was *stupid.* She plumps her pillows with her fists, finding little relief. Just as she doesn't understand the appeal of flouncy outfits, she doesn't understand why Minos seems to prioritise building landmarks that are all looks over substance, leaving destruction in their wake.

How many sun-orbits will pass before they understand the

obvious: that Minos, like most worlds, only has finite resources —of which there will soon be none left—and that it makes zero sense to keep building bigger and 'better' feats of engineering, just to *look good*.

She huffs, planting her head against a pillow so solidly its plush interior envelops her head.

Nanny squeezes into the pillow fort to join her. His gentle smile doesn't upset her; he's not laughing *at* her. He's on her side. Always.

She wants to smile with him, but she's too darn annoyed at *everything*.

"Not only are their proposals logistically convoluted," she says, gesturing in much the manner she had when telling this to the committee, "it's also" —more importantly— "*unkind*."

It's all so easy for them, pontificating about designs and use of resources while sitting beneath the marble arches of the palace. They're not the ones struggling to heat the slums they're forced to call homes. And they're not the ones who'll be uprooted from the Breccia District if the plans go ahead.

Perhaps she shouldn't have called them 'dim as an over-dug mine', or pointed out that it was blind luck of the stars that they won't be the ones to suffer the consequences of such idiotic decisions. But no-one else was putting words to the obvious.

These people could change things for the better—she'd even proposed a technology that *would*—and yet still they're driving Minos deeper into disaster instead.

No-one had welcomed her thoughts. Ari had stared at her with a mix of indignation and disgust that evolved to a hurtful satisfaction when their father had ordered Asterion to leave. It felt—it still feels—like a punch to the gut, one as hard as she's pummelling the pillows right now.

It's always somehow worse when the features judging her are identical to her own.

Asterion rarely suffers boredom. There's always something to be puzzled out, designed, improved upon. When her mind needs a rest, there's an entire library of fiction to lose herself in. But the one thing she tires of—quickly—is being a disappointment.

Yes, she can figure out architectural components until the Minosian bulls come home, but other people are a riddle for which she doesn't have the language or context. And in the puzzle of her royal family, Asterion has always been a piece that does not fit.

She sniffles, and Nanny unclasps something from around his neck before holding his hand out. Curiosity wins, and Asterion cranes to peer at the small, odd-shaped stone attached to a simple necklace.

"You know, most people look at this and see just a lump of stone," says Nanny, his voice soothing as always. "Something to look past—to kick aside, even. But that's not what I see. I see something unique."

Asterion looks harder at the stone. It looks a little like rose quartz, with lines cabled through it that, by Minosian standards, would deem it flawed.

"It looks like a heart," she says, quietly.

Nanny's eyes light up. "It does."

"A heart made of stone?"

"If you look close..." He cups his hands around it, inviting her to do the same. "You see that?"

There's a pink pulse within the pebble.

"It's glowing!" says Asterion, gloom now veering just a little towards glee.

"It has to have the right conditions to do so. Warmth. Happiness." Nanny's gentle tone feels like a hug. "Others only see its flaws. Only those who take the time to look see that it's unique. And it's clever, too."

Asterion pouts. How can a stone be clever?

"Perhaps too clever sometimes, because it puts feelings on show that may not be for sharing."

Asterion cradles the stone in her palm. The pink glow is gentle, but it's there. Her lingering distress threatens to consume her curiosity and the happiness kindled by Nanny's warmth, but she doesn't let it.

"But you know what?" Nanny's words are quiet, with an air of conspiracy. "People are wrong about that, too."

Asterion tilts her head. Wrong about what?

"Feelings should be for sharing," he says.

Asterion nods, processing this. But isn't it sharing that gets her into trouble? Nanny smiles at her, a doting, knowing smile, as if he can see the cogs in her mind turning.

"But there's an art to it," he adds. "You remember when you were little?"

Asterion appreciates that he doesn't patronise her by referring to eleven sun-orbits as 'little'.

"And you didn't know how to hold a paintbrush, a stylus, not even a pen?"

She nods. Dark days, indeed.

"It's like instinct now. But you had to learn. Interaction can be like that, too."

"Ari doesn't have to learn the art of interaction..." Asterion's chin quivers a little. She's always looked up to her sister. Her confidence. Her ability to say the right things. She used to follow Ari everywhere until Ari told her to stop.

She can see it. People are more at ease around her sister, sparkling like a perfectly cut diamond, while Asterion is just the rock they trip on. Ari says the right things, while Asterion can only say whatever pops into her stupid head.

Nanny lowers his voice even further. "You know, it doesn't have to be a competition."

"But... life is a competition?" Asterion echoes the words she's heard from so many in the royal court: words that are ingrained in every Minosian.

"There are worlds out there where winning isn't a priority," he says, and Asterion thinks he's trying to help, but—

"But I live on *this* world," she says, observing the stone's shifting hues.

Nanny nods, thoughtful. "We all have our strengths. Your sister is adept at getting what she wants. But her artistry with architecture, with composition, a stylus and brush, with *kindness*... If it were a competition, my dear Asterion, you would win every time."

Asterion can't help smiling. Not at Nanny's words, but at the enveloping comfort of his affection.

"Just remember, Asterion: no matter how much your surroundings demand you shape yourself to them, inside you are perfect."

And the heart in her palm, and the heart in her chest, both glow a little brighter.

34

A WORLD UNFOLDS

Half a sun-orbit later...

The last thing little Asterion recalls is falling asleep.
Nothing unusual there. Nanny had put her and Ariadne
to bed in their shared chamber, and there had been nothing to
suggest that when she woke anything would be any different.

She's still in her pyjamas, the fabric soft against her skin.
And her feet are bare, but the air drifting against them doesn't
feel like the airflow of the palace. Something is out of alignment;
her head is heavy, and she can hardly see.

Her breathing sounds odd, too—too close and too hot on her
face. And all she can smell is leather and metal. There's something covering her face... her entire head, in fact. She swipes at
it, but her hands are heavy and wrong and all she achieves is
knocking against something unfamiliar.

Her heart rate accelerates, the drumming in her ears accentuated by whatever in the heavens contains her.

She tries to stand, but her inner mass is all wrongly
distributed. Whatever it is that's clamped around her head, her
shoulders, and braced across her chest, obscures her vision, and

she topples. She tries to claw free, but her hands are useless—though why, she can't quite fathom.

Ari sometimes locks her in cupboards as a sort of game. Asterion doesn't like it, but she's willing to put up with some discomfort if Ari wants to be playful. Perhaps this is just another one of her games?

But it doesn't feel like that...

"Ari...?" Her voice emerges as a strange growling bellow, unfamiliar and unsettling. The discomfort tightens about her chest and within it. Because in that moment, she *knows*.

She's in the mask. Ari's mask.

Why is she in the mask?

And her hands, they must be in the hoof-like braces.

"This isn't funny, Ari!" A scrappy screech spews from the mask, echoing back at her.

And everything beyond the mask is in darkness.

Each attempt to stand lands her on the hard ground. The mask anchors her like a weighted die, and her hands aren't much use. On the twelfth try, she manages more than three steps, and it's trial and error from there, but her balance eventually clicks.

Her chest aches. Are the braces tightening further, or are her lungs just constricting? She wheezes through her panic.

"Nanny?" she calls, but a growl is all that emerges.

There must be eye holes in the mask, and there's finally something to see—albeit still obscured by clumsy design—as pinpricks of light spark into existence.

Is this a dream? A nightmare? Is she witnessing the dawn of time itself, the universe's battle of light and dark as it wills itself into existence?

That last thought nooses around her lungs, tighter than the mask. It can't be, can it?

Not the universe... but a world?

Everyone has the inner power to create a world, with direction and the right combination of ingredients. And that's what this is.

The world-engine is activating.

Invisible forces tug at her, pulling her limbs in opposing directions. The pinpricks of light move further away, finding their places in the dark. The shadows undulate as the world-engine expands the fabric of creation in every direction, just as she'd designed it to do.

She'd be thrilled if dread wasn't pulling at her, as insistently as the calibrating gravity.

She crouches, choosing the warming surface beneath her as her ground; lessening the chance of being swept in a different direction by gravity. The flutter and buzz of chemical reactions accompanies the soil churning into existence under her bare feet.

The scent of chlorophyll fills the air. Trees creak as they accelerate from sapling into forest. Grass and wheat, silver and gold, burst from the ground in shimmering waves. A proteus tree sparks to life, leaves rippling and roaring, the colour of flame.

Water sloshes, puddling, then forging a path over her ankles. It, too, is warmed by simmering chemical activity.

They'd said it would be impossible...

But she'd done the calculations.

As her designs had evolved, it had become clear the Sky Labyrinth would be too large to construct on-world. So Asterion had included notations for how it might self-construct in situ. She'd tried to explain her ideas about targeted abiogenesis to Ari: how the primordial soup containing all the predetermined ingredients for a new world might be packaged into one capsule and sent to the sky. Get the right balance, the right combinations, the right order to mix the ingredients; apply the right accelerants, and it should all rise like bread in a cosmic oven.

Her explanation had only made her hungry and Ari dead-head the palace flowers. But now she's surrounded by the proof of her theory: her own world evolving around her. Organic and mechanical, each piece of the labyrinth clicks together, the ground rumbling like shifting tectonic plates and vibrating Asterion's every nerve.

Shadow shapes fly past... various sizes... objects? All too quick to decipher.

Ouch. Something solid smacks into her feet: something oblong and familiar. She fumbles to pick it up between her hooves. A book from the palace library? The library that had been a crucial part of her sky palace design. It only confirms it: this is *her* world.

She'd designed it all to evolve like clockwork: for the world to grow, to build itself in a co-ordinated dance of creation. But the knot of panic in her stomach constricts her excitement. Because there's nothing in her plans to say that *she* should be within the chaos of creation as it all unfurls. In fact, she'd have specified the opposite if she'd known someone was planning to implement her designs.

Whoever calibrated the distribution matrix must have cut some corners, because—evidently—the cargo container has opened too soon, spilling books and furniture everywhere. But even without flying cargo, a world-engine mid-creation is not a safe place to be. There's no telling whether she'll end up on top of one of the newly formed cliffs, or in it.

Lava erupts into existence mere metres from her. She stumbles backwards, away from the sudden burst of heat.

Right now, she feels less like the conductor of possibilities and more like she's dodging cannon fire on terrain that's threatening to swallow her whole.

As her worldly possessions hurricane around her, the stampede of sloshing water knocks her off her feet. She slips beneath the waves. She can't breathe. She attempts to swim up, with her hoof-encased hands, but which way is *up*?

The undertow is strong. The mask is heavy.

As the current whisks her into the depths, the green sparkle of accelerated bedrock forms. The emerald stone puzzles itself into a water well.

Her arms ache. Her lungs beg for air.

A tremendous *crunch* rumbles beneath her. Something flat and solid shoves her from behind, rising up out of the water like a sky-ship taking flight, carrying her with it.

Cliffs...?

Asterion's lungs expand. *Relief*. Air. Finally. She heaves in breaths as the freshly formed rocks tower towards the engineered sky with its pinprick stars and light channels for moons. Only glimpses find her through the mask.

She shouldn't be here, trapped within the lines of her own blueprints. The Sky Labyrinth was only meant to be theoretical, a fantasy of escape for herself and Ari.

But as earth and rock orchestrate into their final formation, the truth sinks deep into her bones.

This isn't an escape. This isn't freedom.

This is captivity.

35

DESIGNS, DARKLY

I f this is a game, it's not a fun one.

Asterion wants to squirm free of the mask, to take a breath that isn't tainted with wet, soil-covered leather and the tang of metal. She wants to shout out and have her voice heard.

She can't.

She recalls Ari's designs: should the mask's wearer try to remove it—interfering with its mechanisms—they risk lobotomy or death. For now, she's stuck with it.

She can barely see the winding, shadow-filled sky tunnel as she lumbers along it. In her designs, it had led to a river with stepping stones and a moat of corridor layers beyond. If she can find the outer gatehouse, maybe she can figure out a plan from there—though that would be risky, given that the mask doesn't possess astro-capabilities. Perhaps she should turn back, discover the meadow and the other biomes, and... is there a fortress at the centre of this world, like she'd designed?

Maybe Ari is there? Perhaps, underneath all the ruffles and scorn, she had wanted to escape too. Maybe this is all just a... surprise?

But if Ari is here, she'd have been with Asterion in the confines of the world-engine, wouldn't she?

Though the mask had obscured her vision then, too. What if Ari had been there, unable to call out, buffeted between the elements of the world creating itself around her? What if she's lost somewhere in the labyrinth?

A wall of heat wallops Asterion, almost knocking her off her feet. She staggers on, blinking against the steaming, cloying air as the dark tunnel opens into—

Bubbling, thick, red-orange...

A river of lava hadn't been part of her plans. Lava for the heating system, all contained and safe, yes—but *this*?

'The ground is lava' had been one of the few games she and Ari both enjoyed, but it had been fun because the ground wasn't *actual lava*.

"Hello?" A warm hug of a voice embraces her from across the molten river.

The scales of her terror counter-balance with relief.

"Nanny?" Asterion calls back, her voice a distorted growl.

It's so hot in here, she's struggling to breathe. But she can't retreat now. The labyrinth is designed to make people lose their way. Searching for a safer route to the outer layers will take too long. She can't risk losing Nanny.

Stepping stones. Is that part of her design a feature of this place?

Sweat stings her eyes, blurring her vision as she locates the stones on the riverbank, the ones she'd specified as pressure-sensitive. And—*relief*—the stones rise up. And they don't melt. At least whoever corrupted her designs used lava-impervious materials.

"Hello?" Nanny's distant voice again. If she can just get to him, he'll know what to do.

It's reckless, but she's desperate. Her legs are wobbly, like they're not her legs anymore, but she treads from one stone to the next as evenly as she can.

Just a little further...

The final step—

Asterion's fear-numbed legs collapse beneath her. She stumbles, landing in an ungraceful heap on the opposite riverbank. Her chest aches with panic and stifled tears as she drags herself away from the unbearable heat.

She scrambles to her feet—her numbness dissipating with each step—and rushes from the river chamber, past the pillars designed to disguise it, and into the more rigid corridor beyond.

A wall of shimmering mist sweeps across her before she can choose an escape route. The sour mist sinks into her pores, scratching beneath her skin and eroding her confidence.

All the nerves jangling through her rattle to the surface. Her breath tightens again, worse than before. "Ari?"

In the mist, her sister's silhouette disappears at the crossroads up ahead, giggling like this is all just some game.

Please let this be just a game...

She can't trust her own senses right now. She knows not to trust anything in the mists: a byproduct from the woodland's bog-fungus. In her designs, she'd calculated the high likelihood of the spores possessing a toxin with hallucinogenic properties. She'd made clear notations about this. And about the risk that the spores could end up in the labyrinth's air circulation system.

But the Quantifiers and Constructionists who've made this place from her plans must have ignored her warnings.

In the mists, everything is heightened.

She's never been scared before. She's been annoyed and upset at injustices and worried that Ari and Father don't like her very much, and those have paved the way to a range of other unpleasant emotions, but none of them were *fear*. The twisty, squirmy knot in her stomach is doing strange things to her pulse, thrumming in her ears like a Righteous Path parade.

As Asterion stumbles forward, at the next corridor turn Ari's silhouette still haunts the mists, still striding away. Even though she can't see Ari's face, her bitter smile twists like a knife in her back. And in this moment, Asterion knows beyond doubt that Ariadne despises her.

She also knows, logically, that Ari isn't really here. The manifestations will wear off once she's free of the toxin. But that doesn't lessen the grip of fear or the twist of the knife. Hot tears spill into the mask, irritating her cheeks, and she can't even wipe them away.

In the shifting mists, Ari's shape dissolves on a haunting giggle. Asterion clamps down on the inconsolable sobs within her chest, begging to be let out.

But, the mists shift again...

And, thank the heavens, there's a familiar, friendly face.

Please don't let him be a trick...

"Nanny!" Asterion calls, relief diluting her fears just a little as she launches toward the one person in her life who has always made her feel like the world isn't against her; and that maybe she isn't so strange and unwanted.

Please let him be real.

But he stumbles away from her, breaking into a run. A little more relief settles in Asterion's veins. They've played chase in the palace corridors so many times.

Maybe this *is* all just a game.

She's always suspected her victories in their games of chase might be more the result of his kindness than her athleticism. But he doesn't know these corridors. He doesn't know which way to turn.

It doesn't take her long to catch up. For her to barrel into him and throw her arms around him in a gleeful burst of relief.

He'll tell her it's all okay. He'll tell her this is all just a game.

She's half afraid he might dissipate the way Ari had, but he remains solid beneath her desperate hug. Painful cries spasm from him and her scaffolded nerves collapse, buried by dread. He shoves at her, trying to push her away.

Asterion tries to pull back, to figure out what's wrong.

But she can't.

As he flails to get away from her, he slips, tugging her down to the hard ground with him. She tries to stand, but he lets out another agonised cry.

"What's happening?" The tear-filled words tumble from her, but her voice is warped, contorted.

Finally, she tugs herself free and stumbles back far enough to look at him through the mask.

He doesn't look right. His eyes are on her, but they're wide with horror. He's never looked at her like this before. He opens his mouth like he's trying to speak, but only nonsensical gargles emerge.

"What's wrong?" Asterion sobs. *Did the mist do this?*

What can she do to help?

Something tickles her nose and she tries to brush it away, only to meet the barrier of the mask. Something sticky trickles through the eye holes. Something from the horns?

The liquid touches her lips.

It tastes like a bitten tongue.

The mists part further, and only then does she understand.

Her breath flails from her. She'd never considered he might not be running with her, but from her. She'd forgotten what she must look like in the mists; what she must sound like through the mask. And in her exuberance, her desperate need for comfort... she'd forgotten the mask's horns.

What's worse than the two deep wounds in Nanny's chest are

his screams. His agony. His terror. But, worse still, is his sudden silence. The light leaving his eyes as he stops clawing away from her. He stops doing anything. He just... stops.

A sobbing gasp bursts from Asterion, turned to a garbled, monstrous roar as she backs away and runs, hurtling down one corridor after another after another.

She only stops when a blade slices out from the wall in front of her, clashing into the metal of the mask's horns and swiping her solidly off her feet.

That wasn't part of her design, either.

Her sobs unleash as she crumples in an inconsolable heap, straining for breath and understanding. She's only ever wanted to make better worlds. She never wanted to be a monster.

PART V

THE WARRIOR

ASTERION

36

FIRST IMPRESSIONS

Nineteen sun-orbits later...

The fortress shudders in that way it does when the outer-shell's gatehouse is claiming a new crop of adventurers? Voyagers? Fools? The damned? Why in the heavens they come here, and whether it's their choice, Asterion doesn't know. They always end up dead before she can find out.

But that doesn't matter right now. She has to get *moving*.

As fast as she's able, she slops dark clay over her pale skin, pulls on her puzzle of armour and grabs her satchel. The mask constricts: talons around her upper body. When the turntable casts her into the labyrinth, she skids out, one knee to the ground. With the momentum, she propels into a sprint. It's taken many sun-orbits of practice to be smooth about it; all to avoid the time-loss from stumbling and pulled muscles.

The connecting corridor is in alignment, allowing her to dart straight into the labyrinth—though that doesn't mean she'll be quick enough to reach the voyagers. At the Labyrinth's current position, she'll have to double back on herself through the maze several times to get to the outer layers.

Every corridor—and its obstacles—has its own timing. She leaps and ducks and rolls: *stride-stride, left, duck, leap, run-run-run* —like a dance she's been cursed to perform on repeat.

And yet, after all these sun-orbits, it's still a dance that trips her. She might know the labyrinth inside out, might know which walls to leap to, each new gravity-flip—but she's not immune to tiredness and glitches in concentration.

Misjudging the speed of a turn, she stumbles to the knee-scraping shingle-covered ground.

At least her trousers absorb the worst of her splayed landing, and the hoof-cuffs protect her palms and wrists. But the fall costs her precious seconds.

"*Flummox!*" The labyrinth roars in an echo of her frustration.

Aligning her muscles to counterbalance the strain of the mask on her shoulders and neck, she launches forward.

Every second counts.

Because if she can't make better worlds, the least she can do is try to save people from this one.

But it's too far, through too many layers, despite her instinctive knowledge of the labyrinth's permutations, despite all her hours of relentless training. Another entire sun-orbit of daily grind, of strengthening her muscles, increasing her agility, to sprint to warn trespassers who don't know which path is safe and which will end them.

She never reaches them in time.

If only she could have reached them before the mists. They might not fear her, then. They might lower their weapons and give her a chance.

Those fumbled few seconds.

She lingers just beyond the mist. She's built up a resistance to it, but there's still a risk that with too much exposure she, too, might unravel.

"Stop!" she yells. "Turn back!" But all that ever does is

produce a monstrous bellow that makes even her own skin crawl.

Her own heaving breath crowds her face.

For a moment, the ill-advised explorers all stare at her as though she's the one brandishing spears and swords. Their trepidation isn't unusual. Her welcoming words are always transformed to beastly sounds, and the result is always the same. Fear. Violence. Death.

It's not like she hasn't tried communicating in other ways. She's created signs: some warning them not to enter the bladed corridor, and some in Minosian that say: IT'S A MASK! But no-one takes any notice, or perhaps they don't believe the messages. One sun-orbit, she'd tried to downplay the mask's ferocity by decorating it with colourful pigments, but that group of voyagers had been as terrified as ever, if not more so. One had screamed something about a 'demon clown' before about-turning and running straight into his neighbour's sword.

Whatever she does, it makes no difference. The mist's toxins disrupt any aptitude any of them have for level-headedness. Now she can only hope her bellows are terrifying enough to scare them back to the entrance gate without them running into each other's pointy objects in the process.

The mist thins just enough to clue her in on the voyagers swiping their weapons blindly in the swamp of mist, mistaking the blades swooping from the walls for attacks from one another.

Asterion's stomach roils. Already several of the group have fallen. But some are still battling the shadows.

A man with face tattoos avoids a wall blade by stumbling luck rather than skill. A blue-haired woman trips over him, narrowly missing her own blade. A man in garish armour grabs one of his fellow voyagers and uses them as a shield.

Before Asterion can consider what to do about *him*, she's

distracted by the warrior who unsheathes her sword and flips it, catching it with practised ease. Her defiant jaw and confident stance promise to battle the universe. There's something in that promise... it has Asterion pausing—her hard and fast breaths, too. But only for a moment, because her body needs to balance out her dash through the labyrinth, and her impossible task has only just begun.

A task that might be complicated by the warrior aiming her battle-ready stare at her. Defiant jaw or not, the blades will get her too if she dares to advance. And Asterion has no doubt the warrior will dare—

Asterion launches forward between the ropes of mist, dodging the blades lancing and swiping from the walls. *Confound and flummox*, the warrior is charging at her. She's going to lose her head if she gets any closer—

Think, think.

There's a loose stone on the ground nearby. Asterion kicks it hard, aiming for the warrior's legs. It hits her shin, buckling her just as the wall's blade swipes through the air above her.

Thank the heavens.

Before the warrior can return to her feet and waste Asterion's efforts to keep her alive, Asterion tackles her to the ground with a heavy *thud*. She loops a forearm about the warrior's shoulders and drags her as fast as she can toward safety.

The blades retreat into the corridor walls as quickly as they appeared, as if they were never there.

Asterion risks a few gulps of air, timing them as best she can between the coils of mist. The weight of the warrior with her armour and shield isn't the easiest to manoeuvre.

Thrashing, the warrior trips her, and Asterion can't stop the groan that emerges as a bellow as they land with enough momentum they skid apart. Asterion returns swiftly to her feet, but the warrior must need a moment, because all she's achieving right now is staring at Asterion's boots.

The reprieve doesn't last long. The warrior leaps to her feet, sword and shield in hand, evidently too busy glaring at Asterion to notice the pressure sensor she's about to stand on—

Asterion lunges to stop her, but the warrior swipes at her, blade first. Asterion deflects with the mask's horns, pulling back to keep the deadly weapons away from the warrior, only to receive a bone-shuddering shield blow to her face. Well, to the mask, but it aches like a thump through her cheek.

The warrior steps back—

Onto the sensor—

No, no, no—

Asterion strikes the sword and shield aside, steps right into the warrior's space, wraps her hoofed arms around her, and lifts—

Just as a shin-level blade sweeps out from the wall, scoring through Asterion's boot and missing the warrior entirely—

Asterion shoves the warrior up against the wall, pushing her high enough and taking the leap herself, hoping—

Gravity plucks them from their previous horizontal. The warrior wriggles beneath her, solid and warm and... distracting. Asterion barely registers the warrior's weapons clanking down around them. She hadn't intended to land on her so intimately. The corridor's lava-gullies must be faulting, because an inexplicable shiver runs through her.

Too many times, she's witnessed fear close up, but never this steely determination. Never like this. Challenge quirks the warrior's brow, and there's something about her vigour, the set of her jaw, it has a giddiness within Asterion pleading to be let out to play.

Which is... strange.

Because this isn't a game.

The warrior's sword comes from nowhere, slashing like a bladed wall, cutting short any giddiness. Asterion delivers a solid strike to her wrist and the sword clatters aside. Her own cry of pain meets her ears just as she registers the sting in her right upper arm.

For once, she agrees with the sounds emerging from her mask.

The corridor lurches and angles, about as off-kilter as she is. She retreats to her feet, but belligerence personified kicks at her from the floor, and Asterion's legs are out from under her.

The air yanks from her lungs as her back meets the stone floor like gravity just got vengeful.

This isn't the first time a mist-addled warrior has tried to kill her. They're just not usually so persistent.

Even from the ground, Asterion can appreciate the warrior's hypnotic physicality, her careful curation of movement for maximum impact.

But Asterion hasn't lasted this long through luck, and with a few fluid movements, she lands the warrior on her back again.

Asterion straddles her, anchoring her flexing arms to the ground. A challenge in hooves, but not impossible.

"Just *stop*," Asterion tries to tell her through a growl. "I'm trying to help you." Frustration vibrates through her body, her breath; even the corridor's lava-gullies.

There's a fire in the warrior's eyes that threats to burn this world down. Her torque blazes with her fury.

She won't give up, will she?

It'd be admirable if it weren't so frustrating. If it weren't making her and her surroundings tremble.

A calm mind paves the way for a balanced world. She knows this better than anyone. She wrote the equations, quantified the mechanics. But finding calm and balance is easier said than done when trying to save warriors whose blades are aimed at her.

She wants to save her, not fight her. But if the warrior won't let her...

Asterion retreats, taking cover in the mist, leaving the warrior to cool off, hoping she herself might, too.

37

TRAPPED

That night...

Asterion waits until the Minosian sun has set and the voyagers are presumably sleeping before she risks clear-up duty. This is the worst aspect of life here: the wounds, the empty-eyed faces, the visceral remains of lives departed.

If only she hadn't stumbled...

No. The Labyrinth would have found a way.

It always does.

She can dwell on that later. For now, all she can do is make the best of a bad situation.

As far as she can tell, the corridor's blades got three of the new arrivals, while two more were impaled on 'friendly' blades in the mist. One has died by their own blade. That happens a lot here, purposefully or otherwise. And the final departure bears no sign of a mortal wound, but there's no life in those eyes either. Probably a heart attack. Mix the shimmering mist with some preconceived fears and the horrors one's own mind can conjure... Her stomach sours. Too many times, she's witnessed the brave scream at nothing until their hearts give out.

She bows her head and offers the fallen a silent send-off. She's sorry their final moments were filled with fear and pain; sorry their paths ended here. And she hopes to Hades in the Heavens that they find a better place in the uncharted worlds of death.

Then she does what she must. She pats each body down, gathering anything and everything from pockets and satchels. She doesn't especially want weapons, and in any case she can't wield them in her arm braces without adapting them first, but she's learned the hard way not to leave such things littering the labyrinth.

Finding coins in the pockets of the fallen, she inspects them. Currency is useless here, of course, but these sorts of artefacts are her only clues to what might be happening on Minos, and the face imprinted on the coins, so similar to her own, tells her what she needs to know. Ari is alive and still on the throne.

Minosian coins are how Asterion discovered that, fourteen sun-orbits ago, Ariadne had taken the throne. It was a fair assumption, therefore, that Father had passed. She'd cried for a week at that, until she'd realised she was crying not because she'd lost her father, but because she'd never really had one in the first place.

She pockets the coins. Metals can always be repurposed.

Asterion steels herself with a deep breath. All of this is far from ideal. Every aspect is nauseating. The death. The scavenging. Dragging the bodies into the lava river for cremation. But another thing she'd discovered the hard way is that *hoping* a corpse will disappear only leads to poor sanitation. The sooner she deals with the departed, the better.

Does she wish she didn't have to? Of course. But wishes don't go far when corridors are armed with blades and soaked with mists that unravel minds.

⁺
∴

AFTER DEALING WITH THE FALLEN, she tracks the remaining voyagers. She keeps her distance; the mist's toxins will accentuate their perceptions for a while yet, and she has no desire to get caught in the crossfire. But she needs to make sure they're okay.

Once they're calm, maybe—*maybe*—they'll let her show them a safe path back to the gatehouse. And maybe they'll tell her why in the heavens they're here.

But the voyagers are not okay.

The tattooed man lies deathly still, abandoned in an outer corridor. His wounds are strange; his punctured torso isn't the work of the labyrinth. A *person* did this. Was it accidental or intentional? One puncture wound could be a grave error, but two...?

Do the voyagers know there's a murderer among them?

Her own breathing—still recovering from dragging the others to the lava river, the immense heat, and the horror of it all —turns all the more ragged at the thought.

For a moment she observes him, his still features contorted with the distress of his last moments. What did he do to deserve this? She doubts he did deserve this.

She bows her head for his final send-off, her hopes to Hades in the Heavens. But, as ever, it's best to get this over and done with. She anchors his feet beneath her armpits, quietly apologising to him for such an inadequate ending as she begins her slow, respectful procession.

Her back and shoulders strain, her arm muscles burn. At least her strict training regime is useful for something. Of course, she'd rather use her fitness to save lives than to cremate the dead.

She's trying.

A distant scuffling stops her and her breath. Did she hear something? Is it just the voyager's armour against the ground? The stupid mask obscures so much. It could even be the adjusting mechanisms within it.

With no further sounds, she continues.

As she tows the body, adjusting the boots in her grip, a shimmer of neon captures her attention. She lowers the man's foot to trace the luminous line. It must have been hidden beneath him before. She's read about thread like this, in both myths and medical journals. It shimmers. Raw power captured in woven fibres.

Following the trail of thread, Asterion looks up and her wonder is eclipsed by the warrior and her targeted scowl.

Okay.

Asterion knows a murderous look when she sees one.

This is a trap.

✛
˙•

Corridor turns and a lava river later...

By the time Asterion reaches the night-time skyscape of the meadow, she's exhausted.

She races along the sky-dome, dappled with light wells of moons and light bursts of stars. To get to the lake and meadow, she'll need to jump into the gravity stream, but first she needs to be in the right position to land near the shallows. She'd jump sooner if she could, but deep water plus the heavy mask is an equation for disaster. Not to mention that disturbing the deeper lake biome will summon the fierce fish that lurk there.

But jumping does nothing. Her legs are heavy with exertion, her lungs lost for breath. *Flummox.* She hasn't the energy left to leap high enough.

Not to panic, though. Well, no more than usual.

The chimney-like moon platforms are tall enough to make a difference, and there's one that's perfectly placed—by luck rather than design. She heaves herself up onto the chest-height circular platform, interrupting its light as she stands. She crouches, then leaps as high as her muscles will allow, elongating her body and diving up... up... up...

—Gravity flips—

Diving down... down... down...

...until she hits the water in an inelegant splash. There's no way to dive gracefully in a top-heavy bull mask. The mask's weight immediately drags her under as it fills with water, but she holds her breath, turning her body upright to wade to safety.

Breaking the surface near the shore, her chest aches as she waits long seconds until the mask drains, and she can finally claim some air. She drops to her knees, gasping, but at least now she can catch her breath in peace.

Once her limbs have recovered a little, she scythes some wheat and bundles it onto her back, before helping herself to a much-needed drink from the lake with her filtration-canister. It's a challenge with hooves and a mask, but not impossible. If she angles right, she can manage a flow that at least stems her thirst, though seldom quenches it.

For a moment, she just lets herself enjoy the babble of the stream, the gentle lap of water against the lakeshore, and the ripple and sway of silver grass and golden wheat. She looks up at the twinkling skyscape she designed—it always helps her find calm—and she reminds herself that this inner world is just hers. No-one has ever found their way beyond the lava river.

Warning prickles at the base of her neck, while goosebumps strain against the camouflage clay smeared on her skin— applied thickly enough that only the top layer has washed away during her brief swim in the lake.

There's commotion in her night sky, too distant, too shadow and mask-obscured to know the details, other than she's not alone.

The invasion sediments unease and panic in her stomach.

She keeps still. Perhaps they haven't seen her. Perhaps they'll go away? She looks to the reflection in the lake, staring until she finds the interrupted stars, and two glinting dots staring down at her. Even at this distance, there's no mistaking the warrior's hunter-like stillness.

She's not sure why she looks up at the warrior, because her body has already decided what's next—

Shirking the gathered wheat from her back, she bolts for the dark woodland and doesn't look back at the pursuing warrior until she's at the tree-line.

It's challenging terrain, but she knows which paths lead to boot-stealing bogs and how to double back without being seen.

But she's not as far ahead as she'd hoped to be when torch-light blazes between the trees behind her; exhausted by her exertions and the lake water weighing down her clothes.

The warrior is catching up.

Asterion takes cover in a hollow tree and waits. Her lungs burn. Her legs and neck throb dully beneath the veil of adrenaline. The wound on her upper arm is smarting, too. It's okay though. Once the warrior races past her, she'll sneak back to her fortress.

But the warrior doesn't charge past her. She stops; close enough to Asterion's hiding place that the contours of the warrior's tense sword-gripping arm are *right there*. All the warrior has to do is turn slightly and she'll be staring into Asterion's eyes. Or, her mask, at least. Her torque's glow through her mask's eye holes is sure to give her away at any moment.

The warrior extinguishes her torches, suspending everything in darkness. The tempo of her breath slows almost to silence, and Asterion stifles her own, too. Which is a challenge, given that she can practically feel her heart thumping against the mask's chest brace, as if demanding to be set free.

In all her time here, she's never fully acclimatised to the silence of the woodland and meadow biomes. There's the background hum of water in the meadow, and the engineered airflow that sways the trees, but the only living creatures are the skeletal fish—not her choice of wildlife. And with the lack of sporadic chirps and fluttering, the lack of *life* in this place, it can sometimes feel... empty.

She hadn't got far enough with her designs to specify what animals could exist here. And it's too late now.

Still, this world is not without wonder. Which must be what the warrior is discovering as, all around them the woodland fungi lights up in an entire spectrum of dancing, shimmering colour.

This is the world Asterion had wanted. The beauty of nature on display. She's never watched someone discover it before. And that's a sight more breathtaking than the midnight forest, as the warrior's scowl unfolds to something more open, and eyes that had been an inferno cool to curiosity. How can something so fierce turn so gentle? How can the warrior have a jawline so strong, when her skin looks so soft?

The wonders of the universe.

And all Asterion can do is watch, hoping the warrior won't turn any further, hoping she won't discover her. And—strangely —hoping she will.

Asterion holds her breath...

The warrior is so close—

But a sudden shove from the shadows sends the warrior splashing into the bog.

Asterion's heart rampages as the warrior whips around, as sharp eyes target only the culprit. The spear-wielding man in gold is apparently just as oblivious to Asterion's presence. He chuckles; the taunting sound aimed at the warrior—and Asterion is tempted to shove *him* into the mud. See how he likes it.

Unsubtle footsteps trip and trudge toward them. *Flummox.* More voyagers. She's already outnumbered, and on borrowed time.

Abandoning her plan to double back, she makes a break from the thicket, winds her way between bogs and tree roots, before springing off the sensor disguised as a rock that triggers the immense sliding doors to open. She just has to get through fast enough to close the intruders out.

Asterion barrels through the narrow opening into the ice chamber, but the hunting party is in fast pursuit. There's no way she can about-turn to trigger the closing mechanism without throwing herself into their path.

It's too risky. She has little choice now but to keep skidding into the chamber, while the voyagers tumble and slip all over the place.

When she glances over her shoulder, the golden man is elbowing his way past his fellow voyagers, while the warrior returns one of the group to their feet.

At least she's not out to get everyone.

Just Asterion, apparently.

Well-practised, Asterion reaches the sideways ice forest and its veil of fog swiftly and without incident, but her stomach swoops. That creaking roar... the chamber doors are closing. Unless the voyagers found the trigger—which is unlikely—that can only mean the Labyrinth is turning.

Flummox. She's so darn tired she's out of sync with it.

They're all in the wrong place at the wrong time.

It's only a matter of moments before the chamber has sloped so much that all the voyagers can do is obey gravity and plummet into the forest of ice.

Each cry and scream spears through Asterion like she's the one meeting a sharp and untimely end. This biome was never intended for death. None of them were.

But she should have been more careful. She should have been quicker. She should have paid more attention... If only she hadn't been so exhausted...

On her new horizontal of the fog-hazed ice forest floor, her own beastly reflection taunts her from a dozen directions.

She has no idea if any of the voyagers survived the fall. She hopes they did, but she also has no desire to cross paths with them right now if all they're intent on doing is chasing her with weapons.

As she winds between the sheer, reflective tree trunks, seeking out the tree that's a hidden door to the space between the labyrinth layers, a flash of gold snags in her vision. Suspect movements, too.

The golden man is levering a beast trap open, obscuring it in the ice fog. Is the trap for her?

Best leave him to it. Let the labyrinth and time deal with him.

Asterion tracks down her tree; always a challenge in the mirror maze, even when she knows where she's going. She'd designed it to be fun, a place to play chase and hide-and-seek. She'd never imagined it devolving into an actual hunting ground.

She reaches for the ice-branch that will trigger her escape route, but pauses.

Is the trap for her? Or is he the one who killed the tattoo-faced man? Is he a danger to the others? Have any others survived? Has the warrior made it into the ice forest? Does she know his nature? Is he a danger to her, too?

So many questions.

All interrupted by the *snap* of metal and a bone-scraping scream shuddering the snow-laden ice branches.

Asterion's gasp meets the air in a plume. That's a depth of pain that cannot be forged. Whoever it is, she can't leave them to the mercy of the golden man. Asterion is quick to retrace her steps to where she'd seen the trap be set.

She peers between frozen branches, careful to not let a wayward reflection give her away. And there, between the cluster of reflective tree trunks, is the warrior.

Her every ragged breath tugs at Asterion, and she loses her own when the golden man closes in behind the warrior, his spear angled downwards, kill-ready.

Without a plan, without a further thought, Asterion launches out from hiding. Not close enough to stop him, but enough to divert his attention to her.

The sudden alarm in the golden man's eyes, and his gasp, lets her know he fears the Minotaur. And, in this instance, she's glad of it.

She solidifies her stance to let him know she's serious.

The warrior's laugh distracts her. It's not cruel, but amused. Which is... a strange reaction. Asterion can only assume the warrior is suffering some pain-induced delirium.

A sudden movement from the golden man—

Asterion twists on instinct. His spear cuts through her left shoulder, ripping a roar from her. *Confound and flummox.* She should have been more focused on the spear than the warrior.

The spear is lodged in the ice-tree behind her, so close the spear's blade still cuts against her—her shoulder flaring— tracking her blood into the jagged lines of smashed ice.

She buckles to one knee, pressing one hoofed hand to her injury. The golden man punches the air in celebration, shouting something that sounds like, "I told her I'd get you!"

But maybe the blood roaring in her ears is playing tricks,

and the mask, too. Either way, she can't think about those words right now.

He still has his broadsword, but he won't be able to get close enough to use it without going through her mask's horns. And they're as sharp as they look. So sharp they stab pain in her gut even when she thinks of it.

And that's not her only weapon.

She snarls, tugging her scythe free from its satchel loop as she stands between him and his lost spear. His unsettled gaze darts between her, the scythe and his spear. Not so tough without it, is he?

Undeniable fear in his eyes, he retreats into the mirror maze with a sneer, and Asterion treads closer to the warrior bleeding into the snow. As she nears, the warrior claws at the fog-obscured ground, her nerve-scouring cries of pain and fury aimed, undeniably, at Asterion.

The warrior puts up a good inner fight, but when her body gives out, when she sinks to the ground in the comparative calm of unconsciousness, Asterion is glad of it.

For the warrior's sake.

38

WOUNDS

As Asterion mixes a new batch of numbing tincture for the warrior's wounds, she can't help but be amused by the bull-headed soft toy wielding a little sword and the most serious of expressions.

Is that supposed to be her?

It begs the question: *Why is there a depiction of her?* But she might not be brave enough to ask. *Don't ask questions you don't want to know the answer to.* How many times had Father scolded her with those words as a child?

Still, the soft toy has a certain charm... It might have more if it weren't covered in labyrinth grime and bog-fungus goo. Once she's cleaned the warrior's wounds, she'll sort herself and the grumpy soft toy, too.

Asterion doesn't make a habit of searching through the belongings of people who are still alive. Which, now that she thinks about it, isn't the boast she wants it to be. But in this instance, she has reason. The luminous thread the warrior had been carrying could be of significant benefit to her right now.

If there's a chance she has it...

But it doesn't seem to be amongst her belongings. She must

have lost it somewhere in the labyrinth. Possibly in the woodland bogs?

The warrior's breathing changes, almost imperceptibly.

She's awake.

Flummox. Asterion had hoped she'd remain unconscious for what needs to happen next.

The warrior is woozy, as is to be expected, but fighting it. She's rigidly watching Asterion. She's gearing up to something, Asterion can tell. The warrior, in her delirium, isn't as subtle as she perhaps thinks she is.

Bracing herself, Asterion steps from the shadows. But the warrior doesn't lunge at her. Instead, her mouth opens in... confusion? Surprise?

She calls Asterion "Princess" in Athenian, then adds something Asterion doesn't understand. She's not had much opportunity to use the language. There's a note of playful familiarity in the warrior's words that's incongruous given their previous encounters.

Though... Asterion does like it.

In the light from the flaming hearth, the warrior's blue eyes twinkle like azurite. Is it strange, Asterion's urge to gaze into them? And there's that shiver again, like the one she'd experienced when she'd been pressed against the warrior in the bladed corridor.

It's possible these sensations are nothing to do with faulty heat-gullies...

She can't help her bewildered head tilt as the warrior rattles off several incomplete—and incomprehensible—sentences. *What* and *How* and *Princess*... What in the heavens is she talking about? Asterion sets her pestle and mortar aside, pulls her chair to the side of the bed and perches to inspect the trap, distracted briefly by the warrior staring at her arms. Is there blood seeping through her bandages, or something?

Never mind that.

They really need to get on with removing the trap from the warrior's leg. It's not the first of its kind to make its way within these walls. Asterion was victim to one herself, once. If she hadn't been quick enough to shove a hoof into the snapping jaws, it would've sliced her leg clean off. As it was, the infection nearly did her in—which is why she needs to get on with cleaning the warrior's wounds. It's frustrating about the luminous thread. If it is what Asterion thinks it is, it would have been so useful.

When Asterion reaches for the trap, along with a wooden lever to make her intention clear, the warrior's clenched jaw says she's as ready as she'll ever be.

As smoothly as she's able, Asterion levers the trap open, prying it from the warrior's shin. The warrior's scream frays Asterion's nerves, as if the metal teeth are biting into her own flesh. Soon, but not soon enough, she casts the hideous contraption aside, cursing the heavens and beyond that such things exist.

The warrior is trying to be still, she can tell. Asterion tries to tell her that pain is temporary, and that she'll be okay, but is that actually the truth? She hopes so. The warrior doesn't understand her, anyway.

Asterion tries to seek permission to apply the balm, but the warrior's azurite eyes are accusing as she gasps something about "killed"? Her vitriol seems aimed at the bull mask on the dressing table. Its sliced exterior isn't pretty, but Asterion's been too focused on tending to the warrior to take the mask to her workshop for repair.

Her insides twist. She wants to tell the warrior she's sorry about what happened to the voyagers in the ice forest, that she didn't intend for anyone to get hurt, but the Athenian words evade her. She reaches out with the balm, but the warrior claws away from her, her words pummelling her as a mix of terror and disgust contort her features.

The warrior wrestles free from her restraints, an agonised cry tearing from her as she knocks her injured leg. The restraints had been loose, intended only to stop her from startling and hurting herself. *Stop this, you're hurting yourself.* That's what Asterion would say if she could remember her Athenian studies.

But the warrior tumbles heavily from the bed before Asterion can stop her, landing with another splutter of agony that makes Asterion's nerves spark and the chamber's fire-torches flare.

The warrior flails upright through pure bone-headed determination. But then she slips, planting weight on her injured leg. She buckles to the floor and promptly passes out.

It's not a great start.

But it's still not the worst interaction Asterion's ever had.

✛

WHILE THE WARRIOR is lost to her fever, Asterion cools her brow with a cloth. Her skin is smooth, light brown like smoky quartz, with occasional marks and divots that could be old blade scars. Her nose is a little notched—a historical break, perhaps?

Asterion's fingers twitch. The warrior's short hair is as dark and inviting as artists' charcoal.

The warrior's features strain with whatever the fever amplified by mist-toxins is dragging her through. Asterion adjusts the cool cloth on the warrior's brow but refrains from trying to soothe her nightmares with her touch.

She cleans her wounds and applies the healing tincture, refusing to linger over calf muscles that would make any sculptor swoon. It wouldn't be right; not when Asterion's breath keeps lodging in her chest, her cheeks heating like she's the one in the throes of fever.

She's just... overreacting. She's been shut away for two-thirds of her life. Of course she's experiencing baffling feelings for the first person within her fortress.

When the warrior settles, Asterion retreats to her workshop with the disgusting—in all senses—trap, setting it on her workbench to deal with later. She could do without having to poke at it, but she'll need to clean it for hygiene's sake. First, though, she needs to finish tending to the warrior.

But before she can wash her hands and source needle, thread and bandages, commotion echoes along the fortress corridor. As she peers out, Bok-bok charges toward her as if fetching her, or warning her something is amiss.

Bok-bok leads her towards the fortress gateway, but Asterion only has to follow the clumsy clattering to locate the wayward warrior. She'd assumed her recuperating guest would sleep for hours yet. With such a severe leg injury, she hadn't thought the warrior would want to leave the bedchamber.

Asterion could have locked her inside the bedchamber, but it just didn't seem necessary or right. She knows all too well what it's like to be locked away on someone else's decision, and she wouldn't wish that on anyone.

But what is the warrior doing, clawing at the door? Is she trying to leave?

Bok-bok hasn't been subtle in squawking her feelings about this stranger, but the warrior now has a burned forearm to add to her collection of injuries. Guilt slinks through Asterion; she should have checked Bok-bok was tucked away in the coop, or at least out in the garden.

Any charm the warrior might possess currently evades her as she wildly swings her sword at Asterion. The only bright side of her guest's delirium is that she currently has no accuracy whatsoever.

Asterion lets the vile behaviour slide; the mist's toxins must be playing the warrior's fear response like a V-iolin. In any case, it's not long before pain or fever wins its tussle with the warrior and she sinks to the ground again as if dragged by invisible tethers.

Hopefully, she'll be in a better mood when she wakes.

+
∴

The next day...

The warrior is awake, and Asterion almost drops the tray she's balancing at the look of longing her guest aims her way. That look... it's for the jug of water and the steaming bowl of soup on her tray. Of course it is; the warrior must be beyond thirsty. But for one stomach-swooping moment, Asterion's breath fumbles in her chest.

Now, though, the warrior's stillness prods her more evolved instincts.

She's up to something.

As Asterion navigates the tray—repurposed from the shield of a past voyager—toward the warrior's bedside, she's never felt so *watched*. She adjusts her posture. Is this normally how she stands? Her muscles are all tight; she hasn't cooled down and stretched as she typically would after a dash through the labyrinth.

And why is the warrior staring at her like that? Like Asterion's been the one chasing *her*?

Something glimmers on the floor near the bed. It looks like broken glass. Did the warrior knock over her drinking vessel? Where are the rest of the shards?

Vitriol glints in the warrior's eyes, matching the fallen shards. *Why?* What did Asterion do to her?

She hesitates just a step away from the bedside table.

But it's too late—

The tray in her hands upends, the hot soup sailing past her. The warrior grabs Asterion's shirt, dragging her closer as she swipes at her with her dagger of glass—

Asterion deflects the attack with her tray—

Her annoyance flares in line with the warrior's hiss of pain. *Enough of this nonsense.* She throws herself on top of the warrior, anchoring her hips with her thighs as she pins her wrist to the pillow. If the warrior's hips can't move, she can't kick. And she looks like she wants to do more than kick.

Does the warrior think she's still in the thick of the mist, fighting the labyrinth? Have the toxins soaked deep into her system? Or does her grudge have nothing to do with the mists?

The warrior's other hand is wedged between their bodies, still clutching Asterion's shirt. If she wants to tussle, they can tussle. Asterion would prefer they stop, though…

She increases the pressure of her grip about the warrior's wrist until the warrior's fist loosens and the glass shard she's clutching clatters to the floor. That flash in the warrior's eyes—is it frustration, or something more dangerous? And why, with the warrior's weapon now on the floor, does Asterion feel like she's the one who's been disarmed?

She should put some distance between them. She shouldn't want to be closer than she already is. It's utterly irrational, this magnetic pull towards a person who's not only on an inexplicable mission to do her harm, but is currently covered in a bog-fungus slime that will soon turn repellent.

There are so many reasons to retreat, and yet—

The warrior wriggles her hand free from between them.

Asterion grabs it and presses it to the pillow, canting herself forward... and closer still.

Murderous. Bog fungus. Two good reasons to not put her body —especially her nose—any closer. What's happened to all her survival instincts?

It's tactical, keeping the warrior pinned like this. There's no knowing what she might do otherwise. But Asterion can't keep this up forever. And tactical pinning has never felt... like *this*. She's never wanted to stay straddling her opponent indefinitely, breathing the same air, pressing so close her heartbeat is joined by another.

It's making her skin tingle in a way that... well, it's not unpleasant.

And it should be. All things considered.

The warrior lets out a gasp so gentle, she probably hadn't even heard it leave her lips.

But Asterion heard it. Her whole body buzzes with it.

Beneath Asterion, the warrior's muscles uncoil and her grimace unwinds to something... different. What does that almost-smile mean? It's not calming, but it's not cruel, either.

Is she enjoying this, too?

Talk about mixed messages...

It's not Asterion's imagination that the warrior is leaning a little closer, her eyes washing over Asterion's face, her throat. She looks... intrigued? It ignites something in Asterion; something that stutters electric through her torque, giving her away.

How *embarrassing*.

The warrior shifts beneath her, pressing her hips up. *Oh, come on. That has to be on purpose.* At the intimate pressure, exhales and moans tangle between them. If her torque wasn't stuttering before... The unfamiliar heat sparks beneath Asterion's skin, branching through her like electricity in water.

Perhaps *this* is why people write and read so many fictions about intimate proximity.

Because, yes, this is a sensation she would pursue.

But not like this.

Asterion releases the warrior's wrists. She can't be having these *thoughts* while restraining the person who's inspiring them. Especially when that person can't be trusted not to turn a drinking glass into a weapon.

But suddenly none of that matters, because her nostrils are trying to collapse in on themselves as they signal the awful truth.

The bog-fungus has turned.

"Urgh. You smell like olfactory evil," Asterion tells the warrior, somehow managing not to gag. "Oh, Hades in the Heavens. I might have to cut off my nose. Snort soap. Oh, *confound* me. It's even stinging my eyes."

But even more than the stench, it's the daggers in the warrior's eyes that turn the lava-gully heat in Asterion's veins to an ice forest chill.

She needs to direct this oscillating energy somewhere, or the Labyrinth will start faulting. Which is why she scoops up the source of her problems and deposits her in the wash chamber. Would she have been less commandeering about it if the warrior hadn't been so persistently vile? Yes. But now she can sort out her stench, and Asterion can have a few minutes to recalibrate without an attractive but unwieldy guest trying to stick her with a blade.

It all has her muttering as she bundles up the bedsheets to wash—or burn—before cleansing her hands and arms in the kitchen and stopping by her workshop to retrieve the crutch she'd made a few sun-orbits ago. Finally, she returns to the bedchamber to put fresh sheets on the bed and source clean clothes for the warrior, being careful to select trousers that won't press her injured leg. The ill-tempered stranger might be annoying, but Asterion's not a monster. She wants her to be comfortable.

The warrior's satchel is among her belongings. She might need things from there, so Asterion takes it and the crutch and braves the wash chamber.

While Asterion has been busy, the warrior has managed to stand beneath the water cascade. Her eyes are closed as she runs soap through her hair, coal-black turned to an anthracite lustre by the water.

But Asterion's not staring. No.

Should she say something, let the warrior know she's there? She's the calmest Asterion's seen her, though she winces as her fingers press the tiny cut in her eyebrow. *Really? Some* warrior *you are.*

But as Asterion's gaze drifts across the warrior's naked form, all chiselled lines and glistening smoothness, those words take on a different tone:

Some warrior you are.

The thought surprises her. She's seen a naked body before, of course. She has mirrors. But the sight of her own body has never made her feel... curious? Is that the right word?

She wants both to be closer to the stranger, and to run away. How in the heavens does that make sense?

And why is her heart thumping like it's hiking up a labyrinth-tilt? Why are her cheeks warm? And what is that fluttering in her stomach, and lower?

Channelling the unfamiliar, baffling feelings into helpfulness, she hangs the warrior's satchel on a hook and sets the crutch within reach against the wall. She's never read anything about the proper etiquette for when a guest is naked in your water cascade and you want to observe them but also suspect that would be creepy. So she makes herself scarce.

39

NOT ARIADNE

With her tray of medical supplies, Asterion returns to the bedchamber. She strides in because it's her room and it's been too many sun-orbits since she's had any reason to knock on a door—and almost fumbles her tray. *Again.*

Carrying a tray should not be this challenging. It's just that—

Undershorts.

Asterion has already seen the warrior naked, albeit partially cloaked in steam. But somehow, the sight of the undershorts—the ones Asterion had left for her—skimming the jut of her hip bones, is more than her mind can handle.

It's a strange reaction to clothing. Perhaps it's to do with the flex of the warrior's stomach muscles. And from there it's only a short upward journey to—

The warrior clears her throat.

Eyes. A short upward journey *to her eyes.* Into which Asterion is very much staring now.

The warrior says something in her lyrical Athenian lilt, but it's her raised eyebrow that communicates her outright smugness.

Well... fair enough.

Asterion's cheeks are hotter than the Seven Suns, and her sparking torque is only fuelling them. How long has she been staring? She zeroes in on her tray, keeping as much distance as possible from the warrior as she sets it on the bedside table.

"You look..." *Distracting.* "...clean."

After pulling on a vest, the warrior is trying to pull her clean trousers on over her injured leg, and making it look like the most challenging task in the universe. Asterion strides around the bed to her. "Here, let me help—" but her guest recoils so fast she almost pings off the bed.

Asterion pauses, raising her hands in placation. She hopes the warrior can see in her eyes that she only wants to help.

The warrior's assessment of her seems to stretch a million sun-orbits—but ultimately, she nods. A grudging nod, but it's the permission Asterion needs to kneel and help guide the trouser leg past her injury.

"Stand," she tells the warrior, as gently as she's able.

This is progress, isn't it?

But then the warrior touches her shoulder, and Asterion flinches. The warrior snaps back to hostility, grabbing for her neck.

And within a half-second, Asterion has her pinned to the bed, disappointment sinking through her bones. *Seriously? Does she never stop?*

The warrior cries out, and Asterion grits her teeth. She hadn't meant to knock the warrior's leg, but what does she expect when she keeps climbing out of the cooking pot and into the flames?

"What is it about me that's so terrifying?" Asterion's voice cracks a little. *Don't cry. Don't cry.* "What am I doing that's so darn offensive to you?"

She might as well be speaking through the mask for all the

stranger's understanding. Communication still isn't her strong suit, apparently.

But the warrior seems to simmer down a little at her outburst. Asterion lets go of her wrists, which is precisely when the warrior discovers she's back in restraints. This prompts a grumble as the warrior observes her bindings, though she settles down again at Asterion's exasperated huff.

Asterion can't trust her, but they need to change her bandages and check her injuries. She eyes her guest pointedly. "Shall we try this again?"

To her surprise and relief, the warrior nods.

Asterion unwinds the warrior's leg bandage, hoping her wary eye asserts *Don't you dare try anything*. The stitches are holding. The wound is red raw, but the tincture will calm it. She seeks permission by showing the dish of tincture. At the nod of approval, Asterion sets about applying it, as gently as she's able. But the first touch to a wound is always the worst. It always takes a moment to sink in.

The stranger tenses but does nothing reactive or stupid. She seems to relax a little after that, and Asterion does too. The warrior calms more after testing the flex of her leg muscles, though Asterion's nerves bristle in sympathy at her wince.

It's a deep wound, but her guest is mostly intact. Hopefully the warrior's patience is better than her ability to trust, otherwise she'll have a long and unnecessarily arduous journey back to health.

As Asterion moves on to re-dressing her forearm burn—*thanks, Bok-bok*—the warrior says something to her with a smirk and a raspy, teasing lilt. Is she making fun of Asterion? Trying to provoke her? Asterion's previously learned Athenian is waking enough that she understands the words "restraints"—thanks to the more... *adventurous* intimate fictions her library houses—and "dinner first."

It's not Asterion's fault her guest decorated the floor with her dinner, is it? It's only when Asterion is making that point clear with a nod to where the soup had landed that the joke she's joining in on has her cheeks burning. Because the joke is a lot like that thing she's read about called *flirting*.

And it has her all squirmy inside.

Perhaps it's because in the fictions she's read, the ones she hadn't fully understood but enjoyed all the same, the characters involved had a foundation of trust. And the terrain she and this stranger share is faulty at best.

But all the warrior seems to care about in this moment is that Asterion understands Athenian.

Keen to get these interactions over with, and oddly drawn to prolonging them, Asterion shrugs and moves on to soothe and re-dress the warrior's injured palm, before giving the same treatment to the cut in a disbelieving eyebrow. Why is her guest staring at her, mouth agape, like she's more puzzling than a Minosian maze? It's enough, at this proximity, for her to seek further permission. And with the responding nod, she continues.

Her pounding heart must be from the residual angst from their scuffle. Nothing to do with her fingers tracing over the warrior's skin.

The fight seems to have melted from the warrior's posture now, and Asterion is glad of it—for her own sake as much as the warrior's. Tearing through a labyrinth and wrestling its visitors in failed attempts to save them, then towing the fallen to their rest—not to mention dragging a well-built warrior to the safety of her fortress—is all exceptionally exhausting. If she had a tether, Asterion would be at the end of it by now.

When the warrior asks, "Why are you doing this?" Asterion understands the words but not the meaning. Because the answer is so obvious, why is the question needed in the first place?

"You—hurt." *Urgh*. Her Athenian accent is terrible.

She's not going to try to communicate the more confusing aspects: her curiosity, the electricity that sparks within her when she looks upon the warrior, the inexplicable magnetism. Chances are that her sparking torque is communicating that for her.

She can admit it's a design flaw: putting on display the emotions that neither of them have asked for. That annoys her enough she doesn't think twice about letting the warrior loose from the headboard.

The warrior's eyes meet hers. *Should she look away?*

"You're not Princess Ariadne." The warrior's words punch the air from Asterion's lungs.

No, she's not Ariadne. Everyone—*almost* everyone—always told her she should be more like her sister... but the irrefutable fact is: *she is not Ariadne.*

But... wait...

That must mean the warrior knows—or knows *of*—her...

"Ariadne? You know Ariadne? Is she okay?"

"Uh..." The warrior's utterance seems to be from lack of understanding, rather than hesitance.

Asterion's frustration is accompanied by disquiet. Between the two, her thoughts race through an entire maze:

What if Ariadne isn't okay? What can Asterion even do about it, locked away in here? Yes, she can get to the outer gate-house, and technically she has a whole range of astro-helmets to choose from. But astro-helmets and a bull mask do not mesh. And unless the warrior has a sky-ship waiting for her...

And all that would mean leaving the Labyrinth...

On the other hand...

What if Ari *is* okay? What would that mean in relation to Asterion's situation?

Well... that's a path she's not willing to—

"You're... her twin?" The warrior gestures to her.

Asterion scoffs. "I—her—twin—she—*my*—twin." Being a twin should at the very least be equal, shouldn't it?

The warrior mutters something and raises her hands in placation, with more snark than Asterion thinks appropriate. Still, at least she's not trying to stab her anymore.

Asterion has so many questions. She might not want to know the answers to a lot of them, but there are some she can't contain: "Is Ariadne happy? Is she making her mark on Minos? Is the mark she makes... good? What is Minos like under her rule?"

The warrior huffs, and Asterion's shoulders sag. She'll need to brush up on her Athenian. It's just her luck, isn't it? The first person to survive the labyrinth, the first person here in her fortress, and there's a *flummoxing* language barrier between them. And a personality one, too.

Out in the labyrinth, the warrior had been brave. She'd taken the lead into dangerous corridors, been kind in helping her fellow voyagers. But all she's done with Asterion is attack.

The warrior fires an abrupt question at her and Asterion repeats the only words she'd caught—'the' and 'fuck...?'—as the warrior hoists up her trousers with an awkward wriggle. It'd pull a laugh from Asterion if the warrior's expression weren't so thunderous. And if Asterion wasn't so... dejected.

Asterion stops her repetition when the words click into the grooves of her memory. It's a crass term for the things the characters in her intimate fiction books get up to. Asterion scowls: why are her cheeks hot again? Reading those stories never makes her blush, so why is it happening now?

"—stop—?"

Asterion understands that one word in the warrior's latest unhappy tirade and promptly steps back, though she has no idea what she's done to deserve those words or their tone. What is she meant to be stopping? The warrior keeps berating her, the unfamiliar words too swift in their smarting delivery. Asterion can only rub her neck to channel her nerves as she tries to piece it together, but the only ones she can understand are 'why' and 'here'.

The warrior points to each of them, then at their general surroundings. *Why did you bring me here?*

Asterion doesn't have enough Athenian words to express that the metal-jaw trap she's just gone to considerable effort to remove from the warrior's leg, had been set by the golden man. And that she suspects he'd been responsible for the tattoo-faced man's death, too. For all of this, she can only think of one word that might fit. She gestures to the window, hoping the warrior understands she means *out there*.

"Monster."

There's a pause before the warrior erupts into joyless laughter that borders on maniacal, followed by another barrage of Athenian. Asterion doesn't get the joke. How strange, to be so *cut* by a language so lyrical.

From the onslaught, she extracts one word:

Kill.

'You kill everyone'? No, that can't be right.

"Perhaps, I... not understand?"

The warrior's sigh is more than frustrated. The next words Asterion deciphers are 'not Ariadne' and 'who the fuck are you?'

"Who...?" Asterion repeats. There's *that* word again... What in the heavens is the warrior talking about? Asterion wants to help. She does. But she just doesn't know how.

Missing the mark, as ever.

The warrior is right. She's not Ariadne. Ariadne would know what to do, what to say. Ariadne would have a translation tincture soothing her ears and sweetening her tongue, most probably, too.

No, no. She won't let those negative thoughts in. Asterion is who she is, and on the inside she is perfect.

With the deepest fortifying breath she can manage, she musters her best Athenian accent:

"My name is Asterion."

And she wants to be defiant, bold and sure... but the furrows in her confidence, etched by her formative sun-orbits of being a disappointment, they run as deep as the labyrinth's corridors.

Ariadne. Is that who the warrior hoped to find?

"Confound and flummox," she mumbles, and shows herself out.

Because no. She is not Ariadne.

40

ENOUGH

Sorting the belongings of the fallen is necessary, but Asterion has had enough. She hates this part. Dealing with the bodies is worst of all, but going through their possessions is a task that twists her stomach and heart together in the worst of ways.

But if life within these walls has taught her one thing, it's to be *resourceful*. You never know when shirt fibres might need to be repurposed as surgical thread; when your boots might split and need to be replaced. It's better to gather first and find a use later than to throw away what's already been created.

That doesn't make the sorting easy, though. She often has to clean the items of blood and grime first. Even the weapons need cleaning before she can repurpose them into tools to tend the garden, or to keep the Labyrinth ticking over.

But it's the keepsakes that are most gut-wrenching. It's those that draw out her tears. Because each treasure of the fallen conveys a piece of their humanity. An image of a loved one, or a family portrait—a still life or action shot within a shard, in ether or print—gives a glimpse of their life beyond these walls.

The people who enter this place are always serious, scared,

joyless. But out there are people who care about them, people who will be wracked with grief when their loved one never returns.

It all makes Asterion want to claw free of this place and roar in the face of whoever was responsible for turning her perfect world into a death trap. And made her the monster within it.

Was it disgruntled Constructionists? Was it Father?

Ari?

No. She can't think about that.

Her chest aches with the sobs shaking her foundations. Even the Labyrinth groans with her distress. At least with her tears, the fortress garden is getting some hydration; an unintended quirk of the alignment between her torque and the Labyrinth.

She reels in her sobs long enough to blow her nose. The hairs on her neck prickle. There's something prodding at the edge of her awareness. A shadow? Her own instinct for survival?

She turns. Blurred through her tears, the warrior is *right there*. The lamp light stutters. Usually, she's better at sensing when someone's within her orbit. It's an instinct that's kept her alive. But she's so frazzled right now, everything's a bit off.

The warrior is gripping a sword in one hand, her crutch in the other. It's the sword that makes her purpose clear.

But she's just standing there. Staring.

Exhausting though it may be, Asterion doesn't begrudge anyone lost in the labyrinth and the mist for overreacting when they encounter her in the bull mask, even when all she's trying to do is help. But the warrior must be free of the mist toxins by now, yet she's still gaping at her like Asterion's murdered her family...

Oh, Hades in the Heavens. She hasn't, has she?

She's never wanted to hurt anyone. Never. But over the sun-orbits she's discovered, in the most visceral ways, that when faced with the choice between a stranger's life and her own, she will do what she must to survive.

She tries to tell herself that's on them. That they might have been suffering the mist's toxins, but when she'd run from them, they chose to chase.

And there have been times, too, where she's ended a person's life to end their suffering. If there had been any other way... But without the resources or knowledge to deal with such complex injuries...

But such details are likely irrelevant to a broken-hearted loved one on a mission of vengeance.

Is that why the warrior is here? Is that why she's been so aggressive?

Renewed tears stream down Asterion's cheeks, and—for the briefest of moments—she resigns herself to whatever the warrior decides for her. Because choosing yet another life over hers is too much.

But. No. She's survived this long. She's not giving up now. She's not letting some ill-informed, bad-tempered stranger decide her fate.

With one solid slap, Asterion sends the warrior's sword clattering to the floor. She shoves her away, but unbalances herself too in the process. Asterion lands on top of her, and the warrior huffs with irritation.

Why in the heavens do they keep ending up this close?

The warrior's body exudes a welcome warmth; the kind Asterion wants to lean into. How many of those who lost their lives to the labyrinth had known the heat of another person?

Her chest aches. It's been so long since she hugged anyone; since anyone hugged her. The last time she'd tried... she hadn't understood that it wasn't a game...

Renewed sobs vibrate within her chest, threatening to unleash. She could really do with a hug—

Something blunt jabs against her ribs. So lost in her grief, she hadn't noticed the warrior reaching for the weaponry pile.

"What more do you want from me?" The words burst from Asterion between sobs, as she buckles and rests her tired head against the warrior's shoulder.

She expects sharp agony... but it doesn't come. When they both look down at the weapon pressed beneath her sternum, Asterion can only blink in confusion.

The warrior has perhaps had one too many knocks to the head, or she has a strange and dark sense of humour, because who in their right mind tries to murder someone with *a spoon*?

Also, perhaps Asterion needs to assess her sorting abilities, because how did that get into the weaponry pile?

The absurdity of it almost eclipses her devastation, but in her inner battle between laughter and tears, her tears win out. Because all Asterion had wanted was to help the warrior heal and be safe. And, after everything, the warrior is *still* trying to hurt her.

What kind of monster does the warrior think her to be if *this* is the thanks she gets?

If this is what it's like to be around people, Asterion just wants to be left alone.

41

TRUCE?

Eyes sore from a sleepless night of tears, her neck aching from her makeshift chair-bed—all because there's an ungrateful, murderous stranger in her *actual* bed—Asterion isn't in the best mood.

But she's determined to treat her guest like neither of them are monsters, in the hope it'll turn out to be true. So she sets out breakfast at the banquet table, preparing the place nearest the doorway for her guest so as not to overtax her injured leg.

Whoever adjusted her designs of the banquet hall was either being kind or cruel. Kind to give her more space; cruel to remind her that she's alone in it.

But in this instance, a bit of distance is welcome. At least then the stranger can't swipe at her and Asterion won't have to land on her. Again.

When Asterion notices the warrior loitering in the entrance-way, her stomach doesn't knot, exactly, but it's ready to.

At least she's not brandishing any weapons today. That's a good start. But Asterion isn't about to let her guard down. There's a tension in the air, the kind Asterion experiences when trying to unstick a labyrinth mechanism, where failure promises catastrophe. She hopes she doesn't get crushed by this faulting dynamic.

Her guest's demeanour is calmer than it has been. As she takes the offered seat without event, Asterion keeps her sigh of relief to herself. When the warrior's wary eyes search the table in front of her, Asterion chuckles to herself. She hopes the stranger has a sense of humour.

With a deep breath for courage, Asterion stands and takes her time in approaching, keeping her guest in her sights in case she returns to being an outright nightmare.

Determined eyes, raw blue topaz, watch her like she's a puzzle to be solved. By the time she reaches the warrior's end of the table, the warrior has done nothing stupid. Maybe there's an unspoken truce? Maybe Asterion breaking down into an inconsolable wreck has shown the warrior she's no threat? Or perhaps the warrior has just had enough of ending up underneath her.

Asterion suppresses a smile. "You smell much better than bog fungus today."

The warrior narrows her eyes a little, but there's no sign of hostility in them. Asterion enjoys dramatically placing a spoon in front of her before backing away from said spoon like it's something terrifying. She amuses herself at the very least, and the dropped jaw of affront and the tint in the warrior's cheeks are their own reward.

She doesn't even mind that the warrior's response is simply to stare at her as she returns to her seat.

"Eat," she tells her guest, though why the corner of the warrior's mouth should be twitching like that at that simple word is a mystery. But soon the warrior is eating like she's trying to dig through the bowl, while Asterion tries not to gawp at her.

Table manners have never been high on Asterion's list of priorities. As a child, she'd been more interested in trying to solve Minos's wealth imbalances and civilian food shortages than learning how to use royal cutlery.

Asterion's face must be a picture of disproval, but that's mostly at the hypocrisy of royal standards rather than at the warrior's manners. Though, etiquette aside, there must be the need to *breathe* between mouthfuls?

A similar thought must strike the warrior, because she chokes a little before slowing her pace.

Usually Asterion eats in relative silence. Mostly because there are only so many conversations you can have with yourself. And a chicken. But now that there's someone here... *Conversation.* She can do this...

"You have—name?" Asterion grimaces. The last thing she wants is to torture her first ever guest with her inaccurate Athenian pronunciation and fumbling sentence structure. She'll have to work on that.

"Theseus."

Theseus. It has a certain Athenian lyricism to it.

Not sure what else to say, Asterion continues eating her porridge. She could tell the warrior that the Athenian lyricism of her name is much more pleasant than her behaviour has been so far. Or that she's glad the warrior is no longer trying to murder her. But she decides silence is best.

She'd make a joke about them starting off on the wrong foot, but she's certain the warrior won't understand, and perhaps it's a little too soon to be making jokes about limbs.

She should ask the warrior why she's here, and what her problem is... but what's the point when the question and answer are likely to be misunderstood, by one or both of them.

Perhaps the warrior would prefer silence?

"Why... you wear... mask?" is what Asterion absorbs from the warrior's next utterance.

And she doesn't know how to answer a question that's so

much bigger than her. Why does she wear the mask? Because someone decided she would? Because they altered her Labyrinth designs to contain her, and made the mask a condition of her limited freedom?

How much of her life has she spent trying not to think about that?

She must take too long to answer, because the warrior acts out the same question. The warrior is curious... and it always calms Asterion to understand how things fit together. And now that the look in her guest's eyes... in Theseus's eyes... has dialled down from murderous to merely suspicious, hopefully it can evolve to something more comfortable.

If Asterion helps her to understand this place, maybe that will help?

"Follow me," she tells Theseus, and leads the way to the entrance hall. The warrior aims her annoyance at the mask now, instead of Asterion. As she inspects the mask, her body rigid like she's expecting a battle, she has questions that Asterion doesn't understand. Asterion demonstrates the camouflage clay and the warrior's eyes seem interested. In her usual routine, she stretches her neck and shoulders, readying herself.

Even though she hates wearing it, she demonstrates the mask to Theseus, showing her that it's a key. Because that's the most literal answer to Theseus's question of why she wears the mask: *because she has to.* If she wants to leave the fortress, she has no choice. And the only way to remove it again is by returning to the keyholes in the fortress gatehouse.

The mask's straps tighten automatically, mechanically, about her chest, her shoulders, her neck and temples—always a couple of notches beyond comfort, compressing the breath in her lungs. Over the sun-orbits, the mask has adjusted to her changing physical form. Though she's grown bigger, it fits her still.

If only the discomfort of the mask were merely physical—but even putting it on is a test of mental fortitude. Aside from being weighted and contained within something that makes her look and sound ridiculous at best and horrifying at worst, she's forever fearful that today might be the day the straps will tighten too much and break her.

And there's the not insignificant fact that someone, somewhere, decided *she* should be the one to wear it; the very idea churns within her like a misaligned world-engine creating only chaos.

But she's not thinking about that.

She listens for the labyrinth's machinations beyond the door, judging the relative positioning of the turntable with the connecting corridor beyond. Once the door is unlocked by the mask's horns, the turntable will spin her out there. Miscalculating means getting a face full of wall at best; a life-ending plummet into the labyrinth's mechanisms at worst.

It's always important to listen.

She gets the demonstration over with, returning to the warrior and the fortress gatehouse within a few dizzy moments. Instead of being calmed by her new knowledge, the warrior is anything but, announcing something about *going*.

It catapults Asterion into panic as she frees herself from the mask.

The thing must finally have cut off the circulation to her brain, because she's the idiot who's just shown a complete stranger with no enthusiasm for her wellbeing *exactly how* to leave her trapped here at the centre of the Labyrinth. Permanently.

"I—go. " Theseus grabs for the mask.

Patience worn thin, Asterion steps in and unbalances the warrior, tethering her to the wall by a satchel strap. It's so easy, she'll bet the plucky warrior is embarrassed about it. Well, good. Serves her right for being a monumental idiot.

"Arrgh. Stop tying me to things!"

"*You*—stop!" Asterion shouts back. She could do without all this drama. Terrors in the labyrinth are enough. She has no wish to add being trapped within her own fortress to the list.

The warrior needs to understand not to go out there without her. Not to take the mask and leave her in here, reducing her world to only its very core...

She won't be able to harvest wheat from the meadow, or medicinal wildflowers, or the fruits that only grow in the woodland. She won't ever again be able to relax at the lake's edge...

Not to mention what will happen if something in the labyrinth snags and she can't get out to repair it...

"You—no—open." She stabs a finger toward the mask, then toward the door. "You open—I here? Trapped."

Theseus gestures too, mirroring her. She seems to be demanding that they *both* go out into the labyrinth. It makes sense, technically. That's how they got in.

Does she think she's a prisoner here?

Asterion points at Theseus's leg; the reason for her temporary captivity. She'd assumed it was as obvious to Theseus as it is to her that she would never make it to the outer gatehouse with such an injury. It's too far; there are too many obstacles. Asterion knows them all. She knows the rhythm of the Labyrinth, but she's never had to guide someone through. It'll be dangerous. Especially with such an injury.

She expresses this in all the Athenian she can muster: "Exit far. Obstacles. Many. Danger. Stupid." Not to mention that at this point in the rotation, the bridge that links the fortress to the outer layers of the labyrinth is aligned the wrong way to reach the external gateway.

"When good... You—go." Asterion points at the loose satchel

straps. *Look. Not captive.* If the warrior wasn't so ruled by her emotions, she might take a breath and realise.

In her exasperation, Asterion slips into Minosian as she tells her, "If you fight only shadows, you can never win."

Theseus is watching her, like she's trying to solve a challenging equation. She can see it in those intense blue eyes. Finally, with a deep breath, Theseus nods and scrambles upright. "Okay."

The tightness in Asterion's shoulders loosens a little. Because in the wake of all the hostility, the sharpness and bite, there's something soft and honest about her demeanour. Though she knows she needs to keep her guard up, her gut believes Theseus.

Okay...

But... What next? She's never done this before. Never had someone else in her space. Never had to look at her world through someone else's eyes.

Asterion wrings her hands a little before she brightens with an idea. "You want... tour?"

42

CARRIED AWAY

Asterion's designs for the banquet hall might have been adjusted by whichever cruel Constructionists got their grubby hands on them, but this garden is hers.

She'd designed the fortress to wrap around the gardens, the stone walls reaching a palatial height before curving into a domed sky, with light wells funnelling in sunlight or moonlight. She'd been thorough in her calculations to figure out how to make something that isn't a sky look like one, but you never truly know whether designs work until they're in motion. And she's pleased with the result.

Enough that she's warmed by pride as she shares her world for the first time. So much so, she can't help prattling on about all the most interesting features of the garden as they make their way through it: the different plant types, and how they grow at an accelerated rate thanks to the world-engine this all originated from.

It's difficult not to get carried away, because there's just so much she wants to show her guest: the twisteria tree's cascading canopy of petals and the gnarly twists of its trunk—oh, and...

"The proteus tree. You see its leaves? Their water-like

surface, the patterns and colours, all change according to external influences. Chemical balances." The leaves are currently solid with no blotches, which means: "Air balance is good."

The colour is informed, some say, by the emotions of those near its branches. But Asterion doesn't mention that, because it's a rather uncertain mix of drab greens right now, with only the occasional leaf of vibrant purple which likely stems from her current exuberance. When she holds one of the palm-sized orbs hanging from its branches, the fruit transforms from pale green to vibrant amethyst at her touch.

Then, gesturing haphazardly, she explains: "These are the sun and moon mirrors. Oh, and over here..." She diverts to her other favourite part of the garden: the water well. "I know the emerald hue might seem a bit opulent, but the specific material was necessary because of multidirectional gravity." Because not only is that well her water source, it channels down to the true centre of the Labyrinth. "Any other material would crumble under the push and pull."

She's blathering. She should take a breath. She should wait for Theseus, in fact. A tour isn't a tour if you leave your tourist behind. Theseus is doing well with the crutch, but the gardens aren't the easiest terrain when you're unsteady on your feet.

Besides—she reminds herself—though Theseus seems to have calmed, she's still a stranger, and one whose mood has been distinctly changeable in her short time here. Asterion still shouldn't turn her back on her.

She halts in the middle of the path, and—*Oof!*—Theseus slams right into her. And yet, Asterion doesn't flinch—well, not much. She doesn't panic and shove Theseus away. Perhaps because Theseus, her arms flailing, looks too startled to be launching an attack.

Asterion catches her upper arm to stop her from falling. "Sorry," she whispers, in Minosian, her heart rate up-ticking.

She should let go of Theseus's arm. She should step back far enough that Theseus's breath no longer tickles her face.

Athenian. Speak Athenian. "I—um—not do—not done this—before."

They're so close. And this time, Theseus's smell is much improved. The soap is familiar: honey and oat milk, from Asterion's own stock. But beneath that is something else; something her nostrils admire, something that sends a tingle through her entire body. The smell of *freedom* is such a ridiculous thought, she can hardly admit thinking it. Even to herself.

Maybe she should check the leaves of the proteus tree; make sure she's not turning strange through oxygen deprivation. But she daren't. The leaves are no doubt a little more colourful than they should be right now, with her eagerness to share her world, and thoughts of Theseus's scent vibrating under her skin.

Enough. Don't be weird. Guests might be a new concept, but she's confident it's not polite or well-balanced to sniff them, even subtly. But with Theseus no longer intent on her demise—or so it seems—it's easy to get distracted by the curiosity sparkling in her eyes. Spotlit by sunlight, Theseus looks like she's from another world; almost impossible in her glow, like she was delivered here by powers beyond understanding. Ridiculous, of course. But apparently that's what Asterion's mind is on lately: the impossible and ridiculous.

Don't get carried away. Just because you've been cooped up alone most of your life, that doesn't mean your guest is interested in anything except getting out of here as fast as possible.

Understandably so. Perhaps instead of apologising for a subpar tour and a glut of Minosian commentary, Asterion should apologise for luxuriating in the smell of Theseus's skin and the way her eyes glisten in the sunlight.

She's loathe to admit that she's overwhelmed because this is the first time they've been this close without Theseus trying to kill her. It's a low and unhealthy bar for attraction; merely her body reminding her that she's been alone here for too many sun-orbits without any emotional or physical connection. Her body's way of telling her she's not dead inside.

A commotion and flurry of feathers.

Oh no!

Quickly, Asterion intervenes and rescues her favourite chicken from the fray, soothing Bok-bok who looks more alarmed than usual. With the bullied creature under her arm, she returns to Theseus and prattles on about how people bring the strangest things into the Labyrinth. Including eggs. The person who'd brought them likely thought them a hard-boiled snack, not already-fertilised Roasting Chickens.

Asterion huffs. Is that interesting? Should she be talking about eggs? In Minosian, no less. Perhaps she should make eye contact with Theseus, rather than looking down at Bok-bok.

When she looks up, Theseus is staring at her. And Asterion is at a loss for what to do with, or say to, *that* captivated expression.

Bok-bok, however, has lots to say about it. Squawking, she flaps free from Asterion's hold and charges at Theseus, who looks about as bewildered as the chicken had been. Bok-bok's flaming blue and orange wings are quite the sight to behold—as are her bellowing fire-squawks, which are best avoided at all costs. Thankfully, the chicken has an inbuilt survival instinct, and normally smothers her own wildfire tantrums by sitting on them with her flame-retardant feathers.

But burning Theseus a second time would be unforgivable, so Asterion douses Bok-bok with a pail of water from the well. Flame hisses to smoke as the chicken cools off.

Theseus continues to stare—though now she's dividing her

attention between Asterion and Bok-bok—apparently caught between terror, confusion and... who knows what else!

"I... Tour..." Asterion continues, picking up the conversation —or rather her monologue—where she'd left off. "I—not—tour —Give tour. First time."

Bok-bok swishes away in the most exemplary huff Asterion has ever seen.

At the warrior's sudden eruption of laughter, Asterion flinches—but calms a moment later. Because Theseus isn't laughing *at her*. There's nothing unkind about it. When Theseus laughs so hard her face creases, it's all so lyrical and such a relief, Asterion can't help joining in.

43

STARTLE

Asterion gets to work in her library while Theseus rests in her bedchamber. If her guest is to be comfortable here, Asterion has some serious Athenian to learn. She checks on Theseus at intervals to ensure she's comfortable and not slipping back into fever, leaving food and drink on the bedside table for when she wakes.

Later, in her workshop, Asterion extracts and disinfects thread from old shirts, as she's done hundreds of times before. As she works, her mind wanders towards troubled thoughts of the golden man.

Most people who venture here and cross paths with Asterion have fear and hesitation in their eyes. But that glint in the golden man's eyes... Asterion's seen that look before, in Father's eyes—and in Ari's. She'd call it *vicious ambition*.

The knowledge that someone like him has made it to the Labyrinth's inner layers sediments in her stomach like rock. It has her skin all itchy, too. She seldom wishes people harm, but with him, it's some comfort to remind herself that no interloper has yet survived this long here, and he's unlikely to be the exception.

She'll need to investigate his whereabouts soon, because she'll need to *sanitise*... At that thought, the sediments in her stomach multiply.

What is it about the Labyrinth that lures ambition to stalk its corridors? Do the voyagers risk their lives here to prove something, or are they sent here as punishment? Are they reluctant, or willing only until they meet the mist? Her musings on the matter always go in circles, and it's never long until they encroach on questions about her own situation she's not willing to explore.

But she does want to know why Theseus is here. Doesn't she?

At the thought of Theseus, her torque pulses, lighting up the threads on her workbench.

Why does her pulse accelerate at the mere thought of the warrior? It's not the same as when it spikes for survival. Well, it's not *not* that, given their early encounters... but there's something more to this strange sensation.

A voice. Movement.

Here. Behind her.

Asterion flinches—but her racing heart stumbles, because the voice is lyrical and sweet, even if the words it carries are not. Her insides scrunch when she processes Theseus's question: "You killed all these people?"

How can she think that? Still, after everything—why does she so easily label Asterion a monster? Why do all the others who venture here? Yes, out in the labyrinth there's the mask... but she's not wearing a mask now.

"No." Asterion tries to keep her voice steady. "They kill— Labyrinth kill." But she has, too. She's ended lives to save her own, and others out of compassion. "I—only—"

The thread on her workbench feels like it's knotting around

her every vital organ. How can a stranger's judgement hurt so much? Asterion shouldn't care what she thinks. She shouldn't. But they've only just found an equal footing, and she needs Theseus to understand.

How can Asterion possibly explain? Especially with her limited Athenian.

Theseus's assessing gaze swerves from the belongings of the fallen to her. Such direct eye contact knocks the air from Asterion's lungs, but she steels herself for judgement. What does Theseus see when she looks into her eyes?

"I—no hurt. But... I choose—my life."

Please understand. *Please.*

Something shifts in Theseus's gaze, like mechanisms clicking into alignment, and Asterion wishes she could decipher that look. Is it horror? Sympathy? Something else?

"What is all this?" Theseus looks at the items on the workbench, the ones Asterion needs to sort through.

Asterion gestures around them, more fiercely than she'd intended. "Is—no use—to dead."

Theseus nods. Good. Nodding is good. It's agreement. Or consideration at the very least.

Her next question is about what happens to the fallen, and if Asterion delved into the recesses of her memories, she might piece together some passable Athenian to describe what happened to them and her part in it, but the words "fire" and "chamber" are all she's willing to voice.

The warrior's widened eyes let her know she understands. That her response doesn't include claiming a weapon—or misorganised cutlery—from the metal pile, is a good sign, isn't it?

But she's clearly wrestling some beast in her own thoughts. Asterion can only imagine Theseus is concluding the sort of monster Asterion is... but when words do emerge from

Theseus's mouth, they're not an accusation or a judgement, they're: "Thank you."

Asterion's eyes connect with hers. Thank you? Does she mean it? That's what a thankful expression looks like, isn't it? Though deciphering such never was Asterion's strength.

"Thank you for rescuing me," Theseus continues. "For stitching my wounds. And, uh... everything. Uh..."

Asterion understands the words well enough. Her Athenian revision must be sinking in. And the rock in her stomach, it's transforming to something fluttery and unfamiliar. Theseus wouldn't be thanking her if she thinks she's a monster, would she?

"Thank you," Theseus concludes in Minosian with a lyrical lilt.

And for the first time in a long time, Asterion doesn't feel alone.

✦

WHILE THESEUS GETS some much-needed rest, Asterion prepares their evening meal. It's refreshing to cook for someone aside from herself and a flock of expectant chickens. There's something warming about it. Which is... strange. Why would having more tasks, more things to prepare, inspire warmth? As Asterion peels carrots, she's rather stuck on the idea.

The growl of caught mechanisms—somewhere in the beyond-fortress bridge layer, she guesses—echo and vibrate the kitchen and its components. Her entire body lifts, just a little. It's such a usual occurrence, Asterion hardly notices. She pauses chopping for a moment, and within the next she lands and carries on.

"The fuck was that?"

Asterion's body reacts to the intruder before her brain can

intervene. Heart in her throat, she whips around with the knife clutched in hand.

The Labyrinth roars, more mechanisms snagging.

Theseus. It's just Theseus.

It's safe here. She'd designed it so. It's okay. Everything is okay.

And at least now Theseus is looking to her for answers, and not throwing grimaces, punches or blades.

Asterion's shoulders relax, though it might take a minute for her heart to do the same. Theseus's eyes, however, are wild, darting every which way like she expects the Labyrinth to fold in on itself.

Admittedly, at the age of eleven sun-orbits, in her designs, Asterion hadn't foreseen the potential impact of aligning her own equilibrium with that of a labyrinth via torque-tech. Sometimes it's vindicating to have the Labyrinth roar when she's startled, or groan when she's mentally stuck on something, but mostly it's just concerning that the structure might fault.

The chamber lurches, and while Theseus clings to the doorframe, Asterion catches the rolling vegetables. She has to hide her smirk at Theseus's overreaction as she explains that the labyrinth is moving and that sometimes it gets a bit stuck.

She doesn't mention that everything's been a little off-kilter since Theseus's arrival.

"Can I... um... help?"

Asterion doesn't turn at Theseus's question because she can already see her through her side-glare. She wants to believe they're in new terrain now, where they can share space without catastrophe. She's made clear to Theseus that she means her no harm. They've shared laughter, awkward questions, and arrived at an understanding, haven't they? But it's difficult not to shake the possibility that she might turn belligerent again.

Asterion doesn't mean for her hand to tighten about the knife, but... well... she's been through some situations.

Theseus is looking healthier. Healing must be taking it out of her still, but she looks better rested. She's more appreciative and approachable, too, if a little easily perturbed by the Labyrinth's mechanics. The tension in her annoyingly perfect jaw has eased, though it's still square enough to measure angles against...

What was her question again?

'Can I help?'

Maintaining a sensible distance, Asterion pushes three carrots along the counter. When Theseus asks for something to chop with, Asterion presents her with a spoon.

What's the point in life if you can't make fun of its ridiculous moments?

And what a discovery: Asterion rather enjoys the amusement on Theseus's face. *This*. This is the warrior Asterion wants to know.

✝
•

THAT EVENING, Asterion likes that Theseus sits closer to her at the banquet table. She likes that Theseus fills the silence with stories of her adventures on other worlds—and that she doesn't seem to mind Asterion's endless questions. Asterion doesn't understand everything Theseus says, but she likes the musicality of her voice. And their silences are no longer filled with worries.

She likes a lot of things about the evening. She even likes thinking about it as she prepares to wash their dishes, singing to herself as she often does when she's happiest.

But then—

A sudden choked sound behind her—

She whirls around, and the plate she's holding slips from her hand and smashes on the slate floor.

Theseus is standing in the doorway. She looks okay—just clearing her throat or something.

"Confound and flummox," Asterion swears. Broken crockery. It's not a big deal, really, but it's not like this place had been fully furnished on her arrival. Thanks to the appalling calibration of the cargo distribution matrix, many useful items were lost—if they'd even been included in the cargo in the first place. She's had to source many basic items from the fallen—and since few voyagers carry their own crockery, she's created most of her plates and bowls from the woodland clay, with Bok-bok's assistance.

But it is just a plate. It's possible she's more bothered by the symbolism of the damn thing. Because everything breaks, eventually.

Asterion and Theseus might not like each other, or they might... but if they do... She doesn't want to *enjoy* having Theseus around, because when she leaves—and she *will* leave, and Asterion will ensure she does so safely—whatever they have will be broken.

What's the point of getting to know someone, only to set herself up for disappointment?

Lost in her own thoughts, Theseus is so suddenly there—right beside her—the breath abandons her lungs, stealing her sanity too as memories stampede her—

A limited view through a mask of shadows—

Nanny's terror-widened eyes—

His waning attempts to claw away—

Gargling last breaths—

Confusion and fear—

Asterion recoils from Theseus and from her memories, her breath tangling in her lungs. She doesn't want to think of Nanny.

Not how things ended. Not now. Not ever. Why does she have to think of it now? Why not when she and Theseus had been battling in the corridors or at every turn since? Why now, when things are finally calm between them?

Is it her body's way of reminding her that proximity hasn't historically gone well for her? That Theseus leaving isn't the problem? That Theseus staying might be?

"This is my mess," she tells Theseus. "I can clean it up."

✦

THE PROBLEM with healing is how *long* it takes. It'll be a while yet before Theseus is up to the journey back to the external gatehouse—which is why Asterion throws herself into running circuits around the garden at first light, and hefting the stone slab left over from the fortress walls thanks to a Quantifier's miscalculation.

As well as taking her mind off Theseus, it's an important routine. Asterion has to keep her body strong, her fitness exceptional, in order to contend with the mask, the labyrinth and its annual interlopers.

"Bok-bokkkkkk!"

The screech alerts her to Theseus lurking in the shadows of the fortress garden's gateway. What is she doing? Does she want to join in?

Asterion's breathing is heavy from her workout. *Mostly* from her workout. Maybe Theseus is waiting for an invitation? But before Asterion can take more than five steps in her direction—because, against her better judgement, she wants to spend time with Theseus—the warrior retreats inside. And now it's not just sweat Asterion needs to wash away under the water cascade, but disappointment, too.

That. That right there is why she can't *enjoy* having a guest.

Because if this is what it's like when Theseus has merely been polite and *not murderous* for only a matter of days, what will she feel if Theseus is civil or more to her for a sustained amount of time?

Asterion doesn't want to be that person: the recluse who latches onto the first individual to show her anything other than outright hostility. She'd like to think she's too strong, too analytical, to be tricked by feelings. But this pesky warmth in her chest would suggest otherwise.

She stomps into the kitchen. No-one deserves to be the target of desperation. She should damn well leave Theseus alone.

And she would, except that Theseus is right here.

Theseus stares at her, looking a little uncomfortable, although all Asterion is doing is getting a mug of water. Is she standing too close? She's drinking normally, isn't she?

"Sorry," Theseus mumbles, before limping hurriedly out of there. She probably doesn't appreciate Asterion's accidental staring, or her *thinking* so damn loud.

When Asterion strides into the bedchamber, pulling off her sweat-soaked clothes, she's so preoccupied with the importance of giving Theseus space that it takes her a moment to notice Theseus perched stiffly on the bed, eyes wide like she's suddenly alert. It's only then Asterion remembers *knocking* is a thing. This might usually be her bedchamber, but it's Theseus's for the time being. And barging in isn't a polite or well-balanced thing to do.

Stupid Asterion. Social conventions—remember those? She stomps to the wash chamber.

Her fortress designs had included a second wash chamber next to the bedchamber that's now repurposed as her workshop. Whoever altered her designs must have decided there'd be no need for that second wash chamber. Or for a second bed.

The heat of the water cascade unknots some of her aching

muscles and her stress. Her neck and shoulders remain tight, however: in part from the mask—always the mask—and in part from sleeping in a nest of chairs.

She hisses with pain as water tracks through her shoulder wound. It must have reopened during her exercise. She's been so distracted by Theseus, she's neglected her own wounds. Time to sort herself out.

Not wanting to take too long about occupying her guest's rooms, Asterion doesn't linger. She marches back into the bedchamber to find Theseus still on the bed, even more wide-eyed than before. Perhaps she's trying to rest and Asterion just keeps on interrupting. Best she hurry up, then.

Asterion sources clothing and pulls on a pair of undershorts, then crosses to the mirror to inspect her shoulder. She tries to be quick, but it's difficult to get a proper look no matter how she angles herself.

In the mirror, Theseus's eyes meet hers. Her face is so... flushed. Does she have a temperature? Is her wound infected?

Without thinking, Asterion hurries over to the bed, leaning close enough to check whether Theseus's brow is sweating—a sure sign of fever. But her brow, apart from being raised to the heavens in apparent surprise, looks the same as always.

Still, her cheeks are heated.

"You—are hot?" Asterion asks her. Theseus is gripping the sheets. Perhaps her leg is painful today. Asterion points to it. "Is —okay?"

"Is fine," Theseus insists, and Asterion narrows her eyes at her. Trying to be brave about injuries that can lead to blood poisoning or worse is nothing short of idiotic.

But Theseus diverts the discussion by offering to stitch Asterion's wound. It's not exactly the definition of 'keeping her distance', but to refuse would fulfil her own definition of *idiotic*.

Especially when Theseus digs into her satchel and a spool of illumi-thread spills out of the bag's secret compartment. Asterion had looked in her bag for this! How in the heavens did she miss it? She lives in a labyrinth of hidden doors and false walls —*she'd designed it*—but evidently one bag's secret compartment is beyond her. Well, that's grounding, isn't it?

Theseus obviously doesn't realise the treasure she holds. Asterion tries to explain that there's no need to disinfect anything, because of the thread's properties, but Theseus is as stubborn as she is captivating. Asterion will just have to let her see the thread in action.

With supplies at the ready, Asterion settles on the bed beside her, shoulder angled, but Theseus takes an age inspecting the wound before soothing her skin with the balm.

A sigh escapes Asterion, because this is the first touch in nineteen sun-orbits that's intended to help her and not harm. She swallows past the strange tension in her vocal cords, strengthening her inner scaffolding. *Don't cry. Don't cry. If you cry now, you might never stop.* It's a relief when Theseus starts chatting about the balm and how it functions.

It could just be the healing magic of the illumi-thread, but there's a definite tingling heat spreading through Asterion's body. And she can't chase away the thought that Theseus being here isn't the worst thing...

But no...

It wouldn't be fair to prolong her stay unnecessarily. Which is why Asterion asks her, "I can—re-sew—leg. Heal—fast?"

She'd thought her meaning would be clear, but Theseus looks... momentarily lost. "Um..." is all Theseus manages to say before she clears her throat and scrambles to her feet—her eyes fixed on Asterion's like she doesn't trust one or both of them not to do something stupid. Theseus's wince as her barely healed leg meets the floor has Asterion's own nerves briefly igniting.

Clearly trying to put as much space between them as possible, Theseus grabs her crutch and stammers "N-no, thank you," as she flees.

Did Asterion mistranslate and say something horrifying or suggestive? Or had Asterion misunderstood something? If Theseus is so keen to get away from her, why didn't she say yes to the thread?

44

SUNSHINE

The next day...

With her ear-piercing squawk and sizzling-hiss, Bok-bok lets her displeasure be known. It's apparent she doesn't want Theseus in the garden—or in the Labyrinth at all. She's probably just being protective. Or jealous. And Asterion appreciates it—mostly—but even so, the chicken needs to simmer down. Asterion could do without a poultry tantrum this morning. And she'd like to solve Theseus's frown, and to figure out—if Theseus doesn't want to be near her—why is she here when there's a whole fortress she could occupy.

"Beak shut, Bok-bok," Asterion reprimands and the glaring chicken obeys.

When Theseus wishes her a 'good moaning' instead of a 'good morning' in Minosian, Asterion is thrilled. Well, she's confused and a little embarrassed at first, to be honest. But once it's clear from Theseus's tinting cheeks and vaguely mortified expression that she's missed her intended target, Asterion can only appreciate her efforts. Because Theseus is *trying*.

It's perhaps this, and the fact that she'd rather there was less chicken drama, that encourages her to introduce Bok-bok and Theseus, officially, to each other. Maybe then they'll get along.

Whether it'll work... well... she's never had to introduce her chicken to anyone before. "Is—Bok-bok," she explains to Theseus. "Is—Theseus," she explains to the chicken.

"Bok-bok?" Theseus asks.

"Bok-bok," confirms the chicken, with a simultaneous side-eye at them both.

Asterion doesn't miss that Theseus winces with each crutch-aided step—her own nerve endings bristle with it. She should respect Theseus's decision not to use the illumi-thread. Or should she, when that decision is stupid? Theseus could be healed by now if she'd accepted it.

Instead of giving Theseus a piece of her mind, or staring at her—*don't be weird!*—Asterion continues harvesting vegetables, murmuring her thanks to them for their sustenance.

"Are you talking to the vegetables?" asks Theseus, and Asterion tenses. She's being weird.

"Yes." But is that so odd? She sits back on her heels. How did her brow get so sweaty so fast? She wipes away the moisture with her forearm. "I—apologise. And thank. I'm thank—for eat. I apologise—no more grow." It's not like she's had anyone else to talk to—apart from chickens and the walls.

Best not say that.

"I know—is strange." *Please let it not be too strange.* Or do; then Theseus will leave faster, which will be better for them both. Asterion digs more forcefully, still whispering to the vegetables to soothe herself as much as them.

From the corner of her eye, something glimmering draws her attention. Is it time? Already? She'd estimated that the buds on the frost-fruit trees wouldn't break for another few weeks—but there it is: blossom catching the morning light. Once they're in bloom, the other trees will blossom, too.

She strides past Theseus to the orchard, forgetting to use her Athenian words as she examines the light blue petals peeking through their protective armour of leaves.

"Is sign—season change," Asterion explains, belatedly remembering herself. "New food—soon."

Not yet. But almost.

Asterion looks back at Theseus, who's so silent. Should Asterion be concerned? "Did I—do—talking wrong?"

At least Theseus looks surprised by Asterion's question. "No. No... Perfect. You did talking perfect."

And although Asterion doesn't want to care what she thinks, Theseus's compliment is like sunshine on her skin.

⁺
∴•

THESEUS INSISTS on helping in the garden.

It's... not productive. There's the minor detail of her having little demonstrable knowledge of how to not behead or crush the produce Asterion works so hard to cultivate. But there's also that furrow in her brow and the way her shirt stretches across her shoulders as she digs, all framed between lettuce leaves and thick tomato stalks...

It's all so... distracting—Asterion has a darn crick in her neck. She gets to her feet, stretching her aching neck. She needs to cool off.

She strolls to the well, silently admiring Theseus's focus on her digging. She must be thirsty, too, so Asterion takes her a mug of water.

Theseus looks up at her, eyes wide. Is she afraid the water's poisoned? Haven't they moved past such concerns?

"Is well—from lake. Clean. Filtered for purity." Asterion takes a gulp to show it's safe.

Theseus accepts the cup. "Thank you," she says, in

Minosian, and the two words have Asterion pleased. Her accent isn't too bad.

As Theseus drinks, Asterion's gaze drifts to the lines of her throat. Who knew watching someone else hydrating could increase her own thirst?

It's ridiculous. She's just had a drink.

The more time she spends around Theseus, the less the universe makes sense.

So why does she like it?

"Did you learn more Athenian overnight?" asks Theseus.

Asterion stifles her smile. She noticed! Last night, her studies had unlocked a whole host of vocabulary she'd learned as a child, and reminded her about Athenian tenses. "I—try. Tried. *Am trying.* Lots to learn." She could work on her pronunciation, but it's such a relief just being able to communicate. And the company is... *nice.* Better than Bok-bok—though she won't tell the chicken that. She has feelings, too.

But she mustn't crowd Theseus. She mustn't get attached.

She returns to her task of planting carrots. The gardens won't cultivate themselves. They could have, if she'd thought of it at the design stage. Or she could have designed something over her many sun-orbits here—but what else would she do without her crops to tend?

But... erm... What is Theseus doing?

Asterion had intended to leave her be, but... is she trying to dig straight through the Labyrinth's core to the lake on the flip side of the sphere? Were Asterion's cultivation instructions not good? Carrots don't need to be planted that deep. Or is Theseus distracted?

Whatever it is, Asterion has to stop her before she collapses the entire vegetable patch—and them with it—into a multidirectional gravity sinkhole.

Theseus squints up at her. The flare of embarrassment

across Theseus's cheeks as she follows Asterion's questioning gaze to the hole and its neighbouring mountain of soil is about the cutest thing Asterion has ever seen.

Not wanting to spook either of them, Asterion kneels slowly beside her and makes quick work of refilling the hole that's practically a ditch. "What's it like in that world of yours?" she asks in Minosian, before being brave… and guiding Theseus's hands in planting seeds to an appropriate depth and pressing the soil.

But Theseus retreats.

Disappointment slinks through Asterion. Her heart hammers like a mining drill that's lost its steering. She wants to re-dig that hole and bury herself in it. She hadn't meant to overstep.

But it's clearer than the purified well-waters that Theseus wants space.

So, over the next few days, Asterion gives her that. She steers clear of her at all but mealtimes. Even in the banquet hall, she eats as fast as possible, so that Theseus won't have to spend any more time with her than necessary. She doesn't try out any more of her Athenian. She doesn't ask Theseus why she came here, or why she'd been so intent on harming Asterion when she arrived. She doesn't ask where Theseus is from, or what her enthusiasms are. She might not want the answers, anyway. And what's the point when Theseus will be gone soon enough?

Besides, if people wanted to be around Asterion, she wouldn't be here, would she?

✝
∴

EMOTIONS ARE UNWIELDY BEASTS. Asterion is trying, really trying, not to let one confusing warrior ruin her mood. Music always helps. Her portable music player arrived here thanks to a past voyager. And—while her garden exercise regime is for fitness—movement to music is for enjoyment.

Multitasking with cooking, she's just getting into it when Theseus stumbles into the kitchen amidst a squawking ruckus.

"Sorry," says Theseus, barricaded in by Bok-bok strutting up and down the corridor, poultry eyes aglow. "I think your chicken hates me."

There's no two ways about it. "Yes." Asterion almost smiles. Such a small creature; such a well-built warrior. She's not expecting Theseus's answering smirk, but after days of avoidance, the cheeky glint in her eye as she lingers in the kitchen is a healing balm.

Maybe she's fed up with being alone. Maybe she's just scared of a chicken. Either way... if Theseus can stand her presence, Asterion's unrequited crush and fear of losing a theoretical friendship doesn't mean they can't be civil, does it?

A knife is seldom a peace offering, but in this case, Theseus—after a face pinched with confusion—accepts Asterion's offering and joins her at the counter to chop vegetables.

She's better at chopping than gardening by a Minosian mile, thank the heavens. In fact, her speed and precision are outright impressive. Asterion stretches her aching neck and returns to stirring the pot on the heat cradle—but not to her dancing. It feels odd now she's being watched. Well, not watched, but not alone. She can't help nodding to the music, though, and it's not long before Theseus starts singing and... dancing? Is that what that is?

Whatever it is, Asterion likes it.

Theseus's commitment to outright foolishness in time to the music evolves and Asterion can only join in. As they bop about, as they laugh together, the tension unwinds from her muscles. It could be her imagination, but even the moonlit garden, framed by the kitchen window, seems to glow a little brighter.

Unsteady on her healing leg, Theseus slips—

Asterion reacts without thinking, her hands grasping Theseus around the waist as she falls. Theseus's quickened breaths brush her cheeks, topaz eyes glinting with reflected moonlight and possibility as electricity flourishes beneath Asterion's skin.

No doubt her torque—and the groaning Labyrinth—is giving all that away.

Asterion holds her breath. She shouldn't be gazing into Theseus's eyes like they're characters bound within the pages of some fiction. She needs to keep a grasp on reality. For both their sakes. Theseus hadn't stepped willingly into Asterion's arms, any more than she'd intended to get caught in that trap. And she's not consistently welcomed Asterion's company since. So what looks like an invitation—like possibility—must be misconstrued.

Best to get her healed and out of here, isn't it?

"I think—we—should—do it," Asterion tells her.

Because, really, why delay the inevitable?

45

SEISMIC

Minutes later...

"On the bed."

Eyeing Asterion unwaveringly, Theseus shuffles into place. Asterion settles on the bed too and lifts Theseus's partially healed leg into her lap to apply the healing balm. She doesn't let her touch linger on Theseus's skin, as much as she might want to. This is a medical procedure, a necessity. To linger would be more gross than poking a healing wound.

Which is what she has to do.

She might have learned enough Athenian to explain water purification, but she hasn't reached the point of being able to explain how illumi-thread works. From what she's read, a long time ago now, it heals from within.

As she smooths the balm into Theseus's raw scars, Theseus grimaces like she's in pain. But there shouldn't be pain, not with the balm sinking in.

"Is—okay?" asks Asterion, concerned. "I—hurt you?"

Theseus clears her throat. "No. Is—okay."

Relieved, Asterion continues, considering aloud the best

course of action. When she suggests removing the stitches first, Theseus nods like she's caught between relief and discomfort. When Asterion wields a knife, Theseus tenses.

"Is just—stitch removal," Asterion explains. Hopefully those are the right words.

"I think I preferred being unconscious for this."

Asterion surmises that Theseus's winces are more about the general idea of her injury being touched than actual pain. "Can—be arranged." She can't help being playful, even while picking out the stitches methodically with needle and knife. Though Theseus is looking rather more grey than usual...

"You—not have to—" Asterion pauses. She's been learning more Athenian. It'd be outright laziness not to use it. "You do not have to watch."

Theseus squints up at the ceiling as if it might hold the secrets of the universe. That tickles Asterion. "You—brave warrior?"

Theseus grumbles something about her leg being cut off. Asterion is reasonably certain she's not making a request. And then Theseus adds, confusion or intrigue colouring her tone: "Warrior?"

"Mmmhmm. Sword. Shield. Armour. Determination in eyes. If not warrior—you are what?"

Too close. Distracting. That is what Theseus is.

Asterion focuses on stitching the illumi-thread over the raw scars. She sews beneath the skin enough—she hopes—that its healing properties will sink in.

Sure enough, the thread is already absorbing.

"You are good." She sets Theseus's leg back on the bed and holds out her hand in invitation. Theseus hesitates, before placing her hand in Asterion's.

Asterion's heart does... *something* at the contact. Not panic, though not a thousand miles removed from that either. It's a good feeling, all warm and fluttery through her body.

How strange.

She turns Theseus's hand palm up and removes the adhesive bandage that's covering the cut. The cut Theseus got because she tried to stab Asterion with a piece of glass. The reminder is enough to cool whatever those warm flutters are up to.

Theseus flinches, and Asterion curses herself. Was she too abrupt in ripping the bandage off? With her thumb, she smooths the salve over Theseus's palm, which seems to relax the brave warrior. Then, at Theseus's nod of permission, Asterion drags a length of illumi-thread across the healing scar, which fades to nothing under the glowing fibres.

Her forearm burn is next. And as the hurt is erased by the thread, Asterion traces over the fibres with her thumb; sinking into Theseus's skin like a perfect scattering of stars.

That something so hurtful can transform to beauty... well... it's captivating. So much so that it's only when Theseus's hand presses over hers that Asterion realises she's still caressing Theseus's forearm.

Has she overstepped?

Theseus's palm is so warm, her touch so gentle. What does it mean to have Theseus's hand on hers? What does it mean for that touch to resonate everywhere?

Theseus's mouth twitches, as if she's about to speak. Asterion steels herself. If only they could stay in this moment, before whatever Theseus has to say halts any beautiful possibilities.

Instead of speaking, Theseus reaches for Asterion's blushing pendant. And Asterion doesn't stop her. She doesn't want to stop her. Because something inside her chest is buzzing, like something winged frantically trying to break free.

It's not comfortable... but it's not unpleasant, either. It's the only discomfort she's ever wanted to lean into.

Sparks. That's what this feels like.

And sure enough, her torque is flickering too, giving her away.

When Theseus's bright eyes meet hers, Asterion feels it down to her foundations. A seismic rumble trembles the chamber and she takes longer than she should to react to her world *literally* tilting.

Thirty-three degrees—

A clatter of medical supplies—

The thread falling... skittering...

Oh no!

Asterion launches herself across the bed, diving towards the flaming hearth where the illumi-thread—without a care for the lives it could save, the many future injuries it could heal—bursts into flames.

Just like that.

If not for Asterion's insistent grip on reality, she might think the crackling flames were laughing at her.

Curses spew from her. She doesn't even know what she's saying; she's just really *flummoxing* angry with the universe. So angry that her common sense and survival instincts must also have landed in the flames.

Which is where she would be, too, if it weren't for Theseus who has her by the belt and is hauling her back up the bed, begging her to hold on.

Theseus's pleading pulls her from her grief, and Asterion clambers up the bed, clinging like Theseus is her own rescue rope.

Theseus wraps an arm around her back, like it's the most natural thing to be holding Asterion close, for them to be pressed together. But she's just being the hero Asterion had observed out in the labyrinth, saving her from the flames. Still, it's difficult not to imagine or hope that being held so close—so close that she can feel Theseus's heart racing her own—is the start of a journey they're both inviting.

It's panic that's vibrating through Theseus's chest. Nothing else. All while the blue light of Asterion's torque dances between them, a bold confession of the electricity charging through her veins.

Body heat and breaths combined, they're as close as two people can be.

So why does Asterion ache to be closer?

She used to have a hold on logic and sense, but now all she wants to hold onto is Theseus's shoulders and this moment. Those eyes, that look... they're not of someone who wants distance. They're inviting her closer.

Asterion traces her fingers up Theseus's neck. *Is this real?* She strokes Theseus's nose with her own before gravitating to Theseus's jaw; she'd be a fool not to verify such a perfect angle. Her skin is so soft, Asterion could luxuriate in it for an eternity.

Or a more realistic timeframe. But all her higher faculties are on hold as Theseus's mouth angles to meet hers.

Confound and flummox. There's no mistaking *that*, is there?

She's read about kissing. She understands the mechanics. But she'd had no idea it'd set her body buzzing like a portable music player just got turned to full volume in her chest.

Theseus's hands glide under Asterion's shirt and over her back. That's not what someone who wants distance would do...

Asterion presses into their kiss, her tongue finding Theseus's. Her inner music player ups its volume, and that winged *something* in her chest flutters from her heart to her head to her toes.

More. Yes. She wants more.

And *Hades in the Heavens*, Theseus's quiet moan could power an entire Labyrinth. Asterion's never consciously had to remember to breathe before. Apparently she's not as good at multitasking as she'd thought.

The Labyrinth groans and the chamber judders as it rights itself, shunting them in different directions and back to reality. Asterion's inner music player cuts to hissing static, and the winged-something in her chest flaps in panic.

So much for keeping her distance.

46

POISON

Soon after...

Asterion's hands, usually so steady, can hardly hold the stick of charcoal still enough to draw on her library's mezzanine wall. Creating stars calms her, but less so when she's reprimanding herself. She resorts to smudging it instead.

She should be berating herself for losing the precious illumi-thread, but her jumbled thoughts are orbiting a far more torturous topic. Because you can only miss something once you know what you're missing, and...

That kiss.

She liked that kiss.

She doesn't turn when Theseus joins her on the mezzanine, a few paces away. She doesn't want to see Theseus's face and the confirmation that their kiss should never have happened. Or perhaps Theseus is here to invite a repeat, but also to remind her that she'll be gone soon. Asterion doesn't want that reminder, either.

"Your sister..." Theseus says.

Asterion's ash-covered fingers pause. It's not the post-kiss opener she'd expected. Well, it's not like she'd had any clue as to what to expect next... but talking about her sister wouldn't have been it.

She follows Theseus's concerned gaze to the portrait in question, on one of the mezzanine's pillars, where she'd committed Ariadne's image twelve sun-orbits ago. She hasn't seen Ari since they were children, but her own face had been guidance enough for what she might look like.

She *knows* that the Ari in the portrait isn't real, but in her time here, talking to the image has been a good alternative to monologues with plants and chickens.

Uncertain what to say, Asterion resumes smudging her skyscape.

"Asterion. Your sister..."

Asterion's insides squirm. Her stomach aches. Her throat hurts. She shakes her head. *Please don't.*

Theseus continues, her words hesitant. "She challenges heroes and criminals to conquer the Labyrinth..."

"No-one—can conquer—Labyrinth—all die trying." Asterion rubs her forehead; maybe she can erase her unwanted thoughts.

The sympathy etched in Theseus's brow only makes everything worse. If it were a blade she was brandishing, at least Asterion could fight back.

"Kill the beast. Bring me its heart. *Set me free.*" Theseus's words land like a kick to the chest. "That is what Princess Ariadne challenges those she sends here."

Asterion's insides stutter. Nothing feels right; like everything is too big to fit in her body—her heart, her lungs, her feelings. The chamber falters, the Labyrinth groaning as if it, too, wants to reject everything Theseus is throwing at her.

It's too much. The pity in Theseus's eyes turns the dents in Asterion's armour to spikes.

"I live—in Labyrinth—*you* talk in riddles." And who else, what else, can Asterion turn to but her sister's image? For as long as she can remember, only cold stone eyes have stared back. Even before the Sky Labyrinth.

In a daze, Asterion reaches out, smearing ash across Ari's face. The stain, like the tightening knots of truth inside her, cannot be undone. Because once she admits to knowing who orchestrated her prison, her punishment... she'll have to wrestle that knowledge by the horns. And it might just kill her.

She grabs a rag and wipes at the blemish, attempting to remove the marks. She's wrong. Theseus is wrong. It's just a misunderstanding—

She has no idea what she stammers in reply to Theseus. Something about her being strong and Ari keeping her safe. The excuses she's repeated to herself over and over for the sake of hope and sanity. But in her own shaking voice and the echoing strain of the Labyrinth, she can hear the cracks threatening to tear her world apart.

"Are you? Safe? Your scars suggest otherwise."

She'd push those damning, sympathetic sounds back into the warrior's mouth if she could. Theseus can throw all the 'logic' she wants at Asterion, but she severely underestimates Asterion's ability to deceive herself.

Somewhere in the labyrinth mechanisms are crying out as her inner world strains at the seams.

"She give—gave—*gives me*—mask. To protect."

"That mask is the reason people hunt you!" Theseus's words land like punches. "You live in a death maze, Asterion!"

What does she know? How dare she, a stranger, barge in here and tear at the seams of Asterion's life? "*I live in a palatial puzzle!*"

Asterion steps right up to Theseus, angling for a battle. But instead of meeting her challenge, Theseus just stands there, regret in her eyes.

"Ariadne sent me here to kill the Minotaur."

How can such gentle, apologetic words spear through her heart and snatch the air from her lungs, leaving them as empty as the space between stars?

Of course it was too much to hope that Theseus had simply happened to stray across Asterion's path. Of course trying to kill her wasn't the result of miscommunication and toxic, mind-altering mists; she'd journeyed here for that purpose.

Ariadne's purpose.

The spear in her chest twists, fury and heartbreak warring in her veins. She can't look at Theseus. Theseus who does Ariadne's bidding. Theseus who came here to kill her. Theseus who won't even let Asterion hide from the truth.

Go away. Everything needs to just... go away.

The building storm inside Asterion breaks, and she thunders into motion. She flees, hurtling down the spiral stairs, out the library, along the curved corridor and to the fortress's gatehouse to grab her mask.

If she risks the labyrinth, if she runs fast enough, perhaps she can escape Theseus, and the truth.

PART VI

LOST

ASTERION

47

TURNED AROUND

Beyond the fortress, Asterion and Theseus slam to the flagstones together in a bruising sprawl. Asterion staggers upright, not waiting for Theseus to recover, nor for more truths to fall from her stupid, distracting mouth.

How had she not seen this monster right in front of her? Is she so desperate for company? Or just too easily tricked by a handsome face?

She can't imagine Theseus trying to hurt her now. But she's been wrong—or in wilful denial—about so much. How can she trust herself?

Best to keep running.

Even though it's illogical, in this place. There's no way out, not for her. Only this endless road to nowhere, looping back on itself like her darkest thoughts.

Asterion hurtles from the turntable, through the connecting corridor to the labyrinth's layers, and Theseus's footsteps follow at a fast clip as she pleads for her to "wait." If she'd timed it better, she could have lost Theseus in the endless rotation and realignment of the layers.

But the bridge is steady, for now.

Which is more than Asterion is feeling with Theseus in pursuit.

The mask pinches her shoulders, squeezing across her chest, her temples and neck. The weight is something she's used to, but somehow it's more cumbersome than usual today, insistent on trying to drag her down.

If she was more in control of her emotions, the labyrinth wouldn't be so off-kilter right now. The unusual slant of the corridor has her clipping against the walls and stumbling. But she keeps on her feet through determination alone.

Kill the beast.

Bring me its heart.

Set me free.

Betrayal chokes tighter than any mask. She might be the one gripped within the mechanisms, but it's Ariadne who wears the mask of deception.

Asterion doesn't want to believe it. In an ideal world, she wouldn't even have to consider questioning her sister's integrity. She'd *know* Ari was innocent. But in that world, she wouldn't be trapped in a mask of her sister's dark design. In an ideal world, Theseus's words wouldn't have flowed into the grooves of truth like lava into heat-gullies.

She's been running from the truth for so long. It was going to catch up to her eventually.

If Ari, Father, or both, had wanted to gift her the world she'd designed—a perfect world in balance, free from royal obligations—it wouldn't be filled with traps, hunters, fear and loneliness. And she wouldn't be cursed to wear this mask, her face hidden, her voice suppressed.

Asterion might not agree with the importance Minos places on visibility, audibility and competition, but she can still see that her precise circumstances are intended as a punishment. By Minosian standards, death would have been less cruel.

She skids to a stop at a crossroad, her breath stumbling from her aching chest.

She knows the labyrinth's tempo, its sinister dance. She knows how to avoid its hidden blades and nightmare mists.

She never gets lost.

But for the first time in a long time, she's out of step, uncertain.

And worse...

The shimmering mists are rolling in from three directions: so fast Asterion is shrouded before she can do a thing about it. The bank of mist is so solid she has no choice but to inhale.

Her heart pounds like an unhinged carnival parade as the mist's toxins needle beneath her skin.

She swings between the three mist-obscured corridors, but her head is in such a spin she can't say from which she's just emerged.

A soothing voice reaches out from the corridor to her left as a figure takes shape in the shroud of mist. She can't decipher the words, but the timbre is familiar and the tone calming.

But.

Nanny isn't there. He can't be.

The figure opens its arms in invitation. But no matter how much she wants to run to him, it can only be a trick.

She turns away, refusing to look, but his rasping breath nooses around her, squeezing the air from her lungs. It can only be an echo from the haunting chambers of her mind, but that doesn't stop grief, fear and shame snagging like horns in Asterion's chest.

The Labyrinth wails.

Blood-soaked, gaping holes in Nanny's chest.

She's been caught in the mist enough times to know that's what she'll see if she turns to look at him.

She never meant to hurt him. She's never wanted to hurt anyone.

But that hasn't saved anyone, has it?

She designed this place. *She* angered Ariadne, her father, or the royal committee—perhaps all of them—enough that they sent her here. And now so many have died.

All because of her.

And the mist runs riot with the fact. The shadows of the fallen—all the people she couldn't reach in time, the people she couldn't save—are multiplying. They wield weapons. Their bodies bloodied, their faces contort with fear, pain, or both. Their voices blur into one mournful, indistinguishable murmur that rises to a crescendo.

She'd tried. Every sun-orbit, she'd raced to reach them. She'd tried to communicate with them, to make them understand the dangers. She'd *tried*.

Asterion's focus veers between the corridors. Which way to go?

But there are so many silhouettes. Too many.

All the people she's failed.

All the people who'd lost their lives trying to kill *her*.

For so long, she's blamed the voyagers' incomprehensible aggression toward her on the mists. But what kind of monster must she be if so many people are prepared to die trying to end hers?

It's difficult to argue for your own survival through a mask that shrouds your voice. It's difficult to argue when so many want you dead.

The voices of everyone she's ever disappointed bubble up around her like noxious swamp gas. Ariadne. Father. The writhing mass of faces within the royal court. All looking down on her now with disgust.

What kind of Architect-in-waiting can't even say the right

thing, please the right people? Perhaps it's fitting that the mask renders her voiceless, because no-one has ever wanted to hear what she has to say anyway. Perhaps that's the whole point.

Another direction. Another silhouette takes shape in the mist: with neon-blue dotted at shin level, and armour shinier than it should be, gleaming like the sword she's casually flipping...

She'd trusted Theseus.

Or she was starting to, at least.

Is she here to finish the task Ariadne set?

Or has the mist got Asterion fighting shadows?

Theseus's sneer ridicules her for trying to help her, for falling so easily into her trap. Asterion stumbles, buffeted—by the tilting corridor, or her emotions? Everything. Theseus's sword may as well already be lodged beneath her ribs.

Amidst the crowded silhouettes and their voices, footsteps clip toward her.

Another direction. Another figure. Her heart rate ratchets to battle-ready as the spear-wielding golden man stalks out of the mist. His gloating laughter is a haunting detail her mind would torment her with, but the theatrical wickedness of his astro-mask framing his snarl... that's a detail too far.

She'd assumed the Labyrinth would have dealt with him by now, but he can't be a conjuring of her fears. For his callousness, his cruelty, he's the one person she's crossed paths with in this place for whom she feels no guilt surrounding his death.

He can only be real.

And protected from the mists by his astro-gear.

She backs away from him, the mask obscuring full view of the other paths as her focus flits between them. She's so consumed by the echoes of torment—crowded by imagined glares and verbal barbs—she can't figure out which is a real and present threat.

She has to run.

But—

Nanny's corridor will take her too close to the golden man. The other corridor—

Asterion chooses the other path, ploughing through the taunting Theseus and her blade. Ropes of mist unspool as the apparition dissolves along with the hordes blocking Asterion's path.

Footsteps—

Fast—

The golden man is chasing her—

She ups her pace, but stumbles in the off-kilter corridor.

Behind her there's a heavy thud and a scuffle, followed by a familiar *oof*. She skids to a stop, turning on her heel as she glances back.

The shimmering mist churns with an almighty tussle, disrupted by Theseus—with no armour, no weapon, no shield —on the ground, wrestling the golden man—

Asterion's stomach drops.

She's not where she thought she was—

As her heel slips—

Backwards over the cliff edge—

48

OVER THE EDGE

P lummeting from the top of the meadow's waterfall isn't something Asterion has tried before. And it's not some-thing she has a choice about now.

The water hits like concrete, swallowing her, filling her mask and barricading her breaths. She splutters, her hoofed hands useless in her attempts to swim toward the rapidly retreating surface.

She cries out, pouring her every inconsolable hurt and frus-tration into the mask and water. Bubbles burst, obscuring her vision until she's left with nothing. No family who care about her. No friends. No *air*.

All she can do is reach helplessly toward the light of the meadow's trio of moons as the weight of the mask drags her down, down, down, until her boots meet solid stone.

Her chest aches with injustice and missed breaths. She's not ready to give up this fight, but that doesn't change the facts of water, gravity, and a weighted mask. Her thundering heart stretches time to its limits, sharpening her senses and filling mere seconds with the details of the biome's depths.

Blue and purple aquatic plants sway with the disturbance of

her sudden arrival. At the perimeter of the lake bed, the plunging waterfall churns the water. It's far enough from where Asterion is that the lake appears almost tranquil.

But there's nothing calming about the lung-aching prospect of drowning. Even if that weren't a problem, soon the fang-fish will be.

Asterion's stomach lurches as the challenges of her situation multiply. On the clifftop, a blurry but distinctive golden figure looms, spear angled toward the surface of the lake.

Where is Theseus?

The thought that Theseus might be injured or worse forces an air bubble from Asterion's lungs. Does that make her a fool?

She should focus on her own survival.

Can the golden man see her from the clifftop? She can see him...

If she can get to behind the churning waterfall, she'll be hidden. But the cliff face beyond the furious water is smooth and sheer, and all she'll achieve is drowning herself.

But hiding is rendered irrelevant as a second figure body-checks the golden man—

A stripe of shadow interrupts the moonlight as the figures plummet from the clifftop, a crackle of luminous blue trailing down with them like a falling star.

The shadow and star crash into the lake in a storm of bubbles before unravelling. As the golden man flails, Theseus leaves him behind, swimming with purposeful, powerful strokes down towards Asterion.

There are no weapons in her hands. And as she nears... The creases in her brow and the worry in her eyes have Asterion's heart full, even if her lungs aren't. Because *Theseus is here for her.* Not to hurt her. But to help her.

Well, she's been in this labyrinth most of her damn life and never needed rescuing. But maybe this once it wouldn't hurt?

But—

Bubbles spew from Theseus's mouth as the golden man tugs her backward, both kicking furiously. The golden man jabs at her with his spear, missing her one quick-thinking body squirm at a time.

Tangling in the lake weeds, Asterion can do nothing but watch as—in the distance—the waters are awake. She tries to warn Theseus, but only succeeds in crowding the interior of her mask with vision-obscuring bubbles.

The froth dissipates and gold turns to silver as the golden man—arm recoiled, ready to jab his spear at Theseus—is enveloped in a frenzy of fang-fish, nipping and gnawing and latching on, sharp as any monster trap.

Theseus fights free, pulling herself through the water and swiping away any fanged outliers, as the golden man is lost within the swirling mass.

Uneasy relief washes through Asterion. Fang-fish hunt as a shoal. Now they've caught their prey, they'll focus on that before venturing to find more.

Theseus rolls into a dive, heading straight for Asterion.

She's fast, but Asterion's lungs lurch, protesting, screaming at her that she's almost out of time.

An illumi-glowing palm reaches for her and Asterion reaches back. Theseus grabs her cuff—but instead of letting Theseus tow her up to the surface, Asterion pulls her down towards the bedrock.

With the—albeit distracted—fang-fish obstructing their path, plus the weight of Asterion's mask, they won't make it to the shore in time to not be next on the menu.

Confusion crowds Theseus's features as bubbles burst from her mouth. If only she could see Asterion's face, she might understand that it's okay; that Asterion has a way out. It's not one she's tried before, but... desperate times...

She tugs Theseus towards the distinctive emerald glow near the bedrock at the middle of the lake, where the water sways nearby plants. Theseus must recognise it, because she takes the lead, pulling Asterion along with admirable speed. Her ability to forge a path through water is a sight to behold, but not one Asterion has the luxury of lingering on right now.

Once they reach the emerald bedrock, Theseus's alert eyes assess the large circular grate, embedded in the bottom of the lake.

Asterion had designed the portcullis at the Labyrinth's centre to be opened by completing a fun, simple puzzle. But now, seeing it for the first time, she discovers that it, like so many of the Labyrinth's features, has suffered from Ariadne's dark revisions.

But, thank the heavens, the keyholes are a familiar design.

Her lurching lungs burn.

Everything is heavy and light all at once.

But they're almost there...

Theseus must understand because she joins Asterion, helping her align the mask's horns into the keyholes, her more dexterous hands assisting Asterion's lagging movements. It takes a second and an age before the grate spins, water swirling, pulling them into an emerald tunnel, the discrepancy in gravity propelling them towards moonlight.

An all-consuming heaviness crowds Asterion. Shadows, too. She's outside of time, where everything and nothing is possible. That moment on the cusp of *what next?*

Momentum.

Moonlight.

Asterion's torso lurches, her every muscle lashing out as her lungs splutter and she finally heaves in air.

Her heart races, her lungs tripping to catch up, as she's

dragged from the well. She lands gracelessly, soggily on soft ground and Theseus's solid warmth.

The mask's braces have loosened in the portcullis keyholes, just as they do in the fortress gateway...

The weight of the mask lifts from her shoulders as Theseus pulls it from her. It lands in a sodden heap in the grass, empty eyes staring at her in the fortress garden's moonlight, as cool air caresses her cheeks.

Illumi-thread fibres twinkle at her from the forearm across her chest, holding her close, keeping her safe. Theseus's chest rises and falls against Asterion's back, chasing her missed breaths.

"You're okay... breathe... breathe..." Theseus's lyrical Athenian is assertive and calming, but Asterion's desperate, rejuvenating breaths stumble with shuddering sobs. Relief at being able to breathe again? Or relief at experiencing her first *proper hug* in nineteen sun-orbits?

"You're good... you're good..." Theseus murmurs, and all Asterion can do is sob and bury her face against the warmth of Theseus's shoulder and the full body embrace. She doesn't bury her tears. She doesn't retreat. Because, for the first time in a long time, she has someone looking out for her.

For the first time in a long time, she can let herself crumble.

PART VII

THE FORTRESS

49

QUESTIONS
ASTERION

Once Asterion's sobs subside into mere cries and exhaustion, Theseus guides her to the wash chamber. The hastily applied camouflage has been mostly washed from her skin by the lake and well-waters, but the water cascade takes care of the rest.

Theseus must think Asterion's quaking limbs to be the result of the cold, because as the water warms her, she smooths her palms over Asterion's arms and back, encouraging further warmth into her.

That Theseus stays with her, supporting her, letting Asterion lean on her shoulder as she cries—is more warming and cleansing than any water cascade.

She vaguely recalls the air-blast drying her. And now she's in bed, wearing undershorts and a long-sleeve. Theseus—also in dry clothes, now—leans over her to adjust the bedcover, tucking her in.

When she steps away, Asterion reaches for her. "You—" She falters. *Don't go*, she wants to say. And: *You should go. You don't need to deal with this.* Indecision chokes her, and all that convulses from her throat are more sobs.

Theseus rubbing soothing circles between her shoulder blades makes everything better and worse.

Asterion shuffles over, and—as if by unspoken understanding—Theseus joins her under the covers. It feels so natural to gravitate to her warmth, to bury her face against her neck as the swell of Theseus's biceps and strong forearms wrap around her. Against her safe and sturdy foundations, it's only moments before Asterion finds sleep.

✦

ASTERION WAKES, thrashing.

Her chest heaves, and it takes several moments to recall that she's in her bed, safe in her fortress. She's not under attack. Bunched up and knotted, the bedsheets have lost the battle. Though, she's uncertain who won the internal war: her, or the shadows in her thoughts.

Her body aches like she's gone ten rounds in the Iolcian Games arena. Pressure niggles behind her eyes; her head protesting from last night's sobs. She reaches for Theseus, but the space beside her is empty. It's probably a good thing, considering the manner in which she awoke. The last thing she wants is to add to Theseus's injuries.

Asterion sits up, trying to stretch out her aches. There's no sign of Theseus in the bedchamber, but drifting in from the corridor there's the distinct smell of cooking eggs and burning bread. Asterion follows the questionable aroma to the kitchen, where she finds Theseus puzzling over a pan of scrambled eggs, a certain consternation to her frown that seems to question why they're defying her.

Theseus moves easily about the kitchen, the thread in her lower leg glowing. She's much more structurally sound now.

Which means she'll be leaving soon...

But before the pang of disappointment can take root in Asterion's chest, Theseus brightens as she turns and sees her in the doorway. That dulls all Asterion's aches, just a little.

Theseus has been industrious. Through the kitchen window, Asterion spies yesterday's clothes hanging on the line. Theseus could have dried them in the air-blast, but she must have noticed that Asterion likes to hang her clothes out in the garden.

"I'm not much of a cook," Theseus warns her with a careful grin as she plates up their breakfast. The slab of bread is somehow both too soft *and* burnt, and the eggs look less scrambled and more... decimated.

But it's perfect.

At the banquet table, Theseus sits closer to Asterion than usual, but not close enough to crowd her. The fresh, colourful proteus-fruit juice isn't cold, but it's not full of pips or pith either, which is a pleasant surprise given the egg and bread situation. The breakfast *is* objectively terrible. But subjectively...

Theseus could have let Asterion run off to get lost in her spiralling thoughts and the labyrinth. Instead, she'd risked her own safety to pursue Asterion, saved her from the hunter and from drowning, looked after her... even made her breakfast. And the way she's glancing at Asterion now, when she thinks Asterion isn't looking, like she's trying to check she's okay but not deluge her with questions...

Asterion's chest swells with warmth. "Thank you." Her voice comes out gravelly from last night's tears. But she has her own questions for Theseus. Firstly:

"You are—okay?" Though Theseus shows no obvious signs of injury, she had quite the skirmish last night.

"All good." Theseus smiles, but then turns a little sombre. "I've dealt with people like him before." She breezes on, not lingering on whatever dark thought must have surfaced. "And I think those fish will have, uh... solved our problem?" Her glance at Asterion is careful, like she's not sure how either of them will feel about this.

"He deserves it." Asterion points to Theseus's leg. "It was his trap. Before. With—spear... He was—to kill you."

Theseus's eyes widen. She speaks slowly, like she's discovering the words for the first time. "And...you stopped him?" She nods to herself, like pieces of a puzzle are slotting into place. "*He's* the monster you were talking about." She rubs her face. "He killed Tattoo?"

Asterion nods. Had Theseus thought her responsible for that? No wonder she was on such a war path when she first got here.

"Yeah." Theseus nods. "He deserves it."

"He not—even have—excuse of mists." If he'd been drenched in the mists, she might understand his proclivity for violence, but... Speaking of which... "The mists... you are okay?"

"I held my breath," says Theseus with a brief but smug grin. Good. *Good*.

"And you?" There's concern and curiosity in Theseus's eyes. "The mists got you too, but... you're okay? Already?"

"Repeat exposure—mists—metabolise faster."

For a moment, Theseus's mouth hangs open. "You know the Athenian for 'metabolise'?"

Asterion shrugs. She likes Theseus's growing smile, but... there are more important things right now. "You kill monsters?"

Theseus's smile disappears, and Asterion instantly misses it. "I do."

"And you are here to kill *me*?"

Theseus pokes at her obliterated eggs before looking at Asterion with such sincerity that Asterion already trusts her.

"I'm here to kill a terrifying Minotaur," says Theseus, matter-of-factly, and Asterion holds her breath like she's back in the nightmare mists. "Let me know if you see one, will you?"

And just like that, Asterion's stress unwinds.

Just as it had become obvious that Theseus had arrived here on a mission to kill her, it's obvious now that her mission has changed. They've weathered so much together already... She *does* trust Theseus. If she didn't, she wouldn't have let herself crumble in her arms last night.

Asterion pokes at the half-charcoal, half-bread lump on her plate. "You murder breakfast instead?"

It's fascinating to watch the mix of surprise and amusement in Theseus's blooming smile. "Like I said... cooking's not my skill set."

No. No, it's not. But officially monster killing is. And that reminder has Asterion's positivity paused. She huffs, annoyed with herself, with her situation. "I did not know..." She hates how small her voice is. How shaky. She tries again. "You are— first person I save. And that—only because you—too unconscious to kill me."

Theseus, to her credit, doesn't protest. She just nods, waiting for her to continue.

"I'm not *stupid*," Asterion says, sharply. "I can—take hint. Swords and spears—thrown my way. But—I—not know they— here—to kill me. That you..." Asterion scrubs her forehead with her palm, her cheeks heating with embarrassment, because Hades in the Heavens, it's so blazingly obvious now. "I thought everyone—afraid... in the mist... my mask—it scares. I understand fear. I... not realise."

She puts her fork down, worried she's clutching it too much like a weapon. "I—not know people *have—mission* to kill me." Her stomach churns, although that could be the burnt bread.

"What did you think people were here for?" Theseus asks, gently.

Asterion shrugs. "To win against—Labyrinth. To find—way

out? Minosians prize solving the puzzle. To triumph against death."

Theseus nods, thoughtful. Something about her rucked brow suggests she doesn't want to ask her next question... "Why do you think you are here?"

That question. It's a vice about Asterion's lungs. It's *the* question; the corridor of daggers she's avoided ever since she awoke here all those sun-orbits ago. She tries to breathe evenly, but her breath stumbles and stutters, her every muscle primed to bolt.

But outrunning the truth is as much a fool's journey as outrunning your fears, isn't it? It's time she faced up to it. She doesn't owe Theseus an explanation, but perhaps she owes one to herself.

"At first I think—it is—game." Her heart rate ratchets, but she powers on. "I think—I had to *solve* labyrinth. I think Ariadne —be here, too. That we will live here, away from—challenges of royal court."

Asterion soothes her sternum with her palm, a fire-swamp of hurt bubbling within her. "But. *No Ariadne.* She—good with politics, always. I never..."

How to sum up that though people might have admired her designs, her architectural achievements—beyond that, there was nothing she could get right? Not in the eyes of Ariadne and Father, and often times the royal court. No-one appreciated being told they were wrong, that they never thought things through. But if something is ill-conceived, egotistical, or cruel, why not call it such?

Asterion might design labyrinths, but the subtle cues of social requirements are a maze she always gets lost in.

"I—not subtle." Her eyes flit to Theseus, searching for any clue, any smirk or tick, to suggest she might be with *them* on this. But Theseus's features hold only understanding. It's the crutch of courage she needs.

"Constructionists—idiots. Father, as well. They waste resources for vanity. Entertainment. I tell them. I question. I give —better way forward. But I—always—sent to my chamber. I think..."

Asterion gazes out of the banquet hall's vast window, overlooking the garden. How many hours of her life has she spent imagining her sister joining her here? How many sun-orbits has she wasted longing for Ariadne's approval... her affection? And how long has she been hiding from the inevitable truth?

Ariadne is not the person Asterion wishes she were. Asterion might be the one with the pebble pendant, but Ariadne is the one with the heart of stone. She always had the sediments of cruelty within her, and with time and pressure they had lithified.

"...they sent me away." The words snag like a fish hook in her throat. She swallows to soothe the ache. "I always—annoy Ariadne. I think she—want me gone."

The sentiment is a bull kick to her chest.

Why had Asterion ever wanted her approval to begin with? Ariadne might be good at getting what she wants, but she was never *good*. Asterion might never have been socially adept, but at least she cares about other people.

She fights back the tears threatening to break through her defences. She should have admitted it to herself long ago. Ari's forte has always been torture.

Asterion draws the deepest of breaths, steeling herself.

"Minotaur is—myth. Story told to children. Ariadne—make real. She want to—make me—monster. And she—sends you to..." She gestures to Theseus, but she can't look at her. She can't say the word *kill*. "Ariadne—not protect me. And I am—idiot. I hide—from truth."

"No." Theseus's reply is so sudden, Asterion's gaze swerves to her. "You're not an idiot," she says, more gently but with the same conviction. "*Hope* isn't idiotic. Your sister might have wanted rid of you, and found a way to elevate herself in the process. But you are not an idiot. This place has death at every corner—but you survive, Asterion. Every sun-orbit, when people try to hurt you, you survive. You thrive. And you try to save them. You hope to make a difference. Seeing the good in people doesn't make you an idiot. Those of us who ever wished you harm are the idiots. You saved *me*. You're a fucking hero."

Oh.

Well...

The fire-swamp inside Asterion simmers down as her heart pendant warms her skin. It's probably glowing, but she daren't check in case she draws attention to the lump of stone that gives away her feelings. As if her torque doesn't do that already.

"I talk to chickens..." she points out. "I—not sure that—constitute—*thriving*."

Theseus's answering smile is so broad; if Asterion's pendant hadn't been glowing before...

As if on cue, Bok-bok—where in the heavens has she been hiding?—flaps up onto Asterion's lap, wiggling like Asterion is her own personal nest.

Asterion doesn't miss Theseus's flinch and glare. In fairness, the chicken is giving good side-eye back. Asterion can't help her amusement at Theseus's huffs. "You sure—you are—monster hunter?"

"I don't hunt chickens!" But Theseus is smiling just a little, too.

Bok-bok flaps in protest as Asterion stands. Theseus's eyes are questioning. And Asterion wants to give her answers, because... it's just... it's important that Theseus *knows*. Because she's right: this place has death at every corner. Which is why Asterion needs her to understand that she's not a monster.

50

NOT A MONSTER
THESEUS

Moments earlier...

Here's a strange 'morning after' nervousness in the air. The kind that hovers in the wake of showing someone intimate parts of yourself. Theseus's clothes had remained distinctly on—well, after she'd changed out of her sopping wet clothes and into dry ones—and yet she feels like she's shared herself for the first time.

Which makes no sense, given that it had been Asterion, not Theseus, who'd let loose her emotions. Theseus was simply *there*.

But *there* is not ordinarily where she is. Even when she forges physical connections, she never stays for breakfast, let alone cooks it—which the evidence on their plates makes abysmally clear. She should really improve her culinary skills there.

Last night, trails of tears had marked Asterion's cheeks. It had broken something inside Theseus to see her so submerged in suffering. As her sobs had vibrated through them both, all Theseus had wanted was to hold Asterion together as she fell apart. If only there was some way for her to make everything better, to give Asterion back the life her sister has stolen. But it's not exactly the sort of problem she can throw a sword at.

How could Ariadne be so callous? Theseus has a thousand questions on the intricacies of the sibling rivalry and how it paved the way to Asterion's imprisonment. She has a sky full of other questions, too. But for now, all she can focus on is Asterion getting abruptly to her feet, her eyes sparkling with nervous enthusiasm as she asks: "You want to see my designs?"

Well... Theseus might not understand what she's asking, exactly, but she'll say yes no matter what.

✦

THESEUS'S CALF muscles niggle in protest as she follows Asterion along the curved corridor. The illumi-thread has healed her leg improbably fast, but it hadn't had time to settle before she'd raced after Asterion into the labyrinth last night.

Adrenaline might have masked the injury then, because it's reminding her it exists now. But she shakes off the discomfort to catch up with Asterion, who's trailing her hand in a purposeful pattern over part of the corridor wall at the site of the hidden door.

Sure enough, an oblong section of the wall opens out, and Asterion leads her into the library. Flames flare to life in the fireplace as they enter, its warmth wrapping around them like a hug.

A tough, monster hunter hug. Obviously.

While Asterion heads to the right side of the sizeable room where there's a massive wooden table piled with books—some open, some stacked—Theseus gravitates to the bookcases to examine the vertical lines engraved in them, spanning the front edge of every shelf. She'd thought them a pattern, perhaps—but now it occurs to her, with unease souring her stomach—what they really are.

She's been in a few prison cells over the sun-orbits; she knows first-hand the elasticity of time when all you have are the walls for company. Those cells had been decorated with lines like this.

She turns to Asterion. "How long have you been here?"

The sparkle in Asterion's eyes dims a little as she looks up from her table of books. "What measurement—you like? Sun-orbits? Minosian? Athenian? Standard?"

Interplanetary sun-orbit conversions were never Theseus's strong point, but when Asterion motions to the markings on the lower shelves and tells her, "I was shorter when—first arrived," understanding thumps like an uppercut to her ribs.

She was a child *when she was sent here.*

Her guide-Shard had told her as much, hadn't it? That the 'Lost Princess' was 'lost' at a young age. She just hadn't wholly... understood it.

"You were—?" The words snag in her throat.

Asterion squints, calculating. "I count... nineteen sun-orbits and seventy-three days. I was—eleven, when..." She trails off as she returns to her books, flipping through the pages with purpose. She gestures for Theseus to join her at the table.

Theseus gravitates to her side but leaves a respectable gap between them. The last thing she wants is to crowd Asterion, even if her brain is teasing her with memories of wrapping her in her arms.

Focus, Theseus. Asterion is telling you something. Asterion has slipped into Minosian in her enthusiasm. Behind the hard sounds, there's an almost soothing rhythm, even if she's talking so fast Theseus can't pin down the individual words.

There are diagrams for *everything* in these tomes: everything within, and relating to, the Labyrinth. The Minoglyphs are lost on Theseus, but the free-form artistic sketches and rigid, precise blueprints—pages dedicated not merely to each chamber, but to each component within— are clear enough, though the details they depict are so complex, it boggles Theseus's brain.

This must be Asterion's analysis of how everything in the Labyrinth works: the records she's kept while trying to figure out how to escape, or to keep herself safe.

When Asterion meets Theseus's eyes, she looks almost bashful. "Sorry. I forget," she says, in Athenian now. "Handwriting is —mess, I know."

Is it? The designs for the light-blocks are as clear as day, detailing how the Labyrinth's outer-shell absorbs sunlight or moonlight, channelling it through to the inner layers through colourful blocks in the walls. Other diagrams seem to suggest that the ice forest is part of a meticulously balanced weather system. Those drawings contain clear hazard markings warning to only enter the chamber at certain points in the Labyrinth's rotation.

In the next notebook are depictions of the meadow's woodland: everything from sketches of trees to equations longer than any sentence Theseus has ever uttered. The fungi are a particular focus, along with a warning about its byproduct.

Asterion must notice the focus of Theseus's attention. "The mists—intended as—positive effect. Euphoric. Like dream. Uh... wish fulfilment. But balance is off. It can bring—emotion— thoughts—um—expectation closer to surface—exaggerated like nightmare. Effects depend on—uh—state of mind. I warn—in notes—but... I think Constructionists not pay attention—or ignore." She wrings her hands like she's nervous. "I promise—I not design—death maze."

She looks at Theseus imploringly, as if begging her to believe her. But Theseus is busy choking on her own breath.

These are the original designs?

Asterion designed this place?

Asterion is the Architect?

That's a snowball to the face if ever there was one. Theseus coughs, still spluttering.

Asterion steps around her to whack her on the back. "I forget —how—to function sometimes—also." She traces her fingertips over an expanse of pages covered with fraught scribbles of Minoglyphs. "I try—stop mists. But is—fungus mutation—issue."

"You *designed* this place?"

Asterion squints quizzically at her, as if they're back to having no shared words. And Theseus can only blink at her in awe. At eleven sun-orbits, Theseus had been climbing trees and getting into scraps. She barely knew her ass from her elbow. Meanwhile, Asterion had been designing worlds.

"This place—meant to be in balance. My design—it is— world that ticks over. Not..." A heavy frown furrows Asterion's features, and Theseus wishes she could smooth it away. "...this." Asterion gestures, indicating the Labyrinth in general.

The Labyrinth creaks as if in agreement.

With new eyes, Theseus re-examines the notebooks. In Asterion's designs, the external gateway is decorative, but not threatening. There's no looming Minotaur, for starters. The ice forest had been intended as nothing more than a cluster of crystalline trees arranged to form a fun mirror maze.

As Theseus thumbs the sketches, Asterion gives a self-deprecating chuckle. "I was—little—when I designed."

Sure enough, among the precision of the blueprints are hints of a childlike exuberance. The sketches are beautiful, the imagination behind them whimsical. They're the kind of images an interplanetary tourist might choose to boast: *Wish you were here!*

The pieces are starting to fall into place. Princess Ariadne's motivations are starting to make sense. Well, not *sense* as in morally right and something that anyone should ever do to someone else, let alone your own sibling, but sense in terms of how the power-hungry shape the world around them to claw to the top.

The Sky Labyrinth is the architectural wonder, the feat of engineering, that won Ariadne the title of Architect-in-waiting. Ariadne wanted her sibling gone.

But why keep her alive?

Murdering someone for a throne is not something Theseus would think to do, but if Princess Ariadne is intelligent and cruel enough to co-ordinate such a complex throne-theft, why didn't she just kill her sister? There are far easier ways to get rid of someone than imprisoning them in a Sky Labyrinth, and challenging oafs on a mission for validation, and criminals desperate for redemption, with the task of killing them.

Does Ariadne want her sister dead by especially creative means? Is that what this is? A horribly creative punishment? A game?

In Theseus's experience, monsters who play games never tire of them. They never change, either. They strive only to bend the universe to their will.

And Theseus is an idiot. She sees monsters everywhere, yet was fooled by one masquerading princess imploring her to set her free?

Honestly, it's embarrassing she'd been so easily led.

Theseus is only scratching the surface of Asterion's designs, but it's clear she'd intended to create something beautiful. This world was designed to be a wonder; playful and perfect.

Until Princess Ariadne stole those designs and twisted them in to something monstrous.

Well, fuck.

It's almost impressive how much Theseus got backwards, isn't it?

She faces Asterion, preparing to ask one of her thousand

questions, or voice one of her thousand apologies... but where in the heavens to begin?

Asterion steps closer to her, her fingers tracing just above Theseus's right cheekbone like she's trying to make sense of *Theseus's blueprints*. Her almost-touch, that curious gaze, whisks the breath from Theseus's lungs.

"Why you—look at me like this?" asks Asterion.

Has Theseus been outright gaping at her? Again?

Shit.

But all Theseus can do is stare. Because just as each new Labyrinth rotation, each new permutation, uncovers new avenues, Asterion, too, is full of surprises. Like the Sky Labyrinth, Asterion is complicated, mighty... beautiful.

"It's j-just—" Theseus begins, nervously adjusting from foot to foot and— *Fuck*. Pain radiates up from her right leg. She stumbles, but Asterion ducks under her arm and guides her towards a wingback chair. Theseus opens her mouth to protest, but—

"Sit," insists Asterion, and Theseus does as she's told.

She must have overdone it, running so soon after starting to heal. The language must be settling in her veins, though, because she understands when Asterion commands, in Minosian, "Let me see."

She lifts Theseus's heel and cushions her leg on the opposite chair. She mumbles something soothing—so much for getting to grips with Minosian—and Theseus needs a moment. To recover from the pain branching up her leg, yes—but mostly to rearrange her brain cells.

She's never been this malfunctional—emotionally, communicatively, physically—around *anyone*. And it's pissing her off.

51

FRAGILE
THESEUS

Asterion must attribute Theseus's scowl purely to the pain, because she kneels to inspect where the illumi-thread stitches have melded with Theseus's flesh. Her gentle touch shouldn't be propelling Theseus's pulse like a well-oiled sky-cruiser, but it does.

She's just seeing to your wounds. Your previously gross and scabbing injury.

Theseus would do well to remember that. And to not think about how, the last time Asterion dressed her wounds, they'd ended up tangled in the bed together. Heavens above, was that only last night? It feels both a lifetime and moments ago.

Theseus grits her teeth. She'd expected to be challenged within the walls of the Sky Labyrinth, but she hadn't considered gentle hands to be the source of torture: hands, apparently, that belong to a genius who designed a monumental puzzle in the sky.

Like, seriously. What the fuck?

"The illumi-thread—it undo damage," Asterion explains. "It heal—admirably—but it need—chance to absorb. So... no more chasing me through—labyrinth, okay?"

Stars above and heavens below, has she always had that mischievous half-smile? Theseus needs to stop staring at her like she hung the Minosian moons. Though... technically...

Anyway. The ache in her leg is probably just cramp. She hadn't exactly done any stretches before pursuing Asterion.

"Is probably—just cramp," Asterion pronounces.

Has that furrow of concentration in her forehead always been this cute?

Stop staring. Focus on literally anything else. She leans back to gain a bit of distance, her palm planting against something soft. A pillow. There's a neatly folded blanket, too.

"This is where you've been sleeping?" Theseus winces: it's not the best change of subject, but at least she can still form a sentence. She shifts in her seat. The chair is comfortable enough, but it's not somewhere she'd choose to sleep. Perhaps Asterion's scowling at neck ache wasn't simply the result of the Minotaur mask.

Asterion looks up at her, wryly. "There was—murderous monster hunter in my bed."

Theseus narrows her eyes. "You didn't know I was a monster hunter."

"*Murderous* is enough to not share bed."

Yeah. That's fair.

"You're telling me this grand palace of yours only has one bed?"

Stop talking about beds. Heavens above.

Asterion stiffens and Theseus kicks herself. She'd said she dreamed up this place as a sanctuary for her and Princess Ariadne. She recalls Asterion's workshop; how its layout mirrors the bedchamber. Had that been its intended purpose in Asterion's original designs?

If Theseus could hunt Ariadne right now, she would.

Umm... So...

It's not her imagination that Asterion's thumb is caressing her leg, is it? She's probably just massaging the muscle to stave off any returning cramp. That would be... logical.

Breathe.

"I—liked it."

What? Theseus's brain isn't working today. Has she missed something Asterion said? Or is Asterion doing that thing where she starts her sentence in the middle of an unspoken conversation?

Either way, now is an entirely inconvenient time to be noticing the shimmering turquoise flecks in Asterion's eyes; like sunshine on a calm ocean...

"The kiss," Asterion clarifies. "I liked it."

Oh. The sky-cruiser in Theseus's chest just switched up a gear. Maybe that'll kick-start her brain. It's kick-starting everything else, that's for sure.

"I have—never kissed before. I would—like to. Again. With you."

Theseus's spluttering inner propeller doesn't know which way to steer.

"I..."

...want to...

"I..."

...mustn't promise more than I can give...

"I shouldn't have kissed you, Asterion."

Asterion's hands drop from her leg, her scowl calling *bullshit.* "Why not?"

"Many reasons." *I don't want you to get attached. I don't want you to mistake your feelings for something they're not.* "You never having been kissed before, for one."

The scowl deepens. "By that logic no-one—ever be kissed."

Of course Asterion will easily out-logic anything Theseus

says. That shouldn't make her want to smile, should it? Asterion sure isn't.

"If—should not have... why did you?"

Theseus clears her throat, because now she's thinking about it: about how Asterion's fingers had traced her skin, how her breath had caressed Theseus's cheeks. But Theseus had been the one to close the gap, to seek Asterion's lips: her soft, warm, curious, keen lips...

She tugs at her collar. Has the lava network ramped up?

"I... Uh... I guess I got a little caught up in our proximity."

Asterion nods, slowly. "Do you not enjoy... proximity?"

Now *there's* a question.

Exasperation bristles in Theseus's chest. "Asterion..."

"*Theseus...*" Asterion mimics.

Seriously? Is Asterion mocking her? Right now?

"I wanted your kiss." Asterion just lets *that* stretch between them.

"Asterion..."

This time, Asterion doesn't mock her; she just frowns. And Theseus hates that she's the cause. "I just... I don't want you to think this is... something it's not."

Asterion sits back on her heels, observing her as though waiting for Theseus to elaborate. *Okay...*

"You've been trapped within these walls for so long. I only seem... *attractive*... because you've got nothing to compare me to."

Asterion's features pinch. "I—crossed paths—many people. I —never want—to kiss any of them."

"The people in the labyrinth? The ones who are either running from you or trying to kill you?"

"Yes. But—"

"Me not running away or trying to kill you is too low a bar for you to want to kiss me, Asterion. We don't know each other.

Not really. You don't know *me*. You've only known for a matter of hours that I *was* initially here to kill you."

Asterion's properly scowling now. Seconds pass, each more damning than the last. Theseus should never have leaned into that kiss. Then they wouldn't be having this conversation and Asterion wouldn't have to try to translate Theseus's emotions when Theseus can't even decipher them herself.

"Was I...unskilled—?" Asterion tilts her head in that way she does when she's trying to figure something out. Theseus scolds herself for making Asterion feel in any way *not enough,* but Asterion continues. "Practice—makes good. And—improve with constructive criticism. But only if you... want?"

Yes. Want. But...

Theseus swallows. The last thing she needs to be thinking about is *practising* with Asterion. She shifts in her seat. Asterion saying all these things... it's making her want to wrap her arms around Asterion and kiss away the scowl that she put there in the first place.

But if she did that, she'd be the worst person in the universe for the crime of mixed signals.

"You've been through so much, Asterion. Kissing you... I shouldn't have... I, um—" Theseus rubs her forehead and sighs. "It's just that—what you're asking of me... Sometimes that sort of closeness can lead to... feelings."

And damn if *that sort of closeness* hasn't been setting her own thoughts wandering lately. She's usually better guarded. She's sure her crush will swagger away if she doesn't do anything stupid, like stoke the flames. She hopes so, anyway. She's not usually prone to crushes.

Asterion's eyes widen as her expression tours from realisation via disbelief to annoyance. "You think I am... *delicate*?"

Theseus almost laughs, because *delicate* is the last thing Asterion is. She's the mighty—if misunderstood—Minotaur who deals daily with the deadly shifting puzzle of the Labyrinth. She's the warrior who dragged Theseus to safety when she couldn't save herself, even though Asterion herself was injured.

Theseus tries not to think about all the wounds Asterion's body has fought to heal. She tries even harder not to think about the strength in those arms, those shoulders. The contours of the muscles that only last night she touched.

Fuck. The sky-cruiser of her heart rate isn't short on fuel.

Asterion's strength is so much more than physical. She's been shut away for so long, yet she holds no grudge in her heart, only kindness. She might be the strongest person Theseus has ever met.

"No..." Theseus cringes at the weakness of that one word. She hadn't intended to patronise Asterion. She'd been trying to avert disaster, only to navigate right to it. Asterion just has her so unbalanced she keeps landing with her foot in her mouth. Fuck's sake.

But before she can kick her stupid brain into gear, Asterion stands, fists clenched at her sides; breathtaking and defiant.

And all Theseus can do is stare in panicked admiration as Asterion closes her eyes and rolls her neck, her muscles slackening, as if recovering from an inner battle.

That's true strength: unravelling negativity before it tangles within you.

"I know I—shut away from—real worlds," says Asterion. Her eyes blaze with quiet fury, though her voice is calmer than Theseus's would be if their roles were reversed. "Separate—from people. But I—not without context. I read fictions. I watch story-reels. I know about—*intimacy*. Obviously, you *not murdering* me —is—crucial component." She scoffs. Her Athenian is getting really good. "But that—is not what attracts me to you."

So... she *is* attracted to—?

Theseus. Behave. That is *not* the point here.

"If you—not want to kiss me, Theseus—is fine." Is that disappointment flickering over Asterion's features? "*I'm* not a monster. But what—*not* fine—is you treating me like I—am naïve, fragile princess—trapped in tower, unable to navigate feelings."

Okay.

Yes. Fair.

Asterion huffs. At herself? At Theseus? At the unsettled flickering of fire-torches and the hearth? She turns and marches away—but then strides back toward Theseus, stopping just out of arm's reach. "You think—one kiss and I—fall in love with you? I—fine before you—in my world. I—be fine—when you gone."

Ouch. That's Theseus told. But... hadn't that been exactly what Theseus wanted to hear? Wasn't that what she was trying to protect Asterion from: the risk that if they encourage whatever it is that's been building between them, it'll hurt Asterion when Theseus leaves?

So why do Asterion's words hurt *her* to hear?

And, more importantly... *Asterion doesn't want to leave?* Is that because she can't? Or won't? She apparently thinks it's possible for Theseus to leave, so why not her?

That's a topic they need to explore.

Later.

If Asterion ever talks to her again.

"Just because I—never *experienced* intimacy..." continues Asterion, "just because I—never been touched, that doesn't make me a fool—"

"Asti, I know that—" Theseus hazards to her feet, her leg a lot less excruciating than this conversation she's stumbled them into.

Asterion arches an eyebrow at her. *Do you?*

Theseus tries not to gulp. There's a sharp intelligence in

Asterion's eyes: a starry winter sky over a frozen lagoon. Invigorating, beautiful... but biting, too.

Focus...

"—And Theseus?"

Asterion steps right up to her, and *fuck* Theseus could kiss her; show her there's only one fool here, and it's an arrogant jerk of a monster hunter. Is she being a sanctimonious jackass in refraining, or just a sensible one?

"...it's not as though I don't know what—hand between my thighs feels like."

Well, fuck. That's an image Theseus could do without if she ever wants to form a sentence again.

Heavens, Theseus, find your tongue and use it.

For *speaking*. Obviously.

But before Theseus can close her mouth and not look like a dazed fang-fish, Asterion marches from the library without a backward glance, muttering in Minosian.

With her departure, the flames in the hearth die, the fire-torches dulling. The library feels suddenly cavernous and cold. Theseus paces, racking her brain for the shape of Asterion's parting words:

Instead... decide... feel... want... ask...

"Instead of deciding what I feel, what I want—perhaps you could *ask*."

Theseus stops pacing, shame writhing within her gut. Theseus, you fuckwit.

52

FRUSTRATION
ASTERION

N*ot some naïve, fragile princess trapped in a tower, unable to navigate feelings...*

Well... navigating feelings effectively doesn't involve stomping off in a huff, does it? Even Asterion knows that.

In her defence, she's not had much need to practise reeling in her emotions when her companions for the last nineteen sun-orbits have been a flock of temperamental and melodramatic chickens. And before that, her demonstrations of interpersonal skill had resulted in her closest family sending her to exist *in the sky*.

It's not a ringing endorsement.

But still—what does Theseus know? Apart from how to provoke a whole host of frustrations?

Asterion grunts, her muscles aching as she flips the giant stone slab from one side of the orchard to the other to clucks of vague encouragement from Bok-bok. Who, thankfully, has just about enough sense to not get in the way of Asterion's weight training; preferring to oversee from a nearby branch.

It's a redundant task, but a therapeutic one: good for channelling her newly discovered excess angst.

She doesn't need anything from Theseus. She doesn't need anything from anyone. This is *her* world.

Aside from Ariadne's deadly adjustments...

Anyhow...

She'll be fine when Theseus leaves.

The massive stone thumps down onto the grass.

Asterion paces, catching her breath. Theseus isn't right, is she? Asterion isn't only drawn to her because she's *here* and Asterion has no point of comparison?

No. It doesn't fit. Even out in the labyrinth, Theseus had fascinated her in a way no other voyager ever has. Perfect jawline and athletic prowess aside, she'd admired Theseus's kindness and bravery.

How was she supposed to know Theseus had come here to kill her?

She hefts the slab one more time.

It would be fair to conclude that she trusts too freely. She'd trusted her family to act in her best interests. Okay; she hadn't *specifically* trusted them not to banish her to a prison orbiting their homeworld—who would even think of that?—but she'd been trusting enough not to see their ruthless self-interest.

Perhaps she had been too eager in inviting a strange warrior into her fortress to recuperate. But epic, life-threatening misunderstandings aside... she'd tried to keep Theseus at a distance, to not know her.

And yet, she cannot shake the idea that she *does* know Theseus. Perhaps not so much in words and shared histories, but in her gut. And in their shared laughter. That had been the most healing of balms.

She might not be able to articulate it, but there's something about Theseus that draws her closer. A moth will always flutter towards the light; only once it's close does it discover whether it's a light that warms or a flame that burns.

Should she have told Theseus she'd been fascinated by her in the labyrinth as she'd never been by others? Or would Theseus think her some strange cavern-dweller?

Perhaps that is how Theseus sees her. Perhaps that's why she doesn't wish to kiss her again.

Fair enough.

Theseus isn't wrong to be cautious. A loner in a sky-fortress is unlikely to be the most well-balanced. But though Asterion hadn't intended to throw herself at Theseus—the Labyrinth had orchestrated that—she had welcomed the sudden embrace.

And Theseus had invited their kiss.

But one 'no' is enough. Asterion would never want to over-step. So all she can do is respect Theseus's words. Respect with a monumental dose of confusion, perhaps. But still respect.

And that's okay. It has to be.

It's just... *difficult* when she's been locked away so long with only the imaginings of fiction for company, and then some warrior with an exquisitely angled jaw and a smile that lights up the heavens, saunters into her world. It's difficult not to want to explore that jaw, and the mouth responsible for those smiles.

Asterion sighs. A few more rounds of stone-heaving and she'll be too tired for such thoughts.

"Bok-bok." The chicken summons her attention towards Theseus, loitering at the garden's edge by the fortress doorway. She's wandering gingerly on her recently cramped leg, avoiding looking directly at Asterion. She must know Asterion is here— she's making rather audible progress with hefting the giant stone, and the nearby proteus tree is awash with intense colours —but she's not venturing any closer.

Is she checking on Asterion? Making sure she's not going to emotionally unspool?

Bok-bok doesn't chase Theseus off, but she maintains a good

suspicious squint from her branch, an expression probably much like Asterion's own. The combination sees Theseus retreat into the fortress, which only adds to Asterion's frustration. Now her leg is almost healed, Theseus could go any day now.

And then that's it.

Asterion sighs.

She can't keep avoiding Theseus. It'd be stupid to miss her only chance in nineteen sun-orbits to make a friend. It might hurt when she leaves, but at least Asterion will have memories; something different to her usual repeating routine.

That is, if Theseus is even interested in friendship. Or if she sticks around long enough for it to be a possibility.

✝︎
˙•

IT'S ALL VERY WELL DECIDING NOT to avoid Theseus, but clearly Theseus knows how to make herself scarce when she wants to. No doubt Asterion's lack of greeting in the gardens was taken as a hint.

When it's time to prepare dinner, Asterion discovers the vegetables already chopped and ready, alongside a note in a scrawling attempt at Minosian:

WAS PROCEED TO CONCOCT FOOD
BUT CONJECTURE YOU WANT MEAL PALATABLE

A scribble in Athenian follows, presumably as backup:

WAS GOING TO COOK
BUT THINK YOU WANT DINNER TO BE EDIBLE?

Signing off the note is a stick figure that seems to be Theseus herself, wielding a little stick-sword and wearing a chef's hat with her tufty hair poking out.

Theseus might not want to kiss Asterion, but she still makes her smile.

+
.•

THE AROMA of vegetable stew must draw Theseus out of hiding, because she peers around the banquet hall doorway, presumably trying to assess Asterion's mood.

Asterion sets their bowls across from each other at the table's centre and gestures for Theseus to join her. Theseus doesn't protest at sitting opposite her. In fact, she looks thankful; though also a little uncomfortable, as though she suspects Asterion might send her away at any moment.

As they sit, something in the mid-layer labyrinth mechanisms groans. Asterion holds her breath as she listens. A tree, snapped by multidirectional gravity, shuddering the woodland floor? Or... No—it's something caught. One of the air circulation rotors, perhaps?

Theseus glances warily around the hall. Understandably. It's not a calming sound when you're trapped at the centre of a moon-sized structure, orbiting a planet that has no interest in your safety.

But the snag, as often happens, resolves itself, and Asterion can breathe again.

"Minosian craftsmanship—more looks than substance," she explains to Theseus. "Quantifiers and Constructionists deviate from—designs." In Minosian, she adds, "Idiots."

Theseus's half-laugh is awkward, like she doesn't know what to say. Perhaps Asterion could have said something less terrifying? Something other than: *Idiots built this place, good luck to us.*

"Is probably okay," she adds, which, judging from Theseus's thin smile, is less reassuring than she'd hoped. "Happens a lot."

Theseus's face falls. Asterion sighs and picks up her spoon. Maybe silence is better.

But as they eat, even the creaking chatter and groaning distraction of labyrinth faults might be preferable to this silence. Hades in the Heavens. Dealing with a disgruntled fire-breathing chicken is easier than navigating the emotional landscape of another person, especially alongside her own feelings. How does one restart conversation after throwing a tantrum about kissing? Or not kissing? Or about being treated like someone who can't control her emotions, only to respond, arguably, by losing control of them?

Theseus clears her throat. "Maybe you could show me a thing or two?"

Asterion looks up. About kissing? About emotions? Or something else?

"I mean," continues Theseus, her cheeks pink. *She's thinking about kissing, isn't she?* "Um... in the kitchen. With cooking, I mean. This stew, it's... You know what you're doing. I don't know how I've survived this long without a single culinary skill."

She's babbling. And it's... cute?

Her on-edge energy should make Asterion nervous, too, but instead she's almost smiling, because Theseus is trying to build a bridge. As much as Asterion enjoys the Theseus who struts and swaggers, awkward, flustered Theseus is just as appealing.

Asterion sets down her cutlery and sits a little straighter in her seat. "It is possible..." she begins, and Theseus looks relieved not to be the one talking anymore. "...I was... bull-headed, before."

Theseus stares at her, her mouth twitching as if trying to work out whether that was a joke. Asterion smiles, and Theseus's cautious smile grows too.

"I responded poorly," Asterion adds, and Theseus's shoulders relax.

"I'm sorry I upset you." Her quiet words hold the weight of truth.

"I am sorry. Chasing me—cause more injury."

Theseus shrugs with a quiet smirk. "Given how I acted when I first got here, perhaps I deserve it. Just a little."

53

SOME WARRIOR

THESEUS

The tension from Theseus's earlier missteps seems to have passed. So much so, they tackle the dishes together in comfortable silence: Asterion washing, Theseus drying. It's so fucking domestic, and yet... oddly relaxing.

Though Theseus isn't sure she deserves to relax. She's apologised for upsetting Asterion—but is that enough? She's not normally one to get uptight about simple physical proximity...

She doesn't want to hurt Asterion; that much is true. But maybe it was unfair of her to assume Asterion might believe their attraction to be something more than it is. Asterion has never asked her for anything, let alone any kind of promise.

So why is Theseus being such an epic fuckwit about this?

Perhaps because she doesn't want Asterion to get hurt.

It *is* Asterion she's worried about.

Right?

Yes, Theseus can admit, quietly, to herself, that she has a crush—but that's not the same as *feelings*. She's just... drawn to Asterion. She admires everything about her: emotionally, physically, academically... She wants to listen to her voice even when she doesn't understand the words. And the very idea of hurting Asterion makes her own heart ache—

Oh.

Shit.

Apparently Theseus can face down a razor-horned creature feared by an entire world—but ask her to be honest about the thread tugging ever more insistently on her heart, and she'll run in the opposite direction.

Some *warrior* she is.

Especially for lumping all of this on Asterion: accusing her of being the one prone to too many feelings and liable to get hurt.

Fuck.

Should she tell Asterion all this? Would it help anything?

It might at least help Theseus feel like less of a chicken-shit.

Or maybe she should just get on with figuring out a way to get them both out of here.

"Monster hunter?" Asterion interrupts her thoughts, nudging a newly washed bowl into her hands. "Is a very specific profession. Why you—choose it?"

Theseus doesn't know how to answer that. Most people want to hear something heroic. And she can give them that, if she's in the mood.

She could tell Asterion about the water-dwelling creature with nine heads and a thousand teeth, or about the time she was chased by a fleet of wrecker ships. How many admirers have looked at her with hunger in their eyes, all because of her fear-lessness (recklessness?!)?

They wouldn't look at her like that if they knew the truth she barely even lets herself acknowledge: that the burr of inade-quacy that latched on early in her life means she never wants anyone else to suffer the poison and brutality of bullies. Which is why she does what she does. She wants to leave each galaxy better than she found it, yes—but also… how else is she meant to prove to herself that she's good enough?

But all Asterion knows of her exploits is from having been the target of her mission in the worst possible ways. She probably isn't looking for inflated tales of bravery and adventure.

Theseus shrugs. "Figured I might as well try to make the galaxies safer, one monster at a time."

Asterion is studying her like she's spotted a snag in Theseus's fabric and is deciding whether to pull at the thread. Theseus dries the crockery so hard she's surprised it doesn't break. Generally, she can joke or flirt her way out of discomfort, but her tongue's gone and tied itself in knots. Running is another option —but as much as she'd like to exit this conversation right fucking now, it's such a relief to be near Asterion, too.

How do those feelings make sense all at once?

"Safer for—people, not monsters," adds Asterion. Though not judgementally. Theseus hadn't thought to clarify. "It must put you in—danger a lot."

Fuck. Theseus can't even think about that. Not the *danger* bit, but the *monsters* bit. Asterion is clear evidence that she got it wrong this time. So fucking wrong. What are the chances she's got it wrong before? How much undeserved 'justice' has she doled out? How many unwitting mistakes that make *her* the fucking monster?

Don't think about that.

"I'm not the brightest." Theseus tries for a winning smile— the kind that charms people when she's in the mood to be charming—but it's a little tight, and Asterion simply nods her agreement.

Rude.

Though Theseus appreciates the honesty.

"Do you enjoy it?" asks Asterion.

"Being not bright?"

Asterion rolls her eyes, and Theseus's smile evolves to a genuine one. "I'm good at it. *Usually*." Though this whole adventure is a rather abysmal example of not just her observational skills, but her prowess with a blade. However, given the circumstances, she's rather thankful for that.

Asterion squints at her, perhaps considering whether to point out that's not the same thing. Theseus tries again: "I like that people and worlds are safer and happier when the monsters are gone." She clears her throat. In all her sun-orbits, she still hasn't found a way of saying that without sounding like a sanctimonious prick. Sometimes she leans into it—but if Herakles were here, she'd be eye-rolling, hard.

Besides, her swagger doesn't work so well with Asterion studying her like she's an equation she's almost solved.

Asterion returns to the dishes. "Have you—ever—killed a person?"

Theseus nearly drops the bowl she's drying as everything in her chest rebels. She tries to hide her shaking hands by pacing as she dries the crockery. She's making it worse.

Such a direct question. Typically, she sidesteps that sort of thing, deflecting to monster hunts that are more... acceptable. She could lie to Asterion, but...

Deep breath. Chin up. She has nothing to be ashamed of, even if her body doesn't always get that message. Even if Asterion judges her. Even though she cares what Asterion thinks... She doesn't want to lie to her...

"Yes." Her voice is smaller than she wants it to be, and her ability to make eye contact has upped and left. She dreads the possibility of disgust or disappointment in Asterion's expression, but she needs to know.

She looks up. Asterion is nodding slowly, thoughtfully. She's not looking at Theseus, but maybe that's because she's focused on the dishes. Maybe she's calibrating how she feels or giving Theseus a bit of much-needed space.

"Did they deserve it?" Asterion asks.

At least on this answer, Theseus's voice is as sure as her conviction: "Yes."

"Good." Asterion gives a single, certain nod.

That's it? That's all she has to say to Theseus's confession? She's just... accepted it? Most people want to know all the gory details of her job. At least, they think they do. Asterion only wants to know the justice of it.

The tension in Theseus's neck uncoils like she's just shed a Minotaur mask from her shoulders, but her relief lasts only a moment. Because if Asterion knew the details, perhaps she wouldn't be so understanding.

Or perhaps... perhaps Asterion is uniquely placed to understand?

"You choose—your life over theirs," says Asterion in quiet solidarity, as if she knows Theseus might spook at any moment. Heavens above and below; how did Asterion nudge beneath her armour?

"Do not worry, Theseus, Monster Hunter. You will be out soon. Back to making worlds better."

Is it just Theseus, or is Asterion sounding a little... flat? And what does she mean, *out*? Out of the Labyrinth? It can't be that easy, can it?

"Have you ever tried to leave?" she asks, and Asterion goes rigid at the sink.

The silence stretches. Perhaps Theseus isn't the only one sharing partial truths. She can't stop herself; she moves to stand beside Asterion, sharing her space for a moment before reaching for the blushing pink stone, the almost-anatomical heart pendant hanging on its long chain around Asterion's neck.

"You have the key to your escape," she says, examining it. It's warm to the touch, she notices, trying not to think about Asterion's warmth as she strokes the stone's smoothness with her thumb. "Why do you not use it?"

Asterion swallows. Is she staring at her mouth to better understand her, or...? Theseus should move away. Talk about mixed fucking signals.

"Mask make—not possible. N-no astro-helmet for mask—"

Would it be wrong to wring Princess Ariadne's neck? "But—"

Asterion turns away, taking her heart-pendant with her. "Is not possible."

Theseus swallows her disappointment; at the reinstated distance and Asterion's assertion. *Not possible?* How is it that a person who's capable of designing an *entire world* can't decipher a mask? But Asterion's shuttered demeanour makes it more than clear that she doesn't want to discuss it further.

Theseus clutches the drying cloth so she won't forget herself and reach for Asterion to soothe the tension in admirable neck muscles. But, as ever, her common sense is one step behind her motor mouth. "I can't imagine being shut away for so long. There must be things you miss."

Shit. How fucking insensitive.

Sure enough, Asterion's shoulders rise a little higher, her posture stiffened. When someone tells you they're trapped in a place—that they've been trapped there for nineteen sun-orbits, no less—maybe don't be the idiot who points out how much they're missing.

To Asterion's credit, she doesn't throw the dishwater in Theseus's face, or shove her out into the labyrinth. The tension in her posture is joined by a ponderous, almost tortured expression. And Theseus hates that the silence between them is stretching beyond the known galaxies. A sure sign that Theseus has fucked up. Again.

Quick. Change the subject. Something light. "Your Athenian is getting to be better than mine."

Asterion's worried eyes flit to Theseus. Perhaps because she's been punished—is still being punished, every day—for her accomplishments by the very people who were supposed to support and encourage her most. Theseus smiles, trying to show her it's a genuine compliment.

Asterion's laugh of relief is like a life-restoring V-iolin. And damn—her blush is about the cutest thing in this world and the next.

"Not better," Asterion corrects her. "But languages are—like puzzle. Once I know rules—it clicks. But you are born to Athenian. Yours—will always be—more real, even—once I am fluent —when mine is technically more correct."

Her eyes flick up to Theseus's as if worried she might be offended, but Theseus's mirthful smirk seems to calm her.

"I'll keep working on my Minosian."

Asterion nods. "You have—good accent. My ears—they enjoy the sound." That thread wrapping around Theseus's heart tugs, and she can't help glowing at the compliment. "Especially when you commit to it."

Yes, if only Theseus could *commit.* But the only thing she's ever committed herself to is hunting monsters.

+
∴

Is it strange that Theseus doesn't want the evening to end?

They're only walking from the kitchen to the library, at a pace that's perhaps meant to accommodate Theseus's healing leg—even though her leg is arguably healed now. But Theseus could imagine she's accompanying someone home after an enjoyable evening in a recreation district. Not that she's done that sort of thing often.

Right now, her heart is thumping harder than any gentle stroll merits. She knows why. It's her own unique combination of misplaced excitement and self-inflicted regret. Because what kind of dimwit warns off a handsome woman in case said woman gets her heart broken, only to get all swoony herself at a simple compliment about her accent?

Theseus huffs inwardly at herself.

They reach the hidden door to the library and she doesn't know what the fuck to do with herself.

"Good night?" Is the questioning lilt to Asterion's words because she's puzzled why Theseus is lingering, or because she doesn't want her to go?

"You should be in the bed," Theseus blurts, speaking before thinking. Big surprise.

Asterion looks at her, perhaps waiting for her to supply some context.

"I mean... it's your bed. You should sleep in it. I'm literally a pain in your neck at this point." Theseus laughs a little too loudly.

Asterion's mouth quirks—either at Theseus's joke or her mortifying awkwardness—as she rubs her neck, confirming the truth of Theseus's statement. "But—you are guest."

The statement stretches between them. And then, just as Theseus is certain Asterion is about to refuse...

"We could share?"

Theseus's heart needs to calm the fuck down. It's all fluttery. *Stop that.* She opens her mouth to insist, gallantly, that she can sleep in the library's nest of chairs... but she doesn't manage anything as advanced as words. Only a nod.

At that, Asterion brightens. Presumably at the prospect of a good night's sleep.

+
˙•

TEN MINUTES and a million heartbeats later, they settle under the covers. It's only a matter of days since Theseus had been busy alternately charging at the Minotaur and clawing away from her in terror. Now she's in bed next to the beast in question, her heart trying to drill out of her chest, wishing she could both run away and snuggle closer to her.

And if there's one thing Theseus doesn't do when she shares a bed, it's fucking *snuggle*.

Why in all the heavens did she agree to this?

Yes, they'd shared the bed last night. Theseus had even held Asterion in her arms. But that had been different. Asterion had been overwhelmed by *everything*. It would be confusing for them both if Theseus were to hold her again now. No matter how much her body buzzes with the inclination.

Asterion doesn't even want that, judging from her positioning right on the very edge of the mattress, as far away from Theseus as it's possible to get.

It's not long before Asterion's breathing settles, and Theseus could be convinced she's fast asleep. But when she steals a careful glance across the bed, Asterion is staring up at the ceiling, her eyes glistening.

Is she having trouble sleeping, too?

"The stars," says Asterion, softly, like it's a secret, and Theseus rolls onto her side to look at her properly. "You asked if there—is anything I miss. I miss seeing the stars."

And she rolls over, leaving Theseus staring at the line of luminous stitches peeking from beneath the strap of her vest; their glow bright enough to illuminate the older scars marking her flesh.

Theseus's heart squeezes, because while her own scars are mostly from her chosen profession, Asterion's are from being forced to fight for her life. Theseus has never before had the urge to reach out and kiss away someone's past hurts.

But that's her problem.

She's a warrior. She should be able to lie next to a kind, intelligent, creative, attractive individual and be able to keep her hands and lips to her damn self.

"Theseus?" Asterion shifts under the covers, angling to her.

"Mmmm?"

"Don't worry. I promise—not to kiss you again." She says it so matter-of-factly. Then she turns back over and falls asleep.

And now all Theseus can think about is Asterion and kissing. Stars above. There's little chance she'll find sleep now.

54

STARS

ASTERION

The stars have never called Asterion names or made her feel like a mistake or an embarrassment or like she's in the way. Then again, she's never offended the stars—at least to the best of her own knowledge, but that's really beyond her scope. She's always enjoyed them blinking down on her. Or up, down and sideways, as they're doing now.

That's why she uses the Labyrinth's raw materials—flint, clay, natural pigmentations—to draw, engrave or paint the stars she longs to see. It's why she'd included as many faux stars as possible in the Labyrinth's false skies; why she included several viewing platforms in the Labyrinth's exterior blueprints.

Those platforms were omitted from the construction—apart from one. Which seems a purposeful cruelty, because the mask's horns are too large for her to get through the access hatch.

Therefore, the stars remain beyond her reach.

She'd designed a place of perfection. A place of safety, of joy and wonder.

Ariadne had turned it into a punishment.

But Asterion doesn't want to think about that. Not while

she's perched in the open gateway of the Labyrinth's outer-shell, staring at the stars she misses so much.

It's a dream. She knows that. There's no other way that she could be observing the strange beauty of space without even an astro-helmet to protect her. Only in her dreams can she roam like this. Mask-less; defying the laws of the universe.

She's had this dream before, many times. It's one of her favourites. There's a peacefulness in sitting and staring at the ever-shifting vista of space.

Theseus is sitting beside her, legs dangling over the edge of the gateway, watching her the way Asterion usually watches this skyscape. That part of the dream is new. And breathtaking in a way she's never before been able to imagine.

Theseus leans in closer, warm breath teasing Asterion's lips before they meet in a gentle kiss...

The heat from where their lips touch travels a direct and pleasurable path down her body as Theseus's mouth roams, exploring Asterion's face, her neck. A stream of Athenian caresses her ears. The words are indecipherable, but their musicality, the affection in Theseus's tone, wraps around Asterion like silk.

With a gentle tug to her open shirt, Asterion invites Theseus closer. If only they could be rid of these layers...

She has no recollection of removing Theseus's clothes, nor Theseus having removed hers, but no fabric separates them now as Theseus's body presses the length of hers and Asterion presses back. Ordinarily Asterion needs to know the precise mechanics of a situation, but right now Theseus's smooth skin and hitched breath, and the otherworldly sensations building inside Asterion's own body, are her universe.

There's no glow beneath their chins. They're free of their torques, but Asterion doesn't need a piece of engineered metal to let her know how she's feeling. Even the backdrop of stars, framed by the gateway of her design, aren't enough to distract her from the perfection—the safety, the joy, the wonder—of Theseus's touch.

Intense azurite eyes reflect the stars, and Asterion cannot look away. It's sure as Hades in the Heavens not the gaze of someone who wants to run away.

Talented fingers caress between her thighs: the reverent touch of someone who wants her close, wants to keep touching her, kissing her, and would fight the heavens for her.

Perhaps it can only be a dream, but... She would fight the heavens for Theseus, too.

Unwilling to be a mere spectator to this adventure, Asterion slips her hand between their bodies and luxuriates in the push and pull of pleasure, in sweet Athenian moans, as Theseus's eyes light up like an aurora.

"Asti..." she whispers, that single word containing the best kind of confession as Asterion's universe expands beneath Theseus's touch—

⁜

ASTERION WAKES in the middle of the night to her own moan and gasp, echoed by the Labyrinth.

Sweat clings to her like the aftermath of a fever dream. She grips the bedsheets, chasing her breaths, blood rushing through her veins in a way that makes her feel alive.

The chamber is sweltering, the hearth blazing as hot as her roaming thoughts. She'll need to do something about that epic design flaw. It's just never been so pronounced before.

She could do with cooling down, too. And with not thinking about Theseus when she's right next to—

Asterion's thoughts stumble as much as her breaths.

Theseus.

She's not here.

The bed beside Asterion is empty.

Is that better or worse? Had she been audible enough in her dream state to scare Theseus away?

Maybe instead of fixing the heating problem, Asterion should just throw herself into the flames.

No, she's being dramatic.

But only a little.

No wonder Theseus has put a stop to any potential intimacy if Asterion's imagination embraces her so readily.

She takes a moment to wrangle her breathing into something resembling calm. She doesn't usually sleep so soundly; it typically takes no more than an out-of-place groan from the Labyrinth to rouse her. But not when she's wrapped in dreams of Theseus, apparently.

Something about Theseus... It has her relaxed...

Too relaxed.

Not that she's feeling any of that now.

Where is Theseus? Is something wrong?

The pragmatist in her checks the fortress entrance hall, just in case discovering Asterion in the euphoric throes of her dream has inspired Theseus to flee into the labyrinth and never return. But—no—that's just Asterion's embarrassment talking. From what she knows of the warrior, if she did hear anything, she'd either smirk knowingly, or blush as profusely as Asterion.

But the mask is still on its hook by the gateway. Maybe Asterion herself should do a few circuits around the labyrinth, just to expel this nervous energy.

The banquet hall is empty too, as is the kitchen. But the kitchen window frames the moonlit garden, and the far end, where the orchard begins, is aglow with colour.

Asterion navigates through the night-time garden towards the telltale glimmer of the proteus tree. Some leaves are vibrant, others drab; but all are in flux, light trickling through them, like they can't decide which colour they should be. The darker patches are a sign that either the air supply is out of balance, or there's someone beneath the branches who's off-kilter with sadness or gloom. But there are brighter leaves, too; pinks and purples, suggesting more positive possibilities.

The closer Asterion gets to the orchard, the louder the familiar snoring purr grows.

There, nestled in Theseus's lap, is a sleeping Bok-bok, her feathers dark save for flickering embers. Unless Bok-bok is having a troublesome chicken dream, it's likely the fluctuations in the proteus tree's hues stem from the person sat beneath its branches.

Theseus looks up, and Asterion wants to comment on Bok-bok snuggling up to Theseus (and not trying to burn her to a husk), but their quiet shared smile says enough.

Theseus is a little hunched; deflated, almost. If not for the fleeting smile, Asterion would think she wants to be left alone. But when Asterion sits beside her in the soft grass, in amongst the tree roots, Theseus doesn't move away.

Sitting side by side, like this, it's not unlike her dream of being in the gatehouse together, staring out at the stars. Apart from the detail of the chicken snoring between them. And the fact that they're both clothed. And that the sparkle in Theseus's eyes is not the reflection of stars, but the shimmer of unshed tears.

Did Asterion cause this? Does Theseus even want her here? What if she was trying to escape her and Asterion's just followed her like some... clingy chicken?

"Did I wake you?" she asks, holding her breath. *Please say no.*

Theseus shakes her head.

Asterion lets out her breath. Quietly.

"I couldn't sleep." Theseus's eyes shimmer all the more as

she lets her head fall back against the proteus trunk. The flourishing leaves dance in her eyes. But so do the shadows.

How can Asterion turn those shadows to light?

If she's not the cause of Theseus's disquiet, perhaps she can help.

"You look like—you are—having thoughts," she says, gently.

"I've never been accused of such a thing before." Theseus grins, but it falters, and a silence settles between them. Asterion lets it, because there's something on Theseus's mind. She doesn't need a proteus tree to tell her that.

She places her hand on Theseus's forearm, and the leaves above them flutter with greens and pinks amongst the gloom. Theseus breathes deep, like she's readying for battle.

"You asked me why I became a monster hunter." Her voice is quiet, as if she doesn't want to wake Bok-bok, or isn't certain she wants to share her words.

Asterion nods, ready to hear anything Theseus is willing to share.

55

PAST
THESEUS

Asterion's gentle touch to her forearm soothes Theseus's nerves. Even Bok-bok snoring on her lap is comforting. Maybe there's hope for her if even a hot-headed, judgemental chicken can revise their opinion of her enough to choose her as a temporary nest.

Theseus takes a deep, fortifying breath to hold her tears at bay. She's never willingly shared this part of herself with anyone, not even Herakles. But here, with Asterion, it feels right. Perhaps because Asterion had simply asked, and Theseus wants to answer. Perhaps because she's been carrying this weight for too long.

Best get on with it before she loses her nerve.

Where to begin?

"My stepfather was a piece of work." She swallows the sour taste in her mouth. It never feels right to refer to him as any kind of *father*. At most, he was the man who'd married her mother. "He never liked me. He reminded me at every opportunity that I was *a mistake*. That my mother only kept me around out of duty. He had a way with words. They were more brutal than his fists."

The strange, inconsistent glow of the proteus tree highlights

Asterion's scowl. It holds not just sympathy, but a protectiveness, like she'd battle him right now if she could. Her support is a buttress, encouraging her to continue. "At least the bruises he gave me—which he always blamed on me getting into scraps— would heal. But his words..."

Idiot. Useless. What even is the point of you? Always when no-one but her was there to hear them. Even now, her hackles are up, her instincts attempting to shield against the erosion of her self-esteem.

Her breath stumbles.

"He promised my mother the worlds. She was so desperate to be loved, so relieved to not be gutter-adjacent anymore. And on the surface it was... good. He had enough status that he could house us. There was even a courtyard and fountain, all large enough to impress his magistrate associates. We no longer had to struggle to make ends meet. He bought her gifts, made every damn thing sparkle. The thing about sparkles is they're a fucking distraction. They stop you seeing what lies beyond."

She'd been naïve, back then. She hadn't learned yet how the worlds worked. When she'd needed the Athenian magistrates to step up, to do something to help her, their response had been... lacking. Yes, the Athenian way is to follow the moral compass, but heavens above and below they'll debate its direction to death, first. And if all you do is deliberate, then the loudest voices—including her stepfather—have no trouble drowning out those who struggle to be heard.

Suffering their inaction first-hand probably influenced Theseus's tendency to get stuck into the fray first and figure out a way forward from there, if she's being all self-aware about it.

"He had a way of turning any complaint I had into being my fault. I was oversensitive, dramatic, or a liar. He excelled at poisoning people to his way of thinking. He was subtle enough."

Theseus hazards a painful breath. Her lungs ache, her throat aches, every damn thing aches, because—

"The authorities believed him. Everyone did. Even my mother. I was *trouble*."

There's a damning judgement in Asterion's scowl, but her thumb stroking Theseus's forearm reassures her it's not aimed at her.

"I put up with his shit for three sun-orbits."

Will Asterion still be on her side when the whole truth is out?

"One night, he drank too much. My mother wasn't home and he was angling for a fight. He did his usual routine, calling me names, going on about how my bio-father outright rejected me, how my mother would be better off without me, how he had better things to waste his money on than me. Why didn't I just fuck off already?"

Rage for her younger self, the same rage she'd felt half a lifetime ago, sluices through her veins. "I packed my bag so fucking fast. I'd fantasised about leaving so many times, I'd planned what to take. I'd kept my sword hidden under my mattress so he wouldn't find it. It was a memento from my bio-father, apparently. I never knew him, so it wasn't sentimental, but I knew I'd need it if I was going it alone."

That exhilaration, the prospect of freedom, had fuelled her. "He kept shouting, louder and louder. I tuned him out enough." But even then, his voice had burrowed into her brain like radio static, spiking into her thoughts. "I didn't say a thing to him. I just headed for the door. But he blocked me in. He saw the sword and accused me of stealing it. Said there was no other way someone like me would have a fine sword like that. He'd taken everything else from me—and he wanted that, too. There was so much I wanted to say back to him—but it was all tied in knots inside me. And I knew whatever I said, he'd turn it against me."

The flicker of gleaming red leaves in the tree of flowing light; it's not far removed from the colour her stepfather had turned when she'd met his tirade with silence.

"He was so fucking mad that he couldn't get a rise out of me. I tried to step past him, and he shoved me so hard—" The air lurches from Theseus's lungs even thinking about it, how she'd fallen to the polished wooden floor. "Still, I didn't react. I knew if I did, he'd call me an animal. He'd convince people I was the aggressor. There was nothing I could do that would've been right."

She swallows the memory of blood on her tongue as he'd struck again, with heavy boots this time. He'd bust her lip, broken her nose and her spirit.

She swipes away her tears. Back then, they'd been tears of pain and all-consuming fury. Now they're for the youngster she'd been, trapped and helpless, with no way out.

"I thought eventually he'd get tired and stop, but... he just—kept—kicking. He started recounting the story he'd tell my mother, about how I got so bruised: the fight I'd started that he'd had to get me out of." He'd laughed, then; a strange twist of bitterness and glee, like it was all a game to him. "He said I could only leave when my mother kicked me out."

Theseus hugs herself and Asterion's hand falls gently to Theseus's thigh. Will she keep it there once she's heard the rest?

"All I could think was: when I'm gone, he'll do this to her. And he won't stop until she breaks."

She swallows past the lump in her throat.

"And then he picked up my sword. And I knew he was going to kill me." She'd come so close to accepting death. "I wanted him to, honestly. *Go on*, I thought. *Show them who you truly are.* But I knew he'd wriggle free, like he always did. He'd make it my fault somehow. And there was no fucking way I was letting him take my life *and* the truth."

Theseus reaches out, like she's defending herself all over again.

"When he lunged at me, something clicked. I grabbed his arm and used the blade against him."

The sound of metal scraping against bone isn't easy to forget. Even here in Asterion's orchard, he haunts the shadows, her sword still wedged in his gut, his face twisted with pain and cruelty—and Theseus's throat burns.

"I just wanted him to *stop*. I didn't want to kill him. But I wanted him dead. I was glad when he stopped breathing. Like the universe had been adjusted for the better."

Asterion's hand remains on Theseus's thigh, squeezing a little tighter.

"*He* was my first monster."

Will Asterion understand? She risks a glance at her—and Asterion's not staring at Theseus like she's a monster. Instead, her hand wraps around Theseus's clammy palm like a lifeline.

"I should have done something... cleaned myself up, at least. But I couldn't move. It was like I needed to keep looking at him in case he came back. I needed to be sure he was gone."

Theseus shuts her eyes, but his bloody corpse haunts the dark behind her eyelids, too. She steadies herself with a slow inhale and exhale but can't shake the rigidity from her muscles.

She opens her eyes, fixing her gaze on their held hands.

"My mother came home. Found him. Found me covered in his blood. I told her what had happened. I don't know how. But..." Finally, the scaffolding holding back Theseus's tears collapses and her sobs tumble out. "Sh-she didn't believe me. She didn't see h-her child finally standing up for herself. She saw a monster who'd butchered the man she loved."

She withdraws her hand from Asterion's, pressing the heels of her palms to her eyes. It's been so long since she cried about this. She doesn't want to shed any more tears.

Maybe her mother had been right all along. Maybe she is a monster. If Asterion hadn't been so determined, so capable... Theseus would have killed her.

How many other lives has she unjustly ended?

"No," says Asterion, with such conviction that Theseus pulls her hands from her eyes and looks at her. Asterion's hand lands on hers again. "*He* was the monster."

A single sob of utter relief tumbles from Theseus's chest at the connection, at being understood, at the weight that lifts from her shoulders. She rubs her aching sternum, daring to look toward the shadows. They hold only the trees of the orchard, blossom and leaves. But it's the gentle pressure of Asterion's hand around hers that grounds and soothes her more than anything.

People are tricksters, always seeking from Theseus more than she's able to give. Her mother's husband had wanted whatever was contrary. Her mother had wanted her to stop telling lies that she never told. Even Theseus's lovers have pretended to be aligned with her offer of temporary entertainment, when they really wanted her to tie her future to theirs.

People pretend to be whatever they think will get them what they want. But not Asterion. Kind, curious, clever Asterion, who's only ever herself.

In different circumstances the nighttime garden—the orchard with its tree with colourful leaves of water and light, and Bok-bok's feathers flickering like embers in coals—and how they're sharing this space together, it would be romantic.

Apart from the epic over-share, obviously.

But romance should be the last fucking thing on her mind right now. Because there's still more to the story.

"My mother told me to get lost. So that's what I did." Theseus clears her throat and shrugs. "Guess that's as far as her maternal instincts could stretch."

It hadn't always been like that. Her mother hadn't always been like that. They might not have had much, before *him*, but they were happy enough—at least, that's what Theseus had thought. But her mother's image of her had been so easily tainted. When the only person who's known you your whole damn life, who's meant to be on your side no matter what, suddenly sees you only through the distortion of someone else's words... that kind of rejection is more damaging than any bruise, more deep cutting than any blade.

"So... you are—on the run?" Asterion looks so damn worried for her. It'd be cute, if the history Theseus is sharing wasn't so dire.

"Technically, in the Athenian Expanse, there's a warrant for my arrest on my homeworld. But I'm shielded a little because of who my bio-father is." And don't get her started on the injustice of *that*. She's all for not being thrown in prison, but she'd rather it was because of the truth, not her lineage. "Still, it wouldn't be wise for me to return."

Asterion nods, her thumb caressing Theseus's palm where the illumi-thread dapples her skin. "Do you miss your home?"

Home. Oof. What a weighted word. There was a time when she hadn't been 'a troublemaker on a wayward path.' Cheeky, yes—she never could resist a prank, or an opportunity to make her mother smile—and life had been... fun.

Yes, there are things she misses. She misses roaming the shorelines exploring rock pools and leaping from clifftops. She misses the specific colour palate of the ocean, from vibrant turquoise in summer to the forbidding grey of stormy seas. She misses the tranquillity she'd always found beneath the waves, and the strange creatures that wanted to play. She misses the friendships of her youth.

But what she misses isn't what *is*.

"I miss the beauty in it," she says. "I miss... I miss what life was, and what it could have been."

But the house she'd left hadn't been a home. And she's not sure if *home* is something she's had since. The closest she's got to that feeling of belonging, of safety, freedom and fun, was voyaging with Herakles.

She takes her hand from Asterion's to touch her coin pendant, the Locator Herakles had given her. Life stories are *long*, aren't they? She tries for brevity: "After my mother threw me out, I became an insufferable cliché for a while. Scrappy drunk aiming to dish out justice but too unco-ordinated to hit the mark." She cringes at herself. "I'd fight anyone who seemed like they deserved it. Possibly some who didn't."

Asterion's eyes are still bright and interested. Thank the heavens. Because the only thing worse than being a monster is being a bore.

"Then one day, this gladiator of a woman dragged me from the middle of a bar brawl I'd started. I was broken, but I was still fighting. And not in a noble way, either. Herakles. She'd done nothing but try to help and my fists were still flying. She bested me so fucking easily."

What a mortifying jackass she'd been.

"She looked after me. Helped me channel my frustrations towards something good. My world was torn apart by a monster and pieced back together by someone who stops them."

And that's the truth of it. Why she does what she does.

"No-one should have to suffer a monster." Asterion's words are a balm as she smooths Bok-bok's feathers. And for a while they just sit, listening to the chicken's contented purrs-bordering-on-snores.

"You say—I don't know you..." says Asterion, thoughtfully.

Yes, Theseus had thrown that in amongst her reasons for

them not to kiss. Damn. She's sure that red glow from the tree is now an echo of the heat in her cheeks.

"...that we—not—know each other. But... I see... I saw—how you are in—labyrinth. How you—carry yourself."

"I think you'll find you *literally* carried me. Well, dragged me." Theseus smirks.

Asterion's responding smile is shy. "I—watch you—in the labyrinth." She cringes. "Which—yes—*sounds* creepy. But you—are monster hunter—here to kill me. So... out of—us—*you*" — she pokes Theseus in the chest— "are creepy one."

Theseus's sudden laughter prompts a startled *"Bok-bokaaa!"* outburst from Bok-bok. But then, after a hefty dose of side-eye, the chicken wiggles her behind into the nest of Theseus's lap and settles again.

It's not at all what Theseus had expected Asterion to say. And she's not wrong. And, yes, Theseus does still feel bad about that. Always will. But Asterion is so playfully matter-of-fact about it, it feels like a game. The good kind.

Asterion turns more sombre. "So many people—victim to this world. I try to stop it. Either they or the Labyrinth—not allow it. I saw you—look after others. You are brave and kind."

Theseus's witty, self-deprecating retort dies on her tongue.

"Minus—recent errors in judgement," Asterion continues with a wry smile, "the Seven Heavens are lucky to have—monster hunter like you."

Above them, the canopy of proteus leaves glows a little brighter. Whatever that's about.

"I was chaos when I first got here," says Theseus, "and you still have positive things to say about me?"

"Is as much—surprise to me—as to you."

Theseus smiles, and there's nothing forced about it. Nothing weighing it down. The Labyrinth's gravity must be fluctuating, because she feels lighter. Or maybe that's just what it feels like to share something important, life-defining, with someone you trust.

Theseus's heart practically face-plants in her chest. *Trust.* That's not something in her artillery. Not usually.

But yes, she trusts Asterion.

She's carried the accusation of being the monster her mother saw for so long, it's become the fault in her foundations. But if Asterion—Asterion, who is only ever honest—doesn't see the monster in her... then maybe it's as mythical as a Minotaur.

Theseus's hand seeks Asterion's and squeezes, just as the first shaft of morning sunlight drifts down the dome's central sky-well, bouncing off the angled mirror-stones of the pathways and sending light soaring to mirrors all across the garden.

Petals unfurl, blossom illuminates, but Theseus is more captivated by the rainbow-flame reflections of the proteus tree flourishing in Asterion's bright eyes, by the warmth of Asterion's fingers threaded with hers.

Because holding Asterion's hand... it doesn't feel like something to run from. It feels like exactly where she wants to be.

56

FICTIONS

ASTERION

"There are fictions," Asterion suggests as she shows Theseus into her sizeable library. She hopes to help Theseus find something to relax her after such an emotionally exhausting start to the day. Not wanting to crowd her, Asterion keeps her distance by a few paces, glancing down at her own boots at intervals, even though Theseus is much more interesting to look at. She smirks to herself; would Theseus think that a compliment?

She must have laughed a little, because Theseus turns from the bookshelves, raising a curious eyebrow. Fire-torchlight flickers in those night-sky eyes with depths Asterion's only just beginning to discover...

Oh, *flummox*. She's gazing. She'd promised herself she wouldn't gaze. Her boots could do with a shine. Yes. Boots. Look at the boots, not into Theseus's mirth-filled eyes.

Also, maybe remember to breathe.

Theseus returns to trailing a finger over the book spines, exploring the possibilities. It's a little nerve-wracking having Theseus in here. Not in a bad way; it's just that she's never shared her library with anyone before. There are books and story-reels, Shard-tech, too. It's quite the collection.

Most of the tomes were originally housed in the Minosian palace library. No-one else had ever been interested in the library or its books, which is likely why, along with her blue-prints for the Labyrinth, its entire contents had been sent up here along with the world-engine. But thanks to the poorly cali-brated distribution matrix, it's taken Asterion many sun-orbits to locate and gather the books from the near and far reaches of the labyrinth. She still finds them even now: embedded in corridor flagstones, up trees. In the winter biome, she's hacked some from within trunks of ice. And a few had ended up in the mead-ow's sky with starlight beaming through them. Others are irre-trievable, wedged into odd places as the world had formed around them. No doubt the rest were consumed by lava, or lie buried beneath layers of rock and soil, never to be seen again.

But her collection still spans everything from the science of rock formation to romance. Most of the books from the Minosian palace are factual, on subjects such as raw materials and architectural design, while most of the fictions about worlds and emotional landscapes beyond her reach were brought in by voyagers.

It's an admittedly strange item to bring to the Sky Labyrinth. Is it possible Ariadne might have had some part in it? And if so, is it intended as a cruelty or a kindness? Are they to keep her entertained? Or to remind her what she's missing?

It doesn't bear thinking about, but she's avoided such thoughts for far too long. The truth of the matter is that Ariadne never wanted a sister.

And now that she thinks of it, in many ways her experiences are not so different from what Theseus has been through. Theseus, too, had been forced to live under the same roof as family who didn't want her, who made her life a misery. Both of them have been condemned by those they should have been able to trust: those who should have cared and didn't.

Around the library, the fire-torches burn brighter in sympathy with Asterion's clenched fists. If she could, she'd throw an entire library of books at anyone who's ever treated Theseus that way. Perhaps she should throw that library at Ariadne, too. Just as it's not Theseus's fault that those around her couldn't see her value, nor is it Asterion's that Ariadne and Father failed to see hers. Asterion might have been abrupt in her critiques of others, uncouth by the standards of the royal court —but she was never intentionally cruel. And now, if she had the choice of whether to be more like Ariadne or herself, she'd choose herself.

It's taken a lifetime—and a wayward warrior bursting into her world—but, finally, she understands what Nanny was always telling her. And the certainty with which she feels it... it's like a hug from within.

Theseus reaches to select a book from the shelves, and Asterion steps a little closer to her. "You—might not—like that one."

Theseus raises a questioning eyebrow. "Oh?"

"They both die in the end."

Theseus returns the book to the shelf. Ironically, given Minos's obsession with appearances, the books' covers give no clue about their contents.

"What about this one? You think I'll like this?" Theseus holds up the book for her to inspect.

"Depends. There is—lot of..." Asterion pauses, piecing together the phrase, "...physical—proximity in that one. A sky full of feelings, too."

Theseus thumbs the pages—which are, admittedly, worn from Asterion having re-read it several times.

"That one you think they—going to die—but—they don't."

"Do you think, maybe..." begins Theseus with a stifled smile,

"...part of the fun is *not* knowing exactly what's going to happen?"

Asterion blinks at her. What kind of stress-inducing madness is that? She likes knowing what's going to happen. She's about to argue her case, but she's distracted by Theseus's wide eyes, gawking at... at what? The full width and height of the library?

"Wait. Have you read *all* these books?" She sounds... stunned? *Impressed*?

"Not *all*." Most of them, though. "There is—book on—observation of—aridity in paint that is...*dry* for my tastes."

Theseus squints at her. Should Asterion really be trying for humour in an unfamiliar language?

But then Theseus's mouth twitches into a smirk. "Is there really a book on watching paint dry?"

⁺₊•

STOOD over her library's table, Asterion is trying to stay focused on her blueprints and figuring out what might be causing the audible snags in the Labyrinth. Has some piece of machinery degraded? Or is it simply an imbalance resulting from her torque-labyrinth alignment? The Labyrinth has been tested by too many negative emotions across the sun-orbits, perhaps it's just adjusting to input that's more... positive.

But it's difficult not to be distracted by Theseus, nestled in an armchair, balancing *A History of Minos* alongside her tourist guide-Shard for translation. She looks more like she's tussling with an overbearing beast than with a history book in an unfamiliar language.

"What are you reading about?" asks Asterion.

It takes a second for Theseus's grimace to soften, like she's relieved to have been pulled from the fray. "Minos's Labyrinth tradition." She sets her shoulders, ready for a new battle as she reads aloud in Minosian: "Offspring of the Architect can only—elevate to become the Architect-in-waiting" —Theseus looks up at her, as though Asterion were the student— "the ultimate power in Minos, and the individual responsible for infrastructure..."

Her accent is good. Asterion encourages her with an exaggerated regal gesture: *you may continue.*

To her delight, Theseus chuckles. "By presenting the..." She traces the Minoglyphs with her finger, squinting at them like she's turned long-sighted, "...blueprints of a puzzle-structure so monumental... it will become—wonder of Minos."

Theseus coughs, perhaps to cleanse herself of all the guttural Minosian sounds before continuing. "An Architect-in-waiting can only—ascend to Architect once a... suitor solves their monumental puzzle. In doing so—the suitor has thereby demonstrated—they are deserving of—throne and Architect's marriage hand..." She frowns, checking her guide-Shard for the translation. "...Hand in marriage?"

Asterion nods her approval.

Theseus looks frazzled, like she's horrified by the concepts, or perhaps simply needs to recover from the linguistic gymnastics. "Your parents were joined under the Labyrinth tradition?" she asks, reverting to Athenian. "Your father solved the Labyrinth your mother created?"

"Mmhmmn." Asterion hadn't witnessed her parents' courtship. Understandably. And Mother's Flame had extinguished not long after she and Ariadne were born. Father never spoke of it. Not in a *it hurts too much* way; more a *it doesn't matter* way. And with Asterion's recent and reluctant acceptance of her sister's personality, and the fact that Father would have to have been involved in the events that had put Asterion here, only now does she consider that perhaps Mother hadn't fitted into his plans, either.

But she can't stomach another scenic route through the chaos of her callous family.

"Your mother's puzzle was a nest of pyramids, right?" Theseus scrolls back through her guide-Shard. "Constructed beneath the planet's crust..." Her eyes widen at that. "Stars above. Sounds like more of a puzzle to build than to solve."

She's got that right. "It had some... tectonic side effects," Asterion admits.

"Are *all* the monumental puzzles death traps?"

Asterion sighs. "Is—Minosian way." It merits so much more than a sigh. "Is also—stupid tradition."

"Yeah... I'm all for respecting tradition, but I draw the line at death puzzles."

Asterion nods. It'd be the first thing she'd change about Minos if she could. She feigns attention on her blueprints and does her best to sound matter-of-fact—aloof, even.

"When you leave here... tradition dictates that..." She tries not to wring her hands. "...you marry Ariadne. She is—Architect-in-waiting. By leaving here—alive, you—will have solved her Labyrinth, officially. By marrying her, you set her free. Free to be—Architect. That is—Minosian way."

"I don't give a damn about solving her Labyrinth!" The words burst from Theseus, which, judging from Theseus's widened eyes and the subsequent flicker of apology, she's startled them both. Theseus clears her throat, then adds, more calmly: "Anyway... it's not *her* labyrinth."

Asterion looks up, but Theseus is staring valiantly at the book in her lap, squirming like a nest of fire ants has taken up residence in her trousers. Is she worried that she's implying that it's Asterion's Labyrinth and therefore, if anyone is to be married, it should be her?

"Anyway," Theseus continues, flipping through the ether-pages of her guide-Shard, "I'm not sure getting dragged to the core to get nursed back to health, then shown the way out, by the 'Minotaur' is the same as being clever enough to solve the labyrinth. Besides..." Theseus's jaw clenches. "I don't care if marriage sets her free. She fucking—" She huffs. "*Kill the beast. Bring me its heart. Set me free.* At no point did Ariadne mention that the heart I was meant to... collect was a *pendant*. She knew what she was doing. She tasked me with *digging your heart out of your chest*, Asterion. Like fuck am I going to marry her."

So... is that a yes to marrying Ariadne... or no? Asterion's face must pinch as she tries to decipher that last sentence, because Theseus clarifies: "I am *not* going to marry your sister."

Asterion's heart pendant glows a little at Theseus's conviction. It's been a long time since anyone was furious on her behalf. "Is also stupid tradition."

As if needing to direct her energy somewhere, Theseus is on her feet and sauntering to the bookshelves. And Asterion absolutely isn't watching the poetry of her movement, the certainty and strength in every step. Her gaze isn't lingering on the glowing scars that highlight Theseus's calf muscle each time it bunches and stretches—

Ting!

Asterion's eyes snap to Theseus's.

Theseus is looking right at her. Her smile isn't *knowing*, exactly, but there's a hint of something...

Ting! She's also flicking a coin in the air. With each flick, it catches the light like a falling star, accompanied by a *ting!*

Asterion refocuses on her blueprints. She's not even doing anything productive anymore. She just needs to not be staring into Theseus's curious eyes or at her exquisite form.

Asterion stretches out her neck, trying to not make it

obvious that she's as tense as a tether-line. Cool as a winter woodland biome. Yes. That's her.

Ting! It's closer now, and Asterion can't help herself. With one stride, one reach, she snatches the coin from the air.

Triumph.

But in claiming it, she's put herself in Theseus's space, close enough to notice the movement of Theseus's throat as she swallows.

"Can I help you?" Theseus's lips quirk into a pleasing shape. Asterion's torque frazzles as the thought sparks down her spine.

Stop staring. "Why do you play with this?" Asterion opens her palm, holding the coin out between them. Her body buzzes to be closer to Theseus, but Theseus has made it clear she doesn't want that, so...

Space. She should give them both some space.

Asterion steps back, toward the library's table... but Theseus moves with her. Asterion holds the coin out to her, and when Theseus's warm fingers close over it, the fire-torches tremble.

That's another tick in the *Asterion's emotions are challenging the Labyrinth* column.

"Sometimes it helps me focus," says Theseus, turning the coin across the backs of her fingers like a magician. "Sometimes it helps me figure things out." She flicks the coin skyward again —but she must misjudge the trajectory, because snatching it from mid-air brings her so close to Asterion, Asterion can see the over-fuelled fire-torches blazing in her eyes.

Something flutters in her chest, like a caged creature desperate to spread its wings. Does Theseus know she has a winning smile? It's lopsided and even more perfect for it.

The Labyrinth groans as though even it is unimpressed at Asterion's unhelpful thoughts. *Just... choose a topic. Any topic. Not about mouths.*

"Quantifiers and Constructionists care little for—how many

backs break in—realisation—ridiculous plans." Okay, so she might have failed at sounding cool and nonchalant. And at maintaining any kind of sentence structure. But at least she's successfully chosen the least alluring topic in all the heavens. *Yes. Good. Keep going.* "Nor do they care—how many resources—consumed by—monuments to royal romance. They—want—bigger, better, with no regard for what's good for—world or people in it."

She's always thought there was a certain irony in Minos becoming a mere husk: beautiful on the outside, but hollow within.

"O-or at least, that's how it was..." Okay, apparently she's discovered how to babble. Why is Theseus looking at her with that glimmer in her eyes? How has the luminosity of Theseus's smile grown even brighter?

"How would you do things differently?" Theseus leans in closer, like she's eager to know... or like she's about to kiss her.

Which she isn't. Obviously.

And it's not a bad feeling, being seen and heard. Asterion only worries she'll misconstrue the intent.

"Is there no hope for Minos?" Theseus asks, and her gentle Minosian growl must obliterate Asterion's good sense, because she reaches out—not for Theseus, but for her torque. The catch of Theseus's breath stills her hand for a moment. But she doesn't withdraw, so Asterion continues.

"I designed these so there would be hope." She strokes her thumb over the twist of metal around Theseus's throat. Her fingers brush against soft skin and Theseus's torque responds with electric blue ripples.

Good. It's not just Asterion who's feeling this... *energy.*

The library lights flutter in line with her breath. *Focus, Asterion.*

"It was... prudent to find—way to not just conserve

resources, but create them," she explains, in a perfect example of nervous energy. "I found—way to turn each individual's Minosian Flame into targetable electrical energy. Like a... biological dynamo, without draining or harming—mortal source—torques fuel the world around its wearer. Homes lit, heated, powered. No-one—without. Resources—finally equal. People can be calm and content."

She perhaps should have withdrawn her hand by now. She does exactly that. Her cheeks are warm. Everything is warm. But just as she drops her hand, Theseus steps closer, reaching to touch Asterion's torque.

It's only fair...

And—oh, *wow*—her heart has only ever raced this fast when she's been sprinting through the labyrinth. Though this is a much better feeling.

She just wishes the glow of her torque wasn't giving her away.

Maybe Theseus won't notice the blue sparks dancing between them, and Asterion enjoys the play of light across Theseus's jawline.

"You designed these? To help people?" Theseus's expression is filled with something like wonder, as though Asterion had done something momentous, rather than just the kind, sensible, necessary thing. "How do you do that?"

"Do what?" Asterion's voice is a whisper. She doesn't want to startle either of them. She wants to exist in this moment for as long as possible.

"Create light in the darkness."

"Do you mean literally? I have diagrams." Asterion gestures to the blueprints scattered across the table behind her, not breaking eye contact.

The corner of Theseus's mouth lifts, and all Asterion can think about, again, is how Theseus's lips had felt against her own. And Theseus's sparking torque, the way her gaze keeps detouring to Asterion's mouth, the way she's lingering within such intimate reach, even though there's a whole darn fortress for them to exist in...

Asterion might not be experienced in these things, but it's clearer than any blueprint... it all adds up to *Theseus wants to kiss her.*

But Asterion had promised not to...

Well, directions can change, can't they? And now they have more shared words, they should use them...

"I want you, Theseus," she whispers. "Even if it's just for a short time."

She watches the battle play out in those stunning topaz eyes, more like flame than stone. She sees the moment when Theseus surrenders—or triumphs—and she leans in, close enough that her breath caresses Asterion's lips.

Asterion's fingers migrate to the smooth skin and short, shaved hair at the nape of Theseus's neck, tracing along to her jaw. "But if you need to toss a coin to decide—"

The rest of her sentence is lost to Theseus's lips pressing to hers. Fuel to Asterion's flame. Her every synapse sings. Fire-torches crackle with the power surge.

Without breaking their kiss, Theseus presses Asterion backward until her legs meet the edge of the table, landing her atop the pile of blueprints.

Yes. Why in the heavens was this table ever used for anything else?

All around the room, the lava-gullies pulse. The fire roars in the hearth.

Heavens above and below. She could power a world with what she's feeling right now.

57

FLAME

ASTERION

Fingers hooked around Theseus's belt buckle, Asterion tugs her closer, and Theseus's responding moan into her mouth could short-circuit the Labyrinth. Or set it on fire. She spares an occasional glance toward the hearth, just in case.

The way Theseus's hands are roaming up and down Asterion's hips like she's trying to know the shape of her, there's no doubt in Asterion's mind that they both want this. Asterion tugs at Theseus's shirt. "Can I—take this off?"

With a smile that's both smug and eager, Theseus guides Asterion's hands to her collar, where Asterion's keen fingers start unbuttoning. Her knuckles brush against heated skin as her heartbeat pulses in her ears, her chest and—Hades in the Heavens—much lower, too.

Undressing has never felt like *this* before.

Theseus is wearing a half-vest beneath her shirt, but Asterion will get to that.

When they break from their kiss for breath, Theseus's attention strays to the surging blue and orange flames heating the room around them.

"It's emotions that spark the flame?" she asks, almost breathless, as Asterion slides Theseus's shirt from her shoulders, her inquisitive hands following its path down Theseus's back. "With the torques, I mean."

Does she really expect Asterion's higher faculties to be working right now?

Asterion nods, refusing to use her mouth for anything other than kissing when Theseus tastes so sweet, like proteus juice and possibility. Perhaps the fruit has fermented, because this is intoxicating... What was Theseus's question, again?

Uh... emotions... flame... "Yes. Just living, breathing—that is Minosian Flame. Channelled through the torques... creates resource..." Is this really the time for this conversation? "...can be used as energy."

"Wait—" Theseus pulls away a little, her arms still bracketing Asterion against the table.

Wait? Really?

Disappointment loops about Asterion's stomach. She'd read Theseus's enthusiasm as in line with her own. Has she misunderstood?

Theseus squeezes her eyes shut as if to re-centre herself. "Heights of emotion are more powerful? Happiness, *excitement—*"

It's not what Asterion had intended when she'd designed the torques, but at eleven sun-orbits old, the effect of intimacies on energy-tech hadn't been on her mind. The heat settings were supposed to balance out, not amplify emotions for all to see. But now is not the time to be thinking about amendments to her designs, nor wondering whether the flaw is in her design, or in the constructionists' execution of it.

"And... fear?" asks Theseus.

What is happening? Asterion's own fire cools abruptly. "I... yes?"

Theseus takes a step back. "Asti... I'm sorry."

Sorry? What...? That's what she'd ask if her brain and mouth were in communication. Does she regret their kiss? Again? Asterion shuffles down off the table, trying to rein in her dejection.

Theseus grimaces. "The torques... aren't used as you intended."

So... this isn't about the kissing? Asterion steps beyond Theseus's potential reach. She can't think straight when they're wrapped in each other.

"The people of Minos aren't calm and content." Theseus's features pinch with apology, perhaps even regret. Asterion already hates where this is going. "And resources are not equal."

Asterion loses her breath. That's not the way it's meant to be.

"Your sister has Minos and beyond terrified into believing some bullshit about how the torques protect them from the Minotaur. That without the torques, the beast would steal their Flame. There are... festivals celebrating your downfall. I'm so sorry, Asti."

Asterion knows that Theseus means it. Every word. But Asterion's mind is racing, tripping on itself. It shouldn't be a surprise at this point that Ariadne's aspirations to the throne aren't for the good of all Minosians, for looking after them as an Architect should.

Any lingering embers cool to ice in her veins as the truth takes grip.

Tricking a world into stealing their resources, then pointing the finger of blame at a mythical monster in the skies: how very neatly *Ariadne*. But why mine people for negative emotions when positive ones will do? Why produce more than is needed?

Asterion never got to comprehensively test the torque-tech, but perhaps because negative emotions demand more energy to create, they generate more output too. And Asterion can only guess that the unequal distribution of resources is to fuel Minosian excess; not for the many but the few.

Sending heroes and criminals to the skies with their own torques... well, Asterion would never have considered it. It hadn't occurred to her that her designs might need to mitigate against brutality or greed. But the horrors of the mist-drenched labyrinth must create enough energy to power the capital for an entire sun-orbit.

Theseus paces, combing her fingers through her hair. "We have to go back to Minos," she says, pausing before Asterion. "We'll find a way—"

We...? Back to Minos? What is she talking about?

Asterion recoils—into the solid table. She fumbles around it to the opposite side. How did she go from wanting to be as close to Theseus as it's possible to be, to her nerves on a knife edge?

"I—not go back."

Theseus stands a little straighter, like she's stunned Asterion isn't leaping to agree with her plan. But she softens a little, her next words imploring: "Your sister uses lies and fear and *your* designs to power her world. But it's not *her* world, Asterion. It's yours. You're the rightful Architect-in-waiting."

"Is—*not* my world." Asterion bites back. "Is not *hers*. No-one owns a world. Architect—is to serve the people. To—steer, only. For the good of citizens."

"Exactly!" says Theseus, with something that sounds a lot like affection. "Minos will be a better world with you on the throne."

Asterion appreciates her vote of confidence, but she hates everything else about this. Yes, Ariadne needs to be stopped. Someone has to protect the people of Minos. They need a leader with their best interests at heart.

But. Has Theseus forgotten the facts?

"I can't leave. My mask. Astro-helmets—not fit underneath."

"You're telling me—" Theseus's words are like a fiery burst, "—a genius who can figure out how to power an entire world with Minosian Flame, who can create an entire other world in the sky, can't figure out how to unlock a mask?"

"You think I haven't tried?" Asterion snaps, a new, unwelcome heat slinking through her veins, mirrored in the raw blue flames of the fire-torches. How did they go from the most joyously exciting moment of her life to *this*? To Theseus implying that she's chosen to spend her life trapped in a labyrinth with visceral death at every turn? "I never ask—for this."

"No, Asti, I know." The fight has gone from Theseus's posture, though the tension remains. "I'm sorry, I..." Her brow buckles, and Asterion can't tell which of them she's disappointed with. "Fuck," she mutters.

And all Asterion can do is pace beside the table like she's an animal, caged. She never asked to be an Architect, nor to be good at designing worlds. She never asked for a sibling so jealous and a father so cruel they shut her away.

No-one had wanted her when she was on Minos. No-one came looking for her. No-one wants her back.

This unsettled energy needs to go somewhere, so Asterion directs herself towards the garden, where there's a stupid giant rock in need of lifting. And Theseus, taking the hint, doesn't follow.

✦

ASTERION'S BICEPS burn as she lifts the rock.

What a load of bullshit.

She's wrong. Theseus is wrong. About Asterion not trying to free herself of the mask. She's analysed it again and again over the sun-orbits, eventually determining that— theoretically—it would be possible to open the mask by striking a key component at an extremely precise angle. She'd also determined that if she misjudges that angle by even a fraction of a degree, a failsafe will kick in and lobotomise her.

Ariadne's design might have been lacking in kindness, but as a device for punishment it is accomplished.

She's also—obviously—tried using the horns to unlock the fortress without actually putting the mask on, but Ariadne had thought of that, too. The door only opens when she's wearing the mask, bowing before the gateway. And the mask can only be safely removed in the fortress keyholes once returned.

If she can't venture into the labyrinth without the mask, she can't wear an astro-helmet. And if she can't do that, she can't enter the outer-shell gatehouse. The gatehouse that she'd designed to be the only way in or out of this world.

But even if she were to solve all of that... it's not so simple as stay or go.

Both are an adventure. Both are terrifying.

Staying means being the hunted; choosing her life over those who seek to end it. But it also means she can stay hidden away in her own world; the world she designed.

Leaving means probably dying in the attempt—and even if she did somehow make it out of the Sky Labyrinth, space isn't an easy obstacle. Nor, for that matter, will Ari be. It won't serve her to have the 'Lost Princess', the living proof of all her transgressions, return to Minos.

Even if Asterion could escape Minos, explore the Seven Heavens... there's no escaping Ariadne and her ambitions. Asterion's own face will always tie her to that world.

All of which adds up to her wanting to be several worlds away from the Sky Labyrinth, and at the same time to never have to leave.

Muscles burning, Asterion flips the giant rock again, refusing to be beaten by something as banal as gravity.

If she's honest with herself, there had come a certain point—

the point at which she'd become familiar enough with the labyrinth to navigate it safely, the point at which she'd settled into her fortress and her routine, her world—when she'd stopped trying to escape.

Asterion drops the slab and it lands with a satisfying thump. Stretching her arms up behind her head, she opens her lungs.

You're telling me a genius who can figure out how to power an entire world with Minosian Flame, who can create an entire other world in the sky, can't figure out how to unlock a mask?

Theseus's accusation rattles around Asterion's thoughts as she paces. It's still a fact that in trying to escape, the mask could be the death of her; that thanks to Ariadne's brutality, her own face could be too.

It's just… difficult to admit that even without those challenges… she still might choose the Labyrinth.

Damn it. Hurtful comments are always worse when there's a foundation of truth to them.

58

SHOOTING STARS
THESEUS

Theseus, you monumental jackass.

Rainbow carrots never did a thing to her, but she's dicing them like they deserve it. With Asterion out in the garden, working off the emotional fallout of Theseus's latest misstep, the least Theseus can do is get dinner started while her own thoughts *wurr* like a sky-motor trying to get back on course.

In light of new discoveries—specifically how Princess Ariadne is using torque-tech to the detriment of Minosian citizens—Theseus *should* be thinking about how to go about dethroning a cruel royal. She isn't typically one for overthrowing regimes and inciting rebellions. Normally, she deals with the monster, then it's on to the next. When the monarch and the monster are one and the same, however... she might need to up her game.

But all she can think about is how she's fucked up with Asterion. Again.

That kiss—that fucking epic toe-curling kiss—had been about to lead to more. And Theseus had ruined it.

"*We* have to go back to Minos. *We'll* find a way." What was all *that* nonsense about?

First of all, Theseus rarely includes anyone else in her missions. Second of all, how dare Theseus try to dictate what Asterion *should* be doing?

But... that's what's so confusing ...

Asterion has the intelligence to envision a better world in her damn sleep. She's the gentlest person Theseus has ever met. *Of course* any invention of hers would be designed to make a better, fairer world. So why, then, doesn't she want to change her homeworld for the better?

And even setting that aside—why stay to be an unwilling participant in endless deaths? Why stay in a place where she can never see the stars? Why not explore them, instead?

Perhaps it was thick-headed to assume Asterion could find a way around the mask if she just applied herself. She's a freaking genius. What does Theseus know?

"Yeah, so..." It's been a while since her last imaginary talking to from Herakles. "Perhaps you should stop being such an arrogant prick?"

Theseus would protest, but Herakles took the words literally out of her thoughts.

It's just...

The mere thought of Asterion staying behind has Theseus all wrong inside.

Asterion can clearly take care of herself. But she shouldn't have to. She shouldn't have to endure the curse of blood on her hands through no fault of her own. And that horror aside... all it takes is one bad day. Sooner or later, she'll end up on the wrong end of a blade.

Theseus can't make her leave. But she can't leave her behind, either.

With a woeful sigh, she adds the chopped carrots to the stew on the heat cradle. In her peripheral vision, Herakles leans nonchalantly against the kitchen counter.

"But what do I do?" Theseus asks under her breath.

"Please, step away—from the weapons…"

Theseus turns to the doorway, hope rising at Asterion's playful tone. She looks freshly showered and in clean clothes. Her posture is a little rigid, her hands stuffed in her trouser pockets, but she joins Theseus at the counter.

Herakles is gone. Well, obviously she was never really there.

"Weapons?" she protests to Asterion. "It's a spatula."

Asterion shrugs, inspecting the bubbling stew. "The way you cook—is definitely weapon."

A relieved laugh escapes Theseus. Asterion's teasing is more rejuvenating than illumi-thread. "I'm not *that* bad…" she mutters.

Asterion's only reply is a raised eyebrow. Fair enough. Theseus chuckles, more to herself; if anyone had told her she'd be dining at the centre of the Labyrinth, she'd have assumed she'd be the one on the menu, not the one being shooed away from the stove and encouraged to peel more carrots.

If Asterion has come to join her, perhaps they're okay?

For a while they're quiet, working side by side. Asterion adds various herbs to the stew, tasting as she goes, while Theseus gathers crockery and cutlery, silently admiring Asterion's culinary instincts. She's tempted to ask whether Asterion wants to talk about what happened—The kiss? Her monarch sister siphoning fuel from a world and its people? Theseus's many fuck ups?

But she's dragged Asterion across more than enough emotional coals for one day. So she keeps it simple and honest: "I'm sorry I upset you."

Asterion stops stirring the stew. There's uncertainty in her eyes, like she's assessing Theseus, or the situation. Finally, she nods and resumes stirring without a word.

Dinner is a quiet, ponderous affair. Theseus doesn't push for conversation. It's only once they're in bed together in the dark, a gap like a chasm between them, that Asterion says, quietly: "I wish you could see this world through my eyes."

Theseus wishes that, too. It takes her a moment to swallow past her dry throat and respond, her whisper matching Asterion's: "You could show me?"

But Asterion either doesn't know how to respond, or she's already asleep, because it's only moments before her breaths turn languorous and deep.

✝
∴

THE GENTLE BREEZE sways the long, lush grass, as rhythmic as dream-filled breaths. The scent of clean linen drying in sunshine teases Theseus's nostrils as she rests, hands folded behind her head, on a soft blanket amidst rolling hills and open fields.

This isn't a place she recognises. At least, not precisely; it's more a concept of a place. A possibility? A hope?

Whichever it is, she's more interested in the gentle growl of Minosian whispers against her neck, and Asterion pressing against her side, her heat spreading through Theseus's body.

Asterion's words are just beyond her understanding, but there's no mistranslating Asterion's lips caressing a path to her mouth, meeting her tongue. There's no misinterpreting the adventurous fingers mapping the canyon of sun-kissed skin revealed by Theseus's opened shirt, before delving with slow certain purpose beneath her waistband.

On Theseus's delighted gasp, sunlight turns to starlight, the world spinning as fast as Theseus's own dizzying thoughts as Asterion's fingers stroke inside her, elevating her higher and higher. *Stars above and heaven's below.* Any questions on her tongue turn to moans on her lips as Asterion growls softly against her ear.

As the planetary spin accelerates, Asterion's otherworldly rhythm crescendos, catapulting Theseus's every synapse beyond the stratosphere and to the stars. Only as cosmic bliss lights the skies does she understand the words on the summer breeze:

"Please, Theseus. Set me free."

$$\begin{matrix} + \\ \cdot \bullet \end{matrix}$$

THESEUS WAKES WRAPPED in a sleeping Asterion, her nose buried in the crook of Asterion's neck, their legs entwined. How did they end up in *this* position?

Asterion's features are so relaxed, Theseus breathes more carefully, trying not to wake her.

Fuck.

No wonder her thoughts had wandered in sleep. Theseus should extricate herself. That's the right thing to do.

With the precision of a renowned monster hunter trying to escape a beast's lair, Theseus disentangles her legs from Asterion's and rolls onto her back. But Asterion rolls over too, her arm draping over Theseus's hip and erasing the inches Theseus had put between them, her deep, slumbering breaths continuing.

Fuck, fuck, fuck.

Her efforts thwarted, her body tingling, all Theseus can do is lay awake and think.

Because if she falls asleep in Asterion's arms, she's likely to embarrass herself. It's surprising she hasn't already.

If there's one thing she hates, it's a confusing dream. Does the dream-intimacy mean something, or nothing? And what the fuck is 'set me free' all about?

Those are the same words Princess Ariadne had used to set

Theseus on her original mission. Are her dreams mocking her now? Or are they reflecting how much she wants Asterion to *want* to be free of this place, to live in a world, any world, that isn't this one?

Or maybe Theseus is just so wound up, that her mindscape was simply trying to grant her some release.

+
•

MORNING TAKES its damn time turning up.

At the first hint of sunlight, Asterion shifts, and Theseus wriggles from underneath her. She seeks refuge under the wash chamber's temperature adjustable cascade, but it does little to cool her imaginings. Water forges its way down her body and she relives Asterion's mouth on hers, and Asterion's decisive tug on her belt buckle. It inspires a daydream of Asterion drawing her closer, her body solid against hers.

Heavens above. If she hadn't gone and interrupted yesterday's kiss, she'd have stripped Asterion on the bed of her labyrinth designs and explored her with fingers and tongue until she'd learned exactly what makes the rightful Architect tick.

Fuck. Theseus rolls her eyes at herself. It's just all this... being in the same space... and their—what is it Asterion calls it?—*proximity*, that has her head in a spin and her dreams amongst the stars. She's never been so wrapped up in someone before. But she's also never experienced a kiss that set her insides on fire so thoroughly.

If only Asterion would join her in here. Right fucking now.

As her own hand follows the path of water down her stomach and beyond, Theseus wonders idly what the escalating energy output of her Flame and torque might be. Hopefully it's powering something worthwhile as she imagines the most basic and beautiful ways she and Asterion might save and create resources together.

+
.•

"WE SHOULD," says Asterion at the banquet table, as if in response to some suggestion.

Theseus waits, smiling. Asterion's habit of starting halfway through a thought and then backtracking triggers a warmth in Theseus's chest that she's trying not to think about.

"You—only seen—labyrinth through mist-eyes. Or in a blur," continues Asterion.

That she's wringing her hands has Theseus's own fingers twitching to reach out and calm her—but she resolves to keep her hands to herself.

But it's Asterion who holds her hand out to Theseus.

"Perhaps—I—should show you?"

The hope in Asterion's eyes, it melts Theseus's resolve and she takes Asterion's offered hand, readily. It's as warm as Asterion's smile, and Theseus's breath goes wandering even before Asterion says: "I want—show you my world."

59

ASTERION'S EYES
THESEUS

I n the entrance hall, Asterion loads her rucksack, complete with attached scythe, onto the gateway's turntable, before reaching for the Minotaur mask. But Theseus steps in to claim it first. Skies above, the damn thing's heavier than she'd expected.

Well. that explains Asterion's exquisite shoulder muscles.

Asterion is scrunching her nose in obvious confusion. Theseus clears her throat. "You've really never been outside the fortress without this?"

Asterion shakes her head.

"Maybe it's time you saw the labyrinth with new eyes, too." Theseus turns the mask over to get a better look at where her head needs to go. "I mean... how else are you going to see the stars?"

Asterion's eyes light up. "You would do that? For me?" Then she tilts her head, that adorable indent forming between her brows. "You're not afraid I'll run off and leave you to be the Minotaur?"

Well, fuck. That thought had not even crossed Theseus's mind.

"I mean, I wasn't..." What in the heavens has happened to

her? She's gone from seeing monsters everywhere to not even considering potential dangers. She takes a steadying breath and tells Asterion the truth. "I trust you."

The words feel more right than anything in a long time. And Asterion's smile... that feels right, too.

While Asterion pieces her dark armour around her torso like a familiar puzzle, Theseus sets the mask aside to tighten her own boot laces. She tries not to look at the contours of Asterion's legs—but she doesn't try hard enough, because when their eyes meet as she stands, there's a touch of knowing smugness in Asterion's gaze.

She's getting confident, and Theseus likes it.

"You want the full experience?" asks Asterion, and Theseus's brain almost breaks.

"Uhh..." Theseus swallows, watching carefully as Asterion steps closer... as Asterion reaches for the bucket of camouflage clay. *Oh. Right.* That's what she's talking about.

Asterion slops it onto her own arms to demonstrate, even smoothing it under the edges of her torso armour. Her lighter skin and the glow of her shoulder stitches are covered within seconds. It won't hide her in the labyrinth's outer corridors or the stark white of the ice forest, but it'll work in darkness and shadow. It worked for her well enough when Theseus had been chasing her.

What a difference a seismic shift in understanding can make. Because, yes, she is still chasing Asterion, even if she refuses to admit it to herself. But not in the way Princess Ariadne had challenged her to. And while the original mission had been to seize a heart, Theseus has a sneaking suspicion she's going to be the one to lose hers.

Theseus tuts inwardly at herself. She's being dramatic. Poetic, almost.

Well, fuck that.

Asterion leaves her face and neck free of the tar-like clay, which suggests she was only demonstrating its application, or trying to drive Theseus wild. Scooping up a fresh handful, she steps closer, a question on her quirked lips.

Theseus nods, because... words... what are words again? If she could find any, she might point out that there's no-one out there now that they need to hide from. Hero is gone. They're alone here.

But she appreciates that Asterion is trying to show her what it's like for her out in the labyrinth. And letting Asterion assist her in slathering on the clay is not something her body will allow her brain to pass up.

Asterion smooths the clay over the splash of luminous freckles on Theseus's forearm, then moves on to travel up her arms, her shoulders, to her neck. Asterion had been so swift in applying her own camouflage, but she's being outright thorough in helping Theseus. Theseus is fairly sure Asterion doesn't need to press so firmly against her muscles, but she doesn't want her to stop.

This might be the best kind of torture.

Theseus grits her teeth. *Don't groan.*

Every stroke against her skin trails heat through her. When Asterion rubs the clay across her throat, bringing them face to face in the closest, most vulnerable way, Theseus's temperature soars.

And fuck if those turquoise eyes aren't alive with a smouldering mischief.

Then, as briskly as if nothing at all had happened, Asterion covers Theseus's torso in armour, fitting the overlapping pieces together around her with masterful deftness. As her brow pinches with concentration, Theseus channels her own into controlling her breathing.

Asterion steps away, letting Theseus twist and turn, testing the manoeuvrability of the unfamiliar armour. When she drifts closer again, Theseus's heart is about ready to climb out of her chest.

Her mouth twitches, hoping to be kissed.

Instead, Asterion fastens a scabbard about Theseus's hips, then slides a sword into its sheath. Theseus isn't sure what use that'll be once she has hooves for hands... Perhaps it's just there for reassurance. Perhaps Asterion just wants an excuse to be close to her. Perhaps she knows precisely the effect she's having on Theseus.

Theseus re-clenches her jaw, trying to stare only at the ceiling. She's sure Asterion doesn't technically have to do all of this. She's quite capable, thank you. But she's not complaining. She's never been so turned on by someone *dressing* her before.

Though, to be fair, it's not something she's let anyone else do.

She instructs her body to *calm the fuck down*. Her body, however, defies her. She needs to hurry up with the mask to hide her flaming cheeks. Since when does Theseus the Monster Hunter *blush*?

Well, apparently more than usual, recently. Fuck's sake. Maybe Asterion won't notice—

Asterion traces a clay-covered finger across her cheek.

Oh. She noticed.

And Asterion's eyebrow raise steals any capability for her to respond beyond a garbled huff, because... *Asterion is flirting with her.* And it's short circuiting her damn brain.

Asterion's features grow serious. "You're certain—about this?"

Theseus can only blink at her. Asterion is talking about the mask now... about going out there... yes?

The labyrinth is a dangerous place, and the weight of the mask plus the cuffs rendering her hands useless will put her at a disadvantage. But she knows she'll be safe with Asterion.

Theseus lifts the behemoth mask over her head. "I am." Heavens. Not only is this thing heavy, it digs in *everywhere*. Her breaths accentuate through the mask layers—metal, leather and fear—into a beastly rasp.

The straps tighten automatically about her forehead, neck, shoulders and chest, pinching sharply enough to force the air from her lungs.

Fuck. How must Asterion have felt when she'd woken trapped inside this thing for the first time? And every time since?

A warm hand on Theseus's camouflaged forearm invites her to calm. Theseus blinks, focusing through the eyeholes. They're difficult to see through, but not impossible. And seeing Asterion's kind eyes, her tension uncoils.

"If you—change your mind," says Asterion, softly, "I understand. I have worn this—most of my life. I will wear it again."

"*No.*" Theseus feels the word before she says it. And when she says it, she hears both it and the *growl-moo* that the mask creates.

Asterion smirks. "With—mask on, you—make even less sense than usual."

Asterion's teasing smile inspires something fluttering in Theseus's chest. She wants to do this for Asterion, even if she herself currently sounds like a perturbed cow. To make her intent clear, she lumbers to the gateway. Her entire posture is off balance, but she somehow doesn't trip.

She takes her place on the turntable where Asterion's rucksack and scythe await them.

"Always remember," says Asterion, pointing up at the mask's horns as she joins Theseus. "Pointy—dangerous."

Pointy. Dangerous.

Theseus nods. She might be an arrogant, swaggering

monster hunter, but she's never above a safety briefing. (And yes, she did learn that the hard way.)

Asterion closes her eyes, and Theseus can only guess she's listening to the Labyrinth. What can she hear that Theseus can't? After a few moments, she nods and helps Theseus lower herself and the mask to the right height to slide the horns into the locks.

As Theseus slots her arms into the other two holes, the cuffs lash about her forearms, pinching as tight as the mask. She *feels* the internal machinations of the mask and cuffs, the cogs clunking into place, realigning and challenging something inside her.

But more distracting than this is Asterion's arms looping around her stomach and chest, hugging her from behind.

"Is—safety," Asterion explains, just before Theseus's whole world spins.

The turntable casts them out into the labyrinth. While Theseus's world is busy turning several rotations, while momentum swipes her off her feet, Asterion is holding on, solid against her.

Asterion landing on her, even while Theseus's masked face is to the floor, is a welcome and frustrating start to their adventure. Is it Theseus's imagination, or is Asterion lingering on her just a little? Is she pressing that little bit closer? Theseus tries to bury her gasp, because she can only imagine how that'll sound through the mask, while Asterion jumps to her feet and holds out her hand.

Theseus accepts. She's not sure whether the extra stumble against Asterion is from Asterion's admirable strength, her own weak-kneed desire to be closer, or because of the stupid mask. Whichever is the tough reason. She'll go for that.

Theseus rights her posture and realigns her neck and shoulders to counterbalance this unfamiliar weight. She wobbles, but Asterion is there to steady her.

"It took me—a while to get—balance right," Asterion says with a smile of encouragement. "This—is good thing, really." And now that smile is knowing, and bright. "At least with you—in mask—beacon of your cheeks won't give you away."

And then, as if that was the most normal thing to say, as if the word "beacon" is the most natural word to know in a second language, and as if all this were just a stroll down a normal non-deadly street, Asterion takes Theseus by the hoof and leads her to the connecting corridor that's in alignment with the fortress gateway. And Theseus might not feel the heat of Asterion's hand, but just knowing it's there through the leather of the cuff, is enough to fuel the fire in her cheeks.

Yeah. It's a good thing she's wearing the mask.

PART VIII

THE LABYRINTH

60

OUT IN THE OPEN
ASTERION

In all the sun-orbits she's been here, Asterion has never wanted to share her world before.

Yes, as a child she'd intended for her sister to live here with her—in a world that was designed to inspire wonder and keep them both safe from any threat. But it's clear now that her wish to have Ariadne nearby was based on the person Asterion hoped her sister would be, rather than the person she actually was. Or is.

Ariadne would never have abided a tour of something Asterion designed. And though that weighs on her shoulders, it's not something she wants to dwell on right now, with Theseus getting to grips with the mask. While Asterion, through practise, can navigate these corridors without incident, Theseus is meandering along like a drunken bull in a crockery shop, each gravity-flip accompanied by a host of disgruntled *moos*.

It's kind of *cute*. Amusing, even, if you ignore the cruelty of the mask and its origins. That Theseus would volunteer to take on the challenge of the mask, for her... that's mighty and heroic. But in showing Theseus her world, it's Asterion's responsibility to keep her safe.

Moving through the labyrinth is a task made much easier without the mask obscuring her vision, or having to concentrate on balancing its weight. She can turn her head as quickly as she wants without bracing for a heavy landing. She can even breathe more deeply, without an ever-present metallic tang.

But as she guides Theseus along the route that's in her moving-mental map of this world, every now and then she has to pause and close her eyes a little to narrow her field of vision and match her surroundings to what she's used to. Sometimes she closes her eyes, to listen, to ensure the labyrinth's rotating corridors are where she thinks them to be.

Sometimes she pauses to just observe: to absorb what the corridors of dark stone, the lava-gully patterns, and the vibrant stripes of colourful wall that pull in light from beyond the Labyrinth, look like with clear vision.

But even with all of this, there's something she's enjoying more than seeing the labyrinth through unhindered eyes...

It is said that all clouds have silver linings. And though Asterion can't recall precisely what natural clouds look like, if she understands the meaning, the silver lining to Theseus wearing the Minotaur mask is the altogether reasonable excuse it gives Asterion to be close to her. To guide her.

Theseus is much more co-ordinated than Asterion had been when she'd first been contained within the mask. But then, Asterion had only been little, then. And even from their first encounter, Theseus has been physically impressive. But if there's an excuse to hold her cuff-clad hand, she'd be a fool not to take it.

Giddiness bubbles in Asterion's chest. Is this what freedom feels like?

No... the giddy-bubbles pop. Anything involving containment cannot be freedom... But it's a glimpse... of what it could be like...

What would it feel like to entwine their fingers, to hold hands without barriers between them as they explore this world together?

Theseus's gentle grumble-moo is perhaps asking what that thunderous tirade is up ahead.

Well, that's the way they're going.

Asterion tugs Theseus through the short tunnel of damp, rugged stone to the roaring cascade of waterfall that drapes over the tunnel's opposite opening.

She guides Theseus along the stone ledge, keeping their backs pressed to the cliff face, until they've sidestepped out from behind the waterfall and are looking out over the moonlit meadow.

The first time they were here together, Asterion had been the Minotaur being chased.

It seems so long ago now.

And if she ignores the lake, and how recently it had almost become her grave and Theseus's, and the golden man's demise thanks to the fang-fish... if she ignores all that, she can appreciate its serenity.

Ordinarily, the sounds and scents of the labyrinth are clouded by the mask. But now the breeze is caressing her face, carrying the aroma of soil and wheat to her while the tall grass tickles her palm.

Her forays into the labyrinth are often for a particular purpose: a material she needs, or a snagging mechanism in need of repair. Or a foolish attempt to save those who are here to kill her. This time, she gets to just *be*.

But they could do with some grain... She cuts a sheaf of wheat with her scythe and affixes it and the scythe against her satchel. It's so much easier without the mask and hooves.

Grinning from ear to ear, she tugs Theseus through the

meadow. Thanks to Theseus, for the first time in her life, Asterion gets to luxuriate in the world she designed.

And she has so much to show her.

61

AGLOW
THESEUS

I t's mighty useful having the Labyrinth's designer guide her path.

How Asterion manages to see through the mask's oddly shaped eyeholes, let alone achieve the speed and co-ordination that had swept Theseus off her feet—repeatedly—to save her from the labyrinth's hidden weapons, Theseus has no clue. Her own attempts merely at walking straight are... well... a bit embarrassing.

Asterion assures her that the paths they're on are safe. As they navigate the corridors and biomes, the joy that lights Asterion's face each time she pauses to touch and experience her surroundings makes the discomfort of the mask worth it. Theseus could almost temporarily forget the Labyrinth's more harrowing aspects. Almost.

Asterion pulls Theseus through the silver meadow with a playful urgency.

"Where are we—?" But before Theseus can finish her sentence, her own moo-growl meets her ears. Stars above, why does the mask make her sound like a confused farm animal, when Asterion had sounded so... terrifying?

Once again, the reality of Asterion's life here burrows under Theseus's skin. But then Asterion turns to her, and the feeling is displaced by her moonlit smile.

Yes. Theseus would follow that smile anywhere.

The thought chokes a startled grumble-moo from her, accentuated by the mask, and she almost trips over her own feet, too. *Focus, focus.*

Her guided path from the meadow through the shadowed woodland is otherwise smooth. Even a couple of days ago, Theseus wouldn't have been able to make this journey, but now a healing warmth buzzes through her calf muscle, centred around where the thread has absorbed into her flesh.

Asterion stops. "Be still," she whispers. Not a warning; simply an invitation to absorb their surroundings.

All Theseus can hear is her own breath echoing within the mask as she tries her best to stay as still as Asterion, who must know what the woodland needs, because as she holds her breath, their surroundings pulse to life.

Leaf veins shimmer, iridescent. Sap effervesces. Water droplets pool within thick leaves, rainbow ripples expanding outward. Luminescent constellations of mushrooms decorate soil and trees alike: discs and domes and every shape in between. Some are symmetrical, some free-form. All of it is *magic.*

Asterion's hand squeezes tighter about Theseus's cuff, and Theseus wishes she could mirror the gesture.

The sight had been beautiful the first time around. But now, watching the ethereal dance reflect like galaxies in Asterion's eyes, this world in balance, this impossible woodland that exists through Asterion's ideas, her designs, the pages of her workbooks... it's *breathtaking.*

Does Asterion have a diagram that quantifies Theseus's transformation into a sentimental fool, too? Her evolution from tough sky-warrior to someone who fucking... *gazes*? Someone who feels the luminescent threads around her heart weaving into a tether-line between them, pulling them closer?

What other explanation is there other than Asterion's ability to achieve the impossible?

62

STARS IN HER EYES
ASTERION

A sterion leads Theseus to the outer corridor that houses the access hatch to the viewing platform. Now, standing beneath it, all she can do is stare up at it.

Theseus gestures at the hatch with an encouraging flourish. Heavens, Asterion wishes she could see her face right now. She imagines Theseus is beaming, thrilled to be giving her this chance. Or perhaps her face is a picture of uncertainty: a mirror of Asterion's own expression.

Because a lifetime of nasty surprises has taught her *it can't be this easy*. Perhaps this isn't a good idea? What if someone has set a trap? Not Theseus. Not anymore. But... Someone?

But *the stars...* She wants to see them. And this might be her only chance. So, she steels herself with a deep breath, pulls her scythe from the back of her satchel, and scales the wall's irregular brickwork.

Without the mask, she can fit through the hatch easily.

The viewing platform is empty: no sign of lurking threat, and everything here is just as she envisioned it. The skyscape is...

"Wow."

It's strange to observe the world of Minos like this; a burnt husk of spherical flotsam, aglow with embers, floating in a glistening dark sea of possibilities. It's strange to think there's someone on that world with a face like hers, ruling like she's Minos's saviour, when she's the one burning it to ash.

Asterion has missed the stars.

When she was a child, it had never occurred to her that there might be a time when she wouldn't be able to look upon the stars speckling the sky; to try to count them, or to wonder what better worlds might be out there.

She'd tried to recreate the heavens through engineering and artistry, but she couldn't. Not fully; not like this. No architectural talent could ever capture the infinite beauty of the skies, their magic and wonder.

And yet... this stunning celestial expanse is nothing compared to the warrior waiting for her in the corridor below; who braved the unknown so that Asterion could have this moment.

Theseus did this. For her.

And that is something more beautiful, magical and wonderful, more breathtaking, than any skyscape. It's the thought that propels Asterion back down through the hatch, her heart bursting with the energy of a thousand stars.

In her exuberance, her scythe catches on the hatch edge and clatters to the corridor's stone floor, beyond easy reach. Theseus must be either alarmed or confused by Asterion's swift, clumsy return, because she scrambles to reach for her with a grunt-moo of what seems to be concern.

Stars above, she's cute. Asterion can just imagine the perturbed face Theseus must be pulling at emitting such a silly sound.

An entire galaxy of feelings orbits Asterion, and the lava in the gullies, patterned all across the corridor, pulses with them.

She grasps Theseus's forearm to steady herself. And, perhaps, to reassure herself that the warrior before her is real.

If only they could be rid of the mask. If only she could look into Theseus's eyes. Would Theseus invite her into her arms? Can she see Asterion's reeling thoughts; feel the true depth of her emotions?

But this thrill, her excitement, spirals off into space, replaced by heart-thumping dread.

Because there's something not right in all this...

Something creeping...

There's a shadow at the end of the corridor.

The silhouetted figure is too far away for her to make out the details, but there's no mistaking the shape of the spear, the predatory tension.

He shouldn't be here. Asterion had been so sure the fang-fish had dealt with him... But this can't be a sensory trick, because they've avoided the mists.

Theseus makes an unwieldy turn, following Asterion's line of sight. And she must forget her ill-equipped status, because she angles her body to shield Asterion with a protective hoof against her chest-plate.

The galaxy of emotions still swirling in Asterion's chest expands in that moment. No-one has ever stood in the path of danger for her before.

But Asterion tempers it. Now is not the time.

She's so used to running. So used to being imprisoned inside the mask, her face hidden and her voice distorted. But... after all... doesn't she have the face and voice of a royal? If the golden man recognises her—or at least if he thinks her to be Ariadne—then he'll stop, won't he?

But he must be too far away to see her face. His spear arm is already recoiling.

Panic twisting inside her, Asterion grabs Theseus's arm and drags her in the opposite direction.

There's no time to retrieve the fallen scythe.

The speed Theseus achieves as she veers through the corridors is admirable, all things considered. But each turn sends her ricocheting off the walls, and her chest is heaving, her breath growling through the mask. It's taken too many sun-orbits for Asterion to learn how best to carry its weight. Theseus must be about ready to keel over.

Asterion could kick herself.

She should never have let Theseus wear the mask.

If she hadn't emerged from the viewing platform when she did, Theseus would be stuck fighting for her life in the thing right now. Or already lost the battle.

And with the golden man and his spear only just beyond a spear's throw behind them, the battle both hasn't begun and isn't over.

She keeps her grip on Theseus's forearm as they run, panic surging through her veins. How to lose him? *Think, think, think—*

She listens for the inner-workings of the labyrinth, aligning them with her mental map as she calculates the rotations. If they can't outrun him, perhaps the labyrinth can help.

The lava river; that's a possibility. But it's too risky for Theseus.

There is another way...

But they'll have to be quick.

Asterion halts, but Theseus doesn't—

Tugging at Theseus's arm to stop her, the bull mask swivels to her, almost overbalancing them both. But Asterion rights them, pulling Theseus along the left corridor and manoeuvring them so that Theseus's back is flush against the wall, pressing her there.

"Hold me close—okay? Don't let go."

There isn't time to explain why—but there's no need, either. Theseus immediately does as she asks. Asterion grips Theseus's sides, ducking her head to nestle on Theseus's shoulder. With a glance to check the golden man hasn't caught up, Asterion toe-kicks the wall.

The hidden door spins on its axis, pivoting them into darkness. Only, this door doesn't have a turntable beneath it.

Asterion knows it's coming—but she gasps all the same as—in the space between the labyrinth's walls—they plummet.

MINOSIAN FLAME
THESEUS

*W*hat the fuck is happening?
Well, falling. That much is obvious.

Theseus's stomach lodges somewhere up in her throat as her armour-encased back scrapes down the wall at break-neck speed.

Asterion is clinging to her, and vice versa. Her hands might not be available to grip anything, but her cuff-covered forearms pull Asterion as close as it's possible to be.

As close as it's possible to be when there's a layer of bull mask and armour between them.

But that's probably not what she should be focusing on right now, since, as they plummet—all around them, amidst a speeding blur of shadow and stripes of colourful light—the labyrinth is in motion.

The mask only allows snippets of visibility, but in amongst the rotating machine parts, cogs and mechanisms, she spies bridges and corridors on their journeys between labyrinth layers. All moving like clockwork.

Trees with sprawling roots cling in furrows and gaps—life

finding its way—while furniture lodged in rock interrupts the design's flow.

Theseus tries to look up, to check they're not being chased, but only succeeds in scraping the mask's horns against the wall behind her.

"We're safe," Asterion soothes, her face a welcome pressure against the mask, somewhere near Theseus's neck. It's difficult to tell precisely where from inside the mask.

Safe? The breath-stealing plummet, the Labyrinth's terrain-quake vibrations—Asterion's assertive embrace aside, if there's one thing this doesn't feel, it's safe.

"The Labyrinth—is turning," says Asterion, raising her voice above the mechanical cranking of this world in motion. "Even if he follows—our paths—not connect."

He. *Him.* They'd been so sure Hero was a goner. That arrogant prick has more lives than a Rosinthorn caterwaul.

How long have they been falling? Why isn't Asterion more panicked about this?

"Is—okay." There's a calming certainty in Asterion's tone as her hand migrates to Theseus's upper arm, thumb stroking her. "Is just—slide."

"A slide?" Theseus's question warble-growls out of the mask.

"Remember, I was—child when I design—this place. Don't worry—be over soon."

Theseus tightens her arms around Asterion, ensuring she's got her. Or that Asterion has got *her.* She grits her teeth at the thought of something happening to Asterion while Theseus is stuck in the mask, helpless to do a damn thing about it.

But Asterion could have left her behind in the labyrinth to deal with Hero alone. She could have guaranteed her own safety. There are few people under the Seven Skies who would risk their own lives to save Theseus. That Asterion is one of those people... that's... more exhilarating than falling through the layers of a moving labyrinth.

"Don't worry—is just water," says Asterion, against Theseus's neck, just a half-second before the angle of their drop scoops them into a horizontal and they barrel through—

Splash—splash—

Yep. That would be the curtain of water immediately soaking her from mask to boot. A colossal *slosh* punctuates the end of the ride as they skid to a stop in a curved-edge corridor, pipe-like in its formation.

Asterion tugs Theseus to her feet, leading her urgently through the knee-deep water. The long corridor houses only the waterfall and the stretch of water that had cushioned their landing. The ceiling is dotted with pinprick lights like stars.

How fun the waterslide and its starlit landing might be, without the terror and chase of it all.

Theseus angles the mask to watch as Asterion approaches an unremarkable section of wall. She pulls her palm across the surface, like a signature, and a seamless door slides open, just above the runway of water.

An engine-like roar and a stifling heat spill out.

Asterion guides Theseus up onto the door's step and into the chamber, sealing the door behind them with another gesture. The slide's landing has washed them both of their camouflage, and the immense heat of this chamber is already drying out their clothes more quickly than any air-blast.

Asterion pulls Theseus along and Theseus is so busy grappling with the weight of the mask and trying to see through its awkward eyeholes, that she can only glimpse details of the chamber.

The metal-grate gangway beneath her feet. The flash of orange from the intricate, heat-hazed lava-gullies far below.

Gauges sitting within the maze-like artistry of pipes across the walls.

There's something uniquely *Asterion* about this space.

The engine-like roar and the gauges put Theseus in mind of a sky-ship, but it's so much bigger than any Theseus has ever hitched a ride or stowed away on.

Hades and the Heavens. It's *so* much bigger.

Finally, Theseus manages to angle the mask to see what this cavernous chamber houses. A towering central column of blazing, blue flame, sparks like a gargantuan lightning rod. Its roar is almost deafening, like air buffeting past eardrums in a skydive.

At the base and the apex, those same sparks dance across the maze of lava-gullies, keeping the rock molten.

This isn't an engine to power a ship. It's an engine to power a world.

And Theseus can't help staring. She can't help stopping. With Asterion's hand still wrapped about her cuff, Asterion is forced to stop, too. She whirls around, distress etched in her face, her torque pulsing with the same rhythm as the monolith behind her.

And the pieces fall into place.

This.

This is Asterion's Minosian Flame. Her spark of life in world-engine form. This is what powers the Labyrinth.

"I shouldn't have made you wear—mask." Asterion raises her voice above the roaring flames, the column's surface kicking out like a sun suffering a comet-collision.

In the light of the epic engine-flame, the ridge of the scar on Asterion's lip is more pronounced. If only Theseus wasn't wearing this mask, she could soothe every scar, kiss away every hurt...

"Asterion, you didn't make me, I—" Theseus steps forward, but her words of reassurance emerge as a growl. Her hands try to curl into fists of frustration, but the cuffs won't even allow that.

It tears into her gut like a blade: what it has meant for Asterion to be cursed to this place. How much she has endured, and yet still sees through the darkness to the beauty. And if that doesn't make the spindle of Theseus's heart glow, if that doesn't have the threads tugging her towards Asterion...

But Asterion is rigid as she paces the gangway, her gestures jerky as though arguing with herself. "It was—reckless. I put you —in danger. I—shouldn't have—"

Theseus steps closer. "Hey, hey, it's okay..." This time, her distorted words are more of a gentle warble, though that's still not much use. But maybe she can do something... maybe she can find another way to show Asterion that it's okay...

She opens her arms in invitation—

But Asterion stumbles back, fear clear in her eyes and in the skittering energy in the flames and electricity behind her. For a moment, Theseus could be convinced that she *is* the monster; the creature from a world of horrors. And for that same stomach roiling moment—with Asterion's every muscle tensed—it seems Asterion will bolt.

Only, then something in Asterion's demeanour shifts; as soon as the panic arrived, it departs. The fear leaves her eyes and her shoulders relax and she steps decisively into Theseus's embrace.

They slot together like puzzle-armour, as if it's the most natural thing. Before, falling through the labyrinth, they'd clung to each other in a kind of desperation, but this... this is different. There's an intensity to Asterion's hold on her, like before, but it tempers into something more like relief as Asterion melts against her.

"It's okay. We're okay," Theseus whispers, one hand moving

in circles against Asterion's back, as though there isn't a hoof-cuff and armour in their way.

Asterion's breathing slows—the engine-column starts to flow more evenly—and Theseus feels the newfound calm as her own. She's almost disappointed when Asterion steps out of the embrace.

But less so when she angles to see Asterion's face; the look in her eyes has evolved to something more positive. Something not far removed from the look she'd given Theseus beneath the skyscape viewing platform. A look of wonder, like Theseus had decorated the sky with stars just for her.

Well, yeah...

If she had that power, she would...

Theseus swallows at the thought, not sure if the concept scares her or invigorates her. Both? For a monster hunter, she really needs to toughen up.

It's not her imagination that the epic monument of Asterion's Minosian Flame is pulsing just a little faster, now, is it? It's not her imagination that the building heat in Asterion's eyes rivals that flame.

If only Asterion could see her face, or even her torque, she'd know she's not the only one sparking inside. Or, perhaps she can tell, because—as the engine's heat thunders around them—Asterion grasps Theseus by the hoof and tugs her along the gangway.

Their path through the labyrinth takes an age. Or perhaps it doesn't. Whichever it is, it's clear that they both can't get back to the fortress fast enough.

64

FEVERISH

ASTERION

At the fortress gateway, it takes moments and an eternity for Asterion—hands shaking, heart dancing—to help Theseus align the mask and hooves to the keyholes before— *finally*—the turntable spins, and Theseus is freed.

Tangled together, they tumble across the entrance chamber floor, the labyrinthine patterns of the under-floor lava-channels spanning out beneath them. Asterion lands on top, her legs straddling Theseus. Vaguely, she registers the *thud* of her satchel landing somewhere nearby, but her body is more alert to Theseus's steadying hands at her hips.

"We are—safe. In here," she tells Theseus. "No way in— without mask."

The golden man isn't a problem she has any interest in solving right now. The puzzle of Theseus, however...

What Asterion wouldn't give for a cooling dip in the water-slide right now. Before Theseus arrived in her world, before she set up camp in Asterion's thoughts, the quirks of her torque-labyrinth connection hadn't been so noticeable. But now? The Labyrinth has never been so damn *heated*.

Theseus's hands drift from Asterion's hips and up her sides

as she sits up to be within a breath of her. There's a question in her touch and in her eyes, sparkling bright and dark like a lake in moonlight.

Asterion pulls back and a flash of confusion and concern crosses Theseus's features, until—*click*—Asterion locates and releases the catch that clips her armour together. At Asterion's fervent nod of invitation, Theseus's hands become willing participants, tugging at Asterion's armour, the *clunk-clank* of metal landing on stone a distant detail under Asterion's lust-fuelled haze as, together, they strip her top half down to her vest.

Theseus's hands return to Asterion's sides in tentative exploration, a flow of blue light pulsing at the hollow of her throat.

Yes. Asterion can relate.

Theseus diverts to fumble at her own armour. The growling huff she lets out when she fails to find the armour catch is so cute, Asterion can't resist kissing her: just the lightest touch, just enough to enjoy Theseus's breath on her lips, to taste the possibilities.

As she presses tighter against Theseus's lap, the combined glow of their torques intensifies. She guides Theseus's hand to the divot in her armour, at the base of her spine. *Click*: Theseus's back plates fall away, her torso plates held in place only by the press of Asterion's body against her.

Asterion takes a moment to steady the race of her heart, letting her touch linger up the contours of Theseus's back to luxuriate in the short hair at the nape of her neck while her thumbs stroke that annoyingly perfect angular jaw. The soft gasp that escapes Theseus's parted lips as she leans into Asterion's touch might be the best thing Asterion has ever heard.

She leans back enough that Theseus's torso-armour falls away, leaving her in a vest so strained by the tight swell of her chest and the lines of hard muscle, it leaves little to the imagination. And at the same time fuels it.

But the absolute best thing about the warrior within Asterion's reach isn't the physique that's taken dedication to sculpt, but the question, the plea, that burns in her eyes, as scorching as blue flame.

And there's no other answer but for Asterion to seize her by her vest straps and claim her mouth in a fierce and feverish kiss.

Theseus's arms wrap tightly around her, pulling Asterion flush against her. Or she tries. The hilt of her sword digs in between them, which has them sharing a smirk even as they kiss.

Asterion fumbles with the buckle of Theseus's belt. Stupid, clumsy hands. Why won't they work? But she needn't worry. Theseus's fingers are working just fine, casting both belt and sword aside within seconds.

They reunite in a frenzy of kisses—a dance of lips and tongues. And when Theseus lifts her, laying her on her back on the warmed floor... *Confound and flummox...* Theseus draped across her while kissing her might be Asterion's new favourite feeling.

65

FIRST TIME

THESEUS

Theseus *loves* that smile: what it represents as much as the feel of it against her lips.

Her forearms bracketing Asterion, pinning her to the floor, Theseus revels in the feel of Asterion, soft and solid beneath her. It's possible that the best place in the universe for her gently writhing hips is between Asterion's thighs; that the best sounds in any or all of the heavens are Asterion's whimpers and moans.

But there's a knock at the door of her mind. Her less evolved instincts urge her to ignore it, but her more noble aspirations remind her to pull back. To let Asterion guide this.

The last thing she wants is to lose this closeness, but she closes her eyes to re-centre herself. Is this what Asterion wants? Every kiss and caress, every audible exhale, says *yes*. But if this is going where her every singing nerve ending tells her it is... there's no need to rush.

But before Theseus can muster the wherewithal to speak, Asterion recaptures her mouth, her warm fingers exploring Theseus's stomach, teasing just beneath her waistband. Heavens a-fucking-bove. Asterion hasn't even touched her yet, and her inner axis is already tilting.

Asterion's desire-darkened eyes search hers diligently, looking for the answer to the question in her own.

And all Theseus can think is: *Yes.*

Which Asterion must recognise, because she delves lower, pressing into the heat that gives away exactly how much Theseus wants this. Wants *her.* Theseus's groan mingles with Asterion's delighted gasp as the best kind of ache travels from her hips to her head and circles all the way back to her toes. She could melt into Asterion; right into the stone floor. But her limbs tense as she remembers herself.

She breathes carefully. She might be on top, but she's far from in control. And it turns out that—with Asterion—it's a dynamic she's into.

But.

Heavens.

A growl of need escapes her. If Asterion keeps stroking her like this, she's going to unravel at any moment, which hardly seems fair...

It's Asterion's first time. Theseus wants her to *bask* in all of this. A quick feverish fuck on a stone floor will not do.

Tenderly, she retrieves Asterion's hand and sits back on her heels. The space between them lasts all of one second as Asterion follows her up to meet her in another world-altering kiss.

Theseus presses a gentle palm to the centre of Asterion's chest. Asterion pauses, her ready-to-kiss lips tugging down with confusion. She covers Theseus's hand with her own in an affectionate caress, and Theseus can't help leaning in to give her the kiss she's been chasing.

Stars above, it's so difficult to stop kissing her...

Focus, Theseus!

Theseus pulls back again. "Shouldn't we... uhh..." What are words? "Shouldn't we talk?"

"No—understand—Athenian," says Asterion, with a cheeky

glint in her eyes, her breath caressing Theseus's lips between kisses.

Heavens and Hades. Asterion's toned arms are a wonder, leading to shoulders to die for... Is she flexing them beneath Theseus's hands like that on purpose?

Theseus clenches a fist around the strap of Asterion's vest as she growls in frustration; at not being able to touch Asterion enough, and at the fact that she should stop. And then again at Asterion's wry smile against her mouth that only makes Theseus want to kiss her more, but—

Focus. Focus. Focus.

"Shouldn't we talk about... uh... feelings and... um... stuff?" *Wow. Way to sound emotionally competent, Theseus.* "I mean... where this is going?"

"I assumed—bedchamber..." Asterion nips Theseus's bottom lip and Theseus swears the universe just turned inside out. Like, in a good way.

Asterion smiles into their kiss, like she knows precisely the effect she's having on her. "Do you want to talk about feelings, Theseus?"

"Mhhhrrrr." *Was that a word?* Theseus herself mightn't understand Athenian anymore. And why does her name sound so good on Asterion's tongue?

"Asti..." Theseus's words are as breathless as she'd feared. "We don't have to rush..." Though her focus drifting from Asterion's sparkling eyes to her inviting lips perhaps undermines her point. "I don't want you to do anything you're not ready for."

"I want to touch you," whispers Asterion. "I want you to touch me..." Theseus's every muscle buzzes at those words. "If that's too much for you, Theseus..." A knowing, playful smile quirks Asterion's lips. "I don't want to do anything *you're* not ready for."

Hades and the fucking Heavens. With a heroic exertion of

self-control, Theseus pauses before Asterion's mouth. "I just... I want to make sure... there's nothing you're worried about?"

Asterion draws back a little, her brow furrowing like she's properly considering the question. Theseus refrains from kissing that furrow. Frankly, she deserves a medal.

"I am a little nervous..." Asterion bites her lip, obviously thinking. "About not being skilled at—at touching you." Her lips brush Theseus's jaw, and Theseus melts. "But... I design mazes. I live at—centre of a labyrinth..." She kisses up Theseus's jawline until she's close enough to whisper in her ear: "...hopefully I can navigate to where I need to be."

Theseus chokes on her own breath. Considering she's the one who suggested *talking*, she sure has lost that ability. "Are you —sure you... h-haven't done this before?" she manages, as Asterion and her wicked smile detour to kiss her neck.

Needing a little space to form noble thoughts—or any thoughts—Theseus stumbles to her feet, tugging at her vest as she retreats to lean against the wall and—hopefully—cool down a bit.

But the lava-gullies are blazing. How is it so hard to catch her breath when both she and Asterion are still more clothed than not? They haven't even taken their boots off yet. From Theseus's weak knees and this weird jelly-like feeling in her body, anyone would think they'd already gone several rounds on the stone floor.

That thought doesn't help her cool down. Nor does the sight of Asterion, knelt amongst their scattered armour, gazing up at Theseus as though imagining her without a stitch of clothing.

With unfair fluidity, Asterion is on her feet, observing her with curiosity or concern. "Is there—anything *you are* worried about, Theseus?"

Pfft. Why would Theseus be worried? That's... ridiculous.

She wants to do this. Heavens above and below, what a fucking understatement.

But if she's being honest, she is a little worried. Which is... new. She's never had any reason to doubt her ability to please her bedmates. She always checks in to make sure they're enjoying themselves. And she's certainly never had complaints. Feedback has been overwhelmingly positive, in fact.

So why is she having... *jitters*... about pleasing Asterion now? Theseus the great Monster Hunter does not get *jitters*. She can stroll into a shadowy cavern packed with terrifying beasts and keep a steady pulse. She can break up a bar brawl and barely raise a sweat. When she's feeling exuberant, she can pleasure three women at once with more than *satisfied* results (because that's what two hands and a mouth are for, right?). But present her with one so-called Minotaur with intelligence, empathy, humour, lagoon eyes, and a smile to die for...

...and Theseus is a fucking damsel cliché.

It's... a lot. Physical she can do. Temporary intimacy, she can do that too. And while what they're doing and about to do is physical, nothing about this intimacy feels temporary.

And that is scarier than a sky full of monsters.

Perhaps she's overthinking it. Perhaps she's just feeling the pressure because this is Asterion's first time, and Theseus wants to make it special for her.

She fidgets. "It's just... what if it's not... *good* for you?"

Asterion's smile is both relieved and mischievous, like she has the answer to all of Theseus's concerns. Stepping closer, she reaches for Theseus's illumi-thread-dappled hand and presses it to her own chest, letting Theseus feel the knocking of her heart.

"What I feel here," she says, her eyes pools of calm. "It's not fear or panic, it's not from running away. For the first time in my life, it's all *good* feelings. Because of you. For you. You..."

Idly, she smooths Theseus's hair behind her ear. Heavens

above, those weak knees and body-jelly just got weaker and wobblier. Anyone would think this was *her* first time.

"...I've been—drawn to you—since I saw your kindness, your bravery. Risking—life for strangers. Putting—oaf in his place." Asterion steps closer, but not close enough. "When you laugh, when you smile..." She squeezes Theseus's hand, holding it just below the fluttering glow of her heart pendant. "...I feel it here."

Such a declaration would ordinarily have Theseus running for the Tartarian Hills, but she's rooted to the spot, welcoming anything Asterion will give her. Asterion's gaze is so full of fondness it feels like an embrace.

"I like when you furrow here" —Asterion smooths Theseus's forehead with her thumb— "when you—are figuring something out." Her fingertips migrate to Theseus's cheek. "And that—furrow here when you are amused." Theseus smirks and Asterion smooths that furrow. "Every day—I am grateful you ventured to my world. I—never wanted—to be close to anyone before. I—never—*wanted*, before..."

Their bodies are almost flush against each other now. Theseus isn't sure whether one or both of them moved closer. It doesn't matter. The warmth of Asterion's body, her words, is somehow both calming and electrifying.

"...I will enjoy being touched, Theseus. It will be *good*, because it is you."

Theseus's heart feels like it's fluttering and glowing like Asterion's pendant.

"Besides..." Asterion leans in, tracing the tip of her nose against Theseus's cheek. "...this labyrinth is touch sensitive. And so am I."

The splutter of unsubtle sparks from Theseus's torque matches her garbled huff of reply.

"And," Asterion adds, with a cheeky glint in her eyes, "may I remind you... I live in the Sky Labyrinth? I learn—long ago—life is about journey, not destination. If either of us—lost, we can ask for directions. Or—we show each other the way."

How can she be so many things at once? How can a smile be both mischievous and wise?

"If you're sure you're ready?" Oh, good. Theseus has finally managed some actual words.

Holding her gaze, Asterion guides Theseus's illumi-flecked hand gently but firmly down to her waistband, then beyond, inviting her fingers to discover...

Slick...

Intoxicating...

Warmth...

"Do I feel ready to you?" Asterion gasps, eyes shimmering with torque sparks and more than a hint of mirth.

Heavens above and below. Theseus forgets how to form words. Did she ever really know? It doesn't matter, since their mouths are suddenly, achingly, wondrously busy with the kind of kiss that challenges gravity and realigns worlds.

66

FINALLY!

ASTERION

Forging a path through the fortress corridors has never set Asterion's insides on fire before. But then, the journey has never been quite like *this* before.

Tangling together, she and Theseus barely keep their balance as they kick off boots and socks, stumbling between kisses toward the bedchamber. It's the first time in her life clothing removal has felt like the most urgent task under the Seven Suns.

Their discarded clothing leaves a trail in their wake, as if they plan to retrace their steps later, to find the way back to where they began. But Asterion doesn't want to go back. She wants to repeat these steps. *Yes.* They haven't even reached the bedchamber, and she already wants to do all of this a thousand times over. But she doesn't want to go back to the crossroads, to the point before they'd chosen this path. Each kiss is a new adventure that leaves her both energised and breathless. She wants to keep pressing forward, to see where this will take them.

But that's what Theseus warned her against, isn't it?

To not get attached. To not get lost in feelings.

If someone else were describing this experience to her, she'd tell them they'd lost their darn mind. She'd never considered that a kiss, a touch, could spark more than physical sensations. But now her heartbeat is thrumming *everywhere*—including the fire-torches and the pulsing lava-gullies—alive with potential and promise—

No. No promises.

Theseus will be leaving soon. And Asterion needs to remember that.

It's just difficult not to imagine the endless possibilities ahead during what must be the most smouldering kiss that's ever occurred under all of the Seven Suns.

Weightless. That's how she feels.

As the Labyrinth groans, her feet lift from the ground, her body drifting with Theseus's like they're on the same orbital path.

It's just a gravity fluctuation, of course: the Labyrinth adjusting to being tugged along by Minos in its geostationary orbit. But right now, it feels like Theseus is a gravitational force, drawing her closer.

They'll fall soon, but Asterion doesn't want to think of that. She only wants Theseus and the anticipation of knowing her, of mapping what lies beneath that distractingly tight fabric and beyond those azurite eyes. Whether there's a path forward for them or not.

Gravity reinstated, they fall—

Asterion's stomach swoops. How they remain tangled in each other *and* upright as they land the knee-high drop is a mystery of the universe.

"Are you okay?" whispers Theseus in Minosian against her lips.

Is she talking about the gravity, or the maze of unfamiliar emotions Asterion is trying to navigate? Asterion squeezes her eyes shut, taking a moment to breathe. Theseus's arms wrap around her, holding her close, tethering her. She opens her eyes, and the passion and care in Theseus's gaze re-tunes the static of Asterion's thoughts to something lyrical and joyous.

Certainty blooms in her chest.

Because what would be worse than Theseus leaving would be Theseus leaving and Asterion never getting to experience this. Never experiencing *her*.

Asterion can't help a satisfied smile at the way Theseus's idly exploring fingers are betraying a particular enthusiasm for Asterion's arms. It has her scheming; mulling over creative situations where they might make use of her strength....

Before Theseus's intrigued expression can evolve to questioning, Asterion dips down beneath Theseus's strong thighs, hoisting Theseus up and against her as Theseus squeals with surprise.

Asterion smirks to herself. Sudden fluctuations of gravity don't startle the monster hunter anymore, but being lifted off her feet into strong arms does? Interesting. It's good to know all that garden weightlifting can be put to use...

Theseus might be as ruggedly captivating as an uncut geode on the outside, but beneath that exterior—to use Theseus's own terminology—she really *fucking* sparkles.

"What? Just because you—brave and noble monster hunter, I can't—lift you?" Asterion's smile blooms all the more when she hears the confidence in her own voice. Theseus's responding look as she wraps her legs around Asterion's waist—half impressed, half begrudgingly thrilled—ratchets up her glee further still.

Theseus dips her head and claims Asterion's mouth in a messy kiss, digging her fingers into the muscles of Asterion's shoulders in the most delightful way. Yes; Asterion would enthusiastically tread this path again. And again.

Without breaking their kiss, without dropping Theseus,

Asterion fumbles for the doorhandle. Failing to find it, Theseus's back meets the door and Asterion luxuriates in the press of Theseus's body against hers.

She hadn't intended to use the door in this way, but... as her stomach presses between Theseus's thighs, and Theseus groans into her mouth at the contact, Asterion could easily forget about needing to open the door at all.

Right here is just—

"Fuck, Asti..." Theseus breathes the words against her lips, and she must have reached back and found the handle, because the door swings open, and it's a wonder—as Asterion stumbles forward—that she doesn't fall or drop her mighty cargo.

The hearth roars as Asterion carries Theseus across the threshold into their bedchamber. More heat isn't what they need, but Asterion's too busy to care.

She might have been rough in sweeping Theseus into her arms, but she's reverent in placing her on the edge of the bed. As they share a languid kiss, torque static teasing the air between them, Asterion leans over Theseus and begins unbuttoning her trousers. No doubt the brave warrior will remember that she likes to take the lead soon enough, but right now Asterion is enjoying undressing her.

When she kneels before Theseus, tugging lightly at her open trousers, Theseus lifts her hips just enough for Asterion to slowly remove them. Asterion is careful to keep the fabric from dragging against the luminous lines in Theseus's lower leg, though she can't help running her thumb across surrounding skin. Because it's this injury that brought Theseus here. It's this that keeps her here. It's this, when Theseus finally admits it's healed, that will pull them apart.

Theseus strokes Asterion's jaw with a single finger, guiding her to look up into her eyes.

Asterion swallows. She doesn't want to think about their

ending. Not when she's got Theseus on her bed in only under-shorts and vest. Not when Theseus is looking at her like that: like she wants to devour her, and be devoured by her.

Asterion lurches forward, catching Theseus's mouth in a kiss, pausing only when Theseus encourages Asterion's vest up over her head. A flicker of uncertainty propels Asterion to her feet. She's still half dressed, still in her trousers, but... she's more aware of her nakedness than she's ever been.

Despite the armour she wears out in the labyrinth, over the sun-orbits, weapons have found their way through to score and glaze her skin. Where burns have healed, the skin has never been the same. By Minosian standards, such a blemished canvas could never be considered anywhere near perfection.

But Theseus's azurite eyes are washing over her with such admiration, Asterion could almost believe she's a work of art. Theseus's speechlessness, her awed exhalation, the way her torque dances with electricity... Asterion feels the compliment down to her toes.

It bolsters her as Theseus closes the gap between them, her lips tracing the lines of her stomach as dexterous fingers banish her trousers to the floor. *Smooth, Theseus; very smooth.* And from Theseus's smouldering grin as she shuffles further backwards on the bed... she knows it.

Only as Asterion straddles her, hovering as she debates how much weight to settle onto her, does she notice that Theseus's expression has evolved to smugness. Before she can start to wonder why—she's already on her back, the full length of Theseus's body pinning her to the bed, the heat of Theseus's skin meeting her own.

Theseus looks pretty damn pleased with herself.

Confound and flummox. If Asterion could choose a feeling to live inside, this would be it.

Her only urge right now is to press closer, but Theseus

clearly has other ideas because she sits, straddling Asterion's hips. Indignant protestations are on the tip of Asterion's tongue, only for words and breath alike to be plucked from her chest when Theseus slowly removes her own vest, unveiling a masterclass of muscle, sinew, and strength.

Like Asterion's own skin, Theseus's is marked with scars: some mere whispers, others heavy dents and ridges in her flesh. How many are from an aspiration to do the right thing? To make all the worlds under the Seven Suns better? From missing the mark with good intentions? From life and surviving another day?

Asterion would invite all the details. Not only the heroics; she wants to know every moment of Theseus's life, everything she's willing to share, because—like her bare skin on show—it's part of who she is.

With a fingertip, Asterion traces a constellation line from a contour of scar tissue on Theseus's right hip, just above her waistband, to a neighbouring scar. Theseus squirms, just a little. But Asterion can tell she's trying to stay still, watching Asterion, letting her explore.

Asterion diverts to the bands of Theseus's stomach muscles. She could never put such perfect lines to paper.

"Is that a good kind of speechless?" asks Theseus, and Asterion's tempted to roll her eyes, or to kiss away that half-smug, half-hopeful smirk. She can't decide which, so all she manages is to gaze at Theseus with naked admiration.

At least it makes Theseus smile. At least it has her leaning down and brushing her lips across Asterion's skin.

When Theseus runs her tongue across Asterion's bare chest, it feels... good... Though not quite what she'd imagined from the colourful descriptions in intimate fictions. Perhaps her body is odd, not responding the way it should?

But her body—every inch—emphatically *is* responding to

Theseus's breathy sounds as she explores. And when Theseus nips at her neck... Asterion's world lights up.

"Confound and flummox...!" Her exclamation slips into Minosian—and did that animalistic moan she just heard come from her? Judging from Theseus's elated grin—further fuel to Asterion's inner flame—absolutely *yes*.

"Interesting." Theseus resumes inflicting sweet torture, dragging her teeth over Asterion's sensitive skin, testing the pressure as Asterion writhes, smoothing her gentle bites with her tongue.

Stars above, Asterion might just implode.

While Theseus continues her exploration, Asterion's hands map Theseus's neck and shoulders. Aware that the mask will have tested her there, she digs into Theseus's muscles with fingers and thumbs, letting out a gasp of her own at each of Theseus's moans. She'd had no idea that the sound of Theseus's pleasure would increase her own.

With a glint in her eyes, Theseus shifts lower. She takes her time in removing Asterion's undershorts, appreciating each new inch with her fingers, lips and tongue.

Hades in the Heavens. Asterion's not sure she'll survive this.

How are her thoughts both racing and calm? It's a strange feeling. A good feeling. A Theseus-inspired feeling.

But as much as she's enjoying the scenic route, a pulsing, insistent part of her is demanding attention. And with each new kiss and caress, close to where she needs it, but not close enough, Asterion suspects Theseus is on a mission to turn her feral.

"Theseus..." she grumbles, in playful reprimand.

Theseus's responding wink is, frankly, infuriating. "Patience, Asterion."

Asterion huffs. *Patience, indeed.* She's half minded to lift Theseus again, to make her squeal... but that thought dies a thousand glorious deaths as Theseus looks up at her, a question in her gleaming eyes.

At Asterion's nod of breathless approval, Theseus slides her undershorts down a little further. Just enough that she can tease Asterion with her tongue.

Asterion's grumbling turns to mewling. "Oh, *fuck*—" *Confound and flummox* doesn't really cut it.

Theseus must appreciate her reaction, because she's quick to remove Asterion's shorts and cast them aside. Asterion doesn't care where they land. She only cares that Theseus returns to where she needs her to be.

Her fingers thread through Theseus's ink-black hair as Theseus's flex against her hips, holding her in place while her skilful tongue explores the most intimate part of her. The glow and spark of Theseus's torque between Asterion's legs feels... apt. Asterion's body is aflame, demanding more. And—thank the heavens—that's what Theseus is on a mission to give her.

But it's been too long since they kissed...

"I—" Asterion sighs as Theseus's tongue strokes her perfectly "—I want to kiss you—" And with a gentle tug of her hair, she guides Theseus back up to her mouth.

Theseus's fingers take over what her tongue had started. And the way she's touching Asterion—the fierce desire and the gentle affection in her eyes when she looks at her... Asterion's never felt so *wanted*.

As Theseus's fingers sink inside her, the guttural groan that reaches Asterion's ears could be her own, Theseus's, or the Labyrinth's.

Asterion's pendant pulses in tandem with her heartbeat as her pleasure soars ever higher. And as they move against each other, their torques ripple electric between them, like illuminated thread in an ever-increasing tangle.

"Is that... usual?" asks Theseus, keeping her heavenly rhythm.

"You—tell—me—" Asterion gasps. Nothing about this is *usual*. Before Theseus, everything in her life had just been ticking over. But now Theseus has found her way into her world, into her waking and sleeping thoughts... there is no usual. Everything is *more*.

At Theseus's particularly sublime caress, Asterion digs her fingers into Theseus's capable shoulders. Theseus's responding moan amplifies the thumping in Asterion's ears, and ratchets up the pressure building inside her, until—

The tangled energy of their torques overspills, orbiting them like an electromagnetic field.

And.

Asterion's inner tethers pull taut. The Labyrinth shudders. The fire-torches blaze. And as her inner thread unspools, the firefly in her chest spreads its wings and soars.

PART IX

THE PATH AHEAD

67

SPOON
THESEUS

I t's been a long time since Theseus fell asleep in someone's arms.

On the rare occasions she's been inclined to stay the night with someone, it's certainly never been to *snuggle*. Especially not as the fucking *little spoon*. It's not how they'd fallen asleep, but it's how they've woken. And... yeah... Theseus doesn't hate it.

In fact, she might have to admit she likes it a whole damn lot. Which is... *yeah...*

It doesn't feel suffocating to have Asterion in her personal space. It's the opposite. Theseus's sleep has been calm. Her *waking* thoughts are only less so because her brain is presenting her with the highlights of last night: how Asterion had unravelled beneath her, on her, beside her... and how she hadn't been shy in learning new skills and doing the same to Theseus, for her... with her.

Theseus lets out a slow breath. Asterion turning her half-lidded gaze on her and insisting mid-kiss to 'show me how to touch you' might be the sexiest moment of her damn life. Or maybe that had been the sight of Asterion's mouth quirking with confidence as Theseus audibly unravelled under her tongue.

Stars above and heavens every which way.

Theseus squirms. Her heart is thumping so hard she worries it'll wake Asterion.

"Do I need—put you in restraints again, Theseus?" Asterion's sleepy voice rasps by her ear, melting Theseus to a puddle at the mere sound of her name. Never mind the mention of restraints.

It's good to know Asterion has a sense of humour about the epic nightmare Theseus had been when she'd first arrived here. But... is she joking about the restraints? Because Theseus could be into that, if—

Asterion nuzzles into her neck. "So wriggly," she mumbles, and Theseus can't help wriggling a little closer, though she scowls at the twinge in her neck, no doubt an aftereffect of lugging that stupid mask.

"You know," Theseus says, her voice hoarse, "now I get why your shoulders are so—"

But Asterion's talented hands curtail the end of her sentence into a not-so-muffled groan as they press between Theseus's neck and shoulders, soothing the exact muscles in need of relief.

"Interesting," says Asterion, a smile in her voice.

Theseus rolls to face her—and then, playfully, nakedly, rolls on top of her. Braced on her elbows, she lowers her weight gradually against Asterion, aligning their bodies... just so...

Asterion's breathless gasp, her eyes widening in surprise, then narrowing with desire, is a look Theseus would invite waking up to every day.

Every day...? All breath exits Theseus's lungs.

But she doesn't panic. Well, apart from the not breathing.

Most importantly, she doesn't *run*. She can't; she's far too captivated, nuzzling against the blush decorating Asterion's freckled cheeks.

"Good—*moaning*," Theseus whispers the purposefully incorrect word choice in her best Minosian accent, and Asterion's chuckle is lost to a moan, and her fingers digging into Theseus's hips, guiding her rhythm, is exactly the reaction for which she'd hoped.

Theseus's sensations sail. They fit together. There's no doubt about that.

"Is this—the way it—always feels?" asks Asterion, her breaths heavy as a cosmos of emotions ripple in the depths of her eyes. Lust, longing... trust.

Theseus has been the giver and receiver of enough passionate touch in her life to know that this is different to anything she's experienced before. It's fun, yes—but there's something more, too. Something that reaches further than the physical.

A lump lodges in Theseus's throat, and she only manages a slight shake of her head in answer, hoping her eyes communicate where her words fail to: that this connection between them... it *isn't* usual. It's not ordinary. That these feelings coursing through her are unique in their strength and combination.

And their heights only remind her how far there is to fall.

Theseus stills her hips and together they chase their breath. It might feel like their racing hearts are converging on the same path, but that can't be what this is...

She rolls off Asterion to lay beside her, giving them both space for their higher faculties to function. Well, almost. Naked Asterion is very distracting.

But. This is something they need to navigate.

"How long do we have?" Asterion asks softly, tracing her fingertips over Theseus's illumi-freckled forearm. And Theseus understands what she's really asking. *How long till you leave?*

The idea tugs on the invisible thread that connects her to Asterion.

Theseus has always been good at leaving. It's easy when she's never had the urge to stay.

But even if she wanted to stay now... she can't. And Asterion hasn't expressed any desire to leave...

"My friend is looking for me," she says, reminding herself. She presses her thumb to the coin hanging around her throat, lighting up the co-ordinates encircling its circumference and the dots on the face depicting her own and Herakles's relative positions. "I can't let her risk her life in this place."

Disappointment and understanding flicker in Asterion's eyes as she reaches out to inspect the Locator.

"She's at the edge of the galaxy of the Fourth Sun, now," says Theseus.

Asterion nods, her brow furrowing. When Theseus smooths the indents, Asterion leans into her touch. Her voice is still soft: "We have—time."

Yes. More than days, judging by the co-ordinates; likely weeks. Probably no more than a month.

It's not endless. But it's something.

But it's also not their only obstacle. Theseus hates to bring it up, but there's the not insignificant issue of:

"The Chosen Hero. We need to do something about him."

Asterion nods sombrely, as if considering the conundrum thoroughly before diverting Theseus's attention with gentle nips to her jaw.

"Labyrinth—deal with Hero." Asterion kisses Theseus's neck. "Time—bring solutions." Her fingers stroke Theseus's ribs, her chest, her abdomen, mapping every part of her. It's no surprise that Asterion is better than her at multitasking. "We are —safe. In fortress."

"But—" Theseus is about to interject that Hero has survived so much already. It might not be that easy. But then Asterion rolls on top of her, setting her thoughts on a much more enjoyable trajectory.

Licking up Theseus's neck—*oh, heaven's above*—Asterion's mouth finds Theseus's as she threads one hand through her hair, while the other slips nimbly between their bodies. Theseus gasps as talented fingers caress her, so perfectly. "Fuck, Asti— how are you so good at that already?"

Asterion's slow smile only heightens Theseus's pleasure—so much so her release sneaks up on her, so suddenly, all she can do is clutch Asterion close, sink into the mattress, and try to tamp down an eruption of giggles.

Yes, *giggles.* That's fucking new, too.

Because *of course* Asterion would surprise her like *that.* That's what this whole situation has been: unexpected. A change of course; Theseus's own demeanour, colder than Iolcian ice, turned to Minosian flame.

"Is laughter the usual response?" asks Asterion.

And all Theseus can do is kiss her.

68

BRIGHTER

ASTERION

As the days tick by...

Technically, activities in the fortress continue much the same as before: cooking, eating, working the garden, exercising, showering, going to bed. But everything is a little... *different.*

The fireplaces burn hotter. Electricity maintains a baseline crackle with frequent surges. Even the glow of the engineered moon and stars is brighter than usual.

Having run some calculations, Asterion is satisfied that the influx of energy isn't going to overload the Labyrinth or suddenly burn out. Which is a relief.

Reading in the library, scribbling notes—about societal structure possibilities, world-engine adjustments, designing worlds—and even painting stars: all are made more enjoyable—and more challenging—by smiles and glances—and, yes, the constant battle to keep their hands to themselves.

Designing theoretical new worlds is fun, but learning how and where to touch Theseus—to bask in her affectionate, heated gaze, to turn her knees weak, drive her wild, and to bring about that satisfied grin—that's more illuminating to Asterion than any world-engine.

As much as the heart-thumping thrill of learning what it is to touch and be touched, she loves the quiet comfort of just being together in the same space.

Sometimes they dance. Sometimes they nestle by the fire. When they read or watch a story-reel together, they curl up with their legs entwined, or within reach of each other.

And Asterion enjoys Theseus's tales of her monster hunting adventures, of where she's from and where she's been. So long as she doesn't dwell on how Theseus's purpose in life is to make the galaxies a better place, and the impracticalities of achieving that from inside the Sky Labyrinth... so long as she doesn't dwell on *why* she's teaching Theseus to read Labyrinth maps and find safe passages through, or why she's explaining the finer details of the outer-shell's gatehouse airlock failsafes... So long as she stays in the moment and doesn't think about any of that...

It's... *good.*

Theseus seems to recognise now when to give her space, and when to do away with it. Even when Asterion says something blunt, Theseus's gaze remains warm and interested. Other people never liked it when Asterion spoke her mind. But Theseus isn't other people.

Asterion has never felt at home in someone else's company before. It seems so improbable. She's always enjoyed her own space, so why is she so open to someone else being in it? Why, when she's on her own in one part of the fortress, does she wonder what Theseus is up to in another?

It's all so... strange.

And food shouldn't taste better, should it? Especially because their inability to keep focused in the kitchen together renders many of their meals more singed than Theseus's solo cooking adventures.

It's a joy and a relief that a spoon is no longer an ill-advised weapon, but a shared implement for taste-testing the meals they prepare together. It's so easy to get distracted. So easy for a look to evolve to a kiss. A lingering touch to turn to a caress. An embrace to escalate to haphazardly discarded clothing.

With their hands and mouths roaming as Theseus's heated body presses hers into the warmed stone of the kitchen floor, Asterion delights in whispering in her ear: "I think we finally found your skill in the kitchen."

Even relaxing in the gardens has never been so... *electric*.

Under the flourishing leaves of the proteus tree, Asterion scribbles ideas for labyrinth alterations, but it's easy for her thoughts to wander with Theseus doing target practice only metres away. Each time she throws a blade, Asterion can't help noticing the definition of her calf muscles, highlighted by the glow of the illumi-thread branching like lightning through her skin; the smooth adjustment of her limbs, every muscle in perfect calibration.

But staring is not the sort of thing you can get away with when you have a heart-stone pendant blushing, a torque sparking, and a proteus tree lighting up like rainbow-fire as energetic and bright as your wandering thoughts.

And judging by Theseus's roguish smile as she strolls over to Asterion, she knows exactly what Asterion is thinking.

A tug of Theseus's belt buckle is all it takes to ignite their torques, their energy tangling in a frenzy of hands and mouths, fingers and tongues. And it's not long before they demonstrate, together, the admirable sturdiness of a proteus tree trunk.

Who knew making love—or something like it—could be an effective method of harvesting proteus fruit?

Not that either of them notice the colourful orbs thumping to the ground around them, as their combined efforts transform the tree's foliage into the most stunning rainbow ever to be ignored...

...and startle a curious chicken into a hasty retreat.

69

TIME TOGETHER
THESEUS

Days turn to weeks...

And everything Asterion does makes Theseus smile.

She enjoys when Asterion interrupts her game of solo catch, snatching the proteus fruit from the air and suggesting a game.

She's entertained when they paint together. It's not a skill Theseus possesses, but Asterion patiently teaches her how to crush and mix various pigments to create different colours. And when Theseus draws stick-figure versions of the two of them, she looks confused, almost horrified—perhaps by the lack of skill? But then Asterion simply scrubs out their stick arms, only to redraw them as cartoonishly muscular.

Theseus even enjoys learning Minosian, though that's likely because of who her teacher is. Theseus can't get enough of Asterion's Minosian growls. It resonates within her; turns her wild. But more importantly, she wants to learn; to meet Asterion halfway and speak her language.

Asterion isn't shy in correcting the shape of Theseus's mouth and the position of her tongue to make the right sounds. So much focus on each other's mouths inevitably leads to kissing. Which, sometimes, leads to more, which—perhaps—is its own language lesson, given the variety of expletives they both utter.

But just being in Asterion's presence is its own adventure. Having spent most of her life journeying from place to place, more often than not the one consistent thing about Theseus's days has been the lack of routine. Change has been Theseus's only constant. But preparing meals with Asterion, tending to the orchard, whispering to seeds, spending time together in the library, chatting about anything and everything, or just existing in comfortable, calming silence... Theseus is never bored.

And so long as she doesn't do silly things...

...like when Asterion asks about Athenian theories of harmonious city design, and Theseus offers to give her a tour of the Athenian Expanse...

...so long as she doesn't comment that Asterion's myriad ideas and plans for world design should be put to better use than gathering dust in the Labyrinth's library...

...so long as she learns from her mistakes and doesn't do those things...

...it's all... so... *good.*

Theseus has seen what mundane domesticity can do to some people, sapping away their happiness until they're stuck trudging through their days. It's something she never wanted for herself. But she wakes each morning looking forward to what the day ahead will hold, because it includes Asterion.

If there's one thing Theseus hates—other than monsters— it's getting her period. It makes her irritable, bloated and sluggish. She literally met a slug monster once that had more energy than she does on her period. But even then, when she usually wants the rest of the universe to please fuck off—snuggling with Asterion is a comfort she seeks.

Bok-bok even willingly occupies her lap like a winged, purring hot water bottle.

As she and Asterion settle into their nest of blankets in the midnight garden, watching the story-reels projected onto the dome of the sky, *comfortable* doesn't begin to describe how Theseus feels.

Happy just about covers it.

And that's more breathtaking, exhilarating and terrifying than any monster hunt she's ever been on.

70

HEROIC-AND-SHIT
THESEUS

"You know I'm already en route, right?" asks Herakles, who can only be an apparition. "That I'm worried enough about you to travel across the Heavens to find you? Because I'm heroic and shit, and I'm your friend, and I care?"

Theseus sighs as she checks there's nothing else to be retrieved from the post-dinner banquet table, while imaginary Herakles smooths her hands through her bright teal hair and leans back on a chair like she's relaxing at a ship's helm. "I mean, *you* know you're having a jolly time, but I need to make sure you're not stuck in the teeth of an epic sea monster like some idiot plankton."

Idiot plankton? Wow. This sounds more like Theseus's inner-critic talking than her friend.

"And I'm doing all this," Herakles continues, "making sure you don't need rescuing, even though you're for sure going to be a sore-ass about it."

Theseus scoffs. But yeah, that sounds about right.

"You don't think she'll leave with you?" Herakles's voice softens, more overtly the manifestation of Theseus's need to talk to someone about this. Bok-bok had been zero help. The chicken had got bored, blinked at her, and wandered off. When Theseus leaves here, she won't be mentioning to Herakles that she talks to her in her thoughts.

Why would Asterion leave here? is Theseus's instinctive response to Herakles's question. *I'm not her world. The Labyrinth is.* And it's not like Asterion has asked her to stay, anyway.

"But you want her to?" Herakles gives voice to Theseus's most wayward thoughts.

Theseus has never wanted to fall for anyone. Because—by the logic of the metaphor—there'll always be a landing. She's always managed to put an end to any potential crush with a goodbye and swagger in the opposite direction.

But she's never been so thoroughly captivated by discovering how someone else ticks before. She's never felt someone else's smile light up inside her chest like their joy is her own. She's never looked to the future and craved someone else in it.

It's been a long time since leaving someone, or somewhere, has hurt. But now... even the idea of saying goodbye to Asterion punches the air from her chest.

But so does the idea of abandoning Herakles and the worlds out there.

She must have stood staring at the empty banquet table for too long, because Asterion's arms loop about her waist, catching her off guard in the best of ways, as she presses kisses to the back of Theseus's neck. Asterion's sneaking abilities always make her smile.

"Your cogs—turning louder than the Labyrinth's." Asterion taps Theseus's temple lightly with a fingertip.

Theseus knows she's being quiet. Any day now, the timer on her stay here will run out. Herakles will be too close. And then there's the knot of Ariadne's reign that needs unravelling.

They should talk about Theseus leaving.

Imaginary Herakles raises an eyebrow at her. *Yes, you damn well should.*

But once those words are out, once Asterion confirms she has no intention of leaving the Sky Labyrinth... that's it, isn't it? This world they've built—this world Asterion dreamed up and Theseus has been growing more comfortable in—will crumble.

"No cogs here." Theseus turns in Asterion's arms, offering her best impression of *nonchalance*.

Asterion studies her, and Theseus is sure she's going to ask her what's wrong. Asterion isn't a fool. She knows as well as Theseus the subject they've been diligently avoiding. Though Theseus's throat is so thick right now she's not sure she can talk about it anyway.

Asterion must see the plea in her eyes, because her own questioning gaze turns heated. She tugs Theseus closer, growling in Minosian against her neck: "I want to kiss you."

Yes. Theseus leans in—but instead of meeting her in a kiss, Asterion pushes her firmly backward until her backside meets the banquet table. And the heat in Asterion's eyes evolves to something... more, as she capably, swoonworth-ily (*...sure*), lifts Theseus onto it.

Fuck. Theseus loves that she can do that.

She glances over her shoulder to confirm that Herakles— even the imaginary version—is no longer present before reaching for Asterion's clothes. But—infuriatingly—her efforts are rewarded with Asterion gripping her wrists and planting them repeatedly at her sides.

Theseus narrows her eyes. Okay... she'll play this game...

With an expertise that steals her breath and makes Theseus forget which of them is the tough, swaggering monster hunter, Asterion unbuttons and removes Theseus's trousers. Theseus would try to play it cool, maybe tone down whatever besotted expression must be occupying her face—but what's the fucking point when the damn torque at her throat is sparking with shared electricity between them?

Again, she angles for a kiss, only to be denied by a smile so confident and scorching, she'd travel the heavens for it. For *her*. Or at least melt and turn into a puddle.

A heroic puddle, obviously.

Curiosity sparks in Asterion's eyes. "Brave Theseus, Monster Hunter. You never—tell me—why you are here... What turned you criminal—sent to—skies?" She hooks her thumbs into the waistband of Theseus's undershorts.

Stars above. Judging by the inferno in Asterion's downward gaze, she's well aware of the galaxy of desire soaking the fabric.

"You never asked—" Theseus loses her breath as Asterion nuzzles along her jaw.

Asterion's lips quirk against her neck. "I'm asking now."

"I... um..." *Use your words.* "...fire. I set things on fire."

On the steps of the palace, no less. She'd lingered after her tour group had left, and bought herself a one-way ticket to a Minosian prison cell. It had been a controlled fire, of course.

Which is more than can be said for the heat in Theseus's veins as Asterion runs her tongue up her neck. When Asterion nuzzles her heated cheeks, Theseus leans closer, certain that Asterion's about to kiss her...

But Asterion only smiles. "I can imagine."

Theseus's heart thrums in her chest and wherever else it pleases. She huffs before growling her own Minosian: "I thought you—wanted to kiss me?"

Asterion nods, seriously—but it's her raised eyebrow that says: *I didn't say where.*

And now, as her mouth and tongue venture lower, as her clever fingers remove the fabric barrier between them, Theseus forgets how to breathe. She might not know what their futures hold... She might never look at the banquet table the same way again...

But one thing is for sure as Asterion *finally kisses her...*

Being eaten alive by a Minotaur isn't the worst way to go.

71

OUT OF TIME

ASTERION

The morning had involved, as it often does, intimate activities between the sheets, followed by similar but more vertical adventures under the water cascade. Asterion had no idea showers could be so... *invigorating*. Breakfast had been their usual; discussing plans for their crops, followed by toiling away on said crops, then another stint in the cascade and relaxation in the library. Now they're kissing languidly in a wingback chair, their torque energy weaving together.

The only thing that isn't energetic and bright between them is the Locator pendant around Theseus's neck. Its surface ripples like the darkest smoke: a silent alarm, announcing that their time is up.

Following Asterion's gaze, Theseus touches the coin and the opposite face lights up with the dots depicting hers and Herakles's relative locations. They're almost upon each other.

Asterion's lungs constrict like she's gulped in that dark smoke.

Theseus had always planned to leave—it's not new information—but there's a difference between a plan for the future and an action in the present. And just like that, a future concern tugs into the here and now, amplifying Asterion's disquiet to outright nausea.

Theseus can hardly look at Asterion, but there's a storm in her eyes. Panic. Sadness. Regret. Resignation? She opens her mouth, but instead of saying anything Asterion wants to hear, her throat bobs. The set of her jaw is less defiant and more... avoidant?

Asterion never thought she could dislike anything about that jaw.

"You're leaving." Asterion can barely force the words out.

"I was always leaving. It's not exactly an info-blast, is it?" The bite of Theseus's words turns Asterion's stomach like a mine drill. The fire-torches crackle like there's a blockage in their supply line.

So that's how it's going to be?

Asterion extricates herself from their nest.

"Asti, wait..." Theseus's warm fingers catch at her wrist. Asterion stops, hoping Theseus will say something, or do something... anything, to show that what they have is special.

But all she says is, "I'm sorry."

Sorry for being short-tempered? *Sorry* she's leaving? Or *sorry* Asterion has ended up in the maze of feelings Theseus warned her about?

But Theseus doesn't elaborate. She only looks... frustrated. Her eyes are pleading, like she's imploring Asterion not to make a big deal out of this.

Not a big deal...

"Asti, please...?" Theseus steps towards her, but Asterion jerks away from her. If this is how Theseus is going to be, she doesn't want to look at her right now.

"Leave me alone." Asterion's voice wobbles as she says it. Her lungs constrict. It's exactly what Theseus will be doing imminently anyway. And there's nothing Asterion can do.

She marches to their bedchamber. No. Not *their* bedchamber. Her bedchamber. She just wants this stupid day to go away. She wants to wake up tomorrow and start their routine again.

Even her clothes prickle uncomfortably against her skin. Which is why she throws them aside, climbs into the bed, cocoons herself under the covers, and cries. It's not useful, but it's all she can do right now.

And perhaps Theseus is giving her the space she demanded, but the ongoing solitude only serves to remind her of how alone she soon will be. Tears burn her eyes as rain splatters against the bedchamber window.

Stupid Labyrinth with its stupid link to her every emotion.

Hesitant footsteps interrupt the patter of rainfall and Asterion has no idea how long she's been under the covers. She might have exhausted herself to the point of slumber, because now she can't decipher if the darkness is night or just the rain shrouding the engineered sunlight.

The covers and mattress adjust and Asterion's over-exerted heart occupies her throat as Theseus and her warmth shuffle closer. Should she pretend to be asleep? Should she tell Theseus to go away? That's where this is all heading, anyway.

But she can't bring herself to push her away right now. Not when the comfort of Theseus's bare skin is adjusting against her back, her arm wrapping around her torso, enveloping her like everything will be okay.

This is what she's losing...

Asterion's tears burst from her anew.

She won't ask Theseus to stay. To curse her friend Herakles to the Labyrinth, all because Asterion wants Theseus to herself, would be unforgivable. And to ask Theseus to return to live here would be no better.

Perhaps this would hurt less if she knew definitively that it all means something to Theseus.

Perhaps it would only hurt more.

Either way, Theseus says nothing. She has two languages with which she could tell Asterion that she doesn't want to leave, but all she does is hold Asterion, absorbing her sobs until she's too exhausted, too empty, to cry anymore.

When Asterion wakes in the night to the Labyrinth's mournful groans, Theseus is there beside her, resting a thread-glowing palm on Asterion's chest. Asterion takes her hand, committing the smooth skin and light calluses to memory. She follows the threads of Theseus's veins up her arms; traces the smoky quartz skin of her chest and up her neck, her jaw, to the gasp on her lips.

Say something, Theseus...

Asterion's throat is sore from tears. She's not sure she can manage words right now. Besides, talking won't change the fact that she has to leave.

Perhaps she should leave Theseus alone and let her sleep.

But in the dark, Theseus's deft fingers echo the journey of Asterion's hand, tracing all the way up Asterion's arm, her throat, to brush her thumb over her lips, before diverting to the nape of her neck, then drawing her close.

Asterion lets out a gentle sigh. The threat of renewed sobs aches beneath her ribs, but Theseus's lips distract her, following the path her hand had taken and ending their journey in an urgent kiss.

Their kiss tastes of tears. Are they Theseus's, or her own?

Theseus's kiss, her caresses, are full of sincerity. And the press of her body, like she can't get close enough... it doesn't feel like she wants to leave.

But what does Asterion know?

Theseus had warned her to not get attached.

Their desperate touches simmer down to slow and unhurried, as if they have all the time in the worlds. But as Theseus's talented hands map her body, it feels like she, too, is committing Asterion to memory.

+
∴

IT'S NOT EVEN SUNRISE YET, but—unable to sleep, her head throbbing like she's had part of her brain scooped from her skull —Asterion leaves Theseus in bed and tackles the day.

The corridor is at a fifteen-degree tilt. She'll have to sort that somehow. Though she has a growing suspicion that it's more to do with her state of mind than anything blueprints and tools can fix.

Gravity is being a little too exuberant today, too, and even the watering system is shedding its own tears all across the fortress garden—which is, frankly, a bit much.

In the kitchen, she hacks into yesterday's loaf like this is all its fault. If Theseus cared, she'd have said so by now. What's the point in learning a language if you're not going to use your words?

Asterion sighs heavily. The serrated blade clatters against the worktop. There's no point in prolonging this suffocating, heart-wringing swamp of emotions. The sooner Theseus is out of here, the sooner Asterion's own inner balance will return.

She and the Labyrinth will be all the better for it.

So she channels her sickly energy into something produc-tive, and saves Theseus the trouble of packing her bag.

+
∴

"HEY," says Theseus from the banquet hall doorway, scrubbing sleep from her eyes. She's barefoot, wearing her usual combi-nation of vest, loose shirt, and three-quarter length trousers, all of which are creased as though she'd thrown them on the floor last night and only dragged them back on again moments ago.

Asterion tries to ignore the possibly tear-induced huskiness of her voice, and the rising urge to wrap her arms around her. Instead, she stays at the banquet table with her untouched frost-berry jam sandwich, trying to pretend her appetite isn't as lost as any voyager in the labyrinth.

Theseus's gaze darts to the empty place setting, directly opposite Asterion at the table's centre. Her slight scowl of hurt pains Asterion. It's worse when she sits, warily, as though dealing with the beast of the Labyrinth she'd once thought Asterion to be.

Drizzle patters against the floor-to-ceiling window, as if its sole purpose is to highlight their shared silence.

Asterion stares at her plate so she won't have to see in Theseus's blue eyes what she already knows, or look at her cute, sleep-mussed hair. She's never been a fan of throwing salt on a wound.

"You want to talk about it?" Theseus's tone is so even, so reasonable, so *gentle.* But she's not offering to share her own feelings. She's pushing Asterion to admit that she couldn't keep her promise.

And Asterion hates her for it.

She was fine before Theseus barged into her life, digging stupid holes in her vegetable beds and burning the produce. She'll be fine again. It'll be good to have some quiet.

She swipes her tears away.

"What—is point? You—are going. I—stay. That is—conclusion. What point is there in—scenic route?"

"Why is that the conclusion?" Dull metal catches the light as Theseus flips her Locator coin over her knuckles. Is she soothing herself from the discomfort of an awkward conversation, or trying to figure something out?

"So you're staying?" Asterion raises a sarcastic eyebrow, underscoring the abruptness of her question. Obviously that's not what Theseus meant, but why should Asterion care when her heart's hurting an unreasonable amount? She'll be a brat about it if she wants to.

"I don't know what to do, Asti."

Asterion flinches. Theseus's affectionate name for her has always been Athenian music to her ears, but now it's only a reminder of what she's losing.

"Perhaps your precious coin can tell you." There's that brat again. She hates herself a little for it. But she hates everything else so much more.

Theseus pauses, but doesn't take the bait. She reaches across the table for Asterion's hand, but Asterion snatches it away from her.

The Labyrinth groans. Somewhere within the mechanisms, something large is butting up against something immovable.

"You're not a prisoner. I—not—stop you from leaving." Asterion's every cell vibrates with tension as she shoves back her chair, throwing her words over her shoulder as she marches from the hall. "I am not—*monster.*"

72

STORM
THESEUS

R ain splatters against the banquet hall window.

Theseus's mouth is agape. How has their conversation veered so disastrously off course before it's even begun?

"Asti—?" Swept along in a whirlwind of confusion, Theseus scrambles after her. She catches up to her in the entrance hall, where she's abruptly presented with her own boots and armour —like a literal gut punch. She fumbles not to drop everything. "Asti, please...."

"You were always leaving." Asterion's words are quiet, cutting, as she fastens Theseus's sword belt about her waist, yanking the buckle a little too tight.

What in the heavens—?

Asterion hardly touches her, doesn't even look at her. It's like she can't even stand to be near her. And that's a chimera kick worse than any Theseus has experienced before. Until the next one lands, the sudden realisation—

Asterion is showing her out.

Now?

But—

They still have time. It'll be days yet until Herakles gets here;

days before Herakles is in danger of barrelling into the Labyrinth. Theseus tries and fails to juggle her armful of boots and armour, to show Asterion the co-ordinates on her Locator. To show her they still have *some* time.

Time to talk, at least.

But Asterion turns her back on her, fiddling with a rucksack.

"Why are you...?" *Showing me out when I have to go? Showing me out when I never planned to stay?* Asterion's right: Theseus has always made it clear that she was going to leave. So why does it hurt so much that Asterion is rushing her toward to the exit now?

Asterion wouldn't do that if she wanted her to stay, would she?

Not worth holding onto. That's all Theseus has ever been.

Fuck. This.

This is why she doesn't get fucking attached.

Idiot.

Useless.

Fuck.

But she can't just leave Asterion here. Asterion might have shown her the Labyrinth's beauty, but it's still a death trap. And if they don't figure out how to solve the problem of Princess Ariadne, then it'll be less than one sun-orbit before Asterion will be hunted again.

There's probably a sensitive, considerate way to convey all that, but what tumbles out is:

"Fuck, Asti. This can't be the life you want to live?"

Asterion stiffens, but doesn't turn to look at her. There's a universe of tension in those shoulders. Damn it. This isn't a winning strategy, no matter what planet Theseus is on.

With a deep breath, she finds a more level tone. "You're always fighting to survive... Please, Asti. You could leave too."

"I can't." Asterion's voice is small as she sets down the rucksack. Theseus aches to reach for her, to comfort her. She would, if Asterion hadn't bundled all this stuff into her arms—

Asterion's next words bring her up short.. "I told you. Mask —not to be tampered with. Mechanisms—dangerous. Will... lobotomise—if—get it wrong."

"That's bullshit."

All around the hall, the fire-torches flare as Asterion swings around to face her, her eyes snapping fiercely to hers as Asterion's torque's energy bites at her neck.

Theseus hates that she has to call Asterion on this. But she has to. "Your mind is astounding, Asterion. Stars above—you *made* this world from nothing. You could find a way out of that mask." She wishes it could be okay for Asterion to keep hiding away, if that's what she wants... but can't she see that this place will be the death of her?

Asterion shakes her head violently.

"Please, Asti. You can't want to stay here. Fighting for your fucking life?"

Asterion freezes, but there's nothing still about the flames and the fizzing electricity surrounding them. Theseus tries again. If Asterion won't leave this place for herself, or for Theseus...

"There's a whole world—your people—suffering under your sister's rule. You're the rightful Architect. Minos is broken, but you can fix it. Even if you won't do it for yourself, don't give up on Minos—"

Asterion lunges at her, fire-torches blazing around them as Theseus recoils. "I didn't *leave*." Asterion thumps her own chest. "I didn't *give up* on Minos." From the floor, she grabs Theseus's rucksack. The button-eyed Minotaur plushie dangles from one strap, her astro-helmet from another. *Asterion already packed her bag?* She thrusts it into Theseus's arms on top of her boots and armour. *Damn, it's heavy.* "Minos gave up on *me*."

As Theseus stands there, stunned, Asterion pulls on the mask.

How did this all unravel so quickly?

Why can't she make it right?

Asterion presses something into her palm.

And Theseus is a mere observer as Asterion pushes her shield against her forearms that are already overloaded with her belongings, forcing her—firmly, but not roughly—onto the gateway turntable. Asterion bows down to the keyholes, her breath heavy through the mask.

"Asti, wait—"

Mechanisms grins and the turntable spins. Asterion must truly want to be rid of her, because in the same moment Asterion is freed from the keyholes, she shoves her, sending Theseus skidding out into the connecting corridor in a clatter of armour and a thud of boots.

Asterion, lacking her usual sure-footed grace, tumbles to the stone floor, remaining on the turntable.

Theseus attempts to stand, but her head is still in motion—

No...

Fuck, fuck, *fuck*.

The connecting corridor is in motion...

The labyrinth is turning, snatching her away from the fortress, away from Asterion, casting her into the dizzying chaos of the unknown.

73

MECHANISMS
ASTERION

Ten seconds and a thousand thoughts earlier...

Asterion thrusts Theseus's satchel into her arms, plucks her heart pendant from around her neck, and pulls on the bull mask. Finally, gritting her teeth against the pain—against everything—she presses the heart-stone into Theseus's palm and pushes her onto the turntable.

Get this over and done with.

But as the turntable spins, panic kicks in. Asterion shoves Theseus away from her, away from the mask's razor-sharp horns, sending her sprawling out into the aligned corridor.

Blood thunders in Asterion's ears. Her chest aches like a gaping wound. Theseus hadn't killed the Minotaur to dig out its heart, but it damn well feels like she did. Asterion wishes her heart *were* made of stone. At least then it wouldn't be hurting like this.

The mask throws her off balance, the internal straps pinching a scar on her neck painfully; pressure to numbed flesh garbling her body's signals.

How *dare* Theseus accuse her of not bothering to find a way out? What does she know? And anyway—why should Asterion leave? This is her fortress. Her palace in the sky. This is where she belongs.

Out in the connecting corridor, Theseus has landed in a heap. And whether it's the way she's crumpled, or the sight of Asterion's precious, dulled, heart-stone clutched in her out-flung hand—

Nanny's bloodied form elbows into her consciousness; the memory tearing into her own chest.

But... no. Theseus is moving; she's okay. And all Asterion can think about is how she can create puzzles and solve them, break things and piece them back together, but she isn't doing that now, with Theseus. She never did so with the mask and the prison of the Labyrinth, either.

Just like she never did when she was four or six or ten, huddled in the darkness of a cupboard locked from the outside, Ariadne's laughter echoing through the keyhole.

Back then, it was always Nanny who came looking for her, rescued her, pulled her back into the light and reassured her she'd done nothing wrong. The same Nanny she'd chased through the labyrinth, so desperate for his comfort. She'd only wanted a hug. But that doesn't make the outcome any less her fault, does it?

And what else can that mean other than she deserves to be locked away?

That.

That's why she's never really tried to free herself.

She's had the key this whole time. And she's solved far more challenging problems than a mask before. If she'd put her mind to it... she could have rescued herself long ago.

But what would have been the point? Her own family had put her here. Even if she'd refused to admit it to herself, the facts are inescapable. In all these sun-orbits, nobody on Minos—family or otherwise—has ever tried to free her.

At least here she can be herself. Hidden away, yes—but she knows the rhythm of the Labyrinth. She knows how this world ticks. Outside there are people, and others who seek power over them. Monsters who lurk in the shadows, pulling strings for their own enrichment.

How *dare* Theseus be right?

Theseus might truly want her to be free of this place...

Theseus might even want *her*...

But it's one thing for Theseus to want her when they're alone together in the Sky Labyrinth. In here, Asterion and her blunt opinions can't bulldoze people's delicate egos. In here, Theseus will never see how ill-suited to politics, to people, and the way of the worlds, she truly is.

At least if she stays here, she can live in the memories and the fantasies of what could have been.

Perhaps. Or perhaps she'll only remember the raw hurt in Theseus's eyes: proof that Asterion has not only disappointed her, but met her expectations in doing so.

Whatever is clenching around Asterion's heart grips tighter. Does Theseus think her a coward for not trying to leave? Or—worse—a monster for wanting to stay?

Asterion never wanted to hurt anyone. But this place...

From every scar embedded in her flesh, every bruise, every injury: this was never a home. It's a cage. A cage that's turned her into an animal, claws ready even when she isn't.

How can she expect Theseus to embrace a life that's hold is a death grip?

Dread creeps through her, turning her breath ragged. Not only at what Theseus must think of her, but...

She knows that mechanical *clink-clunk*. She shouldn't be

hearing it. In her turmoil, she's forgotten the timings. She *always* remembers the timings.

Theseus is out in the connecting corridor. She's only metres from the turntable. But it's far enough.

Even as Asterion hears it, it's too late.

"Come back!" she shouts, but the mask turns her warning to a roar. She lurches toward Theseus—to haul her to safety, to join her, to do *anything*—

But the movable corridor swoops sideways toward its new destination, whisking Theseus with it.

And Asterion is left staring at an empty archway, the labyrinth wall scrolling past behind it in a blur of speed.

No, no, no, no, *no*—

She hadn't meant to send Theseus out there alone.

74

THE WAY FORWARD
THESEUS

Downward spiralling. Water down a plughole; that's what this feels like.

Flattened against the wall a mere metre from the corridor's opening, Theseus swallows her nausea—just—as the labyrinth whips past far too fucking close to her face.

There's nothing she can do but let the momentum pin her and her fallen worldly possessions in place, rattling metal against stone, and wait for the corridor to land at its next location.

Tears, hot and unforgiving, smear across her cheeks. It *hurts*. The unrelenting force of the labyrinth's momentum, yes—but she can deal with that. It's this heart-hammering rejection that she hasn't a fucking clue what to do with.

If Asterion wants to stay locked in here forever... If she wants to shove Theseus out the fucking door... Theseus needs to respect that. Doesn't mean she has to like it. Doesn't mean her breath isn't dizzy in her lungs at how it's all unspooling.

As the labyrinth thunders past, Theseus strains her neck to look at what Asterion had pressed into her palm. Her thumb encounters its smoothness before she's able to see that it's Asterion's pendant; the one shaped like an anatomical heart. The one that usually blushes pink but is now an dull, lifeless grey.

The Heart of the Minotaur.

Princess Ariadne's riddle. The key to the Sky Labyrinth.

Should she try to look past Asterion's serrated words and bludgeoning actions to what lies beneath? The hurt and fear that Theseus would leave her anyway, so she may as well hurry it along?

Theseus's chest tightens. Had those last roars from the mask been Asterion shouting for her to get out, or begging her to come back?

Perhaps she's overthinking it. Perhaps she should just take things at face value: that Asterion would rather stay in a world that threatens her with death, than even try to live free in any world with Theseus?

The thought pinches against her chest like too-tight armour. That's what's happening here, isn't it? They're both trying to protect themselves.

Shit, shit, shit. How has it come to this?

As ever, Theseus could have been better with her words.

You complete and utter fuckwit.

Minos needs you. Never mind that—how about *I need you*? Instead of piling another world of responsibility on Asterion's shoulders, how about *We can take on the worlds together*? That's what Theseus should have said. That's what she *meant*.

Stupid oaf. Find a damn dictionary and use it.

The corridor's momentum slows, then comes to a halt, clunking into its new position. She might have stopped spinning, but her mental equilibrium seems to have spiralled off into space. Falling flat on her face would fit right now, but her muscles tense against it.

From the ceiling, moisture drips into puddles. She stands unsteadily—multidirectional gravity strumming at her in the shadowy, intestinal tunnels, lit only by pulsing clusters of glittering green mushrooms.

More fungus. Great. Please don't let the mists be an issue down here. Or up here. Wherever she is, it has a certain subterranean feel to it. Something sewer-like.

It could be her delicate self-esteem meeting motion-inspired tinnitus, but it sure feels like the Labyrinth is having a laugh at her expense.

Theseus wheezes. Is her panic infecting her lungs, or is the air here thin?

This new location offers seven directions to choose from: four sprawling one way, three the other. Wherever she is, these aren't part of the escape route pathways Asterion had gone over with her in the blueprints.

Shit.

First rule of monster hunting: Survive first. Have feelings later.

Yeah. That's an important one. The unknown is not somewhere she should linger unless she wants the Labyrinth to decide the end of her path for her. She'll have to figure out how to deal with her heart being ripped in two later.

Theseus tucks the heart-stone reverently into her rucksack's safest compartment, scrubbing away a renegade tear. She's all for the first part of Herakles's advice. No matter how tough she pretends to be, she's never quite got the hang of the second—as fucking well evidenced by recent events.

First rule of monster hunting: If you've got armour, don't be an arrogant prick—fucking wear it.

That's a direct quote from Herakles, actually.

Theseus pulls on her armour—her own, this time; at least she knows how to put this shit on. She completes the ensemble with her astro-helmet—open-faced by design—and hinges the jaw guards in place to trigger the invisi-visor, and to unveil the whisper-mesh across her body, enveloping her from shoulder to boot.

Through her mask's invisi-visor, she draws a deep but ragged breath. The mask is doing its job of filtering her oxygen; the stuttering is just her stumbling over the tripwire of her emotions.

The drip-drip of moisture into puddles still reaches her ears, and Theseus's tears threaten to unleash anew. Because Asterion cared enough to adjust her astro-helmet to repair the auditory feed.

Fuck. Asterion is so kind and clever. And she shouldn't be shut away here, not unless that's what she truly wants. It's understandable that she doesn't want to go back to Minos, but—

Urgh. Theseus could do with throwing some blades right now, to get rid of the pent-up chaos churning her insides. But no lingering!

Keeping one eye on the tunnels, she crouches to rifle through her rucksack.

She digs out a thick tome of Labyrinth designs. Asterion's gone through the blueprints and maps with her several times over the last few weeks, but they're so intricate and crammed with conditional positionings, it makes Theseus's brain itch. Usually, maps aren't quite so... detailed. They don't typically feature equations. There's a highlighted through-line that suggests a route from the core to the gatehouse.

But she's not at the core anymore. She has no idea where she's landed.

She'll flick through to try to figure out where she is, but first... what else is in the rucksack?

There's a well-stocked medi-kit, including bandages, numbing balm, a sewing kit, and a sedative syringe. Heavens, she hopes she won't need all that. There's charcoal, perhaps for marking the map? And in the side pocket, there's even a cloth-wrapped sandwich, which, ridiculously, has her battling tears again.

Because someone who doesn't care wouldn't bother making you a frostberry sandwich to send you on your way, would they?

Fuck. Fuck. Fuck.

The Minotaur plushie clipped to her rucksack stares up at her with its button eyes. Is it judging her or feeling sorry for her?

Oh, for fuck's sake. It's a damn toy.

And no more sniffling and what-ifs.

First rule of monster hunting: (the most instinctive one for Theseus) *Don't wait to be saved.*

But even if she reaches the exit alive, she can't just leave. It's been weeks since they crossed paths with Hero, and he should have snuffed it by now, but *should* isn't enough.

Theseus doesn't have an ounce of admiration for him, but he has survival instincts. It's not impressive. The worst of creatures are often the ones who best know how to survive. Hero may be a loser, but he's also either resourceful or unfairly lucky.

There's no way in the heavens Theseus is leaving this place without first dealing with the monster who's after the Minotaur.

Keeping a careful eye on each of the seven passages, she wraps a bandage about her lower leg to hide the illumi-thread stitches. She hadn't planned to navigate the labyrinth in three-quarter length trousers; and the last thing she needs is to be a lit-up target.

Even her forearm's smattering of thread-freckles is glowing through her shirt sleeve. She covers them with another bandage. Finally, she digs her neckerchief out of her rucksack to cover her torque.

Now. Which way to go?

First rule of monster hunting: Always have a plan.

Yeah... Theseus has never been good at that one either. She always preferred charging into chaos, challenging it to charge back. But if she wants to guarantee Asterion's safety, and Herakles's—and even her own—she needs to not fuck this up.

She assesses the pathways as she considers her battle plan.

One: Remove the real monster, by sword or reason. Then at least Asterion can have her world back.

Two: Keep Herakles from charging into danger on a misunderstood mission to save her.

Three: Sort Minos and its monarch.

Four: Tackle her broken heart.

She inspects her Locator. Herakles's current co-ordinates place her only one star system away. In her sky-cruiser, if she hops through the shortcuts, it'll be maybe three days until she zeroes in on Theseus.

Three days. That should be plenty of time...

She is a monster hunter, after all.

75

SOME MONSTER
THESEUS

Theseus has an idea of where she's most likely to find the Chosen Hero. He'll be where he's encountered the Minotaur, and where he can source food and water. She just has to get through the labyrinth first.

It's not a straightforward journey.

Just as she finishes grappling with one corridor's over-exuberant gravity that has her slow-sliding along the floor like a slug monster, the next has her untethered and treading air thanks to the lack of gravity. And the wind tunnel that follows undoes her every step of progress. Enough that she retraces her path and looks to the maps for a workaround.

It's a bizarre selection of experiences, no doubt designed to hinder trespassers. But thanks to Asterion's map, Theseus doesn't stray across any deadly additions.

In her current corridor, the lava-gullies flow erratically. Perhaps Asterion's labyrinth-linked equilibrium is as sideswiped as Theseus is right now.

And Theseus has no idea what to think or feel about that.

Oof! Her upper body lurches, her legs yanked from under her.

Fucking multidirectional gravity.

Her journey feels like it takes forever through endless corridors folding back and under and over on themselves, made worse every time she's forced to wait for the Labyrinth to tick and turn and realign—but it's likely only a few miles before she finds what she's been looking for...

The secret passage that leads through the cliff face to behind the meadow's waterfall. She sidesteps along the damp stone ledge, her back pressed to the rocks, her rucksack temporarily on her front, until she's beyond the waterfall and onto familiar, meadow terrain.

She's never seen the meadow sunlit before.

The waterfall shimmers. The long grass and wheat shimmer. The lake shimmers. Okay, there's a lot of shimmering, but it's just all so... fucking... *magical*.

Asterion *created* all this. She imagined it, put her ideas to the page. And this is the result.

Heavens above and below, she's so fucking incredible. How can one person possess endless kindness, humour, sass *and* the ability to casually design worlds?

Theseus sighs, her chest aching again.

Okay. Enough. If she wants Asterion to have her world back, she needs to focus. The Chosen Hero will be here somewhere. She's sure of it.

Theseus keeps still, trying not to give away her position before she discovers his. She expects to have to go knee to the dirt to find clues, to listen for any sounds that don't fit.

But none of that is necessary.

Up on a silver-grass knoll near the lake sits a cluster of fruit trees, including a proteus tree like the one in the fortress orchard. And in amongst the tree cluster, there's a hammock hanging between the trunks. And on that hammock is a person, ostensibly lounging like they're basking in the sun.

Between the hammock and Theseus, an almost direct path has been cut through the golden wheat.

Well, this sure feels like a trap.

Perhaps Hero thinks he's alone here? Or perhaps he's given up hunting for them and made himself at home while they've been wrapped up in their own world.

She shrugs free of her rucksack, nestling it beneath the gnarly branches of a hedge at the edge of the wheat field. She keeps her shield, but leaves her astro-helmet with her rucksack; it's not ideal being without the whisper-mesh, but she can't risk her helmet getting damaged if there's a scuffle.

Her short-sword presses at her hip as she follows the path through the wheat, her lower leg aching to remind her of the danger of hidden traps.

Partway to the trees, clean-cut wheat gives way to folded stems clomped into submission by heavy boots. Theseus pauses. Did Hero lose patience here? Or is there something hidden in the wheat?

The trap that snapped about her leg is in Asterion's workshop. What's the likelihood of Hero having a second one?

Silently, Theseus unsheathes her sword and pokes at the wheat-covered path.

Nothing.

She's close enough to the fruit trees now to catch the glint of metal in the sunlight. Asterion's scythe. The one she lost. Hero has given the display a good go—but the 'person' lounging in the sunshine is in fact a neatly-arranged shell of golden armour, topped with Hero's astro-mask.

In her peripheral vision, the tall wheat near the lakeside, a sword's throw away, twitches. Does he think he's hidden? How embarrassing for him.

He's not covered his torque well enough, either. It's sparking like an irate electric eel.

She could hurl her sword and be done with him before he even realises she's seen him.

Ordinarily, that's the kind of outcome she appreciates. Vanquish the beast and ask questions later. But if this world-upending excursion to the skies has taught her one thing, it's that appearances can be deceiving. Before, when he'd been chasing Asterion, she'd body-checked him to the ground without pausing to reason with him. And yes, he might have tried to kill them both last time their paths crossed, but she's willing to let that slide if he'll listen to her now.

At least now she knows some Minosian. Hopefully enough to help them avoid any misunderstandings.

She sheathes her sword and turns in his direction but doesn't move closer. "I just want to talk," she says in her best Minosian. Lowering her shield, she holds out her free hand in a gesture of—well, not surrender. More *I won't stab you unless you stab me.*

He stays crouched in the wheat. He perhaps can't quite fathom that his decoy hasn't worked—

Sure enough—

A spear sails toward her head.

Fuck.

Theseus whips her shield up. The spear rebounds with a *clang*, landing nearer the tree cluster, beyond her reach. It's half the length it should be, its wooden end blackened and charred. Victim to the lava river, perhaps?

The half-spear snakes jerkily back to its owner, reeled in on rope.

Well, that wasn't intended for her health and happiness, was it? Theseus huffs, but refrains from drawing her sword. He's no doubt been through a lot. She can give him one more chance.

"Myths—not what you think," she calls across the meadow. "There is no beast. Heart of—Minotaur—is key to escape. I—

have—key." Though she's not going to tell him it's in her ruck-sack, is she?

That gets his attention. The Hero straightens, popping out above the wheat: spear and shield in hand, broadsword at his hip. There's a dagger tucked in his belt, too—only just visible in amongst his shirt ruffles. He's so weighed down with weapons. *And he thinks he has stealth on his side?*

Not to mention his shirt—previously hidden by his golden armour—isn't exactly subtle with its chequered black and red diamond motif outlined in gold stitching.

He doesn't look like he's gone into battle against a swarm of fang-fish. Though he'd been wearing his astro-mask...it must've been equipped with a sturdy whisper-mesh. But—Hades and the fucking Heavens—he's turned savage. Or, at least, he's lost his enthusiasm for washing, brushing his hair, and shaving; he's not over-coifed like he was before.

Now that she can see her target, she'll have her sword soaring through the air before he can even flex a muscle.

Still... one more chance.

"You can—go—from here," she tells him. "I—show you the way."

"You speak Minosian." It's not a question, more an accusation. His voice is gravelly, like he's not spoken in a while.

"I've had—time." *And some good incentive.*

"You would *give* me the prize?" The suspicion remains in his narrowed eyes until his mouth upticks into a surly smile. That can't be good. "You think I'm foolish?" *Best not to answer that.* "You would trick me? To steal the prize for yourself?"

Theseus stifles her sigh. Nothing's ever easy, is it?

"I—give you—way out." She grits her teeth. "I am not here for—prize. The beast—not what you think—she—"

"She?" He starts circling closer, like she can't see what he's doing. *Fuck's sake.* "You are well acquainted with the creature?"

Theseus categorically hates his tone. "She is not—creature. She is—person. How—you think—I learn Minosian? She—"

"The Labyrinth has made the *great Monster Hunter Theseus* soft, I see."

Shit. Has she gone doe-eyed talking about Asterion or something? His taunting laugh is as dangerous as the predatory glint in his eyes. He's not wrong, but... yeah, whatever. He can throw verbal weapons all he wants.

"And where is your precious Minotaur now?"

Oof. Okay, that bites.

And he's favouring his right side, clutching his spear tighter—

Which can only mean—

Raising her shield, Theseus darts right as his spear soars—

It misses—

And now he's charging with his broadsword. Fucking great.

"Listen. She—not deserve—"

He swipes—

Theseus dodges, and in an almighty clash she meets his blade with hers.

"I don't care *what* the Minotaur is," he growls, muscles bunching as he gears up for his next strike. "I'll claim my prize. To rule over Minos. To occupy the Princess's bed."

Yuck. She preferred when she *couldn't* understand him.

Swipe—

His broadsword misses her neck by an inch and—with her shield, the edge of her blade, and his own momentum—she shoves his sword into the ground.

He yanks at his blade but it catches, buried, jolting him off balance. As he stumbles, Theseus boots his wrist, knocking him further off course and losing his weapon.

He growls, his grimace deep as he throws his shield down.

Shit—

The Hero crashes into her like an interplanetary ether-tram, slamming her against the trunk of the proteus tree so hard her sword and shield thud from her hands onto the root-meshed ground.

Shit, shit, shit.

Before he can reach for his dagger, she grasps his wrist.

His acrid breath hits her as his other hand lashes about her neck as—above them—the proteus leaves ripple from grey to black, orange, yellow and red funnelling skyward like rage-filled flames.

The ground shudders, vibrating through the tree trunk and armour as the sun shorts out, turning everything to darkness.

Everything but the blazing proteus tree, Hero's electric-barbed torque, and Theseus's illumi-flecked palm grasping at the tightening hand around her throat.

76

TRIPPED
THESEUS

Pinned against a proteus tree with Hero's hand around her throat is not where Theseus planned to be.

She digs her illumi-flecked hand beneath his thumb, snapping it back with a stomach-lurching crunch. As he cries out, she tamps down the urge to puke on him and knees him in the gut instead.

He buckles and she boots him in his side. He stumbles backwards, tripping on the thick proteus roots, landing with a thud as he clutches his middle and injured left hand, his breath seething.

Hades and the Heavens, that's some kick. Her illumi-thread stitches pulse brightly through her leg's bandage, surging beneath her skin.

The proteus tree's colours evolve to shimmering blues, purples, and pinks. Guess that's the colour of triumph?

But more importantly... where are her sword and shield? And what in the Seven is going on with the Labyrinth?

She reaches for her weapons in amongst the tree roots, but the ground vibrates so hard, she falls to her knees as her weapons tremble beyond her reach.

Beyond the proteus tree, everything is lost to inky darkness. Up in the dome of the sky, the trio of moons flicker, then bloom, dappling light across the lake and the waterfall beyond the meadow, and giving soft definition to the edge of the woodland.

It's all so fucking beautiful.

Apart from Hero groaning through his pain. And that ominous creaking from the depths of the Labyrinth, like a seafaring vessel under strain.

Is this what the Sky Labyrinth sounds like when it's pulling at the seams? Is it Asterion's suffering that's causing this?

The wheat is swaying like there's a storm building and the woodland shivers like a thousand unsettled birds are rustling its branches.

That can't be good...

The ground lurches a little, then a lot. Twenty degrees—

Theseus stands but keeps her centre of gravity low, while Hero flounders at the other side of the knoll.

Branches jostle. Colourful orbs of proteus fruit tumble from them, rolling across the grass and down the tilted terrain. Her sword lands on the ledge of root, down beyond her reach.

Thirty degrees...

Asterion's scythe clatters across the tree roots, snagging on one.

Forty...

The lake's usually calm surface is choppy, sloshing across the shore. Now downhill from where Theseus is, the waterfall bows at an odd angle, hammering the meadow.

Fifty...

Theseus's boots slip against the hard soil. As she skids down the knoll, she snatches up Asterion's scythe and axes it into the ground, straining to keep her grip on its handle.

Behind her... Above her... Hero stabs into the ground with his dagger, but the angle's wrong. As he slips, he grabs onto the proteus roots. He hangs on, but his dagger skitters downhill and is lost to the wheat.

The Labyrinth warbles and cries as the inclining ground shudders to a stop.

Thank fuck.

But it's still too steep.

At the bottom of the hill, displaced fang-fish flop in the lake water spilling across the meadow, teeth gnashing at nothing. They splash in the swirling water as it drains through the secret tunnel behind the waterfall like an epic plughole.

Theseus's shield tumbles and skims down the waterlogged meadow, splashing into the water and disappearing in the whirlpool.

Well... shit.

Theseus's breath lodges in her throat. At the idea of falling into *that*, yes—but also at the idea that the displaced water might threaten Asterion, too.

How fast can Theseus get to the fortress from here?

The woodland stops shivering and Theseus only has time to swallow her dread as—

Whoosh—

A bank of shimmering mist sweeps out of the woodland like a flock of birds on a sudden migration.

She knows that mist. She peers down at the angled meadow, seeking the hedge where she'd hooked her rucksack. Her astro-helmet would be mighty useful about now. Her stuff should still be there. She'll just need the right trajectory and to not tumble into fang-fish infested waters.

Right...

But her focus pulls back up to Hero, scrambling up the roots like a ladder toward his astro-mask hanging in the swaying hammock. But he fumbles, then drops it. The golden mask plummets past Theseus, too busy holding on to grab it.

It skims the meadow's waterlogged surface, then *plunks* into the displaced lake and is lost in a churn of fang-fish.

In a perfect replica of his lost astro-mask, Hero snarls down at her, like its loss is her fault. There's a glint in his eyes. He's about to attack—

Theseus unhooks the scythe from the ground and answers the command of gravity, launching down the steep hill and—somehow—staying on her feet.

She reclaims her dropped sword and slots it back into its scabbard as she goes. Pretty fucking smooth, even if she says so herself.

A glance over her shoulder, and—yep, she was right—Hero is staggering after her and—oh, great, he's found his spear.

Her soles slip on the steep ground, loose with grit and cut wheat.

Fuck, it's *too* steep.

Her armoured back thuds against the ground, shuddering through her. As she skids through the meadow, the scrape of dry ground against her back turns to skimming through marshland, where lake water has overflowed through rich soil.

And Hero, despite flopping about like a fish, *is right behind her.* He lunges, but she deflects his spear with the sturdy metal of the scythe.

The ground lurches, knocking them off course and out of range of each other as they both lift from the ground. Hero's spear paddles at nothing.

The moment of weightlessness stretches as the meadow's angle reduces. Who the fuck knows by how many degrees! But it's enough for Theseus to land upright in the wet soil, scythe in hand, like an absolute fucking warrior.

Hero fumbles the landing.

And then the mist descends like a shroud.

A shiver works through Theseus. Her heart rate steps up a notch. Is that the effect of the mist, or her body preparing for it?

This should be interesting. The last time the mist got her, her terror-drenched brain had amplified the Minotaur's beastly qualities tenfold. And Hero was an outright eyesore.

The mist sweeps across the meadow and up through the sky hatch—the one that had first brought her to this inner-world—where, now, an unsteady stream of orange-red is bleeding into the sky.

Great. Sky lava. That's... an unwanted escalation. But at least it's pooling in the engineered heavens instead of raining down on them. For now, at least.

The Labyrinth groans, deep and shuddering, like a mythical beast in pain, as Hero lumbers to his feet and staggers toward her, spear ready.

"Enough." Theseus raises her voice over the labyrinth's chaos.

But he advances.

Wet soil and spilled silt suck at Theseus's boots. She wobbles, splashing to her knees into the surface water. She kicks free of the mud, but Hero is right there, standing over her—

He's a fast fucker.

His spear jabs down—

With the scythe, she deflects.

He jabs again—

She rolls aside and grabs the broken shank of the spear, but his grip remains firm. She'd hit him in the face with a fang-fish if she could grab one. But a boot will have to do.

She kicks her left leg up and he stumbles back, out of range, hands over his face.

Weighted by water, Theseus heaves to her feet. Her clothes aren't the auto-drying ones she arrived here in. She won't be feeling smug this time around.

Catching her breath, she weighs the scythe in her hand. She's intact and functional. Her skin tingles from the mist, but it's more of a low rolling shiver than the needling of her first encounters with it.

Hero is on his knees in the mud, facing away from her.

That was some kick. He probably needs a moment. Or perhaps he's finally given up on his obnoxious, power-grabbing murder crusade. Which is... good, if so?

But if he still plans to hurt Asterion in any way, Theseus will kick him out of the fucking skies. Her healed leg pulses with the truth of it.

He splutters and, though Theseus can't see his face, she can assume there's blood involved. For a moment, she thinks maybe he landed on his spear, but—

"You broke my nose!" Has his voice always been this whiny? He sounds desperate, like it's not just his nose that's broken, but his spirit too.

"Yeah. That's what fucking happens when you try to kill someone." She doesn't bother speaking Minosian right now.

"How is Princess Ariadne to take me seriously... how are the people of Minos... with my face like *this*?"

Is *that* why he's hunched? He's looking at his reflection in the surface water?

Heavens above. How to put this kindly?

"I think your face is the least of your problems, to be honest."

Hero stands but doesn't turn to face her. He keeps staring at his reflection. Seriously? Has he forgotten they're kind of in a battle right now? Hasn't he noticed the world tilted at the wrong angle, water spilling one way, lava the other?

Whatever. Theseus has more important things to be getting on with. Like making sure Asterion is okay. And somehow stopping her world from falling apart.

But Hero still has his back to her. And Theseus won't stab anyone in the back. That's not even a rule of monster hunting, it's just common decency.

"Is—time to go." She raises her voice. His one last *last* chance to leave this place.

"How are all the worlds to hear my words," Hero continues, as if she'd asked, "if they're distracted by my profound looks?"

Profound... what now...?

"This injury... it will only make me more distinguished."

Hang the fuck on. He's worried that he's... *too good-looking?*

For fuck's sake. Is it too much to ask for him to get a mist-fuelled existential crisis that *doesn't* feed his over-inflated ego? Over how intimidating and impressive Theseus is, perhaps? But no; this tracks. Beneath Hero's over-preened exterior is a void lined only with arrogance.

It must be freeing to not be cursed with self-doubt.

Theseus scoffs, and only then does Hero whip around, glaring at her. *Yikes.* What a mess. His nose isn't so much a question mark as an expletive.

Well, there's something to be said for self-confidence, isn't there?

And it's absolutely the mist twisting things, but the blood from his crooked nose smeared around his mouth, against his pale moonlit skin; his garish, bloodstained shirt... he looks like an escaped sideshow from some horrific circus.

The first laugh that escapes Theseus is one of shock and disbelief. The second is pure derision. Because... seriously. *This guy.*

Hero's almost comically woeful expression morphs to pure rage. Hades and the Heavens. How can an ego be so strong and fragile at the same time?

Hero lunges at her—

She hits his spear aside with the scythe, ducking so fast, his legs clash against her body. Carried by his own momentum, he sails forward, landing in the newly created marsh with a heavy splash.

The ground trembles as she stands. Hero is on his ass in the water, that scrunched look on his face. That's a building tantrum if ever she's seen one. He's reaching into his waistband, hidden by his shirt ruffles.

And her focus doesn't adjust fast enough to the weapon in his hand. A new weapon that upends the scales.

Pain punches through her chest, sending her stumbling. Only then does she hear the reverberation of the gunshot.

77

SHOT
THESEUS

The scythe falls from her grip, landing in the ankle-deep water with a splash, but the fact that Theseus stays on her feet after the bullet's impact deserves a round of applause. The blood surging behind her eardrums gives it a good go as she claws for the breath that's been catapulted out of her.

Hero is still flailing in the marsh-water, fang-fish gnashing around him. He must have dropped the pistol.

Pain is a strange beast. It's difficult to differentiate between a standard wound and a mortal one. It's not Theseus's first time taking a bullet, but it's not a *usual* occurrence, either, so it takes a moment to wrangle the crucial details of the ache radiating through her chest, across her shoulders and up her neck. It might hurt like there's a lump of metal lodged in her flesh, but her fingers seek answers...

There's no blood.

What a fucking relief.

The bullet hit her torso armour. It's an impact injury only.

Hero's groping arm goes rigid in the water, triumph scrawled across his face. *Shit.* He's found the fallen pistol.

He's too far away for her to boot him again. Running at him will be waterlogged and slow.

She draws her sword, ready to fling it, but—

The whole meadow lurches, throwing her off balance. The ground's tilt sharpens abruptly, sending them both tumbling downhill and through the surface water.

Ahead of Hero, Theseus scrambles left and right as much as possible, hindering his ability to take aim.

He might look like a clown, but pistols are no fucking joke.

Up ahead is the hedge where her rucksack and astro-helmet are stashed. She angles her body, using herself as a kind of rudder to slide in the right direction.

It's times like this she's glad she spent so much time as a kid in lakes and under the waves. Water doesn't scare her.

Bullets, however...

Water spits up at her as a bullet narrowly misses her.

Thankfully, Hero's aim is all over the place.

Theseus tugs her rucksack from the hedge, pulling it onto her back in an ungraceful but practical squirming manoeuvre.

The whirlpool below churns with fang-fish.

On her current trajectory, she's still speeding toward the spilling lake water gathering where the meadow biome meets the cliff. Unless she can change course, she'll be sucked down through the waterfall plug hole into flooded labyrinth corridors.

The width of the water expanse isn't insurmountable, but—

Now or never—

At the water's edge, she digs her heels in and leaps—

Please don't fall in...

Her stomach flip-flops—

Gravity tugs her towards the cliff—

Her forearm lashes out to protect her and she holds her sword away from herself, just in time, as she face-plants. Her armour *thunks* against the cliff face and the air *oofs* from her lungs.

At least she's not here to win prizes for grace.

A gunshot claps behind her. Theseus grits her teeth—but no pain follows. Hero's a terrible shot. Or the Labyrinth's unpredictable gravity knocked his bullet off course. Or he's being buffeted, like she is, by the uptick in chaotic airflow.

Theseus springs to her feet and runs horizontal on the cliff face as fast as her drenched clothes allow. She needs to find Asterion, but she's sure as Hades not bringing Hero with her.

Instead of racing up the cliff to the opening above, the one that, at certain Labyrinth rotations, leads more directly to Asterion's fortress, Theseus diverts to the sky wall, its inky terrain with its scattering of twinkling in-ground lights. If this were a snow globe, she'd be running up its dome.

She glances up to the meadow, now behind her and at a right angle to her current position. The proteus tree hangs like a distant, unsettled lantern.

But Hero is still in pursuit, and closer than she'd expected, his silhouette already interrupting the pinprick stars. Fifty strides away. Fewer, maybe.

She ups her pace. She has no desire to get any closer to the spilling lava, but she needs to get lost in the night sky. If she can get behind one of the three chimney-like moonlight channels, she can shield from his bullets and even sneak up on him.

More bullets skitter past, each one a whetstone against her nerves as she ducks and swerves. She's almost at the first moon, but—

A hiss of pain escapes her before her conscious brain even registers it. The force of the bullet's impact sends her stumbling. She catches herself—just—against the nearest moon channel. When she looks down, there's a red slash scored into her left arm, just below her shoulder.

She swings around to face Hero.

He's only strides away. Even a bad shot wouldn't miss from there... And beyond his raised pistol, beyond his bloodied nose, are the eyes of a hunter who savours the kill.

Well, he can fuck right off.

Theseus's hand squeezes tighter about her sword, ready to throw—

But the sky quakes—or something does. A world-shaking roar from the depths, or from above, so sudden and so close it vibrates her insides into new alignment.

Hero's inevitable bullet clips against the moonlight channel.

That roar... it might be a harrowing bellow, but there's something comforting within its layers, enveloping Theseus like whisper-mesh.

Fear ignites in Hero's eyes. His gaze is aimed not at her, but above her, as he stumbles backwards, dropping his pistol.

In one smooth motion, Theseus kicks the weapon away. It skitters to a halt, blocking out the light of a single star. But Hero, in his terror, remains frozen.

Putting distance between them, but keeping him in her eyeline, Theseus looks up.

If Hero weren't so transfixed, she might think it an apparition; a trick of the mind-bending mists.

Because atop the towering stack, uplit by moonlight, is the monumental form of a Minotaur, eyes aglow like flourishing blue flame, shirt rippling in the gusts, shaping to her impressive physique. She's not wearing her armour. She must have rushed from the fortress. But what's most captivating of all, is the defiance and confidence in the stance that says, plainly: *Get your fucking weapons away from my monster hunter.*

If Theseus were the kind of person who swooned, she'd damn well be swooning right now.

Because Asterion is here for her. To save her. To fight for her.

Oh, fuck it. She's completely swooning.

And in any other time or place, she'd be questioning her life choices if she found a bull-like creature utterly beguiling and *totally fucking hot*. But in these precise circumstances... she figures it's okay.

78

TOGETHER

ASTERION

Theseus's arm is bleeding, but she doesn't appear to have other injuries. Good. That's good. Asterion's shoulders lose a bit of their tension. And Theseus is grinning up at her like she's pleased to see her? That's even better.

Asterion finally lets herself breathe. She'd rather offend the great Monster Hunter by rescuing her than risk her death.

She never intended to leave Theseus's safety to chance.

Nor to this oaf.

The golden man is not so golden anymore. His shirt is stitched with gold thread, but he's lost his over-shined armour and his face is grim with blood. No doubt he deserved it. His spear is shortened, but in any case he's too stupefied, staring up at her, to do much with it. For all his strutting, he must really believe the myth of the Minotaur—and perhaps have had a dose of mist—to be so awestruck by her.

Well... best give him a show.

Asterion leaps from the chest-height platform to Theseus's side, unleashing a roar so sinister, so rabid, even she herself is a little chilled by it.

"Confound and flummox, Asti. You look—so fucking hot—

right now." Theseus's Athenian and Minosian is jumbled, and murmured like maybe she hadn't meant to say that aloud. Her smile is a little dopey, too. "I could kiss you."

Her words are a balm to Asterion's ears... but... is now really the time? Isn't this man trying to kill them both?

"I don't have a thing for, like, animal masks. I promise." And now Theseus looks... bewildered, like she's only just realised she's talking *out loud* in a way that's making her sound like she *absolutely* has a thing for animal masks. "It's the whole heroic war-cry thing. Not the mask. Although the mask is beautiful because—behind there—I know it's you."

Okay... It's possible Theseus got a dose of mist and it's amplifying the *good things* in her brain chemistry.

"I'm saying a lot..." Theseus runs a hand through her damp hair. The resulting angle it's sticking up at has Asterion's hoof-encased hands itching to smooth it. Theseus puffs out her chest and lifts her chin like she's reminding herself she's a stoic, tough monster hunter, actually.

Chatty, mist-drunk Theseus is pretty darn cute. But it really is terrible timing as the embers of fear in the golden man's eyes flare into fight as he leaps for where his pistol landed.

Theseus launches herself at him legs first, skidding across his path and tripping him like she's done it a hundred times before.

Stars above. That's a move.

But there's no time for ogling.

The golden man is still scrambling toward his pistol. Theseus climbs to her feet, but Asterion's mask and the shadows hide her. Only the interrupted stars hint at her location, and his.

There are thuds and groans, but all Asterion can see is silhouettes battling against a backdrop of stars. The thought of Theseus getting hurt churns her insides. Her breath trips from her lungs, which only makes hearing what's happening all the more difficult.

The golden man steps over a star channel, up-lighting the pistol he's holding. And he's not aiming at wherever Theseus is, he's aiming at—

Asterion's heart barely has time to start hammering before he pulls the trigger.

But the lurch of her body isn't a bullet strike. It's Theseus. Suddenly. There. Against her. Arms around her, body shielding her. Theseus's shout of pain may as well be a bullet through Asterion's chest.

The Labyrinth roars as the deepest dread slinks through Asterion's veins. She folds Theseus into her arms, clutching her close. *Please, not like this...*

Asterion squeezes her, holding her close, and Theseus's breathless 'oof!' is oddly soothing. More so is Theseus telling her: "I'm okay, Asti." She groans, then adds, hurriedly: "It's just my armour and pride that are dented. I'm okay."

Armour...? Pride...?

Oh.

Theseus is wearing armour. Of course. Asterion had been too focused on ensuring Theseus's safety, to pause to affix her own. Theseus must have noticed and stepped in.

Hades in the Heavens. If Asterion were wearing her heart pendant right now, it'd be glowing so bright.

Theseus whirls around and charges at the golden man like *she's* the Minotaur. Impressive. Terrifying. Asterion feels too many things about it as her heart pulses in time with the strobing starlight. She has some Labyrinth functionality analysis to do—but right now all she cares about is the golden man taking aim—

Theseus ducks and darts between the stars, intermittently found and lost to the light. The golden man, by contrast, is a clear and stationary target in his upward shaft of starlight. His bullets punch into the skies, one after another. Each one jabbing into Asterion's fears, but Theseus continues her erratic dance between stars and shadows.

Click-click. He's out of bullets.

His face twists with frustration—and then his eyes widen with panic as Theseus bursts from the darkness and body-checks him to the ground with a heavy *thump*.

Theseus remains on her feet as he hurls his pistol at her with a growl. Theseus's arm whips out, catching it with remarkable ease.

That's my Monster Hunter.

The words catch in Asterion's chest because... well... it's complicated, isn't it?

But never mind that. Up-lit in her own beam of starlight, Theseus's smirk is more distracting than anything under the Seven Suns. She's in full warrior-jock mode as she pitches the pistol up into the air, high enough that the meadow's gravity steals it away and lands it in the lake water with a satisfying *plunk*.

And here Asterion had been thinking Theseus needed rescuing.

She joins Theseus, wishing she wasn't encased in this stupid mask so Theseus could see just how impressed she is. But a confident smile illuminates Theseus's face, more smouldering than the not insignificant detail of the lava river spilling into the sky behind them. Yes, Theseus knows how impressive she is.

And that only makes Asterion smile, too.

When she'd designed her Sky Labyrinth all those sun-orbits ago, she'd never imagined she'd be battling amongst the stars, side by side with the one person with whom she could take on the heavens.

She just needs a moment.

But, really, they do need to escape the lava...

And the golden man is scrambling backwards, grabbing something out of the dark. He brandishes his half-spear at them as though trying to ward off wild beasts.

Then, instead of running away, he charges.

Theseus's muscles bunch. She's going to sprint for him—

And Asterion can't let Theseus risk herself—

Her own muscles piston into action—

Four strides. She ducks, horns lowered. Metal meets metal as she deflects his spear. The impact jars the mask's internal braces, straining her neck as it all accordions against her shoulders.

The groan from beyond her mask confirms: target hit.

Bound by her momentum, she keeps going, lifting him. She stops so abruptly, it propels him backward. His body hits the ground with a sickening thud and several gasping splutters.

Asterion gasps, dropping to her knees as his silhouette blocks out the stars like spilling ink.

Triumph churns with nausea. *He can't hurt Theseus anymore.* Grief and anguish turn up uninvited.

Even the stars falter.

Two puncture wounds spilling blood...

Nanny's features had contorted with horror and shock. Not dissimilar to the golden man's current expression.

A sob bursts from her, echoing back as a beastly warble. Her breath claws within her throat. She hates this place. What kind of world demands that she choose her life over another's, again and again?

She never wanted to be *this*.

And now Theseus has seen the monster... Well, she already needed to leave—for her safety, and for her friend's... but there's no world in which she'd want to stay after witnessing the death Asterion deals, is there?

"Asti..." That soothing voice; it's so welcome. "It's okay. It's okay." Those gentle words, and the hand rubbing circles against her back, could convince her it *is* okay. "He was never going to stop."

A breath breaks through Asterion's storm of emotions. If Theseus thought her a monster, she wouldn't be soothing her, would she? She wouldn't be kneeling next to her. She wouldn't be removing her neckerchief and wiping the mask's horns clean like any warrior might clean their blade.

"You're my fucking hero, you know that?" Theseus stands, holding her hand out to Asterion.

Asterion risks a glance at her. Theseus is gazing at her with the kind of wonder generally reserved for celestial mechanics. Well, that *is* Asterion's forte.

The reverence bolsters her. Theseus is right. She might not want to end lives to continue her own, but in this instance... at least the Minotaur got the monster.

Still, Asterion has no desire to watch him lose his battle to his mortal wound. She takes Theseus's hand and invites her to climb up onto the nearest moon platform with her. The trust in Theseus's eyes as she joins her is *everything*.

Asterion draws Theseus closer, aligning their bodies and tucking Theseus's head to her shoulder for safety.

"Ready?" Her question can only emerge as a growl, but Theseus holds onto her, bunching her hands in Asterion's shirt as the moon platform opens, and they drop—

79

PATHS DIVERGE
THESEUS

O nly Asterion would dream up a moonlight channel that doubles as a slide. As they plummet through the labyrinth like an immersive game of Serpents and Stairways, Theseus hasn't a clue where they're going, but she trusts Asterion. And frankly, it's a good excuse to hold her close.

Her palm migrates to the centre of Asterion's chest, finding the heartbeat of a fucking warrior. It's racing—but under Theseus's touch, it slows. And in that, Theseus finds comfort.

If only she could kiss Asterion right now.

Fuck. Asterion is outright, undeniably amazing.

And yes, Theseus is aware that the mist's toxins might be amplifying certain emotions... but that buzzing beneath her skin has gone, and she's no longer blathering on about whatever damn thing pops into her head. Her body must be metabolising the toxins faster this time around.

She should be embarrassed about her previous lack of filter, but to be honest, there's not a thought in her head that she minds sharing with Asterion.

The slide ends in a curtain of water. They splash through it and slosh to a stop in a familiar pipe-like corridor with pin-prick stars, flickering in the wake of the Labyrinth's chaos.

They help each other to their feet and wade through the water to the wall where Asterion smooths a pattern across the surface and the seamless door hisses open. They step up into the engine chamber.

The heat is more sweltering than Theseus remembers. And she's not even the one in the mask this time.

Asterion presses her palm to the wall, but instead of closing behind them, the door jams halfway with a metallic groan. The whole Labyrinth is creaking like a sea ship challenged by unrelenting waves.

Is Asterion the source? Or has this world reached a tipping point? Is there anything Theseus can do to help?

She'd ask, but Asterion is striding along the metal gangway —past steaming pipes, and the circulatory system of lava-gullies, towards the blue flaming world-engine. She's on a mission, and Theseus trusts she'll discover what that mission is soon enough.

The low thrum of the world-engine is a heartbeat, keeping urgent time with Asterion as she pulls at pipes and inspects gauges.

Whoosh. The gangway swings out, aligning with the monolith column of the world-engine, and Asterion gestures for Theseus to stay 'stay there.' Despite such passivity being totally against her usual style, Theseus nods.

Asterion gives her a lingering look, presumably checking Theseus's sobriety and understanding. Which is... fair enough.

"I won't move. I promise." Theseus grins and winks as she adds: "It'll be like I'm in restraints."

Okay. Maybe her filter's still lacking a little. Now is not the time to be getting playful—as confirmed by the no-nonsense manner in which Asterion climbs over the gangway's railings, holding onto the edge.

Theseus's heart and stomach jostle in her throat. The drop to the bottom of the engine column is plenty far enough. But she follows Asterion's instruction and stays where she is—until, that is, Asterion leaps from the repositioned gangway.

What the actual f—?

Theseus lunges for the railing, almost tumbling after her.

But Asterion lands on the side of the world-engine column, at ninety degrees to where Theseus stands, with more grace than she has any right to in such a top-heavy mask.

"Fuck, Asti, are you trying to give me a heart attack?" Theseus runs her hands through her hair.

But Asterion simply gestures for her to join her.

Right.

Okay… No problem. Theseus has leapt without looking for most of her damn life. This should be fine.

She climbs over the railing and holds tight. *Don't look down.* Her heart rages in her chest; it must be the dregs of the mist in her system over-exaggerating her fear of falling. Well, not the falling, but the bit that follows.

Tough monster hunter, remember?

She grits her teeth and leaps. *Don't fall. Don't fall.*

Fuck, fuck, fuck—

Her stomach swoops as the engine's gravity grabs her as she plummets. She meets the column ass-first, skidding to a halt like a sky-ship fumbling its landing. *Fuck's sake.* Theseus dusts herself off. Is a bit of dignity too much to ask?

The gangway is above and behind them now. From this new angle, the column—now that Theseus is within its roaring energy—is flat, and feels more like a bridge.

Urgh. She bends double, trying to stop her head spinning. Multidirectional gravity will never not be a headfuck.

What now?

Asterion points to the opposite end of the now horizontal

column. Moments ago, Theseus would have considered this direction *up*, but now it's *along* the platform. About twenty paces from their current position, there's a wall covered in a network of lava-gullies, apart from a large circle at its centre.

Theseus can't help drifting closer, staring in speechless wonder as the circle begins to rotate. As it spirals into itself, an opening appears, widening until it meets the platform like a circular doorway.

Even from here, the chamber beyond is familiar: the cavernous vault-meets-sky-ship adorned with glowing constellations.

Heavens. It's been so long.

Now Theseus understands why Asterion has brought her here. This is the way out. Her escape route. She's only twenty paces, an outer-shell gateway, and a shuttle journey away from Minosian soil.

And she's never wanted anything less.

It's a way out, but not one Asterion can access in her mask. If she wants to at all.

Theseus turns back to her. *If only... I wish... Please...* She can't decide where to start her pleas, or whether it's too late altogether.

If only she could see her face..

Asterion is still imprisoned inside the mask, her hands bound by its cuffs—but the mist must still be lingering in Theseus's system, because when Asterion reaches out, she sees not the hoof-cuff, but Asterion's hand. And not the electric-eyed mask, but kind eyes sparkling like a starlit lagoon.

How is Theseus supposed to leave her behind?

Asterion wants her gone. She wants her to be safe. Theseus understands that. Asterion's not pushing her away, she's trying to set her free. But does it have to be like this? What Theseus wouldn't give to tuck a fallen lock of hair behind Asterion's ear and rub her nose against Asterion's like some sentimental sap.

Theseus opens her mouth, but no words emerge.

Instead of goodbye, she can only press her palm to the centre of Asterion's chest, right where the mask's braces cross each other.

Under her touch, the Labyrinth calms. The distant groans fade. And Asterion's racing heart drums to the rhythm of her own. The same rhythm as the platform beneath them as its threads of energy orbit them, as if trying to draw them together, not pull them apart.

Please don't let this be goodbye...

Once Herakles knows she's safe, once Theseus has done something heroic or stupid to save Minos... she could return, couldn't she? The Labyrinth is chaos, but chaos isn't so bad when you're with someone you love.

I'll come back, if you'll have me...

Yes. Finally. Those are the words—

But—

The Minosian Flame, the platform beneath their feet, flares with a sudden surge, sparking sharp all around them, just as Asterion lurches and Theseus's palm ignites with fierce pain. She can't withdraw her hand because Asterion crashes against her, her masked head thrown back in an agonised cry.

Metal screams, threatening to rupture. But the platform's gravity holds.

Heat joins the pain in Theseus's palm—a sticky wetness, too —as blood blooms beneath her hand, spreading across Asterion's shirt. Theseus retracts her hand to find the glint of sharp metal. And so much blood.

Theseus blinks.

It can't be a spear tip gleaming through Asterion's chest.

No... no, no, no...

It's the mist. Just the mist. It has to be.

"Asti?"

Asterion's body jolts sickeningly as the spear tip retreats with a sharp yank. Asterion's pain-drenched roar rips through Theseus. The platform surges, dulling only a little as Asterion slumps against her.

Theseus tenses to hold her weight, lowering her to the quaking platform.

The spear twitches. It's still within reach, tethered by a rope from the gangway above, where a pale, blood-drenched Hero slumps against the railing. His sour laugh bursts fresh blood across his contorted face.

Theseus's sword is in her hand, slicing the spear from its tether with one slash. With the flick of her blade, she knocks it off the platform edge.

She should've thrown all his weapons into the lake. She should've thrown *him* into the lake.

She drops her sword with a clatter and presses her own bleeding palm tight against Asterion's chest, but the blood won't stop. It unfurls from beneath Asterion's body, a dark, deadly, spreading bloom across the glowing runway.

"No, no, no, no, no, no... Asti. You're the one who knows how to fix things. You have to fix this."

What is she saying?

Don't fucking die, that's what.

Unsteady hooves paddle at her. Asterion's trying to tell her something. Theseus tries to hold her hand, her cuff, but Asterion pushes at the mask, and Theseus sees it: the odd angle of the broken chest brace. The spear must have hit some critical part, because inside the braces, hidden cogs are grinding and *wurring*, and—with Theseus's swift but careful help—the mask lifts away. She casts it aside and it lands with a heavy *thunk*.

Asterion's eyes are wide, staring up at her, her mouth agape, choking on panic or...

Theseus presses her hands to the puncture in Asterion's chest again. There must be some intrinsic link between the mask and the cuffs, because the hooves fall away, too.

Blood keeps spilling...

And Asterion clutches Theseus's hands to her chest, holding on like it's a lifeline. Her torque's energy tremors in tandem with the platform's weakening, pulsing glow.

The inevitability of what's happening sinks through Theseus's veins like burning ice.

"Asti..." *Don't die don't die don't die.*

Do. Something.

Theseus presses Asterion's palms to her wound, rips her rucksack from her shoulders and dumps its contents onto the platform. But there's no medi-kit for this kind of wound.

The chill in the air is sudden; Theseus shivers as it claws down through her teeth to her bones, rerouting to grip around her heart, turning it brittle.

"Hold on, Asti. We can figure this out—"

With shaking hands, she rifles through the medi-kit again. There's a needle—but what use is the standard thread she's got?

"You're going to—be okay. You've—survived so much. One spear is—not going to be the end of you." Theseus tries to smile, but hot tears burn down her cheeks. She's not even sure what language she's speaking anymore.

Asterion reaches for her, clumsily wiping away Theseus's tears and tracing her smile as if she's found something precious. There's blood—fuck, so much blood—all over both of them. But it's the adoration in Asterion's eyes that breaks her.

"I'm such a fucking idiot..."

"You'll have to be—more specific." Asterion's voice is weak, but her words tug a laugh through Theseus's tears.

"When I warned you about feelings? I should've known it'd bite me in the ass."

"You—wasted as a monster hunter. Should—have been— poet." Asterion's eyes twinkle up at her as her breath wheezes.

"Asti?"

A distant thud shudders the platform. A shadow moves in her peripheral vision. Hero? Is he still armed?

Theseus doesn't fucking care.

Because as Asterion's hand drops from Theseus's cheek, her torque frazzles out. The frigid air sharpens as lava-gullies cease to flow. Mechanisms creak to a protesting halt. And deep within its innermost foundations, the Labyrinth shudders and the lights of Asterion's world-engine, finally, go out.

PART X

THE PRIZE

PRINCESS ARIADNE

80

HERALD

Perhaps Ariadne shouldn't have made her adjustments to the Labyrinth *quite* so deadly...

Discussing the price of siphoned torque energy with her export dealer always brings out such rumination in her. If the criminals lasted a bit longer up there, but with the same ongoing fear levels, she'd have more to sell.

Intriguingly, though, this sun-orbit has been a little different. The quantity of fuel generated by the group sent to the Labyrinth has been higher. And judging from the continuing flow gathering in the barrels to be shipped to neighbouring worlds—in exchange for whatever price she demands—at least one of the skyfarers is still alive.

Still, they'll expire soon enough. They always do.

The Righteous Path events always generate a glut of fuel. The mania of the citizens' celebrations always spikes energy levels. Each Sky Labyrinth death results in a reduction of the fuel-flow, but it's more than made up for by the surge of emotions from citizens when Ariadne announces the latest loss. And there's always a continuous low-level hum that stems from fear of the Minotaur and the consequences of straying from the Path.

It's a lucrative business. The fuel exports fund materials to build more attractions. Minos has to stay looking its best to lure in the tourists. The construction and the tourists keep the citizens of Minos busy, and Ariadne and the upper echelons in the comforts to which they are accustomed.

She wouldn't be an Architect's daughter—she wouldn't be the Architect-in-waiting—if she didn't keep searching for ways to be better. More attractive. And richer. She'd ether-stream the whole damn Labyrinth escapade to bring in more mania-fed fuel, if not for the risk that citizens might learn the truth of the Minotaur.

But right now, as her export dealer details the kind of mouth-watering numbers that would usually hold her full attention, something's niggling at her. There's something off-kilter about the world... like she's wearing her five-buckled ankle boots on the wrong feet, or her tuxedo-gown inside out.

She tries to get comfortable in her throne, but something just isn't *right*. What *is* this strange feeling?

The palace fire-torches have dimmed fractionally. That could be it. Upkeepers will need to deal with that.

A knock at her chamber door precedes the royal herald stumbling in, babbling apologies and greetings. Pathetic creature. He's about as useful as... whatever. He's not even worth a metaphor. The stammering wreck had better remember how to use his tongue soon, or she'll rip it out.

But then she'll have to manufacture some righteous reason. *Urgh*. It's not worth the fuss.

While he takes the verbal scenic route to getting to his point, distant shouts and cries carry on the night-time breeze through her open window. The uproar draws Ariadne out onto her balcony. Is it positive or negative? Applause or dissent?

Is it for her?

The night sky snatches the breath from her throat.

Because up there beyond the stratosphere, where for nineteen sun-orbits a light-etched sphere has loomed over her like some ominous, judgmental bauble... now there is only a void.

The void bypasses her throat and plucks the air from her lungs.

No. It can't be.

Impossible.

The light in the skies has gone out.

As Ariadne tries to reclaim her breath, the herald stammers through world-changing facts. The Minotaur is dead. The gateway to the Labyrinth has been opened. Preparations for the celebrations are already underway.

But all Ariadne can focus on is her own heart writhing like a gagged prisoner in her chest, as she tries to figure out how she feels about it.

81

THE MASK AND THE MINOTAUR

Nineteen sun-orbits ago...

"Ariadne couldn't design a meaningful maze if her life depended on it." That is Father's conclusion to the royal court as he compares the blueprints she'd worked tirelessly on against the ones Asterion 'threw together.'

Ariadne bites her tongue hard enough to draw blood. Sometimes she could swear he's goading them both to see how they'll react. That Asterion's first instinct is to insist that Ariadne *tried her best* is worse than the most savage criticism.

Asterion doesn't even *want* to be Architect, for heaven's sakes. That's what Ariadne would yell at the lot of them, if it wouldn't land her locked in her chambers for the best part of a week.

Even as the court discuss at length the inadequacies of Ariadne's 'imagination and accuracy', her 'admirably talented' sister, at eleven sun-orbits old, can't sit still, as if all she wants is to hole up in the palace library drawing and reading fictions.

And *this* is the genius they want ruling Minos?

Asterion might know her way through the intricacies of engineering, but she can't show up to a parade wearing the right attire. She doesn't even know not to talk to servants. It's *embarrassing*.

Do they truly think the candidate who's always saying the wrong thing—without even realising she's doing it—is cut out for ruling a world?

Why can't Father and the court see that?

Besides, there's no way under any of the Suns—*probably*—that Asterion created those designs without help. In any other competition, Ariadne might respect her sister for enlisting someone else's assistance and then claiming their work as her own.

But for the throne?

That's not a prize Ariadne will let her win without a fight.

+
∵

ASTERION IS PONTIFICATING to the court about her designs for some *necklace* that will solve fuel supply issues for all citizens. Yes, there's a shortage of fuel available to heat and power Minosian homes... and *yes* there's a bigger crisis because the mines have already been dug deeper than they should have been... but who does Asterion think she is? With her *ideas* about changing Minos for *the better*?

The court deems Asterion's designs as *groundbreaking*; a *revolutionary discovery* that will *save their world*.

Show-off.

Well, Ariadne has ideas too.

It isn't unusual for Ariadne to daydream about what horrible accident might befall her sister. Or how she might teach her a lesson. Locking her in cupboards just doesn't cut it anymore. The great Asterion can design engineering 'masterpieces' and intricate puzzles, yet she can't find her way out of a simple cupboard?

What a joke. An Architect needs more mettle than that. If Ariadne could eject Asterion into space, she would.

While her sister prattles on about her designs (snore!), Ariadne puts pen to page and works out an appropriate punishment. Something to rectify nature's cruel joke in cursing them with the same face. A face that only reminds Ariadne of all the skills nature has given her sister and withheld from her. She *despises* that she and Asterion share a face.

So she designs her a new one.

She hates Asterion's voice, too; hates that their intonation and even the rhythm of their sentences are so similar. The only time Ariadne enjoys hearing her sister speak is when she's making Father and the court flinch with interjections about stuff like 'sensible use of available resources' and 'considering human impact'. At least *reading a room* is something Asterion fails at, perfectly.

Well, no-one will have to worry about her saying the wrong thing anymore. The mask will make her every utterance incomprehensible.

As a finishing touch, Ariadne gives the mask the visage of a bull and matching hooves, inspired by the farming history and myths of Minos.

She smiles to herself, soothed by the justice of it all. Try impressing the court with your blueprints when you can't even hold a pencil, dear sister.

It's a private flight of fancy. She doesn't intend to share it. But Father, demanding to know whatever's fascinating enough to have Ariadne so gleefully distracted, insists that she present her designs to the court right there and then.

Her audience gasp at the cruelty of it. Face hidden. Voice garbled. Hands rendered useless. Its wearer would be nothing.

Asterion never likes Ariadne's designs, so her criticisms are no surprise. But the overt horror and disgust in her eyes—that's a bit much, isn't it? And to top it all off, she even calls the bull-inspired features *unimaginative*. In front of *everybody*.

Ariadne had neglected to specify the mask's intended recipient during her presentation. Maybe she should have mentioned that detail. See what Asterion thinks of her *inhumanity* then.

But at least her presentation offers the court a reprieve from Asterion's lecturing.

And all isn't lost...

Because even as Father condemns the mask designs, making a show of his disappointment, Ariadne sees the glint of intrigue lurking in his eyes.

She is her father's daughter, after all.

⁜

THE ABSOLUTE RAGE-INDUCING AUDACITY.

Scrap paper? That's all Ariadne's designs are to Asterion. They must be. Otherwise why would she scribble over them with her inane *sky palace* designs?

Asterion prattles on about how the two of them can live there together like it's some magical storybook, about the garden that'll be just theirs, about the viewing platforms in the outer-shell that will frame the depths of space, about how there'll even be moving shortcuts and scenic routes, like a real-life version of that stupid game she's always trying to get Ariadne to play. Serpents and something. Whatever.

And the idiot-genius doesn't even realise that with every word, she's taking a sledgehammer to Ariadne's aspirations.

Because she doesn't realise that she's *done it*. That this is the monument Minos has been waiting for. The monument that will crown Asterion Architect-in-waiting.

She's just... *doodling*. Imagining. Exploring.

And she's won.

⁂

IT WAS ONLY EVER GOING to be a matter of time before Asterion got too big for her shamefully scuffed boots.

Laying out for the entire court their—in Asterion's opinion—collective and individual failings, in minute detail, is precisely the kind of public ineptitude Ariadne had hoped for from her. The murmuring of displeasure that builds during Asterion's diatribe on how civilians 'deserve better than a court of self-serving fools who care more about looking good than doing anything of substance', crescendos to curses from the court.

And that is what pure joy is made of.

Because if there's one thing Father cannot abide, it's public humiliation. Inflicted by his own child, no less.

When he orders Asterion to go to her chambers, his quiet snarl is more chilling than any bellow. Asterion, of course, is as oblivious as always. Only when he hisses, "Get out of my sight," does she shut her stupid mouth and do as she's told.

Predictably, Nanny goes after her. He's always preferred Asterion. He thinks he hides it well, but Ariadne sees straight through him.

She lingers outside their shared chambers to listen in as Nanny comforts Asterion through her tears of weakness. He's giving her some nonsense speech about her *not needing to change*. Peering from the shadows, through the partly open door, Ariadne can just about see the gift he gives her: some misshapen lump of rock.

He never gives Ariadne gifts. It's not like she wants an ugly piece of rock, anyway—but that's not the point, is it?

It's not *fair*.

Her gut-souring mix of anger and jealousy churns into resentment. And inspiration. She can incorporate Nanny's stupid keepsake into her amendments to Asterion's 'revolutionary' plans. It might take a bit of plagiarism... but who said winning had to be fair? Getting rid of your competition is an art of its own.

If Asterion can't anticipate an opponent's next move—if she can't then find her way out of her own Labyrinth—then that just proves she never deserved to be Architect in the first place.

Saving Minos from her sister's lofty, impractical ideals... well... it's really the only Righteous Path to pursue.

:
•

WHERE ASTERION's designs focus on manoeuvring through the Labyrinth like a game, Ariadne's proposed amendments are more... challenging.

There are aspects her sister had noted as needing further work: the mind-bending fungi byproducts that are liable to drift into the ventilation system; the picturesque ice forest that becomes a death trap at certain rotations. Ariadne sees no reason to do away with these aspects. Asterion should be flattered that Ariadne has the vision to turn her faults into features.

And, of course, she adds her own flourishes too.

Once ready, she presents her carefully constructed plan to Father. And only to Father.

A landmark in the sky. With a mythology built around it, with celebration and spectacle—especially something devastating and heroic—tourists will travel from across the Seven Suns to marvel at the Sky Labyrinth, putting Minos more visibly on the sky map. Where it should be.

Father's eyes light up. She has his attention.

A method of control. The intricate monument will offer Justice:

a perfect punishment for disruptive citizens. If fear of the Minotaur doesn't keep people on the Righteous Path, the Labyrinth
will end their path altogether.

The spark of interest in Father's eyes remains.

The trick. Channel that fear to the skies, and Minos will reap
the benefits. Every citizen will be required to wear torque-tech
(which Ariadne begrudgingly admits has its uses). They will be
told it protects them from the monster in the sky who feeds on
their energy. Their terror will generate far more energy than
hope or equilibrium ever would, thus ensuring a steady supply
of fuel.

Father's eyes glint like gemstones but give nothing away.

For this next part, she's counting on one of their shared
attributes: a vicious practicality. Ariadne presses on to present
her final proposal. The piece of the puzzle that brings it all
together.

A solution to the problem of Asterion. An accomplished but tact-
less offspring who—ad nauseum—points out the perceived
inadequacies of Minos, its court, and Father's decision-making...
will not do. If only there was somewhere she could be hidden
away?

"And the Nanny?" asks Father. That is his follow-up question. Not *what in the heavens are you thinking?* Not *how could you
propose something so monstrous?*

And he hadn't said *your* Nanny, but *the* Nanny. He, too, must
have noticed their servant's favouritism.

Ariadne holds her chin high. "He's too short-sighted and
sentimental to recognise the benefits of such a practical
outcome. He's a loose end. He needs tying up."

The silence that follows is perhaps the longest in the history
of sound. And in it, Ariadne stays rigid and strong. Not a flicker
of weakness, no hint of the apprehension souring her stomach.

Or of excitement that the prize of the throne could finally be within her reach.

Will he scold her for trying to pass off Asterion's work as her own? Will he focus on the cruelty instead of the practicality?

And then. Finally.

At Father's twisting smile of approval, Ariadne masks her inner glee with a subservient nod. For the first time, she knows how it feels to truly outmanoeuvre an opponent.

For the first time, she wins.

+
∴

By sixteen sun-orbits old...

The Sky Labyrinth has been in its geostationary orbit with Minos for five sun-orbits. The myth of the Minotaur is going strong. The citizens are generating unprecedented levels of fear-induced flame-energy. Or torque-energy, as it's also called. And Ariadne has grown bored of waiting for Father to die.

It's partly because she wants his throne, yes—but if she's honest, it's mostly because of his persistent indifference to any of the efforts she presents to the royal court in her official role as Architect-in-waiting. Which is... rude.

And. If he'd bothered to pay more attention to her, he might have noticed her slipping the undetectable poison into his food.

Ariadne becomes the Architect.

Well, *technically*, she's still Architect-in-waiting, because she's yet to marry, yet to find someone capable of solving her Labyrinth. (Which is the most euphemistic of euphemisms under the Seven Heavens.) She has the power to change the archaic nature of Minos's rules of succession now, but the tourists eat that old-fashioned bullshit right up.

What matters is that she is in charge, and Minos is hers to do with as she pleases.

+
∴

THE THREAT of being thrown into the Sky Labyrinth to face the judgement of a mythical beast is, evidently, an effective deterrent to crime. In fact, citizens have become so law-abiding, Minos has developed an intergalactic reputation for peace.

And Asterion had been so adamant that 'rehabilitation', not punishment, was the way to a better world. *Ha.*

But despite the benefits of such a reputation, it does mean they're sometimes in danger of running out of criminals to punish. Ariadne even has to invent a few complicated and obscure new laws, the kind it's impossible *not* to break occasionally, just to ensure they have the required thirteen criminals (and one Chosen Hero) per sun-orbit to meet the ceremonial quota.

Initially, Ariadne had expected the light in the sky to go out soon after the Labyrinth's creation—after which, of course, new Minotaurs could quietly be selected. When that didn't happen, she'd expected it to extinguish shortly after dispatching the first ceremonial fourteen, assuming that the incentivising challenge of killing the Minotaur would seal Asterion's fate. But if anything, the light of Asterion's Labyrinth has, sun-orbit after sun-orbit, grown defiantly stronger.

Knowing that her sister is still up there, obnoxiously surviving against every odd Ariadne could find to stack against her, gives her indigestion on a good day and the urge to throw silverware at her servants' heads on bad days. Because there's always the possibility that she'll finally solve the puzzle. That one day she'll show up and be the same Asterion, blurting out things she shouldn't. Things like: *I designed the Sky Labyrinth. It's me who should be your Architect.*

On some days, Ariadne tires of the court's endless demands for solutions to tedious infrastructure and civilian issues. Asterion would have had answers. Not only that, she wouldn't have cared how she'd conveyed them or whether the political puppets surrounding her approved of them. Occasionally, when Ariadne is particularly weary, it occurs to her that she's sent away the one other person under the Seven Suns who was born into the same life as hers. The only other person who might possibly understand the burden of its frustrations and expectations.

But then, of course, she pulls herself together.

And time ticks on...

Puffy-chested 'heroes' with a glut of confidence, and not much else, seek the challenge in the sky. Criminals fear it. Tourists flock to behold it.

No-one returns.

And her sister's light keeps on shining.

82

WHAT NOW?

The light has gone out above Minos...

The Minotaur is dead. Preparations for the celebrations are under way. And Ariadne's stomach hasn't stopped aching since the news.

The victor has found the Heart of the Minotaur. Does that also mean they saw the creature's true face?

The situation will need careful management, if so. If the victor has a problem with it... well... it won't be a reach to convince people that surviving the beast of the Labyrinth could turn someone's mind to mush. Then she can have them carted off to whatever facility deals with that sort of thing. And if that doesn't work, she can spin some tale about a heart attack triggered by Minotaur-induced stress.

Still, there *is* cause for celebration. The citizens' joy at being rid of the Minotaur will create a steady stream of fuel for a while. Minos's trading partners will be pleased.

Only time will tell whether the death of the deterrent in the sky results in increased lawlessness. It might even make Minos a little more interesting. And any uproar will generate more torque energy. There'll still be plenty of fuel to harvest.

But Ariadne will have to invent some new explanation for why the torques must still be worn. Torques must be worn at all times to stave off the return of the Minotaur. *Yes.* She can always send someone else up there if necessary, and blame the Minotaur's resurrection on the selfishness of disobedient citizens. The mass outrage will flood the fuel barrels to overflowing.

Ariadne has mythology on her side. The truth will be whatever she chooses it to be.

And if anyone's unconvinced... she'll have them in gravity-cuffs soon enough. Their ire will boost fuel production, too.

It really all is for the greater good.

For now, as she stands on her balcony staring up at the darkened relic in the sky, her stomach calms. She has a plan. She's in control. She has triumphed over Asterion.

And this time, her victory has a warming finality.

83

VICTORIOUS

If there's one thing Minosians know, it's how to throw an elaborate spectacle at short notice. Within hours, arrangements are in motion, the royal nuptials are scheduled for the following morning, and Ariadne's ceremonial gown is already fitted.

In her chamber's many mirrors, the raw obsidian crystals adorning her waistcoat catch the light, its labyrinthine details picked out in gold. The elegant cut of her golden tuxedo-gown is to die for. The tiered pleats of her coat-tail train glimmer, while the elaborate folds of her pearl-white shirt invite exploration.

Flanked by her polished ceremonial guards, seven each side, decked out in the ceremonial ruffles of royalty, Ariadne graces the drawbridge at the palace gates. She lets the masses gathered below catch glimpses of her. With the exuberant pulse of their torques, the crowds fill the night-time streets like a dark sea of jar-trapped fireflies.

Ariadne smiles to herself. All these people, here to appreciate her. And the return of the saviour who conquered the monster.

As the incoming sky-shuttle approaches the runway, against

a visually pleasing backdrop of amethyst night sky, Ariadne channels all her energy into maintaining the royal poise of her chin. She's already put her guards on high alert in case the so-called hero does anything unhinged.

"Even the strongest of hunters can lose their minds in the chase," she'd told them with believable empathy. "If the champion has unravelled, then it will be a kindness to extinguish their Flame."

A bit flowery, maybe, but her guards had bought it. Should the returning hero show any signs of having lost touch with reality, they'll be put swiftly out of their misery.

Ariadne's hand lingers at the hilt of her sword. It might be for ceremonial purposes, but she keeps it as sharp as her, frankly, dapper tuxedo-gowns. Just in case.

But never mind the potential chaos of whether the winner knows the hidden truth. Who triumphed in the impossible task?

Pistons hiss as, at the far end of the drawbridge, the shuttle touches down. Lava-furrows ignite, cascading between the shuttle and the palace, lighting up the entire monumental palace in the process. Fireworks—silver and gold—burst like a crown across the skies.

Ariadne's upper lip twitches. It is pretty. Crowd pleasing, too. Tourists are here for a show and—sure enough—the crowds roar their applause and capture the event with sparks and clicks and smoke-puffs from several galaxies-worth of devices.

Who is it?

Ariadne doesn't especially want to be promised to someone. But the wedding celebrations will be good for tourism, and give Minosians something to get over-excited about. And if Ariadne likes the look of her betrothed, she'll keep them around for some nocturnal fun until she gets bored of them. She'll see how long they can keep her entertained.

By her estimation, there are only two potential candidates

for who is beyond the shuttle doors. The Chosen Hero or the daughter of the Athenian Expanse.

When she'd summoned the Chosen Hero to her chambers for a pre-Labyrinth audience, it had become clear within minutes that the foundations of his character had either crumbled to nothing under the weight of his over-preened exterior, or had never existed in the first place.

Confidence isn't always attractive, she'd thought, as he'd boasted about how he was stronger and faster than any other. And when he had declared he would bring her the Minotaur's head as well as its heart, she'd had to rein him in straight away. She could do without that sort of over-enthusiasm, though she's reasonably certain that even if he did discover the truth, he wouldn't let such a detail obstruct his path to the throne.

She'd given him the beast trap to make him think he held her favour. But he's so tediously self-obsessed that, if he does turn out to be the victor, she might have to consider making his actual personality a crime.

He's pretty enough to be good for publicity, but it won't be long before some 'ailment' from the Labyrinth brings their union—and his life—to an abrupt and tragic end. She'll find a way to make her citizens adore him first, of course. That'll make their grief and the royal funeral ceremonies all the more potent. In the meantime, maybe he'll at least offer some temporary fun in her bedchamber. Though she suspects he will, indeed, prove to be 'faster than any other'.

The shuttle doors slide open and a cloud of engine fumes obscures the answer to her question as her citizens fall into a strange, reverent silence. The kind usually reserved only for her.

Ariadne raises her chin a little more. Right now, all she wants to know is with whom she's sharing her stage.

What if it's the daughter of the Athenian Expanse?

Handsome, strong, and reckless enough to be entertaining...

Automatic claims of greatness from her subjects and captives started to echo in their hollowness long ago. Out of respect or fear, they'll tell her up is down and forward is back, so long as they think it's what she wants to hear. Not the monster hunter, though. She'd been *dangerously flirtatious*. A treat for the eyes, too. Not to mention the Athenian connection. Perhaps Ariadne might wring some political advantage from the relationship, too.

Yes, she'll do. So long as she doesn't do anything stupid. Under that bravado, under that chip on her shoulder, there's a moral compass that—if she's not careful—might lead the monster hunter to an unfortunate end in a disused mineshaft.

The fumes part.

Finally.

Blood-covered and grime-smeared, the brooding, dashing daughter of the Athenian Expanse steps forward.

Oh, *goody.*

The monster hunter's features are difficult to read from across the drawbridge. Her arms hang at her sides, but her back is straight, her posture taut. Defiant, almost.

In a sea of sparkling celebration, the cheering crowds might greet the monster hunter as though she's perfection personified, but Ariadne sees the truth. A warrior broken by the horrors of battle. A masterpiece of sculpted marble, threaded with fault lines threatening to crack.

Not to worry. Ariadne will piece her back together—into the shape of her choosing.

"The Labyrinth has given you back to us." Ariadne's opening declaration rings out across the ocean of spectators, silencing her Minosian audience as tourist translators convey her words into so many languages, the clash is deafening.

The Minotaur killer starts across the drawbridge. Her movements are a little stiff—not quite limping, but not as limber as she was before—even in gravity-cuffs.

"You have succeeded where so many have failed," Ariadne continues, drawing out her words to accompany the hunter's slow procession towards her.

Is a bit of enthusiasm in her step too much to ask?

Though, at least it gives Ariadne time to take her in. Thank the heavens for astro-safe whisper-mesh, allowing the Athenian to make the journey from the skies to Minos with her accomplished contours on show.

Those arms... She'd invite being as tight to those muscles as the hunter's whisper-mesh. Three-quarter length trousers ending just below her knees frame notable calf muscles...

With all the citizens' torques sparking, it's only now Ariadne notices the glowing blue perforation in the hunter's lower leg.

Interesting.

It's become a fun game, giving the noble ones redundant tools to 'help' them on their journey; making them think they alone are special enough to win her favour. Ariadne had only kept the strange thread, seized from some off-world visitor by skyport control, because it looked pretty. But evidently the hunter has put it to good use.

Soon, Ariadne will put her to good use, too.

"On behalf of the citizens of Minos, I thank you for saving us from the terror in the skies."

In the sea of fireflies, the crowds cheer. Only strides away now, the monster hunter's knuckles tighten around the hilt of her holstered sword, arm muscles on parade. There's a tremor in the light of her torque. Is it exhaustion, or something more combative?

The Athenian doesn't puff out her chest. She doesn't play to the crowds. She stops only a stride away from Ariadne, and her eyes—unblinking, stormy, and as shimmering as precious stones—lock with hers.

No-one dares look at her like that.

Ariadne doesn't know whether to be turned on or terrified. Her body shivers at the prolonged eye contact.

"Your Minosian Flame burns bright." She presses on with her pre-rehearsed bullshit. "You have proven yourself worthy of my hand. Worthy of being a ruler of Minos."

Still the hunter's face shows no flicker of emotion. Did the oaf miss the Athenian translation? Or has her ordeal in the skies made her dim?

The crowds are waiting. *Ariadne* is damn well waiting.

Unsettled whispers from the crowds below are joined by the awkward creak of armour from the guards either side of her.

Ariadne clenches her teeth. Would it kill the monster hunter to look happy about the honour she's being granted?

What lies beyond that stony mask?

Does she know the truth?

A mischievous glimmer enters the Athenian's eyes.

What is she playing at? Is she making Ariadne *wait*?

A dangerous game, indeed.

Finally, the Athenian speaks. Her voice is deep, lyrical and sweet. It takes only a moment for Ariadne's translation tincture to heat behind her ears, just as translator voices vie for position in the crowds.

"I did as you asked, Princess."

Ariadne's teeth unclench. If the Athenian can still be roguish, it likely means she departed the Sky Labyrinth content in the belief that she's righted a wrong of the universe. Perhaps she even considers herself deserving of the prize of Ariadne's hand in marriage, a place by her throne, and in her bed.

Ariadne can work with that.

As attendants descend on the monster hunter and guide her away to be scrubbed and suitably prepared for a more intimate royal introduction, Ariadne maintains her perfect mask of regal propriety. But behind it, she's already imagining how she'll put those muscles and that steely determination to excellent use.

84

BETROTHED

In her chambers, Ariadne admires her many reflections. Her servants fuss over her, but their stream of compulsory compliments annoy her less than usual. She does look pretty-handsome. There's no denying it. Her gold, black, diamond and pearl-effect garments hug her frame in ways that should set the heart of even the most stoic monster hunter racing. Her torque sparks with the anticipation.

Three heavy knocks thud against her chamber door.

It is time.

Tradition dictates that the night before the wedding, the Architect-in-waiting and her betrothed are to give themselves to each other. They must remain undisturbed until sunrise, when the binding ceremony will take place.

Ariadne dismisses her servants, and they depart hastily via their hidden entrance.

Once alone, Ariadne swiftly reapplies the linguistic tincture behind her ears and around her mouth, before approaching her chamber door, the tiered pleats of her coat-tail train trailing behind her.

Keeping one hand on the hilt of her ceremonial sword, she

answers the three knocks with three of her own. The door responds automatically, sliding into the wall.

The monster hunter's gleaming waistcoat buttons and glistening black hair greet her. The saviour of Minos is no longer ingrained with blood and grime; the servants have scrubbed her clean. Her face is unreadable, her back rigid—but she's fidgeting, tugging at her silver royal sash that's cutting across her snugly tailored charcoal waistcoat and jacket.

Ariadne drinks her in. Her coat-tails reach to mid-thigh. The knees of her graphite breeches are decorated with a silver embroidered band. Ariadne's fingers twitch, itching to grip the flesh beneath the finery.

But those thoughts are somewhat soured. Because, below the breeches and the strange glow of thread embedded in the Athenian's lower leg, are not the shiny buckled brogues Ariadne had expected but a pair of ugly, un-polished boots. And lumped beside them is a tattered, grotty satchel, some stupid tourist-tat stuffed toy dangling from its strap.

Not only that, the hunter's hand is bandaged, which is unsightly.

The chief servant of ceremonies has a lot to answer for when Ariadne next sees them. But at least the injuries can be pointed to as further proof of the monster hunter's dedication to Ariadne, and to Minos. And while her betrothed is dashing enough to display in public, she won't be outshining Ariadne at the altar.

The saviour of Minos is giving Ariadne's attire—or the hints to what lies beneath it—a similar once-over. Her face is impassive, but her sparking torque betrays her efforts to play it cool. There's the faintest glimmer in her eyes, but whether it's mischief, or merely a reflection of Ariadne's torque and attire, is unclear.

"You've been polished." Ariadne injects a dose of coyness

into her smile; the monster hunter seems like the type to go for that sort of thing.

But her only response is an unimpressed eyebrow raise.

"As I told your servant of ceremonies—" She speaks! Her lyrical Athenian strokes Ariadne's ears, heating the translation tincture and echoing back to her in Minosian. "—I can wash my damn self."

Stoic *and* feisty? A bold mix.

Her betrothed steps forward as though expecting Ariadne to move aside and let her in—but Ariadne blocks her path.

"I have no doubt, Monster Hunter—"

"My name is Theseus." The Athenian maintains her cool stoicism, despite their faces now being within leaning distance of each other. "In case you've forgotten."

There's that bite Ariadne remembers. She's not certain whether to reward or punish it. If anyone else dared speak to her like that, they'd be on a one-way trip to the Sky Labyrinth.

With all things considered... She lets it slide. For now.

The monster hunter's torque sparks, just enough to be intriguing. *What is fuelling your Flame?*

"Theseus. Daughter of the Athenian Expanse." Ariadne's gaze flits between the Athenian's eyes and her mouth. "It is customary to greet your betrothed with complimentary remarks before they allow you into their chambers."

"You look..." At the Athenian's slow, assessing once-over, Ariadne's heart knocks as loud as a ceremonial summons. Finally, the monster hunter blinks. "...shiny."

"Yes." Assuming a compliment, Ariadne steps aside in invitation... but as her betrothed crosses the threshold, Ariadne hesitates. *Was* that a compliment?

The door slides shut behind them. The monster hunter flinches.

"Ready for battle, I see." Ariadne's teasing tone is intended to lighten the mood, but the monster hunter merely grunts, dropping her grimy satchel in the middle of the polished floor. Still, Ariadne can't help admiring the swell of the hunter's biceps as her hand rests on the hilt of her own ceremonial sword.

Ariadne designed the sword herself. Unlike her own sword, her betrothed's is gleaming metal with blunt edges and a blade that retracts into the hilt upon impact: it's all looks and no substance.

"I hardly recognised you without gravity-cuffs." Ariadne offers her best flirtatious smile as the monster hunter stares from the throne to the expansive terrace beyond the tall windows. In response, she gets... nothing. And then even less as the Athenian meanders over to the window.

Is she *avoiding* her?

Ariadne buries a sigh of frustration. It won't stay buried for long, however. There's a fine line between a challenge and tedious hard work. Perhaps the monster hunter is as dense as osmium: pretty to look at, but difficult to work with? Bad luck for her if so. Being attractive will only get her so far.

Time to cut to the chase.

"Tomorrow we are to be wed." Coy but calm. A calculated edge of nervousness. Perfect. "Does that please you?"

It's impossible to interpret the crackle of sparks in the monster hunter's torque, reflected in the window. From her comments during their pre-Labyrinth encounter, Ariadne would guess the daughter of the Athenian Expanse to be suffering an attack of moral ambivalence about winning a princess as a prize. Or has her stint in the Labyrinth changed things?

"Anything for my princess." The hunter's words are so quiet, Ariadne's not even sure she hears them correctly—but whatever they are, they sound like a promise. Which is all very well, but the sudden leap from stoic to—well, whatever *this* is... it's a bit too... intimate. And it's making Ariadne itch.

She presses on. She didn't get dressed up like this for nothing.

"Are you aware of our customs?" she asks, as gentle as pretence requires. "I assume you have been informed...?"

The Athenian swallows. "They said something... euphemistic. I think I got the gist of it."

She's *still* staring out of the window. What's so interesting? Is she captivated by Ariadne's royal sky-motor? Or, after all that smouldering confidence and straining against gravity-cuffs... is the great Monster Hunter *nervous*?

How... disappointing.

But there's hope yet. If she treads carefully, perhaps Ariadne can coax that roguish champion back out of her shell.

"It's unique," she says, drifting closer to her betrothed. "I told the engineers I wanted a mode of transport like no-one else's. Something that would dazzle." And they had met her specifications. With its golden shell as shiny as a mirror, her oversized sky-motor never fails to make an entrance. She pauses within arm's reach. "Would you like to go for a ride?"

Maybe that'll loosen her up.

She's close enough to the tailored jacket shaped to admirable muscles, that when the Athenian turns to her, Ariadne sees her pupils dilate. Sapphire lost to an oil spill. Her gaze washes over Ariadne's face; and the confirmation of her attraction pulses through Ariadne with a thrilled shiver.

That's more like it.

She'll have the monster hunter between silken sheets soon enough. Maybe if she plays a bit more at being the blushing, bashful bride, it'll hurry things along.

"In Minos, it is tradition..." She clears her throat, shy enough to keep the Athenian's gaze on her, "...to consummate the marriage the night before the wedding." Euphemisms are all well and good, but there's no harm in spelling things out.

The Athenian's eyes narrow. "I assume that is why I was to be so thoroughly scrubbed."

Ariadne is within an arm's reach and the monster hunter isn't backing away. Her torque is sparking, in fact. And, if Ariadne's not mistaken, the hunter keeps looking at her mouth, her gaze fixing on Ariadne's face like she's finally realised she can't get enough of her perfect form.

As an excuse to close the distance, Ariadne reaches boldly for the coin-like pendant hanging below the hunter's open collar. *That* gets her torque flaring, and Ariadne knows a gasp when she hears one.

Not so impassive now, are you, Monster Hunter?

And still, the hunter doesn't retreat.

Ariadne takes her time inspecting the pendant. Even that needs a polish. Its dull surface is more like the Athenian's scuffed boots than any precious metal.

"My friend is looking for me," says the Athenian, looking down at the pendant. "She'll be here soon."

What is she blathering about?

Half turning back to the window, the Athenian's gaze returns to the amethyst sky and the disc of shadow that now hangs there. Ariadne's jaw clenches. Another change of tactic, then...

"It must have been so difficult up there. You must have been terribly afraid." Ariadne bridges their distance with a sympathetic hand on her solid forearm. The monster hunter observes her hand, before returning her gaze to the sky.

"Isn't that the point?" Her words are almost a whisper. Ariadne should probably have an answer, but before she can come up with something noble, the Athenian continues, softly: "How do you feel?"

What?

The question jams the mechanisms within Ariadne's brain. The words themselves were clear enough—but what in all the heavens does she mean? How does Ariadne *feel*? Why in the ever-expanding heavens would she need to know such information? Is she testing Ariadne? Probing for weakness?

"Now that the Minotaur is gone," the monster hunter clarifies. "How do you feel?"

Does she know something? Or is she just one of those people who—*urgh*—asks about feelings? Perhaps it's not such a bizarre question, given the Minotaur's lengthy and well-publicised reign of terror. But it's still an unsettling one.

The monster hunter watches her closely. The *audacity*. Who does she think is in charge here?

How does she feel?

Her thoughts keep ticking over on it, whether she wants them to or not. So many voyagers have tried and failed in the Labyrinth. So *surprised* might be one word for it. *Disappointed*, too. Now that the game she's been playing with her sibling is over.

But she can't trust the monster hunter. Ariadne cannot be anything other than an exemplary Architect. Which is fine. No problem... Spinning truths and sculpting the marble of her personality and appearance into winning form is what she's been doing since childhood.

"I am relieved that Minos is free of its tyrant," she says, inching closer to her prize: close enough to lean in and kiss her, or recoil and slap her, depending on how this plays out.

The monster hunter doesn't even blink. Other than a single spark of her torque, she doesn't react at all.

"If you had to do it all over again, would you choose the same path?" The Athenian's voice is even, giving nothing away, but her torque...

It's sparking up a storm. And yet, her gaze holds none of the desire and reverence Ariadne had expected. It's more like anger. Frustration, perhaps, but tempered with something... gentle?

Ariadne huffs at the question. Who does this oaf think she is? She's not Ariadne's equal, she's decoration. She's here to warm Ariadne's bed and look good on her arm. Nothing more.

She's about to tell her as much, too; to let her mask slip. But as a bandaged hand reaches out to trace Ariadne's cheek, all words evaporate. Ariadne has spent her life reading people, understanding how they tick and manipulating them to her advantage. But she has no idea how to play *this* game.

The way she's looking at her—half gazing, half trying to solve a riddle in Ariadne's features—there's admiration and warmth.

Ariadne has never had anyone look at her like that. Her insides squirm. Which is... not the *worst* feeling...?

Oh, enough with this monumental nonsense.

"I'm content with my choices," Ariadne grits out, more breathily than she'd intended.

Why is the Athenian looking at her like that? And, for that matter, why are they both still clothed? And why is she being forced into stupid conversations about her *feelings*?

Time to get things back on track.

"I am thankful my path converges with yours," she says, liable to give herself a cavity, as she reaches to push a stray lock of inky hair behind the monster hunter's ear.

But a strong hand grasps her wrist—

Ariadne's heart and stomach leap for the Sky Labyrinth. A gasp exits her lips. She should remind the monster hunter of her place in the natural order—

But as capable fingers tighten about her wrist... Ariadne doesn't hate it.

The Athenian's crackling torque gives her hope. So does the electricity dancing in her oil-spill eyes as her gaze flits to her mouth. Ariadne's entire body sparks with it. Her own torque is heating inline with her fluttering anticipation.

"Am I to claim my prize now, Princess?" The Athenian's voice is rough as gravel.

Oh, *yes*. That's more like it. Ariadne leans closer, closing her eyes. Ready.

And waiting...

But nothing happens.

She opens her eyes.

Sexually frustrating Minosian Royalty isn't officially a crime, but Ariadne will make it one. But before she can throw a ceremonial sword about it, the Athenian's hands are at her waist, turning her to face the balcony window.

Ariadne exhales, just as suddenly. The monster hunter pressed deliciously against her back is... a surprise. Not a bad one, but...

"Do betrothed not kiss in your world, Monster Hunter?" Heavens above, she can hardly catch her breath. Keen to move this game to the next level, she reaches behind her, stroking up the smooth fabric tight to her conquest-to-be's muscular leg, seeking the apex between her thighs. But her wrist is caught before she reaches her target.

"Tell me, *Architect*..." The Athenian's breath is hot against her ear. "When you look in the mirror... who do you see?"

Dread slinks down Ariadne's spine. Her voice, there's a strain to it. She grabs for her sword—but a stronger hand closes around her wrist. Both wrists gripped, she struggles against the hold... Is this what gravity-cuffs feel like?

"Do you see her face?"

Ariadne's breath stumbles from her at the hunter's Minosian growl. *She knows.*

"Or do you only see the monster in your own?"

For an endless moment, the cool fingers of dread squeeze about Ariadne's chest. Her torque light trembles and the hunter's sparks, sharp and unforgiving.

But then the hunter gasps, her features in the window's reflection transforming to an inexplicably bright and genuine smile; aimed not at Ariadne, but at the sky.

Ariadne's stomach sinks.

Because where the void of the Labyrinth had overshadowed the sky, a beacon of colour is flaring to life. Labyrinthine stripes splutter across the dark sphere before erupting into unapologetic vibrancy.

But before Ariadne can understand the implications, there's a sharp pinch at her neck, a coolness flooding under her skin. Within a dozen stampeding heartbeats, it drags her beneath waves of darkness, turning her world to shadow.

PART XI

LOOSE ENDS

85

MIGHTY
ASTERION

An undertow of darkness.

Time is elastic... stretched and tangled.

A sudden rush—

A monumental gasp— A lungful of air—

Every cell awakens, every capillary refills... Extremities revive, and Asterion's shoulders levitate from the ground, as—beneath her—the world-engine blazes into flaming blue illumination.

Mechanisms lurch back into motion. Vibrant lava scalds through the cooled stone as the lava-gullies begin to flow, as her own veins pulse hotly into wakefulness.

If she and the Sky Labyrinth weren't so viscerally linked, she'd think it all a heavy-handed metaphor.

The bull mask lies next to her, its empty eyes staring, its braces broken, and Asterion exhales her relief.

She's free of it. Finally.

And—even more impossibly—she's alive.

With shaking, hoof-free hands, she fumbles beneath her ripped shirt to where the spear had pierced right through her. No... it had punched— stabbed—smashed: at exactly the point where a glowing line of illumi-thread now holds her torn flesh together, thrumming in time with her heartbeat.

Which is... unexpected, to say the least.

Her chest aches and buzzes with a hive of healing activity. She can feel her skin absorbing the thread, *feel* its industrious warmth sinking deep within her flesh, repairing ruptured veins, knitting torn muscle back together, returning her every atom to its rightful place.

It's a strange sensation... pressure butting up against pain... but she'd rather this than to feel nothing, to *be* nothing...

"Theseus?" Asterion whispers.

Did she do this?

Asterion thumbs the haphazard stitching holding her together. Theseus will never impress a master surgeon, nor a seamstress, but Asterion sure as the heavens isn't complaining.

Where did Theseus get the thread? Wasn't it all lost to flame?

Where is Theseus?

Asterion strains to look around the chamber, squinting against the vibrant blue of the world-engine platform, but she's thwarted by a sweeping wave of dizziness.

She takes a few careful breaths. And then a whole host more. Because she can. Because she *should*. She might have risen like a bewildered phoenix, but any creature that's had the good fortune to return from ashes should probably take it easy for at least a minute.

Once the frenetic buzzing in her cells has subsided to a background hum, once dizziness makes way for a basic level of sure-footedness, Asterion hazards to her feet.

There's a stillness in the Labyrinth, an emptiness, that tells her she's alone here. If her chest weren't already aching, it would start doing so now.

The circular hatch that had opened at the end of the glowing bridge of the world-engine, the shortcut to the outer gatehouse, is now closed.

Asterion's breath lodges in her throat.

The airlock failsafes mean that any internal entrances to the outer gatehouse must be sealed shut before the external door will open. That the hatch is closed... well... that means someone has left via the gatehouse. *Someone* has used her heart-stone and exited this place.

The pool of her own blood congealed across the platform turns her stomach. But it's the dark smudge further back, near the edge of the platform that escalates her panic, strobing around her in a tangle of world-engine energy.

The golden man must have survived long enough to launch his deadly attack... but her wounds have been stitched...

That can only mean Theseus survived, too.

But—Asterion tries to swallow her dread—the golden man has survived so many things... She needs to know. Whose is the blood at the platform edge?

"Theseus...?" Her throat is so dry, she can barely form the word. Palm pressed to her chest, Asterion focuses her sights beyond the flaming electricity of the platform and peers over the edge, along its horizontal.

And there is her answer.

From this perspective, Minos's Chosen Hero looks pinned to the wall; limbs skewed awkwardly against the labyrinthine lava-gullies. Theseus must have shoved him out of the platform's gravity, only for him to plummet to the 'base' of the column.

Her heart rate slows to a jog, the chamber calming as Asterion gasps her relief.

Theseus made it out. She escaped.

That's... good.

But...

Asterion's raw heartache tests her internal integrity. Theseus can't have known the illumi-thread would work, but she must have hoped. Did she stay with Asterion for a time, waiting to see if her impossible efforts would work? Did she leave believing Asterion was dead? Would she have stayed if she'd known otherwise? Or did she save Asterion's life only to leave her behind?

Asterion presses where her chest aches the most, unable to differentiate hurt from healing.

Even if Theseus had changed her mind, would Asterion have let her stay? In this world that always threatens death...

She steels herself.

Theseus is gone.

That was always the plan.

It's a good thing. It means she's safe.

And yet... it feels like she's taken a part of Asterion with her. It's illogical, this sense of *lacking*, of being less than she was before, yet in other ways stronger, bolstered, seen and heard... How can all those things exist at once? How can she regret everything and nothing?

Asterion rubs her sternum. If these are the feelings Theseus warned her about, maybe she should have listened.

But no.

She hasn't a single doubt. If she had to do it all over again, she would. Even though it hurts to lose her, Asterion is glad for the pain. It means she got to be with Theseus for a time. Just as the Labyrinth will keep on ticking, Asterion will, too. Even if everything is a little off-kilter. And Theseus, wherever she is, will be out there making the galaxies *better*.

True as all of that might be, it doesn't resonate yet. She'll get there. In time, she'll appreciate that Theseus was here and why she had to go. For now, though... it doesn't half fucking hurt.

And there's no shame in the tears that burst from her. She presses her stitches, trying to distract herself with the pain or from it. She lets the sorrow settle in her veins. It hurts because it matters.

But her sobs dampen...

Because there's something... different...

Asterion wipes her eyes.

Further along the platform, near the closed exit hatch, is something she hadn't previously noticed with her eyes startled by the electric blue of the world-engine.

She ventures closer. Only when her focus adjusts fully to looking past the pulsing platform light does she understand what she's seeing.

Charcoal markings. Four sets of scrawled images, all in Theseus's signature stick-figure style. The stick figures look *ridiculous.* Each stick-figure Asterion has freckles, while Theseus has a stick-sword and a daft look that may or may not be intentional. She's taken some creative licence with both their muscles, too.

And Asterion can't help smiling, even before she's interpreted what they mean.

The drawings start with a large Minoglyph question mark, which leads to a fork in the road: four different options.

One path leads to just Asterion, at the centre of a circle networked with labyrinthine markings: *Asterion alone in the Sky Labyrinth.*

The next shows her and Theseus side by side, holding stick-figure hands inside a circle: *Asterion and Theseus together in the Labyrinth.*

Asterion's breath catches. Theseus would stay here with her? Theseus would choose that life, for her?

The third depicts them further apart, with no circle around them: *Freedom from the Labyrinth, but separate?* That one makes her stomach knot.

The fourth and final path: Asterion and Theseus side by side again, holding hands. Except this time, there's no circle around them, only stars.

Asterion and Theseus, free from the Labyrinth. Experiencing the stars together?

A new way forward.

An adventure.

Excitement blossoms in Asterion's chest, pulsing in time with the lights of the Labyrinth before settling into a steady, confident *whoosh... whoosh... whoosh...*

Theseus wouldn't have left these here if she didn't intend to return, would she? It's not clear when that might be—but when she does, Asterion will be ready.

There's no need for deliberation. Not anymore. She might be no less fearful of what's out there in the vast unknown... but the certainty resonates in her chest, as strongly as the illumi-thread pulling her organs back into alignment: she wants a better world. She'll make one, if she has to.

Minos has been the monster in her thoughts for so long. It's time she unmasks it. She wants to fix what is broken. Not just in blueprints and theories. Not just for herself. Minos might have given up on her, but that doesn't mean she should give up on Minos. Her homeworld might think her a monster, but perhaps it's time she showed them she's not.

Heavens above, she can feel her inner flame burning, and the Labyrinth glows all the brighter for it.

In the past, her downfall has been in not seeing the monsters lurking in the shadows and in plain sight. It's fortuitous, then, that the warrior who wants her, who's suggesting they tackle the worlds beyond these walls together, just so happens to be a mighty monster hunter.

86

SKYWARD
THESEUS

I t would be really fucking stupid to die right now.

But it's not like this is the first time Theseus has challenged gravity to a duel. Though it might be the first time she's cared quite this much about the outcome. Also, if she can help it, she'd rather not make an epic tit of herself.

Fuelled by the kind of warm and fuzzy thoughts she would previously have fought off with a sword, she refuses to let something as prosaic as gravity versus machinery be the end of her journey.

"Come on, come on—" She grips the sky-motor's steering wheel so hard her spear-impaled palm starts bleeding into her bandage.

Miles below, Planet Minos is a dark, light-veined mass. She's already made it through the stratosphere... she's almost within reach of the Sky Labyrinth...

Just a little further...

At least she and Princess Ariadne—who is currently unconscious in the back seat, anchored by a safety harness and nestled among her own excess of golden fabric—have the atmosphere and oxygen provided by their astro-helmets. Not that that'll be much use if this lump of metal falls from the sky.

Ariadne's gleaming sky-motor docked right outside her chamber window had made the mad dash to the skies almost too easy. And it turns out that when an entire world reveres you —rightly or wrongly—for saving them from a terrifying, if fictional, Minotaur, not even sky-control will ask too many questions if you commandeer a princess's sky-motor for an impromptu flight to the stars.

Unfortunately, Ariadne's custom sky-motor, being very much looks over substance, is—*evidently*—not built for journeys to the stratosphere and beyond.

Which explains why the three tonnes of supposed Minosian-engineered perfection is juddering and croaking...

Dash gauges and alarms throw blaring tantrums as the sky-motor stalls, yanking the power out of her steering and rendering the controls heavy. In the throes of shutting down, without momentum, gravity pulls at the motor's tail.

Okay, maybe it's time to worry a little...

Come on, just a bit further...

Don't flood the engine...

Theseus eases off the controls, counting five long seconds...

"We're going to make it," she tells the Minotaur plushie sitting on the dash, its button eyes staring out of the cockpit into space.

Lit up with stripes of colourful, cosmic light, the Sky Labyrinth is tauntingly close.

Theseus's chest tightens with tears.

If the Labyrinth is lit up, that means Asti is alive.

She hopes Asterion can forgive her for leaving her alone in the choking darkness of the powered-down Labyrinth.

Theseus swallows against the lump in her throat and the

memory of herself huddled over Asterion's body, Hero's footsteps thudding closer through the dark.

Something in her had snapped, then, bellowing up from the darkest part of her with the kind of throat-scoring scream that could rip the heavens in two. She'd flung her sword without even looking.

A sickening crunch. A single exhale. A distant thud. In the end, that was all the send-off the universe had cared to give Minos's Chosen Hero.

Her heart had felt like it hadn't just broken, but burst into shards, tearing her apart from the inside. In that moment, she had known she would do anything for Asterion. If she could have dug the thread from her own flesh and stitched it into hers she would.

And then...

An idea had sparked.

She'd known it was probably too late. But she had to *try*.

She'd hurtled across the darkened, inert platform of Asterion's world-engine, through the circular hatch and into the gatehouse, the gravitational flip barely a background detail as she'd launched herself at the external gateway.

With shaking hands, she'd reached into the heart-stone shaped hollow and reclaimed the off-cut of luminous thread she'd left there so long ago now, oblivious to its potential.

And now the Sky Labyrinth is lighting up the heavens.

Asterion is alive.

But that doesn't mean she's okay, or that she's safe. Which is why a malfunctioning sky-motor won't fucking do.

Theseus finally revs the engine—

"We've got this." No-one needs to know she's talking to a soft toy.

The dash gauges power up, revitalised, as—

With a splutter—*yes!*—the sky-motor conquers its fight against gravity, summiting against the odds.

Thank the Seven fucking Heavens.

Now—beyond its functional capabilities, beyond the Minosian atmosphere—the sky-motor is adrift. And Theseus would be too, if not for her safety harness.

From here, it should be smooth sailing, so long as she can steer this damn thing.

The steering defiantly pulls left, the hull pitching downward. It's taking all Theseus's strength to keep them on course. Those damn gauges are blinking again, alarms bleating warnings she's already well aware of.

But the Sky Labyrinth must sense her approach, because the entrance runway is rolling out to greet her...

Just. Don't. Crash.

Though that might be a challenge given that the Labyrinth's auto-magnetism is reeling her in, accelerating the momentum of this glorified tin can.

One arm straining to keep the steering in line, Theseus strikes the landing gear release. The gears grind, and don't do much else.

Fuck's sake. Where's a good mechanic when you need one?

She tries again, with the same result.

Great. Looks like she'll be putting her crash-landing skills to nail-biting good use.

Still wrestling the steering, she swivels the engines, blasting them forward to slow their approach to the runway as, at the far end, the Labyrinth's monumental gateway opens.

As it always has, the Minotaur statue looms at the gateway's apex, its otherworldly glare aimed at all who approach.

But that's not what has Theseus's exhale whispering against her invisi-visor. Because standing in the mouth of the Labyrinth is a lone figure in an astro-helmet, a blur of glowing blue pulsing in the centre of her chest.

A giddy laugh of pure glee erupts from Theseus.

She's alive.

And she's upright, standing strong.

She's even waving.

"Woohoo, yeah!" Theseus punches the air. She throws a grin over her shoulder, but unconscious Princess Ariadne isn't the most appreciative audience, so she redirects her joy to fist-bump the button-eyed Minotaur plushie.

The hull dips. The steering jerks—

"Shit!" Hastily, Theseus rebalances the sky-motor with the reverse thrusters.

Almost there.

She just needs to take the heat out of the landing...

87

THESEUS AND THE STARS
ASTERION

A short while ago...

In the Labyrinth gatehouse, Asterion checks her astro-helmet to ensure her missed breaths are only from her holding them rather than a technical malfunction. She's chosen an open-fronted helmet from the stash in her workshop, complete with invisi-visor and protective whisper-mesh.

She's never been in here without the bull mask before. Even with the mask, she'd never lingered for fear the external gate might open without warning and suck her out into space.

But now... now that she's free from the mask, she can explore this vaulted chamber with new eyes. She holds out her hand, letting the multicoloured shafts of light from the external shell dance across her palm: a whimsical detail dreamed up by her younger self. She's pleased, too, that her constellation designs have survived.

But it's not long before her exploration evolves to nervous pacing. It's an excited kind of nervousness, though. Theseus will be here soon.

From the viewing platform further along the labyrinth path,

she'd seen a sky-motor soar beyond the Minosian stratosphere, its trajectory distinctly on course for the Sky Labyrinth. And her heart has been beating excitedly ever since.

She rubs her sternum and takes a breath. Probably best to not challenge her death-defying stitches too much.

Finally, the gatehouse's internal doors close, as they're designed to before the outer gate can open. The vehicle must be preparing to dock.

Please be Theseus. Please be Theseus.

Slowly, purposefully, the two doors of the gargantuan outer gate slide open. The doors' height is a bit excessive for her tastes; either someone interfered with her original designs, or her youthful self had been rather exuberant with the measurements.

The open gateway frames the skyscape and all the epic, endless possibilities within it. Including a gleaming eyesore of a renegade sky-motor that *categorically* should not be all the way out here, weaving haphazardly toward the Labyrinth's runway.

This crime against good taste can only have been dreamed up by one person.

But does that mean Ariadne is the one at the helm?

Ariadne was never interested in the fine details of engineering, but even she would have the sense to know that such a vehicle has no business being beyond the stratosphere.

There's only one person who would try to fly that thing up here...

Well...

That's Theseus's silhouette wrangling the controls, isn't it?

The sky-motor crunches down—

Asterion's legs twitch, like they want to throw her at the wreckage grinding along the runway. But at the sky-motor's current speed and rate of deceleration... she just needs to stay put beneath the gateway arch... and wait.

The hissing pile of metal grinds to a stop just metres from her.

That's one way to land a sky-motor.

Asterion rushes toward the vehicle, but before she can reach the partly buckled side hatch, Theseus is already tumbling out of it. And within a dozen heartbeats, she's on her feet.

Theseus can stand.

She can run.

She's running to Asterion.

It's only a short distance, but still too far. Though close enough to find relief in Theseus's beaming grin.

As they collide, Theseus absorbs the impact as though instinctively cushioning her. Theseus wraps her arms around her, pulling her even closer, and everything clicks into place. Her inner mechanisms are in alignment; her inner cogs have found their grooves.

"Are you hurt?" Asterion leans back to inspect her, but Theseus steps closer, threading their fingers together.

"Not anymore," she says, her eyes bright with tears. She grins, even as tears stream down her cheeks and flitter against her invisi-visor as she leans close enough for their astro-helmets to clunk together.

It only makes them both smile.

Asterion reaches through Theseus's invisi-visor to wipe away her tears, and Theseus takes over the task herself. "It must be the altitude," she protests. "Or the crash landing, or..." She huffs, pressing the heels of her palms to her eyes. She's so cute when she's embarrassed. "I just need you to remember that I'm a tough monster hunter, okay?"

Asterion nods, seriously. "And I'm a terrifying monster."

Theseus's laugh is sudden and genuine, her eyes sparkling in the starlight. The all-consuming warmth in Asterion's chest isn't just from healing anymore.

As their noses touch, their invisi-visors connect, keeping them oxygenated and safe. Thank the heavens for open-faced astro-helmets!

As they take a moment to breathe together, basking in the calm after all the chaos, Theseus's breath caresses Asterion's lips perfectly. When their mouths meet it's gentle... tender but certain, and Asterion's senses soar higher than a sky-ship as she —*finally*—discovers the dizzying, path-altering feeling of kissing Theseus, of being kissed *by* Theseus, against a backdrop of stars.

88

JUSTICE

PRINCESS ARIADNE

E ven before her groggy eyes open, Ariadne is certain she doesn't want to find out what happens next.

The groans and gripes of her surroundings are strange to her ears. Everything reeks of damp and metal. When she reluctantly opens her eyes, she can hardly see.

Until there are bulbous eyes and sabre fangs—

"What...?"

A growl echoes around her. Her body lurches as she tries to bolt upright, to properly assess whatever game the idiot monster hunter is playing, but her head is so heavy she can hardly move it.

What kind of nightmare is this?

No. No, no, no—

Her heart thumps hard enough to vibrate her breath. Each exhalation returns to her as something ridiculous... animalistic.

"No!"

A sudden moo-grunt reverberates the air around her face. She reaches to touch her cheeks, but her hands are as useless as
—*no, no, no, no, this had better be a joke...*

Hooves?

The last thing she recalls is the sting at her neck. Before that, she'd been in the Athenian's grip...

The monster hunter had called *her* a monster...

The Labyrinth had burst back into life, illuminating the sky...

Which means...

Asterion is alive?

How?

Instinctively, Ariadne looks up to check the sky. But the movement unbalances her, squeezing at her neck, anchoring her to the ground, staring at the dead-eyed fang-fish, its skeletal form lying lifeless on the stone floor, half in and half out of a puddle.

Ariadne's wheezing breaths are as deep as a wild creature's. She's about to pull at the mask, to try to wriggle free of it. But she knows better than anybody the damage the mask can do if it's manipulated the wrong way. She designed it.

And yet...

Her sister managed to free herself from it...

It was supposed to be inescapable... To curse its wearer to accept captivity or death.

"Stop playing games!" Her own bellow turns to a roar, so percolating and rough Ariadne lurches forward, only to topple headfirst—*thump*—to the unforgiving ground.

Who is responsible for this? The monster hunter? Or Asterion?

When they were children, Ariadne had never worried about the consequences of toying with her sister. Asterion was always too weak, too trusting, to even consider retaliating.

But perhaps nineteen sun-orbits in a sky-prison might change that?

Ariadne tries again and again to climb to her feet, falling too many times to count. When she eventually staggers upright, her legs are shaking from the exertion. Not just her legs. Every muscle. Some she didn't even know she has. And there's not a thing she can do about the sweat on her brow.

A sudden gust knocks her off her feet again. Her neck muscles strain. Her temples ache. She tries to catch her breath, but her world is off-kilter. In motion.

No, wait...

She's not in motion... but *something* is.

She tries to focus through the limiting eyeholes.

The labyrinth layers speed past. She retreats from the startling momentum, only for her heel to catch. She stumbles backward, landing heavily, painfully, on what can only be the entrance turntable to the fortress at the core of the Sky Labyrinth.

She shouldn't be here. The monster hunter will answer for this. But presumably there's a reason she's been dumped at this gateway. And this bit she knows how to do. She designed the lock and keys, after all.

Her body and her patience exhausted, it takes several attempts to angle and align the horns of the mask into the keyholes. With each click, the shifting door mechanisms shudder through her until the turntable spins, casting her free of her bindings and into the core fortress with an unceremonious clatter, her knees and elbows protesting as she hits the stone floor.

She can breathe more easily without the mask, but it does little to calm her.

Outside the gatehouse, the Labyrinth still clicks and groans. But here, inside the fortress, there's nothing but the kind of silence that speaks volumes.

Alone. That's what it says.

The flicker of the chamber's fire-torches is more unsettling than the monster hunter's rebellion. Ariadne tugs at the torque around her neck. Her fingers close around the familiar, decorative metal.

It's her torque, but...

The torches flame. How *dare* Asterion align her with the Labyrinth?

Ariadne explores her neck and sternum, but there's no heart-stone key. Nineteen sun-orbits ago, she'd given Asterion the key to her prison, but no way to use it. And now, even if Ariadne could free herself from the mask, she doesn't even have a heart with which to escape.

She stumbles to her feet. There's a note on the entrance hall mantle, addressed in precise Minoglyphs to:

SISTER

The handwriting is Asterion's. Ariadne snatches it, her panic building as she skims its contents.

It's... nothing.

It starts with DON'T WORRY, THE CHICKENS ARE OKAY —*whatever that means!*—before rambling about how the labyrinth had flooded recently, including the fortress, but the lava-gullies are quickly drying it all out... and about how the Labyrinth as a whole will right itself soon enough...

And then there's a list of crops and chicken care instructions, along with some helpful reminders about which areas of the labyrinth to avoid for health and happiness.

And worse—Ariadne's horror devolves to pure venom—the note is signed not just by Asterion, but by *Theseus*, too.

They orchestrated this together?

Ariadne screws up the note and hurls it across the hall. Only then does she realise she's not as alone as she'd thought. Standing in the shadows, watching her in silence, is Asterion.

Ariadne strides swiftly toward her sister. "I'll rip you to

shreds," she hisses, pulling back her arm to strike as Asterion stands there, serene. "You stupid, arrogant little—"

Ariadne strikes and pain flares as her fingers meet the cold, hard, flat face of her sister. It takes a moment for reason to catch up.

The familiar eyes staring back at her aren't real. Her target is nothing more than an—admittedly accomplished— life-sized portrait of... *herself*?

That steals any remaining air from her lungs. Silence stretches around her, disturbed only by the distant creak of metal and the *tick-tick-tick* of the Labyrinth.

The nausea of dawning reality churns inside her.

No servants? No-one to handle the tedium and drudgery of endless basic daily demands? No-one to admire her, to fear her, to leap to fulfil her every need?

The bellow that erupts from her is as beastly as the roar of any Minotaur.

The fire-torches flicker. And only her painted image stares back.

Of everything she's ever done to claw her way to the top, to make herself untouchable, to *win*... she never once considered that she might actually have to live with herself.

89

ADVENTURES
ASTERION

The gatehouse groans with a worldquake-strength shudder. It's only as Theseus's hand finds hers that Asterion recalls that it's not her emotions the Labyrinth is echoing. Not anymore. Hers are happily entangled in more positive things.

Amidst the life-changing excitement, sitting side by side with Theseus in the open gateway of the Sky Labyrinth, it's strange to be doing something as mundane as waiting for transport. But she's definitely not complaining as she divides her time between gazing at the stars scattered endlessly before them, and gazing at Theseus. As she finally reads Theseus's tourist guide-Shard, absorbing all the ridiculous inaccuracies about Minosian mythology—including her own—they discuss what a better future might look like. For themselves, and for Minos.

A lot needs to change for Minos to become a place where people can live their best lives. Attitudes will need to adjust. No longer can the emphasis be on winning at others' expense.

Asterion's first act as Architect will be to officially cancel the nuptials, which are scheduled for today. A tradition based on the winning of a person's hand in marriage as a prize is the sort of event she'll be steering Minos away from.

Instead of marriage, Asterion and Theseus will use the ceremony to announce the truth: that there is no Minotaur to fear, and never was. That Asterion, the Lost Princess, is the rightful Architect, and will ensure that each individual's Flame will be shared for the benefit of the world around them, and no longer siphoned off to indulge those who live under marble arches.

But politics is its own labyrinth. Careful navigation will be key.

And between the planning—thanks to the unique properties of the astro-helmets' invisi-visors—there's an admirable amount of kissing, too.

When that escalates to Theseus straddling her, it's the best feeling. Theseus is so gentle; Asterion is recovering from a deadly wound, after all. Her heart-stone blushes as the glowing stitches in her chest pulse steady and strong.

They might technically have Ariadne to thank for the illumi-thread, but Asterion and Theseus have concluded that the thread's use in saving Asterion's life doesn't quite balance out the whole *leaving Asterion in a death-trap for nineteen sun-orbits and repeatedly sending people up there to kill her.*

Asterion isn't one for holding grudges, but there's something to be said for experiencing a taste of one's own medicine. Theseus had been all in favour of leaving Ariadne to combat her own deadly adjustments to Asterion's Labyrinth, but Asterion had chosen to leave clear instructions that, if her sister has the sense to follow them, will keep her from straying into the path of anything deadly. Ariadne might deserve many things, but that doesn't change Asterion's unwillingness to dole out morbid punishments. Perhaps her sister might even come to appreciate Asterion's compassionate traits, now that she's the one benefiting from them.

Ariadne will be consigned to her own company for a while. That is more than curse enough. Whether a power-hungry brat of a princess can change for the better, they'll find out.

But right now, all Asterion wants to focus on is being *this close* to Theseus; how utterly captivating it is to experience her adoring smile, and the stars in her eyes, as they contemplate the future together.

90

ADVENTURES
THESEUS

I t would be fair to say this has been no ordinary monster hunt.

When Theseus had first entered the Sky Labyrinth, ready to slay a Minotaur, she hadn't imagined that she and the 'monster' might end up making out on the drawbridge overlooking the heavens.

Theseus smiles into their kiss. No matter where their paths take them, she'll never tire of the stars dancing in Asterion's eyes.

They're so busy getting... well, *busy* (though unfortunately no clothing can be removed without falling victim to the less awesome aspects of space), they don't even notice the sky-ship touching down on the drawbridge until the hatch levers open. Oops.

Bigger than a sky-motor, smaller than a sky-boat, the sky-cruiser is sleek—the vessel of choice for anyone on a galaxy-hopping mission who doesn't want to have to make many stops along the way. Theseus grins as its captain steps out, her mesh-armour straining against her muscular build, her unruly neon-pink curls escaping from under her astro-helmet.

"Don't mind me," Herakles calls as their comms remotely connect, and Theseus jumps off Asterion's lap and helps her to her feet. "I've only journeyed across the galaxies to come to your rescue."

Asterion reaches for the spare astro-helmet and her bag. The latter of which is stuffed to bursting with as many blueprints and fictions as she could cram into it—but Theseus gets there first. "You're healing. Let me." She follows this up by fumbling Asterion's bag and her own. Asterion's kisses don't half make her dizzy. Thankfully, zero-gravity masks her misfiring co-ordination. Mostly.

Asterion accepts. Theseus slings both their rucksacks over her shoulder, then gathers her sword and rediscovered shield —which they'd found lodged in the tunnel behind the waterfall after the Labyrinth's equilibrium had mostly been restored.

Asterion tucks the extra astro-helmet under one arm.

"Ready?" asks Theseus.

Asterion squares her shoulders and nods. As her hand finds Theseus's, Theseus is certain her own torque must be obliterating any air of mystery surrounding her world-altering crush on Asterion. But she doesn't care.

Together, they step out from the shadows of the Labyrinth and onto the runway.

"Looking dapper, Thee." Herakles smiles good-naturedly as they approach, arms folded nonchalantly across her chest.

Theseus winces. She'd forgotten she's still wearing her charcoal and silver ceremonial suit. "Where's your co-captain?" she calls back.

Herakles rolls her eyes. "Good to see you, too. She's off adventuring. Like you've been, I see." Herakles's eyeline traces up the monumental Sky Labyrinth with an understandable dose of wonder.

"Asterion," Theseus says, nodding between the two of them, "this is Herakles."

"Welcome aboard." Herakles holds out a hand to assist Asterion aboard. Minos is going to *love* the sky captain with her strutting confidence and winning smile.

Instead of accepting the offered hand, Asterion presents Herakles with the spare astro-helmet. From inside comes an indignant: "*Bok-bok.*"

Herakles looks down at the neurotic eyes staring at her from within the helmet, then up at Asterion and Theseus. Her expression is delightfully puzzled.

"*Bok-bok.*"

"Is that... a chicken?" asks Herakles.

"*Bok-bok*," confirms the chicken.

It's not the strangest thing Herakles would have ever seen. It's not even the most unusual creature she's transported on her sky-cruiser. Which might be why she simply straps Bok-bok and the astro-helmet into a seat before welcoming Theseus aboard with a slightly sarcastic bow. "Your highness."

Theseus rolls her eyes. Herakles *knows* she hates that.

"I saw that." Herakles smirks. "Do you want my astronomical chauffeuring or not?"

"Yeah, yeah." Theseus affixes Asterion's book bag to the seat within Asterion's reach, which Asterion looks entirely pleased about.

After adjusting a series of flight controls and inspecting the necessary gauges, Herakles has the door lever shut behind them, followed by the hiss of air adjusting.

"You know, I expected to find you in several pieces." Herakles removes her astro-helmet, unleashing her bright pink mohawk. "Don't get me wrong, I'm glad you're in just the one piece..." Her bright eyes land on Theseus's and Asterion's held hands. "In fact, you're looking positively... *sparkly.*"

She's clearly referring to more than just Theseus's collection of illumi-thread stitches. And Theseus refuses to be embarrassed about it.

"I take it the elevated heart rate wasn't all bad?" Herakles smirks as she holds up her darkened Locator coin. She holds it out, and Theseus taps her own Locator to it. And—just like that—its dull surface restores to a shine, somehow even brighter than before.

Theseus lets go of Asterion's hand to wrap her arms around her friend, thankful that she's here, thankful for the many moments Herakles has got her through that she'll never know about. Because Theseus might have gone on an *emotional* adventure, but she's not going to inflate Herakles's ego any further if she can help it.

"Shit," says Herakles. "You must have some story to tell. The last time I tried to hug you, you were squirmier than a Thessalian alley cat."

"It's... been a journey." Theseus smiles at Asterion, who's watching the two of them with interest, before punching Herakles playfully on the shoulder. "Took you long enough to get here."

"Excuse me for being *a few galaxies away.*" Herakles rubs her shoulder theatrically. "Right." She claps her hands together, settling at the helm. "Once you're belted in, I want every last detail of your adventure—"

Asterion nods happily.

"Maybe not *all* the details," Theseus mutters to her.

Herakles's eyes light up gleefully as she turns to Asterion. "You tamed the beast, huh?" She throws Theseus an infuriating wink.

Fuck's sake. "I'm not a beast," Theseus mumbles. "*Or an alley cat.*" She really needs to change the subject... "Oh, hey—" She reaches for her rucksack. "I got you something."

She unclips the battered Minotaur plushie and presents it to Herakles; its stuffing bursting from the seams, one of its button eyes hanging off.

Herakles inspects the gift, opening her mouth before apparently settling for a quizzical look.

"Like I said," says Theseus, "it's been a journey."

With a chuckle, Herakles settles the plushie on the helm's dash, looking to the way ahead. Well, sort of. "Right. Speaking of journey..." She sets the take-off sequence in motion. "Where are we headed, Princess?" Her eyes connect with Theseus's in the rear-view mirror, making clear exactly who she's addressing.

Asterion's head tilts curiously. "Why is she calling you Princess?"

Oh, yeah. That. By the time Theseus and Asterion had been able to communicate properly, her royal heritage had hardly seemed relevant.

"Uhhh... I'm kind of a... princess. Of the Athenian Expanse. It's not a big deal."

Asterion looks, frankly, less than bothered. "Okay."

Okay? Okay.

In the rear-view, Herakles watches them with what might be vague amusement. But she's still waiting for Theseus's response.

"Ready to reshape a world?" Asterion asks, and Theseus grins. Upending an entire world for the greater good won't be easy. But she's never been more sure of her path.

"To Minos, please," Theseus announces, as though Herakles is merely a hired transport service.

"Are you serious?" Herakles huffs as she guides the cruiser smoothly upward. "You hauled me across two galaxies to take you to a planet that's—in cosmic terms—*right fucking there*?"

Theseus shrugs. "Serves you right for giving me your sentimental, creepy tracking device."

"You better have a good story for me," Herakles grumbles.

Asterion perks up at the mention of stories. "You and Theseus have—been on adventures—together?"

Herakles chuckles. "We'll need a longer journey for all of those." A mischievous glint enters her eyes. "Although... did she tell you about the time we tried to wrangle a nine-headed water creature on the shores of—?"

"Asterion doesn't want to hear all that," Theseus interrupts quickly.

Asterion sits forward in her seat. "Asterion *absolutely*—wants to hear—all that."

"Excellent." Herakles grins. "But first, since we're heading for Minos from its notorious Labyrinth, and one of you looks remarkably identical to its monarch... I think you'd better get me up to speed."

She does have a point.

"And Thee? Is there a reason you're wearing a Minosian ceremonial wedding outfit?"

Asterion tugs lightly at Theseus's lapel. "You look nice."

Theseus can't help mirroring Asterion's smile. And blushing, apparently. Which, of course, Herakles delights in. And while she and Asterion recount their tale, Theseus is warmed inside and out by Asterion snuggling against her.

They tell Herakles about Ariadne and her lies, about the unhinged Hero, about illumi-thread, about all the misunderstandings that pushed them apart and brought them together—glossing over several key moments involving a bed, a library table, an entrance hall, a kitchen, an orchard, a banquet table, and so on.

And for the first time, Theseus doesn't feel like she has to charge into battle with the next monster. She might be sailing the heavens in a sky-cruiser, but she feels like her feet are on solid ground, because—for the first time—she wants nothing more than to build a life with someone.

Thank the heavens she stumbled into the path of an Architect.

✦

SIGN UP FOR UPDATES AND A FREE SHORT STORY!

If you'd like to hear more about my writing adventures (bonus materials, behind-the-scenes insights, new release announcements, special offers, and more!), the best way is via my author update emails:

SIGN UP at:

gwenhyver.com/sign-up-theseus

REVIEWS WELCOME!

 Hello! Gwenhyver here. I hope you enjoyed your adventure with Theseus and Asterion! I'd really appreciate it if you'd leave a review—wherever you bought your book and/or on review sites like Goodreads.

Reviews are great for encouraging others to take a chance on me and the stories I write. Your review doesn't have to be long, or a literary masterpiece, just a few sentences sharing your thoughts/experience. And—though reviews are not for me but for other readers—I'll be very grateful indeed!

Thank you!

ACKNOWLEDGMENTS

I'll keep this brief, because if you're reading this you've already read about 140,000 words! I'd first like to *acknowledge* my utterly awesome wife, Jen, who not only is a lovely human being (the best!) but also very kind in reading through my *Theseus and the Sky Labyrinth* drafts from the early-waffle stage, to the final-but-oops-typos stage! And in between those stages, Jen has been *so patient* - listening to my thoughts about the book, discussing them with me, and being an all-round good egg! Yes, an egg!

I remember when we went to a cafe with our laptops to do some fun writing, when I had ideas for *Theseus* that were 'definitely' going to be a short story or novella... well, I failed at writing the novella, and this beast of a book happened instead. And it wouldn't have happened in the way that it did without Jen always being so... *Jen*. Thank you for making writing adventures so much fun :-)

I'd also like to enthusiastically acknowledge Kat Stainforth of Foxglove & Folio Editorial Services. Her edits at developmental and copy/line edit stage have been not only helpful, but an education. I always feel like I learn a dozen new things (more!) about how to improve my writing each time Kat gives feedback or edits. Thank you, Kat, for your conscientious approach! Writers talk about when people just 'get' their story, and I feel so grateful that you 'got' *Theseus*. And I enjoyed your... *appreciation* of Asterion! :-) It's been such a treat working with you, and I'll be forever recommending your editing expertise to anyone who'll listen!

Now for the cover art! As always, artist Alyssa Winans has done an amazing job of taking my scribbles and deciphering my ideas and turning them into cover art so beautiful I have to actively stop staring at it in order to get writing done!

And thank you to everyone who spreads the word about this book. Whether that's through reviews, on social media, or just telling people about the book... I appreciate you. *This book appreciates you.*

And, finally, thank you for reading the acknowledgements!

ABOUT THE AUTHOR

Gwenhyver is the author of the sapphic, swords & sorcery in space novel series *Jasyn and the Astronauts* where the skies are a wonder and love can move the heavens. She loves writing adventures with fantastical elements and queer characters. She lives in a village on Dartmoor, England, with her wonderful wife. When she's not happily hermit-ing in her writing den, she's exploring cycle trails wearing too much hi-vis!

www.gwenhyver.com

patreon.com/gwenhyver

instagram.com/gwenhyver

facebook.com/gwenhyver.author

tiktok.com/@gwenhyver.writes

goodreads.com/gwenhyver

ALSO BY GWENHYVER

JASYN
AND THE
ASTRONAUTS

THE SERIES

Book 1 - *Under The Ice Skies*

Book 2 - *The Sea of Stars*

UPCOMING RELEASES (as of February 2026)

Book 3 - *Two Faced Planet*

Book 4 - *The Ice Princess*

Book 5 - *The Sky Circus*

Book 6 - *Out of Orbit*

STANDALONES - OUT NOW

Theseus and the Sky Labyrinth

SHORT STORIES - OUT NOW

The Ice Princess and the Gladiator - via the BY HER SWORD anthology, or my Patreon (details below).

Uncharted - FREE when you sign up to my author update emails at **gwenhyver.com/sign-up**

For works in progress, other short stories and more in-depth behind the scenes insights, sign up to my Patreon at **patreon.com/gwenhyver**

CONTENT NOTES AND TRIGGER WARNINGS

This list may be added to in future. An up to date list can be found via www.gwenhyver.com/theseus-notes.

> On page intimacy/sex.
> Injury detail, including blood.
> Violence/use of weapons.
> Being captive.
> Parental/familial mistreatment.
> Death.
> Discussion of bodily scars.

If you feel something should be added to these notes, please contact author@gwenhyver.com

www.ingramcontent.com/pod-product-compliance
Lightning Source LLC
Chambersburg PA
CBHW031728180726
48283CB00005B/1419